THE
DELHI
DECEPTION

ELANA SABHARWAL

QUADRIJUGIS

First published in 2013 by Quadrijugis Books
Cape Town South Africa
33 Church Street
Cape Town 8001

Copyright © 2013 Elana Sabharwal

www.elanasabharwalbooks.com

All rights reserved. No part of this book may be reproduced or transmitted by any person or any entity in any form or by any means, electronic or mechanical, including photocopying, recording, scanning or by any information storage and retrieval system, without prior permission in writing from the publisher.

Cover design: Melody Deas
Typesetter: Kathryn Webb

Printed and bound by Hirt & Carter (Pty) Ltd

Set in 12 pt on 14.4 pt Metrics

The characters and events in this book are fictitious and any resemblance to real persons, living or dead, is purely coincidental.

ISBN-10: 1479105597

DEDICATION

This book is for

SOMARA

My daughter, my inspiration

GLOSSARY

Foreign terms used in this novel

Ayha	Nanny.
Anjee	Term of respect, meaning Yes, sir/madam.
Afghan choora	Large handmade knife usually bone handled.
Bhai	Brother, also used as term of endearment between close friends.
Bharra	Large or older.
Betel nut	Seed of betel palm, chewed with betel leaves as a digestive stimulant.
Bas	Enough.
Buaji	Oldest aunt in the family.
Beedi	Hand rolled tobacco cigarette.
Beta	Child.
Bungalow	Single residence house set in a garden.
Baba	Father.
Biryani	Rice dish made with meat or vegetables.
Charpoy	Wooden framed string bed.
Chappals	Sandals.
Chowkidar	Gatekeeper or watchman.
Chapatis	Stone ground flour flat bread.
Chacchi	Aunt.
Chai	Tea.

Chikankari	Type of embroidery origins from Lucknow.
Curd	Thick yoghurt.
Dupatta	Large scarf worn with traditional women's clothing.
Dhobi	Laundry man.
Dhoti	A rectangular unstitched cloth, 4.5m long, wrapped and tied around a man's legs and waist.
Dhaba	Casual eatery.
Eunuch	A man that has been castrated, typically early enough in his life for this change to have major hormonal consequences. Castration was typically carried out on the soon-to-be eunuch without his consent so that he might perform a specific social function; usually as guardians of women or harem servants.
Ghulam Bazaar	Slave market.
Hamman	A Turkish bath.
Havelli	A gentleman's residence, usually Moghul in style.
Hijab	Head covering worn by Muslim women.
Jali	A perforated or latticed screen, usually in front of a window opening.
Jaldi	Hurry up.
Jula	Indian swing usually made from wood and hanging off brass chains.
Jalebi	Indian fried sweet.
Kurta	Traditional lady's shirt, usually mid-calf in length.
Kurti	Short version of Kurta.
Kichry	Bland dish of lentils and rice normally for the infirm.
Khanna	Food.
Kufi	Scull cap worn by Muslim men.
Lassi	Yoghurt drink.

Mali	Gardener.
Nimbu pani	Lemon water.
Naan	Leavened bread baked in a clay oven, usually shaped like a teardrop.
Pathani	Long men's shirt worn over pants, more common in North India, Pakistan and Afghanistan.
Pashmina	Woolen shawl usually made from cashmere.
Peon	Male secretary.
Pomfret	Ocean fish similar to sole.
Prashad	A semolina, sugar and butter dish served at religious occasions.
Palu	Edge of sari worn over the shoulder.
Pataka	Fire cracker.
Rupee	Indian currency.
Rogan josh	Lamb curry.
Roomali roti	Very thin, flat bread.
Salwar kameez	Traditional dress/shirt worn over pants.
Sahib	Sir.
Sangeet	A musical evening, one of the many traditional wedding events.
Sastrikal	A traditional Sikh greeting.
Tuk Tuk	A three-wheeler taxi.
Tandoori murgh	Chicken cooked in a clay oven.
Tiffen	Food in an assortment of steel containers with lids, usually for eating away from home.
Yogi	Yoga teacher or instructor.
Zardozi	A type of embroidery made with metallic threads.

*T*he man glanced at his reflection in the bedroom mirror and frowned. The gray in his beard made him look old and frail. He made a mental note to tell his wife to dye it black before they made the video. He then walked to his bed, where he sat down cross-legged in his white Pathani suit. He was thinking of the broadcast. It had been many months since he had last appeared in a video. How shocked they would be to see him looking fit and still in control.

His sons stood in one corner of the room, discussing the latest plan their beloved father and leader had come up with. But the leader did not join in the conversation; he was still distractedly looking at himself in the mirror while practicing his smile.

A woman dressed in full black burqa entered silently with a tray of milky, fragrant tea in glass cups. Another woman dressed the same followed with a plate of potato pakoras and butter biscuits. The men stopped conversing and sat quietly, accepting the refreshments with their eyes respectfully downturned.

When the women left the room, the bearded man looked at the courier standing meekly at the doorway and said, "You have the train schedule?"

He nodded.

"And it will remain the same for the next year?"

He nodded again.

With his left hand pulling gently on his gray beard, he said, "And our martyrs? Are they in place?"

Again the courier nodded nervously. The bearded man smiled, almost coyly, and then, as if gaining confidence, the smile reached his brown eyes, which were soft and gentle. Then he was laughing. A cruel glint flitted across his eyes, but it was so brief it was lost in a blink.

CHAPTER 1

The sun was setting over the ancient city of Hyderabad, its watermelon rays painting the white muslin in her fingers a soft shade of peach. Its warm light shone on the embroidery needle, flashing long-short, short-long, as if signaling distress. The delicate paisley pattern slowly came to life as tiny, deft stitches filled the blank spaces on the finely woven cloth. She yelped in pain and watched in terror as ruby-red blood spread across the fabric at an alarming rate. Her father noticed, his mouth twisted in anger.

"You careless girl, hurry to the basin and wash off the blood before it ruins the whole piece."

Her feet felt like clay sucked to the floor. Swallowing her tears, she bit her lip and said, "Sorry, Baba, I'm so sorry."

"Don't just sit there; get up and clean it."

Nazeema looked at her mother, pleading. "Give it to me," her mother said kindly, and put her own embroidery in a basket on the cement floor.

Nazeema tried to escape her father's glare by picking up the empty glasses sticky from the sweet chai they had drunk earlier. Carrying them to the kitchen, she saw her older brother arrive home from school. He was almost bent double from the weight of his schoolbooks in the tattered gray rucksack on his back. His face was dirty, but the gleam of joy in his large brown eyes pulled and twisted something inside her. Envy had her clutching the edge of her dupatta, twirling and scrunching the fabric so tightly between her fingers that she felt it tear.

She knew her father's eyes would light up with pleasure as they always did when he saw his oldest son. She watched from the kitchen doorway as her father greeted her brother.

"Ah, there you are, Beta. How was school today? Did you do well on your science test?"

Her brother threw the heavy bag onto the floor and sat down next to his father. "Full marks, Baba, full marks."

Were those tears glistening in the old man's eyes as he kissed the boy on top of his head? Nazeema watched the scene, a sardonic smile twisting her beautiful lips.

She turned her back to her father when she heard him call out to her mother, "I want you to add the best piece of goat's meat to our son's biryani tonight, do you understand?"

"Of course," she replied and glanced at Nazeema, but Nazeema couldn't meet her mother's eyes. Instead she walked away, taking the washed cloth from her mother to hang on the roof of their apartment building. She hoped it would dry in the last warm beams of the afternoon sun.

Later, when they had finished their dinner of goat biryani, thick curd, and onions, Nazeema listened to her father and brother discussing an IT College in Bangalore, where they were hoping to get admission for him. It was expensive and one of the reasons Nazeema's own education had been halted indefinitely. She had been taken out of school at fourteen and put to work with her parents instead, embroidering fine cotton muslin and silk in the Chikankari method, an ancient and traditional handicraft from Lucknow. That day, her dream of becoming an English teacher was crushed. It was pointless trying to argue; boys were still the hope of their families' future in the new India. Its economy was growing, along with its strong, up-and-coming middle class, but for many girls in poor families, little had changed.

After cleaning the kitchen and packing away the worn pots and cooking utensils, Nazeema said good night and went to bed with a copy of her brother's English homework.

The following morning Nazeema was sent to buyers with a bundle of their embroidered cloth. They bought the best pieces for export, while some were discarded or bought for a bargain price. She placed the folded rupees in a red plastic wallet decorated with pink crystals and worried about the low prices their work had fetched that morning. She walked slowly, trying to delay the inevitable scolding she knew she'd get from her father.

Passing an ice cream wallah, she stopped and studied the pictures on the side of the fridge. She licked her lips and, with a rebellious flick of her long dark hair, bought herself mango ice cream in a plastic cup. Eating it with closed eyes and abandoned pleasure, she didn't notice the middle-aged man watching her in the doorway of the barbershop.

When she arrived home, she was relieved to find that her father had gone out. Her mother was quiet and didn't volunteer to fill her in on her father's whereabouts. He returned much later, singing an old Bollywood love song, gave his wife an uncustomary kiss on the cheek, and announced that he would take them out for tandoori chicken and roomali roti at a dhaba not far from their house. Nazeema was surprised at this generous gesture, but excitedly changed her clothes and braided her hair.

Nazeema felt a glow of pleasure, sitting on the white plastic chairs of the bustling street restaurant and watching her mother laugh loudly for what felt like the first time in a long time. Her eyes shone on her father as she listened to him tell stories about his childhood in a small village on the border of the Punjab. They were licking their fingers, mopping up bits of masala with the last of the roti.

While they were drinking hot, milky masala chai, her father looked at her and said, "Beti, I am so happy to be telling you that I have found a very good husband for you."

Nazeema choked on the hot liquid and looked up at her mother. Her mother seemed to be just as surprised as she was. *She doesn't know.* Her mother avoided looking at her, pretending to clean an invisible spot on the sleeve of her kameez. Nazeema eventually found her voice. "But, Baba, I'm only fifteen. I'm not ready for marriage..."

"Nonsense! You will do as I say and be bloody grateful. Your mother will prepare you for the marriage, which will take place the day after tomorrow." His voice was cold... final. Paying the bill, he glared at Nazeema and then got up heavily, burping as he walked away. Her mother followed him, but her brother, with a sympathetic gesture, helped her up, gently supporting her by the arm as they walked back to the apartment. Nazeema asked him if he knew the prospective groom, but he shook his head and avoided looking into her eyes.

She cried herself to sleep and in the morning rose from bed with swollen, red eyes. Her father looked perturbed, and then barked an order to his wife as he left the apartment. Nazeema's mother tried her best to be cheerful while removing a vermillion silk sari from a wooden chest. She held it against Nazeema's face and smiled. "You look beautiful, Nazeema. This was my mother's sari, and I have kept it all these years for you. You will make your father proud, and I know you'll be a wonderful wife."

They embraced, tears streaming down her mother's face. But Nazeema's eyes were dry; her fate was sealed.

The day and night passed like a movie being fast-forwarded. The henna artist painted an intricate pattern on her hands and feet. The initials of her groom were also painted on the soft flesh of her palm. Her mother oiled and braided her hair. A cousin outlined her large, liquid brown eyes with kohl, and then it was time.

Her family took her to a small hotel on the outskirts of Hyderabad. They were shown into a dark room stinking of old cigarettes. Someone had tried to decorate it with gladioli, but the stems were bent and the flowers were wilting in the heat. Two metal chairs adorned with strings of marigold were set slightly apart. On one of the chairs sat a man, tall and still. His face was covered with tinsel, his features dark and indiscernible in the gloom of the room. Nazeema was seated next to him, and then the ceremony began.

From under her veil, she tried to look at her groom, but his face was turned away from her. She started feeling faint and hot under the layers of silk. The room was spinning, and if it weren't for her mother supporting her by the arm she would have collapsed. The cheers and laughter shocked her out of her daze, and the rich, milky sweet her groom fed her made her nauseous. She was weighed down under the garlands of flowers well-wishers had placed around her shoulders before she was led away by her cousin, upstairs to an airless room in the hotel. The bed was covered in red rose petals. Sticks of strong-smelling incense on the windowsill burned dangerously close to the tattered curtains.

Her cousin left her sitting alone on the bed, and then Nazeema's husband came into the room. He offered her a glass of tea, pouring it from a brass samovar. She accepted with shaking hands and looked up at him as he sat down next to her. He lifted her veil and studied her features intently. With what sounded like a grunt of satisfaction, he stood up and removed his headdress.

Nazeema's eyes widened in horror. It was the face of an old man. A deep scar ran down the center of his face, disfiguring his hawklike nose. His eyes were small and very dark, unreadable, and his mouth was thin and pale, twisted by the scar into a cruel expression. He tried to say something to her in heavily accented Hindi, but she didn't understand. His smile, revealing gaps in his uneven, stained teeth, was repulsive.

Instinctively, Nazeema shrank back and covered her face with her hands, but this angered him. He hit her in the face with the back of his hand, sending her sprawling. She tried to reach the door, but he was remarkably agile. He picked her up easily and continued beating her. Blood was flowing into her eyes, and in the red haze of pain and disbelief, he tore the precious wedding sari off her young body and forced himself onto her.

Nazeema felt her adolescent body being violated and ripped apart. She tried screaming, begged him to stop, but his eyes were dead.

Eventually, in agony and shock, Nazeema passed out, but her blessed stupor was short-lived. In the early hours of the morning, he started raping her again. Exhausted and with no will left to fight him off, she lay still like a rag doll, battered, damaged, and soon to be discarded.

As the bleak dawn light crept silently though the holes of the threadbare curtains, Nazeema's husband got up, groaning slightly as he walked to the bathroom. Noticing her naked body smeared with blood and semen, she pulled the floral cotton sheet across herself, shivering. Her mind was dull, and she concentrated on her breathing, listening to the odd whistling sound of air through her swollen, blood-caked nose.

The bathroom door opened, and she watched him return. He had changed into clean clothing. Picking up a small suitcase, he sauntered over to the bed. He leaned across her leeringly and then licked her face. In halting Hindi he told her he was divorcing her. She closed her eyes, past feeling anything. When she opened them a few moments later, he was gone.

Nazeema stood in front of her family's apartment for a long time. Her face was bruised, and her head hurt each time she moved it. She was dressed in a faded yellow salwar kameez a size too big, lent to her by the appalled young servant girl who found her unconscious on her wedding bed. She had bathed her gently and disinfected her wounds with carbolic soap. Stung by the soap, Nazeema had regained consciousness. She had survived this unthinkable ordeal.

It seemed natural to return to her father's house, yet she was afraid; she opened the door and slipped in. Her mother was standing in the kitchen with her back toward Nazeema. From the bedroom she could hear her father snore. She walked quietly to his room and sat at the end of the charpoy, watching him sleep. An empty bottle of local whisky was discarded on the floor, and the room smelled sour. A loud, spluttering snore made her father move his head off the pillow.

Nazeema saw the wad of rupee notes stick out from under him. She pushed him aside and gaped at the money. It was more than she had ever seen, and she picked up a handful. Hearing her mother gasp behind her, she let go of the notes, and they fluttered down, covering her father's torso.

Her mother's eyes were wide and shiny with unshed tears. "Beti, please try to understand. Your brother has to go to college; there was no other way."

"So you sold me?"

"No, it wasn't meant to be like this. They promised your father that the man would take good care of you; you'd have a future."

A loud ringing noise in her ears made her dizzy, and she sat down heavily on the charpoy. Her father sat up and watched her with guilty, shifty eyes.

"Are you sorry for what you've done?" Nazeema was sobbing. "I'm soiled; no one will marry me now. What will I do?" She fell down and held her mother's feet. "Do something, Ma, please."

Her mother looked at her father, and then turned around and walked back to the kitchen. Her father then shifted his gaze to stare out the window. When Nazeema eventually pulled herself to her feet and walked out the room, she did not see the tears of remorse rolling down his cheeks, chin, and onto his chest.

Nazeema spent the rest of the day in stunned silence. Her home was no longer a place of safety; betrayal seeped from its walls. She didn't know where to go and walked the streets aimlessly. At the ice cream wallah's fridge, she dropped to her haunches and leaned against it. She had no idea for how long she sat there, but when a middle-aged man with a kind face asked her if she'd like some tea, she followed him through a dark alley and into a room reeking of sex.

CHAPTER 2

She tried to run, but her legs were heavy; they wouldn't move. The suffocating heat of the dark, dank alley replaced the ice-cold sensation of fear. They were watching her; she could sense them. Finally summoning up the courage to look back over her shoulder, she saw nothing but overfed rats scurrying like a repugnant tide of vermin, edging closer. Her skin crawled as she pushed open a heavy wooden door, using her shoulder to shift it.

Stumbling and using every muscle in her body to prevent herself from falling facedown into the filth, she looked up and was met with smiling Indian faces drinking from tall glasses. The beautifully dressed women were strolling around in an exquisite garden. Unknown creepers and exotic flowers floated above and around her. She looked desperately for her grandfather, searching for the sky-blue of his starched turban, but every time she saw what she assumed to be a familiar figure, it turned out be a stranger. The yearning to see him was so strong that she felt herself suffocating.

Carla woke up to find her mother's overweight, graying Labrador lying on top of her. The dog was snoring loudly. She tried to recall her dream, rubbing her eyes vigorously. With a groan she remembered the recurring nightmare and pushed the dog off her. He responded by wagging his tail and joyously licked her face. She had been having this dream about her father's birthplace since the sudden death of her grandfather seven years ago. It was always the same: the urgency to reach her grandfather's house, but being unable to find it, lost in an alley and then a garden of smiling strangers. The colors and smells of India were so vivid in her dreams that she had to marvel at the fact that she had never visited this ancient land of her father's heritage.

Her parents had met each other on the cobbled street of Via Cavour not far from the Duomo in Florence in 1972. Carla's South African mother, Sara, was on the customary European tour, a gift from her parents for her twenty-first birthday, while Carla's father, Dilip, was visiting Italy with some of his American college friends. According to him, it was love at first sight; Sara claimed he wooed her with such fervency that she had no choice but to fall in love with this dashing, daring Indian man. But like all great love stories, theirs was fraught with difficulties. The ultimate sacrifice was to walk away from one's own culture and embrace a new one, alien and sometimes cruel.

Carla's reverie was broken when Ben, the Labrador, jumped up and with his tail wagging barked a warning, staring at the door. A second later the door opened, and her childhood nanny, dressed immaculately in a traditional cotton dress and headgear, walked in carrying a cup of steaming coffee. Carla noticed how she had aged: her dark complexion was still smooth, but fine lines around her kind eyes and her weakened posture confirmed the indomitable advance of time.

"Thanks, Prudence."

"Your brother said to get up now; all children are ready and waiting for you on the grass."

Stretching her long, golden arms above her dark blond head, Carla smiled and remembered the cricket match. It was an annual family tradition on her father's birthday that her brothers and nephews observed with solemn obligation.

Dressing hurriedly into shorts and a collared T-shirt, she joined them on the vast lawn of the family farmhouse. Their wine farm was nestled in between the magnificent Drakenstein Mountains in the Franschhoek Valley. The farm had belonged to her mother's family for generations, and it was on the sudden and unexpected death of her grandparents in an airplane crash that her parents had moved back to South Africa from Gabarone, Botswana, in 1989.

Luckily, this had coincided with the election of the new South African president, F. W. de Klerk, who began the process of dismantling apartheid. The Prohibition of the Mixed Marriages Act of 1949 had forced Dilip and Sara to marry and settle in Botswana, a small, independent state on the South African border. Sara's parents had been worried about the union but gave their blessing and helped Dilip secure a job at one of the new diamond mines at Orapa in Botswana. Returning to India was not an option, as Dilip's family vehemently opposed the marriage. A union between him and the daughter of a powerful family in Delhi had been prearranged before he had embarked on his education abroad. Informing his family of his decision to break off the engagement and marry Sara, a white South African girl, outraged them. After an ugly argument, Dilip, young and very much in love, packed up his belongings and left his family home, vowing he would never return.

The cricket match ended in tears after the second innings. Brandon, her youngest nephew of five, hit the red cricket ball with surprising strength. It flew right past his uncle, who dived for it dramatically. The little boy, dressed in his older brother's school cricket kit, was jumping up and down with excitement. He screamed, "It's a six, it's a six!" The checkered dishcloth no longer held up the oversized cream-colored cricket pants, and they fell down in a heap around his ankles, exposing his skinny legs. His cousins burst out in raucous laughter as he fell to the buffalo grass, his face crimson with embarrassment. Carla ran toward him, trying her best to hide a smile. He was devastated, tears of humiliation shining in his jade eyes.

"It's OK, Brandon," Carla said as she pulled up the pants and secured them firmly at the waist with a double knot. She handed him the wooden cricket bat and gave her laughing nephews a look that silenced them instantly. The umpire, her sister-in-law, ruled the match a draw and suggested lunch on the veranda after the players had cleaned up.

Later that evening, while sitting at the long, yellowwood dining table, Carla's father, Dilip, still handsome at seventy years old, raised his glass of Kanonkop Cabernet Sauvignon and said, "To all my sons, their charming wives, and my five wonderful grandsons, thank you. Thank you for joining us as we celebrate this old man's seventieth birthday." Then, lifting his glass toward Carla, he said, "And especially to you, my only daughter, who gave up a few days in her very hectic schedule to fly down from London to be here with us. I appreciate it greatly. And tell that husband of yours, Andrew, next time, war or no war, in bloody Afghanistan or wherever, he must be here. Where is he exactly?"

Carla smiled, wiped a tear from her eye quickly, and said, "In Peshawar. Happy birthday, Daddy."

There was a brief moment of silence; then, as the rowdy

bunch continued their noisy conversations, Sara smiled at her daughter gently and said, "Come back soon, my darling."

The thought of London's gray skies, present even in April, depressed Carla so much that she had decided to extend her trip. She had leave due anyway, which she had saved for a trip to the Caribbean to celebrate Andrew's fortieth birthday, but the night before leaving for South Africa, he had confirmed that he wouldn't be able to make it. Andrew had told her that he was working on an important story, and they had to postpone the trip indefinitely. *Being married to a war reporter has its challenges,* she thought glumly.

As her family continued chatting, teasing each other and laughing about the cricket match, Carla stared at the food on her plate. She yearned to start a family of her own, but it was so difficult with Andrew and her traveling so often for work. After Carla completed her degree at Harvard University, she had moved to Washington, where she became a junior political correspondent with CNN. She had met Andrew at a party at the White House. A tall, handsome British war reporter for the BBC, he was everything she had ever hoped for, and luckily he felt the same about her. After a whirlwind transatlantic courtship, which had left them both breathless, Andrew had proposed. They were married on the family's wine estate on a perfect summer's day surrounded by the magnificent mountains and lush vineyards, grapes glistening as they ripened in the sun.

After their idyllic honeymoon, they had moved into Andrew's flat on Harley Street. CNN had been happy to transfer Carla to their political desk in London, and life for the newlyweds was bliss. But then the shadowy clouds of war darkened the sky on that warm autumn morning of September 11, 2001. Andrew was assigned to Afghanistan and Pakistan to cover the war against Al Qaeda and the Taliban. He was often away for months and weeks went by with no contact between them. Carla realized that she couldn't ignore the fact much longer that after ten years of marriage they were beginning to drift apart.

Carla looked up from her plate at the suntanned faces of her family and smiled wryly. It was no wonder she had welcomed the chance to join her family in South Africa to celebrate her father's birthday.

After dinner Carla asked her father if she could join him in his study for a Cognac. "Of course," Dilip replied and stood up, following Carla to his walnut-paneled study. She sank down in the old, leather armchair.

Dilip handed her a crystal glass. "So what's on your mind, honey?"

"Daddy, please hear me out. Don't say anything until I'm done, OK?"

Dilip frowned. "OK, I'm listening."

"It's about India. Daddy, I really want to go—"

"But you won't be welcomed," he said, interrupting her. "Just because you had a relationship with your grandfather...the family's attitude toward us has not changed."

"Please, Daddy, let me try."

"I suppose you'd like to see the property your grandfather left you."

"Well, yes, I suppose, but that's not the only reason. Daddy, you have told me such amazing things about India."

Sighing, he looked at her and said, "What's the use? You've made up your mind. You've probably already planned the trip and everything." Carla blushed, confirming his suspicions. "You want my blessing, right?"

She stood up and hugged her father. "Thank you, Daddy. I'm flying via Pakistan. I thought I'd surprise Andrew for a day or two."

Disentangling himself from her embrace, he looked at her with noticeable concern. Then he opened the desk drawer, took out a business card, and handed it to her.

"This is the name of a senior advocate in Delhi. He is one of the best and a dear friend. We were roommates at college. Explain the situation to him, and if he needs to speak to me, call. OK?"

"Thanks, Daddy."

"When are you leaving?"

"Tomorrow. I'm flying to Peshawar on Emirates via Dubai. I've called Elouise; I'll stay with her and Harry."

He looked at her for a long time. His eyes were saddened and concerned as he kissed her. "Good night, my sweet. I'll take you to the airport."

The next day, after hugging her childhood nanny for the umpteenth time, Carla kissed her mother and hurried to the driveway, where her father was waiting impatiently in his vintage 1969 silver Mercedes Benz 280 SL Roadster. Her father drove fast, and they were at the airport earlier than expected.

After drinking a coffee, they proceeded to check in. For the first time, she noticed tears in his eyes as he hugged her. Sometimes she wished she could remain in his bear hug forever, and now was one of those moments, but he pulled away, kissed her on the cheek, and walked back to the entrance.

While checking in, Carla bit her lip and briefly considered phoning Andrew. *No, I'll surprise him.* She smiled and thanked the agent who handed her the boarding pass. An unexpected queue at immigration made her late for the flight and she ran to board on hearing the final boarding call.

She breathed a sigh of relief as she finally sank into her window seat. Droplets of perspiration had formed on her brow. Using the towel given to her by the flight attendant,

Carla wiped her face and then sat back, closing her eyes. The anticipation of surprising Andrew made her smile. She tried to ignore the slight, uncomfortable flutter in her stomach.

After almost fifteen hours of traveling, including her three-hour stop in Dubai, Carla had lost some of her exuberance. Thoughts that Andrew could have left Peshawar troubled her, and she regretted not calling him first. The chaos at the airport did not give her a chance to dwell on these thoughts—she had to keep her wits about her to fight off all the pushy porters and taxi drivers. She called to an elderly taxi driver, who was smoking calmly and not vying for her attention, and they set off for the Pearl-Continental hotel. This was the only decent five-star hotel in Peshawar, according to Andrew.

When they reached the hotel, Carla was relieved to see Andrew's name on the hotel register, but the receptionist did not want to give her the key, as she had no proof of her marriage to Andrew. Carla always traveled to South Africa on her South African passport, which was under her maiden name. Not wanting to spoil the surprise, she decided against calling him on his satellite phone and waited in the coffee shop.

On the table lay a brochure advertising the reopening of the hotel following the terrorist attack in June 2009. She shivered as she read about the Abdullah Azzam Shaheed Brigade claiming responsibility for the attack, which had left the hotel almost completely destroyed. Carla drank her tea in one gulp, scalding her tongue. Her mind was distracted: she worried so much for Andrew in such an unstable country, conducting the type of investigative journalism he did.

By early evening Andrew had still not returned, so she went to her bedroom and lay down to rest. When she woke up it was almost midnight; in a panic she rushed downstairs to reception to enquire after him. A young, rather inexperienced-looking girl had replaced the receptionist of earlier that day.

One corner of Carla's mouth lifted mischievously; she had an idea. She walked toward the desk, searching frantically through her purse. Then, sighing dramatically, she said, "I think I lost my keys in the market. Those little kids were hassling me for money, and my key must've fallen out when I searched for small change in my bag."

The girl smiled sweetly. "Those kids are such a nuisance. Madam should not give money. This is making the problem worse."

"Of course, you're right. Thank you, I will certainly take your advice. I am Mrs. Andrew Riseborough."

"Just a minute," said the girl, and peered at the computer screen. She jotted down the room number and provided a new key with the room number on the little billfold. Carla thanked her and walked away, smiling smugly.

As she stepped out of the lift on the second floor, she realized how much she had missed Andrew. *I'll kiss him gently on his eyes to wake him,* she decided, as she swiped the key through the door lock.

The bedside light was on, but it took a few seconds for Carla's eyes to adjust to the dimness of the room. The urgent movement and whispers under the crisp white cotton sheets confused her, and she realized she must have entered the wrong room. She turned around and made for the door, but bumped over a floor lamp, which went crashing onto the marble floor.

Scarlet with embarrassment, she turned her head to apologize, and then she froze. As though in slow motion, she saw Andrew gently pushing aside a slim, dark-haired woman, golden nakedness against his fair chest. At first the golden body had no face, but suddenly it came into focus: the beautiful features of the Parisian-born, Lebanese colleague of Andrew's...Leila. Carla felt that she had been punched in the midriff.

She ran out of the room and stumbled into the lift. She pressed the button for her floor, but forgot to get out. The lift went down to ground level, and she tripped out. The lobby was empty, and the receptionist, who looked like she was gossiping on the phone, gave her a curious glance. In a daze, Carla walked toward her and asked for the bill for her room. Without checking it, Carla handed her an American Express card and signed it. The receptionist asked her if she needed help with her luggage. This galvanized Carla into action and she said, "No thanks, but please order me a taxi for the airport." She went to her room half hoping, half dreading that Andrew would find her, but the corridor was empty. She collected her suitcase and went back to the lobby, scanning it for Andrew, but he wasn't there.

She walked to the waiting taxi at the entrance to the hotel; she wouldn't let herself cry in front of strangers. Nodding politely at the taxi driver, she slumped down in the back seat and heard a voice that sounded like it was coming from a great distance asking, "Which airline?"

Somehow she managed to say, "I'm not sure, drop me anywhere, I'll find it."

He looked at her strangely in the rearview mirror, shrugged, and started winding his way through the quiet streets to the airport.

The airport was almost deserted, and with a groan Carla watched the last flight for Lahore taxiing down the runway for departure. The next flight was eight hours later. As she sat down on a metal bench, her phone rang. It was Andrew, but she ignored the call and switched off the phone. She had a bitter taste in her mouth and hoped she wasn't going to be sick.

She stood up abruptly and walked to the self-service coffee dispenser. A couple of Americans dressed in flak jackets were hovering and conversing genially around the machine. She had to ask them quite loudly to move. One of them, a curly-haired, blond giant of a man, looked at her in surprise and said, "Hey, Carla, what are you doing here?"

Frowning, she looked up at him, recognizing him as a CNN cameraman. "Todd. What are *you* doing here?"

"We're working on a story. This is Evan Robertson, a freelance journalist temporarily in CNN's employ," he said, and then introduced Carla.

"Where to now?" Carla asked.

"We have a chartered eight-seater to Delhi. Evan is stationed in India, and boy, he's well connected. We have permission to fly straight over Indian air space and land at the international airport in Delhi. Where are you going?"

"Delhi, but I'm afraid I missed the last flight to Lahore, so now I'll have to wait."

Todd turned toward his friend. "Hey, Evan, do you think we have space for another passenger to Delhi?"

Evan, who had walked away and was talking urgently into his mobile phone, looked up and smiled. "Sure, but does she have credentials?"

Carla searched her purse and showed them her press badge.

"Cool, you can bunk up with me," Todd said casually, but perhaps a little too quickly.

Carla laughed. "It's OK. My best friend from college lives there. I'm staying with her. I'll just give her a quick call to tell her I'm on my way."

Todd blushed. "Sure, take your time. We're not taking off for another couple of hours."

The Cessna 441 waiting on the runway was battered, and evidence of bullet holes near the tail end made Carla waver. She stopped and studied the aircraft with a dubious expression. Todd noticed and pushed her gently toward it. "Don't worry. This girl just looks a little rough on the outside. Believe me, she'll give you a ride as smooth as butter."

With a raised eyebrow, Carla decided anything was better than sitting on those cold metal benches for another eight hours. "Of course, you're right. Who's the pilot?"

Todd looked behind her and pointed to a long-haired man dressed in jeans and a shabby, khaki Afghanka jacket, the type worn by the Russian soldiers during their Afghan war. He walked past Carla and with a mock salute greeted her in Russian. Carla looked at Todd in despair, but he smiled and said, "Vladimir is the best pilot ever to come out of Mother Russia."

A couple of Afghans dressed in Pathani suits lifted heavy camera equipment into the plane. A Pakistani official checked all the metal suitcases and ticked off the items from the list he was holding.

"I hope we don't overload it," Carla said, but Todd laughed heartily and helped her inside the aircraft. The leather seats were tatty and dirty, but Carla didn't notice; she was too busy watching a Pakistani airport mechanic sticking his fingers through the bulletholes and laughing loudly.

When all the passengers were onboard, Evan passed her a bottle of Russian vodka wrapped in a paper bag. She was about to refuse, but changed her mind when she heard the shrieking whine from the engine. Much to the surprise and delight of her fellow passengers, Carla tipped her head back and took a massive swig from the bottle. Vladimir got the plane off the ground without any hitches, and Carla felt herself relaxing. Her lids were heavy, and she fell asleep within the first five minutes of being airborne.

Elouise Singh replaced the phone on the charger next to her bed and smiled. Harry sighed and turned onto his side on the king-size bed. "Does Carla not realize it's not very polite to call at such an ungodly hour?"

Elouise frowned at her husband. "Don't be such a grouch. Poor Carla's in a state. She's at the Peshawar airport and will be flying into Delhi in a couple of hours."

"What on earth is she doing in Peshawar?"

"I don't know. Does it matter?"

With a grunt he turned the other way and went back to sleep. Elouise switched off the bedside lamp, but couldn't go back to sleep. She was so excited to see Carla and realized it had been more than five years since they had last seen one another. Carla hadn't said much on the phone, but Elouise knew something was amiss. In her mind she started organizing the guest bedroom, making a mental note to tell the driver to pick up some decent gin from the bootlegger.

An immigration official and airport security met the Cessna on the runway. The official checked Carla's visa and welcomed her to Delhi. His smile, wide and genuine, somehow reassured her. Todd gave her a hug and told her to call him. She said she would and then she thanked Evan and Vladimir for the flight. She waved good-bye and walked out of the Delhi airport arrivals lounge. The morning was already hot and a cloud of pollution hung over the city. A thick layer of dust blanketed everything, even the large, heart-shaped leaves of the peepal trees, normally a vivid green, now a dull khaki like that of desert army fatigues.

And then the anticipated smell of India: exotic spices trying their best to mask the stench of excrement, body odor, decaying flesh and vegetation. Spiraling wafts of smoky-scented incense and the sight of welcoming parties, drivers, and coolies greeted her as she waded through the chaos.

Carla scanned the faces of the crowd. Some were standing behind a metal railing, controlled by a fierce policeman in a drab brown uniform, carrying an ancient-looking rifle. A young man peered anxiously at her. Having caught her attention, he pointed to a cardboard sign with her name on it in bold red script.

"Mrs. Carla Gill?"

Carla nodded her head and walked toward him, where she was rewarded with a wide smile.

"I am Om Prakash, being the most devoted driver of your very best friend, Madam Elouise Parker Singh. I have been instructed to pick you up and convey you safely to her residence in Delhi."

Carla smiled in delight at the accent and rather old-school English.

"Thank you so much, Om Prakash. I'm very happy indeed to be traveling with you into the city," she said, mimicking him.

With a coy smile and no words rehearsed for an appropriate answer, he grabbed her suitcase and tried to take her purse from her, but with a firm tug she managed to hold onto it.

On the way to the car, he expertly managed to ward off the dozen or more helpers keen to assist with Carla's small suitcase. The white Ambassador, with little lace curtains in the windows, was surprisingly spacious, and it wasn't any wonder that it was still the preferred car used by politicians and ministers in India.

As Carla gazed out of the window, she saw traffic everywhere: cars of most descriptions; three wheelers, or "tuk-tuks"; cargo trucks painted with garlands of bright flowers, carrying loads three times their size. Between the honking and chaos, a couple of white, dirty, and painfully thin cows sauntered along, oblivious to the noise and threat of the traffic.

After forty minutes the scenery started changing. The traffic eased up. The wider roads were lined with beautiful flowering trees.

"The diplomatic enclave," Om Prakash said, beaming.

"This must be Lutyen's Delhi," Carla muttered to herself, having read extensively about Edwin Lutyen, the British architect, commissioned by the Raj to create the new administrative center known as New Delhi. With many of these buildings still in use today, Carla had decided to add it as a must-see while in Delhi.

They passed a massive park with some impressive ancient architecture, and Carla asked Om Prakash if he knew what the buildings were. Sitting a little taller in the driver's seat, he said, "It is the tomb of Mohammad Shah, last of Sayyid dynasty rulers. Building in the early fourteenth century. It was all village around tombs from Lodhi dynasty to defeat of Moghul dynasty. It was at the time of the English in 1936 that the village was moved and big garden was made by Lady Willingdon, wife of Governor General.

"After independence of India in 1947, it was changed from the Lady Willingdon Garden to Lodhi Garden." He slowed down and pointed out the original name, Lady Willingdon Gardens, still at the entrance.

"Thanks, Om Prakash. You know your history," Carla said with a smile, genuinely impressed.

Om Prakash grinned modestly. "I am always number one in history at school."

A uniformed guard saluted as they drove through wrought-iron gates down a short driveway of neem and peepal trees. Rows upon rows of terracotta pots, a single Delphinium in splendid canary yellow in each, lined the walls of the Colonial-style bungalow.

CHAPTER 3

Elouise Parker Singh was sitting on a rattan chair in the middle of her large garden, reading the *Indian Times*. The lawn, manicured to perfection, equaled the most respectable golfing greens in the city. She wore a cream cotton kameez over a pair of skinny jeans with Indian beaded chappals. Her long, dark hair was casually knotted under a wide, frayed straw hat. As the Ambassador coasted up the driveway, her hazel eyes lit up with joy, and she jumped up to open the car door, much to Om Prakash's dismay.

"Carla! I'm so glad you're here," she said as she pulled Carla out of the car.

As they hugged one another, Carla said, "Oh, Elouise, you have no idea how happy I am to see you!"

Elouise looked at her beautiful friend and noticed that she hadn't aged a day in the past five years. Carla's dark blond hair, with a few golden highlights framing her oval face, was pulled into a long ponytail. Her aquamarine eyes were almost translucent as she lifted her hand to shade them from the bright Indian light. The contrast with her golden complexion was startling.

"Is it possible we're going to be thirty-five this year?" Elouise teased.

Carla smiled wryly. "Too old for my husband, I guess."

"What do you mean?" Elouise asked, concerned and noticing the quiver in Carla's bottom lip. She put her arm around Carla's waist and led her to a rattan chair on the lawn.

Carla sat down heavily, the tears now flowing freely, and told Elouise what had happened in Peshawar. Elouise listened intently without interrupting her. A servant appeared and was waved away. When Carla had recounted the previous night's events, they both sat quietly for a few minutes.

"Oh, Carla, you poor thing," Elouise said, shaking her head. "Andrew is a fool. In no time he will be back looking for forgiveness."

"I don't know. I had no idea it would hurt so much. We haven't been very close lately, but I just presumed it was because we were spending so much time apart. Not the case, it seems. I feel like such a fool." And, laughing self-consciously, Carla added, "I'm not going to bore you with all my problems, Elouise. We haven't seen one another in ages, and I think we should have fun and worry about Andrew later."

"I agree, but please, Carla, if you want to talk about it or need a shoulder to cry on—"

Carla squeezed her friend's hand and said, "I know, thank you."

"Are you going to try and see some of your dad's family?"

"I'm not sure. I'll consult with an advocate-friend of my dad's regarding my grandfather's will. I told you he left me quite a valuable property. My dad said this is certainly going to stir things up, especially with my step-grandmother."

"Oh my God, the Enchantress! Is she still alive?"

"Oh yes, she was much younger than my grandfather; don't you remember that time she came with him on his first visit to me in the States?"

Elouise threw back her head and laughed loudly. "Of course, how could I forget?"

They had been roommates for most of their college education in Boston: Elouise, with all her American confidence and self-assured manner, and Carla, the foreign student, shy and in awe of her surroundings and fellow students. They complemented each other perfectly, becoming firm friends. At that unannounced visit, Elouise had accompanied Carla to dinner with her grandfather. Carla was awkward and unsure of how to handle the situation, as her father had not spoken to him in more than twenty years. At first the stately, bearded man wearing a starched blue turban seemed stern and formidable. But her heart very soon opened up to him when she saw the streaming tears streaking his gray-white beard. It wasn't long before he became one of the most important people in Carla's life.

Noticing the wistful expression in her friend's eyes, Elouise said, "Come, let me show you your room."

They walked through a huge, carved wooden door. A white jasmine creeper in a terra-cotta pot climbed up the doorframe, pregnant with the weight of its heady, exquisite fragrance. Once through the cool, single-story bungalow, they crossed an open courtyard of paved sandstone. The bedroom to the right of the courtyard boasted high ceilings from which an enormous fan rotated lazily. As Carla followed Elouise to the en suite bath and dressing room, she marveled at the pleasing décor of green and white marble floors, the cool, white, marble-clad walls in perfect harmony.

"I hope you'll be comfortable here. Rest a little, then come and have some breakfast with me. Seema, the maidservant, speaks a little English, and she will be at your service the whole day."

Carla stared in wonder at Elouise, who spoke to the maid in fluent Hindi before heading back to the other side of the house.

The houseboy—his name quite escaped Carla—put her suitcase in the dressing room, and Seema started unpacking. The cook, Kishan, knocked gently and with a friendly smile presented her with a cup of tea on a silver tray.

"What for breakfast, Madam? I, Kishan, can make Indian breakfast or conti-style. You like to have some fruit?"

Carla had to smile. "Thank you, but I'm fine with a cup of tea for now." But, observing the disappointment on his face, she changed her mind and said, "Actually, some fruit and Indian breakfast sounds wonderful."

Beaming, he rushed out, scolding Seema in Hindi on his way to the kitchen.

Muttering something under her breath, Seema smiled at Carla and said, "Madam take bath now? Clean towels in here." She pointed to the wooden glass cabinet.

"Thank you, Seema."

"You call me if Madam need somethings," Seema said, and left, closing the Burmese teak double door behind her.

Carla kicked off her shoes and sank into the oversized dark wooden bed, little carved cherubs framing the sides at the head. On the opposite wall, a display of framed lithographs depicted scenes of life in Delhi during the Raj. A carved chaise longue, upholstered in mink silk, rested under the artwork. To one side stood a table on which an ornate silver vase boasted a cascade of watermelon-pink roses.

She sighed. It was a contented sigh, not happy, but at least not one of desperation, hurt, and betrayal. She still could not think of Andrew and Leila in bed together, not consciously, at least. But the image kept resurfacing, making her feel sick in the pit of her stomach—the skin tones contrasting and glistening in the dim lamplight. She quickly shook her head, as if the movement would make the memory disappear forever. *India is the perfect distraction.* With that she put her head back against the pillows and breathed deeply. *I have a good feeling about India,* she thought as she drifted into a dreamless sleep.

When she woke up, she was surprised to realize that she had slept for almost an hour. She yawned lazily and decided to take a bath. After her bath, she dressed quickly in a white linen dress with a narrow brown belt and matching flat sandals. Lifting her chin resolutely, she brushed her hair and pulled it back into its signature ponytail.

The moment she stepped through her door, Seema and Kishan were standing with a ready smile, beckoning her to the wide veranda. Kishan pulled out a chair for her under a large fan, and to her surprise, a cup of hot tea and a plate of cut mango and melon were set on the table.

"Aloo paratha coming presently, Madam," Kishan said and disappeared into the kitchen.

Carla picked up her teacup as Elouise walked in, smiling brightly. Carla's spirit warmed immediately—she was so grateful for special friends like Elouise; she knew the bright smile was purely for her benefit, to cheer her up without mentioning anything about Andrew.

"Good, you're up," said Elouise, as she took a seat opposite Carla.

"How did they manage to time all this to such perfection?" Carla asked amused.

"Seema was posted outside your bathroom, and the minute your bathwater was heard running out, Cook was told and breakfast was started." Looking up she saw Kishan walking over with a tray. "Oh good, here's your breakfast. Thank you Kishan."

"I could get used to this all too easily." Carla laughed and bit into the steaming hot, spicy, potato-stuffed flatbread. "Delicious." Feeling her stomach grumble appreciatively, she realized she hadn't really eaten since leaving for Peshawar two days earlier. "Do you have this every morning, Elouise?"

"Would love to, but I'm afraid of outgrowing my wardrobe."

Carla surprised herself by eating every last bite on her plate. Kishan cleared their plates and discussed something with Elouise in Hindi.

"We were just discussing lunch," Elouise explained.

"Your Hindi is pretty good."

"I guess it should be. I've been here for over three years."

Carla smiled, but noticed a strange undertone in Elouise's usually upbeat voice and wondered if she was happy living in Delhi.

After breakfast, Elouise suggested a trip to Khan Market, the local shopping market near their house. As Elouise was calling Om Prakash to bring the car around, a Jeep pulled into the driveway, and Harry got out. He was still a handsome man, with his Indian clean-cut cricketer looks, Carla thought.

He embraced Carla and said rather formally, "Welcome to India. I hope you enjoy your visit."

Carla watched the married couple as they greeted each other. Elouise smiled and greeted him warmly. He did not return her pleasantries, but asked her to see to his packing, as he had to leave for a conference in the early afternoon. Carla was concerned for her friend, and a thought flashed across her mind that perhaps no marriage was perfect.

Carla noticed the fleeting shadow in Elouise's eyes as she smiled and replied with forced cheerfulness, "Of course, darling. How long will you be away?"

"Not sure. Pack for a week to be safe." He said this without looking back as he went into the house and headed for his study.

With an apologetic look, Elouise told Carla to continue on to the market and that she would join her later, as soon as she had completed Harry's packing. She waved awkwardly and hurried into the house. Getting into the car, Carla couldn't help but think of the confident, independent Elouise at college. This woman being ordered to pack for her husband conflicted so with that image. She decided she would talk to Elouise when an appropriate moment presented itself. Until then she would concentrate on distracting herself from her own heartache by taking in everything India had to offer.

Arriving at Khan Market, Carla's ideas of an "Indian market" were dealt a brutal blow. Khan Market was more shopping mall than side stall-market, selling international fashion and electronics. But on exploration she found some quaint shops selling local handicrafts and many fabric merchants with a resident tailor in the back of their long, narrow shops.

Carla was relieved when her phone rang and Elouise told her to wait where she was, that she would see her in a minute. She would have a guide to help her find her way in this new environment.

True to her word, Elouise caught up with Carla, who was admiring some ethnic home textiles at Fabindia.

"I must introduce you to Sanjay, my tailor. He can copy any designer item in your wardrobe, beautifully and at one-third of the price."

"That's a great idea. I would love to have this Armani dress copied—I've had it for years and it's still my favorite," Carla enthused.

"Did you pack some party dresses?" Elouise enquired, her eyes laughing.

"Not really. Why, should I have?"

"Absolutely! Delhi is a happening place. I've been to more parties since I've been here than my whole life in the States. In fact, we're going to a party tonight at a friend's house. That's if you're up to it?"

"Yes, why not?" Carla wasn't convinced she would be up to it, but she had to try.

"Good, one of my favorite Indian designers has a shop here. Let's find you something special."

Walking through the large glass doors, Carla stared in awe at the beautiful collection. On the one side was a long rail of exquisitely embroidered traditional Indian suits and on the other side, a rail of Indo-Western style evening suits and dresses.

"Oh, wow, this is shopping nirvana." Carla became aware of excitement building up inside her—a welcome relief to the nausea she had felt since Peshawar. She browsed through the collection and picked out a cream, silk crepe, one-shoulder dress, draped in a flowing Grecian style. Gold, pearl, and Swarovski beading on the left hip completed the classy gown. Feeling like Aphrodite, she admired herself in the floor-length mirror to the delighted approval of Elouise and the shop assistant.

"Yes, you have to have it!" Elouise said and started bargaining with the young salesgirl.

"Nothing like some retail therapy to mend a broken heart." Carla beamed, sitting at a coffee shop in the center of the market. Elouise looked at her sympathetically, and Carla thought this might be the moment to broach the subject of Elouise's relationship with Harry.

After ordering their coffees, Carla tried to talk about Harry, but Elouise was evasive. Eventually, with a pained expression, Elouise said, "Please, Carla, can we discuss him another time? He is a busy man, always working on some or other important government project. I think I preferred it when he was a physics lecturer in the States. India has been a big adjustment, and Harry is different here. I guess we all are, in our home environments. The worst part is that we don't spend much time together, and things are a little tense."

"Of course. I'm sorry, I didn't mean to pry." Carla silently chastised herself; she wouldn't want people asking her too many questions about Andrew before she was ready to talk about him. She couldn't even face the subject herself, never mind speak about it with someone else. She swiftly changed the subject, discussing possible travel plans to Rajasthan after she had contacted her father's advocate.

Elouise insisted on paying the bill. "I'm afraid I'm busy this afternoon with my kids. They have dance classes, but Om Prakash will be with you the whole day. He knows Delhi really well, and I think he quite fancies himself as the ultimate Indian tour guide. So you carry on, OK?"

She gave Carla a hug and said, "We'll have drinks at eight on the veranda and leave for the party around nine. Have fun. See you later."

Carla smiled at Elouise, but afraid that her prying had upset her friend, she was about to apologize. Sensing Carla's discomfort, Elouise said, "I almost forgot; Cook will have lunch ready at two, but if you prefer to stay out, you'll find a great Caesar salad at the Imperial Hotel. Oh, and you must try Rajah at the Imperial's beauty parlor—he is great with almond oil head massages."

Carla knew this was Elouise's way of letting her know there was nothing to feel bad about. They hugged each other good-bye. Then, glancing at her watch, Elouise smiled at the waitress and rushed out.

The suggested visit to the Imperial Hotel appealed to Carla, so she phoned Om Prakash to bring the car around to the front of the market. As they turned into the king palm–lined driveway to the white colonial hotel, Carla recognized the distinct architecture of Bromfield, Lutyen's associate in 1931.

A handsome, turbaned Sikh opened Carla's door with a flourish and welcomed her to the hotel. The lovely sense of luxurious calm was briefly interrupted when Carla was requested to go through a security check. She suddenly realized that this must be in consequence of the terrorist attack in Mumbai in November 2008. Since the attack, hotels all over India had stepped up security measures, vowing to not have another massacre. Carla remembered having to report on the casualty figures: 173 killed; 300 wounded. A tight band of unease gripped her, but she resisted with a determined effort.

As she looked around the plush hotel lobby, her unease began to abate. The cool, jasmine-scented marble interior greeted her like an oasis in the Gobi desert. It was beautifully renovated without any loss to its colonial style. Antique furniture and old black-and-white photos transported her back to an era of gracious indulgence.

A friendly concierge directed Carla to the beauty parlor, where she asked for a head massage. Hesitating for a brief second, she also decided to spoil herself with a manicure and pedicure. *Perhaps I'll charge it to Andrew's credit card.* The thought was somehow pleasing.

The vigorous head massage left her surprisingly drowsy, but Carla had a feeling that the therapists were gossiping about her in Hindi. A sweet, round-faced man did her pedicure, and it was the manicurist who eventually asked her where she was from. When she told them her father was Indian and her mother South African, they were incredulous but continued their heated debate in Hindi. Carla had her mother's features and blond hair, with the exception of large, almond-shaped eyes and golden complexion reminiscent of her father.

After a relaxing foot massage she chose a deep red polish for her toenails and a clear polish for her fingernails. Rajah, the head masseur, asked Carla to sit in front of the mirror while he expertly blow-dried her hair and admiringly brushed it over her shoulders.

Carla tipped them generously and, feeling rejuvenated, headed for the restaurant where she decided to try some local Indian snacks instead of the recommended Caesar salad.

As she relished the snacks, she looked around the restaurant, fascinated by the many guests dining there. Well-heeled tourists and a large table with elegant Indian ladies almost filled the restaurant, which looked out onto a magnificent lawn.

The waiter startled her as he presented her with the bill. She sighed and, feeling slightly depressed, paid and left the restaurant.

As she headed for the exit, she passed the Chanel boutique in the lobby. Impulsively, she went inside and asked for advice on their fragrances. The impeccably dressed sales assistant suggested that she try the limited edition called Maharani, available only in Delhi. She told Carla that the fragrance was especially created for an Indian princess who used no other fragrance until her death five years ago. Chanel had released the last few bottles exclusively in India in keeping with the tradition.

Whether influenced by the romantic tale or by the intoxicating fragrance of delicate oriental spice and jasmine, Carla handed over her American Express card and paid a small fortune for the handmade Christofle crystal bottle wrapped in layers of tissue and satin ribbon. Feeling ridiculously pleased with herself, she called the driver and headed back to the bungalow.

As the car slowed down in front of the house, Carla witnessed an obviously intense argument between Elouise and Harry. Without acknowledging Carla, Harry got into the backseat of his car, said something to his driver, and drove out the gate.

"Everything OK?" Carla asked as she got out of the car.

With a shrug Elouise answered, "Nothing serious, let's have tea."

That evening, Carla slipped on her gold-braided high-heeled sandals and sprayed the exquisite fragrance of her Chanel perfume in a lavish cloud around her. She felt every inch the princess poised to make an entrance into a world of glamour, politics, and intrigue. Catching a glimpse of herself in the mirror, she shook her head in mild amusement at her overly fertile imagination. If nothing else, she was grateful for this capacity to fantasize—it certainly lifted her spirit, distracting her from the fact that she hadn't received one phone call from Andrew since she had left Peshawar. She wondered if he even cared that she had caught him with Leila; perhaps he was relieved he no longer had to be with her. Taking a deep breath, Carla fought back the tears that had been threatening all day and smoothed the skirt of her dress. She would have fun tonight; Andrew wouldn't ruin another moment of her time in India.

When she reached the veranda, she saw that citronella candles and lanterns had been placed in and around the garden. Eastern music drifted its sentimental chords from the drawing room. Kishan saw her and smiled his broad, happy smile.

"Madam care for a drink? I can suggest very good gin fizz; Madam Elouise teach me very well."

"That sounds wonderful," Carla replied with real enthusiasm as she seated herself on the rather antique-looking plantation chairs. Alcohol would definitely numb her senses and help her forget.

"What a perfect evening," Elouise said as she joined Carla on the veranda. "I'm afraid enjoying an evening outside without big air coolers won't last much longer now—it's been surprisingly cool this April."

Kishan returned with the drinks and handed Carla hers on a silver tray.

"Cheers, and it is so good to see you after so many years," Carla said as she raised her glass to Elouise.

They drank quietly, and then Carla said, "This really is the best gin fizz I've ever tasted."

"It's the Indian limes and mint. Their flavor is incomparable anywhere in the world."

Elouise's daughters, looking well scrubbed and smelling of jasmine, ran onto the veranda in their pajamas and hugged their mother lovingly. "Come on, girls, say hello to Aunty Carla."

"Wow, you girls have grown, and you're way more beautiful than the photos you sent me last summer," Carla said as she gave them each a hug and good night kiss.

The eldest, Zara, in her early teens, had inherited her mother's fresh-faced "all-American" looks, while her younger sister by three years, Chanda, resembled her father in every way. *In a few years she will be able to take Bollywood by storm*, Carla thought as she admired Chanda's beauty.

The ayah came looking for them and took the girls to bed. Carla asked if they weren't a little old for a nurse, but Elouise explained how some of the ayahs were mostly spinsters or widows, and they chose to stay with their wards, sometimes following them to their marital homes.

Then Elouise asked Kishan to have the driver bring the car to the front of the bungalow.

"So, whose party is it?" Carla asked as they got into the back of the car.

"The Kapoors are well-known industrialists, and Ronnie is the honorary consul for Honduras. His wife, Preeti, is quite a famous designer and popular socialite. She's divine; you'll love her."

"So Ronnie is South American?" Carla asked, baffled.

"No, he bought his title," Elouise laughed. A smiling Carla thought that with hosts like these, this was bound to be an interesting party.

The drive was remarkably short, and as Om Prakash dropped them at the entrance, Carla noticed diplomatic flags on many of the luxury sedans. The smartly dressed guard welcomed them and, holding open a heavy curtain of white roses and jasmine strung together, showed them the way inside.

Carla was amazed: the entire garden was a vision, lit with fairy lights and torches. Waiters with trays of drinks and aromatic kebabs were weaving expertly and quite unobtrusively between the guests. An Asian-looking female vocalist and Indian band occupied a corner platform, marginally higher than the parquet dance floor on the lawn. In a dreamy haze, Carla felt quite overcome, no doubt the combination of her surroundings and the gin fizz. Just then, the vocalist began to sing one of Carla's favorite numbers from the sixties.

An Indian woman, wearing an exquisite navy chiffon sari embroidered in silver zardozi, smiled warmly as she greeted Elouise.

"Preeti, please meet my dearest friend, Carla Gill. She lives in London. We were college roommates."

Preeti took Carla's outstretched hand. "You are most welcome. Is this your first visit to India?" Before Carla could manage a reply, Preeti continued, "Please let me know if you need anything at all. Come. Let me introduce you to some of our guests. I think the British ambassador might have arrived already."

Still holding Carla's arm, she led her away to a group of beautifully dressed women and introduced her to her "kitty" circle. Carla raised an eyebrow in slight confusion at the name. This delighted the ladies, as they giggled and explained that they were merely a group of ladies who met once a month for lunch. They urged Carla to try the different snacks every time they saw a waiter, but with a glass of Chilean Chardonnay in hand, she protested and excused herself in search of Elouise.

An interesting mix of people filled the garden: socialites dripping in extraordinary jewelry on the arms of well-to-do businessmen and industrialists, ambassadors and embassy staff of different nationalities, and some bohemian-looking artists and poets.

Carla found Elouise chatting with a group of dignitaries from Nepal. Elouise introduced Carla to the Nepalese ambassador and then asked her, "Do you remember the Nepalese royal massacre of 2001 in Kathmandu?" Carla nodded, and Elouise continued excitedly, smiling at the ambassador, "Well, His Excellency was at the party on that horrific night."

Carla clearly remembered the story; one of her colleagues worked on it and had filled her in on all the gory details of how the crown prince had shot dead ten people, including his parents, members of the royal family, and then himself.

Sensing the ambassador's discomfort at the memory, Carla changed the subject by asking, "Would I need a visa for Nepal?"

Elouise gave Carla an amused glance, mouthing, "Always the diplomat."

The ambassador was obviously relieved and replied kindly, "You'll be granted a visa at the port of entrance to

Nepal. I do hope you will visit us." He handed Carla his business card. She smiled and thanked him.

Elouise then excused herself and Carla, and together they headed over to the bar.

A tall, broad-shouldered man stood with his back to them but turned around as he heard Elouise asking Carla what she would like to drink.

"Ah, it is the enchanting Mrs. Singh. How are you?" The man saw Elouise trying to catch the bartender's attention and said, "Please, allow me."

Elouise smiled and said rather hastily, "Thank you, George, make it two glasses of Chardonnay."

"Of course, but you will first have to introduce me to your lovely friend," he said, smiling at Carla. His dark brown eyes narrowed in their smile. The visible appraisal made Carla feel slightly self-conscious.

"This is Carla Gill; she is visiting me from England," Elouise said politely.

His grip was firm as he shook Carla's hand. "Welcome to India. This is not your first trip, is it?"

Carla smiled. "Yes, it is, even though my father was born here."

George looked at her intently. "And your mother?"

"She's South African. My parents still live there."

Still smiling and studying her for a moment, he lowered his voice and in a convincing tone said, "You are exquisite."

Quite unsettled, Carla felt herself blushing, but luckily he had turned to order their drinks. Carla now took the opportunity to study him. *American, early forties, athletic build, steel-gray hair cut short, but not unfashionably. Strong jaw line, yet there is softness to his face. Yes, definitely a handsome man,* she concluded as he handed her a glass of wine.

About to ask him how he knew Elouise, Carla heard her friend saying, "Thank you, George, we'll see you around." With that, Elouise tried to steer Carla away from the bar.

Carla choked slightly on her first sip of wine, not having anticipated this sudden departure. She cringed as George handed her a napkin to wipe the wine off her chin. In hasty retreat, she murmured, "Thank you, nice meeting you."

He raised his glass and said, "Until we meet again."

Carla went in search of Elouise and found her on the other side of the garden, chatting with a distinguished Indian man who, once Carla had reached them, was introduced as Ronnie. Now was evidently not the time to ask Elouise why she hadn't wanted to chat to the handsome American instead of this older man. Stuck for just what to say, Carla gushed, "What a lovely party," feeling decidedly tipsy.

"You are most welcome," he said.

The dance floor was packed as the band started playing energetic Bollywood music. Carla stared in awe at the skillful dancing of some of the guests.

"Do you enjoy dancing?" Ronnie asked Carla.

"Yes, I do, but I'm not sure I could manage these Bollywood moves."

"Of course you can. I'll show you," Ronnie said as he dragged her onto the dance floor. Ronnie obviously loved dancing and seemed quite the expert, Carla thought as she awkwardly tried to copy his moves. Smiles of encouragement from Ronnie and some dancers around her helped her to relax, and surprising herself, she found her rhythm, loving the extravagant Bollywood moves. After a few energetic numbers, the band was back with a slow jazz classic. Ronnie thanked her, and as she followed him, strong arms encircled her waist and drew her back onto the dance floor.

George smiled at her wickedly, and to her annoyance the telltale rising warmth in her face betrayed her outwardly cool demeanor. He steered her gently to the middle of the dance floor, holding her firmly, but not too close. They danced slowly, and Carla relaxed in his arms.

"Is your husband joining you later?" George asked, watching her closely.

"No, he isn't," she replied, avoiding his gaze. *No point boring him with my sob story,* she thought. "What do you do in Delhi, George?" She looked up and held his gaze.

"I work at the American Embassy, issue visas and so on."

"Oh, yes, I remember driving past the American compound, quite impressive. Do you live inside the compound?"

"No, luckily the American taxpayers pay for a very comfortable ground floor apartment opposite Lodhi Garden. I have a great cook who takes good care of me. You should come for dinner." As he said this, he looked up and frowned. "I think Elouise is looking for you."

Carla was surprised to see Elouise beckoning her, looking rather irritated. "I guess she wants to go home. Thanks for the dance."

"The pleasure is all mine," George drawled, reaching into his blazer pocket and taking out his business card. He gave it to her and said, "I would love to show you around. I know Delhi quite well—give me a call."

Carla took his card and slipped it into her evening purse. Turning around, she felt a stab of guilt in her chest as one word echoed in her mind: *Andrew.* Then the image of Andrew in bed with Leila resurfaced, and Carla shook her head; she wouldn't feel guilty for just dancing with this man and taking his card—it wasn't like she was sleeping with him. She smiled at Elouise as she walked toward her.

"I'm sorry, Carla, but I need to get home. My yogi is coming at six tomorrow morning."

"That's OK; I'm pretty tired, too. It's been a long day."

They thanked their hosts and left with a promise to meet soon for dinner.

In the car, Carla said, "Thanks, Elouise, I really enjoyed myself this evening."

"I'm glad, but watch out for George—you don't want to

go straight from the frying pan into the fire."

Carla nodded knowingly. "You're right; he's quite the charmer. So you know him well?"

"He hangs out in the same circles as Harry and I," Elouise said casually as they arrived home. Carla could sense that there was more to it than that, but she brushed the niggling feeling aside. She wouldn't be calling George anyway, so there was no point in asking any more about him.

They went inside, and Carla was surprised to see Kishan still awake. He asked her if she would like some tea.

Carla chuckled. "No, thanks, Kishan."

"What time Memsahib would like tea in the morning?"

Carla realized that she was extremely tired and decided a sleep-in would be a great idea.

"Ten o'clock, thank you, Kishan."

Elouise had already disappeared into her bedroom, so Carla closed her door and got ready for bed.

Later, sinking into her comfortable bed, she replayed the evening's events. She sighed dreamily and smiled. As she drifted into a deep sleep, an image of George—and not Andrew—filled her mind.

CHAPTER 4

Carla woke up to the persistent calling of the green parrots in the mango tree. Sunlight filtered through the blinds, and she had to adjust her eyes to the light. Memories of the previous evening flooded her thoughts. She felt strangely happy. Could she be healing so soon after Andrew's betrayal? Was India somehow spiritually regenerative?

She reached for her watch on the bedside table and was surprised to see that it was only ten past eight. Checking her phone and e-mail for any messages from Andrew, she felt unexpectedly relieved to find none. Well rested, she decided to get up and take a walk in Lodhi Garden adjacent to the bungalow. She dressed hastily in her Ralph Lauren track pants and T-shirt, socks, and tennis shoes, and tied up her hair in a messy ponytail.

Upon seeing Kishan, she requested him to ask one of the chowkidars to direct her to the entrance of the gardens. Some argument ensued between the guard, the mali, and Kishan. Finally, settling their disagreement, all three showed her the way to one of the side entrances. Carla thanked them and, laughing, declined their offer of further accompaniment. She waved to them as she started her walk, following the footpath around the garden.

Quite a number of walkers and joggers were on the path, including some ayahs with their young wards in strollers. They greeted Carla politely as they passed her. Tall palm trees lined parts of the pathway leading up to the beautiful Moghul tombs. The lawns were well maintained, with a variety of shrubs and flowers, but it was the trees that had her in awe: large, old, and wise. If only they could talk, Carla thought, all the wonderful stories they'd recount: lovers meeting in the shade of the banyan tree or children making oaths and promises of lifetime friendships.

Some children were playing cricket on the lawns surrounding a magnificent, domed, red sandstone tomb. They giggled as Carla caught a ball bowled too high for the young batsman. With a mischievous smile, she tossed it playfully back to the bowler. The young bowler, dressed in dirty white cricket trousers, beckoned her and indicated that she should take over from the wicket keeper. He was a scrawny young boy who wore sad khaki shorts and an expression to match. Laughing, she declined by shaking her head firmly, aware that any ambiguous shaking of her head might resemble that of the Indian quaint head wiggle—a gentle nodding and shaking at a slight angle, meaning "yes" or "I agree with you."

Some curious onlookers tried to cajole her into the game. Feeling a little silly, she decided to be a sport and took up a fielding position, much to the relief of the young wicketkeeper. The batsman looked at her with an expression of mild amusement. He shuffled his feet into a ready position and waited for the bowler. He did not take his eyes off the tattered, faded-red cricket ball. The bowler, who was determined to impress Carla, bowled short, and the smiling batsman hit the ball high and long in her direction. Unprepared, she ran backward with arms outstretched and eyes intent on the ball. As it started its descent toward her, she tripped over a broken branch and fell flat on her back, winded. She lay still for a moment to regain her breath. The boys and the interested spectators rushed toward her, talking and gesticulating all at once. They helped her up with much concern.

As she sat up, she noticed two Afghani men in Pathani clothes, sitting in the common haunch position of the subcontinent. They were watching her with interest. She got up and, feeling embarrassed, looked away. She thanked her teammates, dusted herself off, and made her way back to the exit, passing the two Afghanis. She kept her eyes on the path in front of her, but as she was about to pass them, she looked up and, with a little shock, realized that the darker of the two was familiar. His eyes were downturned, but the other, fairer Afghani was watching her with pale gray eyes, his expression indistinguishable. She walked home hurriedly, strangely unsettled. Then, reliving her comic fall, she laughed, much to the amusement of the chowkidars she passed as she walked through the bungalow's gate.

Elouise was sitting on the veranda, drinking tea and reading the paper. "Good morning! Come join me for tea."

"Sounds great," Carla said and flopped into the plantation chair, wincing.

"What happened to you?"

Carla smiled. "Playing cricket."

"You're kidding me!" Elouise laughed and shook her head.

"I kid you not. Where's the wonderful Kishan? I need a

cup of tea."

"What are your plans for today, Carla?"

Besides moping over my failed marriage and searching the Internet for the most ruthless divorce attorney in London? Carla said wryly, "Nothing in particular, yours?"

"I have some errands, but you could join me. I'm going to South Extension Market to pick up some silk lining for a jacket the tailor is making up for me. There are some great shops. You could browse around."

"What time are we leaving?" Carla asked.

"No rush. Let's say in an hour."

South Extension had a market on both sides of the main road, with more shops at each end. Om Prakash dropped them in front of an impressive white building, which housed a shop called Heritage. The ground floor carried menswear, mostly formal or traditional wedding outfits, and imported suiting from Italy and Germany. On the first floor Carla was mesmerized by a dazzling display of traditional ladies' formal wear, saris, exquisite silks, and hand-woven cashmere shawls.

She indicated to the handsome young shop assistant that she was interested in pashmina shawls. He asked her to sit on a wooden bench in front of a large, raised platform covered in white cotton sheeting and offered her something to drink, which she declined.

A soft drink in a glass bottle, called Limca, was brought to her anyway, on a stainless-steel tray. The suave salesman started unfolding shawl after shawl, each more beautiful than the last.

After he had unfolded scores of shawls, Carla asked him to stop so that she could make a selection. But he continued opening more, discarding the ones he assumed she didn't like. The pile behind him resembled a large cashmere rainbow collapsed in disarray. At last he stopped, and Carla managed to select three. But, unable to make up her mind, she settled on all three, much to the sales assistant's delight.

Carla and Elouise then wandered through the rest of the market and lunched on delicious, exotic, street food. Carla particularly enjoyed a savory snack of puffed rice.

Drinking sweet, spicy chai out of a small glass, Carla finally plucked up the courage to ask Elouise why she had advised her to "watch out for George."

"He is a charming man; don't get me wrong. But he plays the field and never seems to stay in a relationship for longer than a few months. Then there are all the rumors of the wives—all married to important men, politicians, industrialists…But, then again, I'm not sure; Delhi likes to gossip."

Carla caught a glimpse of a wistful smile that Elouise tried to hide as she quickly dialed Om Prakash, who was then asked to pick them up at the predetermined meeting point. Carla realized the subject was now closed and decided not to ask about or discuss George again. It seemed to Carla that Elouise had a far more complicated life than she was willing to admit to. How could one think that life was perfect, or even covet another's seemingly perfect life? Nothing was as it seemed. Harry had appeared to be the perfect mate for Elouise and had given her this luxurious life in India. But beneath all this façade—servants, fine clothes, and fancy parties—there was an undeniable sadness in her friend that Carla hadn't seen before. She hoped that her time in India would provide solace not only for herself, but also Elouise.

At home an excited Kishan greeted them, informing Carla that a delivery had been made for her, which he had placed in her bedroom.

The fragrance of fresh flowers welcomed her on entry, and then she gaped in wonder, as the entire bedroom was filled with bloodred roses and delicate white sprigs of jasmine. "Oh my goodness!" she said out loud, taking the note from the large bouquet next to her bed. That it could be Andrew apologizing crossed her mind, but she dismissed the notion immediately. Flowers had never been his style.

The note was from George. It read,

Desperate to see you again. How about having dinner with me tonight?

P.S. Could you possibly refuse someone who bought you every red rose in Delhi today?

Carla flushed with annoyance to find Elouise reading the note over her shoulder. With a peculiar expression, Elouise turned on her heel and left Carla's room. Exhilarated and against her better judgment, not even considering the consequences, Carla picked up the phone and dialed George's mobile number.

He answered on the second ring. "George Alexander, hello?"

In a rather constricted, squeaky voice, Carla said, "Hello." Totally flustered, she added, "The flowers are beautiful, thank you."

"So you'll have dinner with me tonight?" he asked. His voice was calm, his tone measured.

Regaining her composure she thought desperately of something witty or clever to say, but could only manage a "Yes—what time?"

"Excellent, I will pick you up at eight."

As Carla put down the phone, she realized what she had committed herself to. She was going to dinner with a man other than Andrew for the first time in many years. It was strange, though—she didn't feel as guilty or as sad as she thought she might. Had she been expecting an end to her relationship with Andrew even before she saw him with Leila?

Carla thought about why she had decided to surprise Andrew in Peshawar. She had made that decision because she felt so distant from him. Perhaps that distance had less to do with physical space and more to do with how they had grown as people. She hadn't felt excited by a man's voice on the phone for so long—not until she had called George, that is. And anyway, Andrew was the cheat, not her. She smiled to herself and said, "What the hell? Life is short."

Kishan knocked on Carla's door at quarter to eight to inform her that George had arrived early and that he would be waiting with Elouise on the veranda.

Carla began to panic. Not only was she nervous to go to dinner with George, she was now making him wait. She stood naked, staring at her closet in disdain. The choices were so limited! She finally settled on a pair of black linen trousers and a sleeveless black silk-jersey top with satin trimming. Her hair was knotted in a casual chignon at the nape of her neck. With a last look in the mirror, she smiled to herself in approval and hurried to the veranda while scanning her phone one last time for messages from Andrew. Frowning, she studied her phone for a second, smiled, a little disheartened, and switched it off.

George stood up when Carla joined him and Elouise. He kissed her on both cheeks and said, "I'm afraid we have to leave immediately. I have a reservation at San Gimignano, and they are not in the habit of holding tables for more than twenty minutes."

"Sure." Carla looked at Elouise and smiled, feeling a little embarrassed.

George said good night to Elouise, thanked her for the drink, and suggested a get-together on Harry's return.

The air was heavy with the fragrance of the jasmine creeper at the front door. Carla breathed in the scent and felt a slight stirring of excitement. A well-built, fair-skinned Indian opened the car door for Carla, greeting her politely in English. George joined her in the back seat of the jeep and introduced her to his driver, Kamal, who was from Kashmir.

"Imperial Hotel," George ordered. He looked at Carla, smiled and said, "I hope you like Italian. San Gimignano is possibly the best Italian restaurant in Delhi. It's pretty authentic, as they fly in most of their ingredients. And, of course, the chef is Tuscan."

"I love Tuscan cuisine. I've spent quite a few summers in Tuscany," Carla replied, "and I have wonderful friends in Florence and Forti dei Marmi on the Mediterranean coast. Have you spent much time in Italy?"

"A reasonable amount. I would like to retire there one day." George narrowed his eyes in mock concentration and said, "A small seaside village. I'd fish in the morning, nap in the afternoon, and in the evening play backgammon on the village square."

Laughing, Carla said, "Yeah right. I can't picture that—more like Positano on the Amalfi Coast, eating fish at lunchtime and chatting up some well-heeled ladies on holiday."

George threw back his head and laughed a deep, satisfying laugh. Drawn in by its spontaneity, Carla abandoned herself to the hilarity of the moment. When she regained her composure, George handed her a Kleenex from a box in the middle glove compartment. She looked at him in slight confusion, but he leaned in closely, took the Kleenex from her, and carefully started wiping some laughter tears from under her eyes. Tiny little shocks exploded in her body, like miniature fireworks. Her legs felt lame, and suddenly she had the need for air. She pushed him away rather abruptly. Taking the Kleenex from him, she avoided his direct gaze and said, "Thanks."

Opening her evening purse, she rummaged through it, looking for her purse mirror. Apart from a fleeting quizzical expression, George was unfazed as he leaned back into his seat and announced their imminent arrival.

Carla looked up and recognized the Imperial Hotel. George led the way through the lobby and to the restaurant. Warm amber wooded paneling with framed black-and-white photographs of San Gimignano, crisp white tablecloths, and the unmistakable aroma of Tuscany greeted them. The elegant maître' d offered them a table inside or one outside in the courtyard.

"What do you prefer, Carla?" George asked politely. With Carla's preference for the cool, air-conditioned interior, they sat inside.

The food was delicious, and Carla found herself relaxed and comfortable in George's company. After they discovered that they had both attended Harvard, he amused her with stories from his college days. Then he asked her about her friendship with Elouise and how well she knew Harry.

"Not well at all. I was already in Washington when Elouise met him in New York. And apart from some weekends together, I haven't really seen much of him. Oh, and of course they came to my wedding in South Africa." She flushed and looked at George, a guilty expression in her eyes. "I'm married. He is in Pakistan, I think. Uh, well, he was there a few days ago. At the moment we're not really in contact."

"You don't have to explain yourself. Elouise filled me in," George said gently, taking Carla's hand in his.

"I shouldn't have surprised him in Peshawar. I've been looking forward to this trip to India for such a long time, wanting to meet some family members, getting to know some of my own culture, and now…" She paused. "Now I'm pissed off. Not only did he cheat on me; he spoiled this trip for me. I had so much to do, so much to see. I don't know what I'm supposed to feel or do. Should I just wait until the end of my trip to worry about our relationship and try to enjoy myself? Or should I start divorce proceedings? Carla could feel a lump rising in her throat. She couldn't believe she was divulging such private information to this stranger. "Enough about me. Elouise has told me something about you. Why are you still a bachelor? Did someone break your heart and forever destroy your faith in the institution of marriage?"

"No, not at all. My parents are celebrating their fiftieth wedding anniversary at the end of this year, and I almost envy them." George looked at Carla with a bright light in his eyes. Seeing this sincerity, she wondered why Elouise had painted such a different picture of him.

Just then his phone beeped. He looked down at the message he had received and, with an apologetic look, quickly typed a reply on his iPhone before putting it in his pocket and saying, "Please excuse me for a minute; I must take care of something. I won't be long—you decide what we should have for dessert."

He stood up as his other pocket started vibrating and headed for the courtyard. She watched him take out a large, clumsy-looking satellite phone as he walked outside.

Carla asked for the dessert menu and decided on the tiramisu with an espresso. She wondered whether she should order the same for George and decided to go to the courtyard to ask him. At first she couldn't see him, as the gazebos were heavily covered in jasmine creepers. A lion-headed fountain spewed water into a trough, adding to the luxurious charm of the courtyard.

She then saw him at the far corner, away from the al

fresco diners, a serious expression on his face. He was speaking quietly but sternly into the handset. He didn't see her approach as he turned his back on the diners. A couple of meters away from him, Carla changed her mind and turned to go back to their table. But then she heard some of his conversation. He was speaking fluently in a foreign language. Was it Arabic? No, she couldn't understand what George was saying. She had taken Arabic for a couple of years at Harvard to help with her Middle Eastern studies. This enabled her to communicate with the Arab-speaking correspondents at both CNN and BBC. Puzzled, she now walked back to their table. A few minutes later, George returned.

"So sorry, had to deal with an urgent visa query. Have you ordered?"

"Yes, a tiramisu to share. Are you OK with that?"

"Perfect, and I'd love an espresso."

Carla called the waiter and asked for another coffee. "Sorry, I wasn't sure if you drank coffee this late at night."

"No effect on me whatsoever. Plus, I still have some work to do later."

Carla looked at him in surprise but made no comment. She hadn't thought his job at the embassy would be quite so busy.

As they ate the creamy dessert, she wanted to ask him about the language she had overheard him speak. But, thinking it might be an intrusion, she started chatting instead about her time in India. George seemed to listen with interest, but Carla detected the distracted glimmer in his eyes. Nervous, she feared she was boring him.

While waiting for their car, George looked around with a guarded expression. He seemed relieved when Kamal arrived, and waving away the doorman's offer to open the door for Carla, he opened it for her and followed her into the back seat from the same door.

They were both quiet on the drive home. But, as they turned into her road, George leaned closer to her. He touched her face briefly and said, "I had a wonderful evening."

Carla felt her cheek burn from his touch and muttered, "Thank you, me too."

When they arrived at the bungalow, the guards let them through, and Kamal opened her door, George getting out on the other side.

He walked her to the front door where one of the chowkidars was unlocking the large antique brass lock.

George shook her hand a little formally and said, "Carla, I would love to see you again. Can I call you?"

Carla was confused by the mixed signals coming from him but found herself saying, "Yes, of course."

Kishan was waiting up for her. Refusing tea, Carla asked him to wake her at eight the next morning.

That night her dreams were filled with George, Elouise, and Andrew; they were strange, uneasy dreams. Carla did not feel rested when Kishan woke her up the following morning with a steaming cup of fragrant tea.

CHAPTER 5

Carla did not sleep well. She only saw Andrew's missed call on waking after she had switched on her phone. Not quite ready to return his call, she decided to phone the advocate instead. He was away in Calcutta, and his secretary told her that he'd call her back in a week or two. Aghast, she wasn't sure she could wait that long but left her number anyway. Feeling miserable, she decided she'd phone Andrew much later, maybe in the evening. He'd taken his time in calling her; he could wait.

She lazed about wondering what would make her feel better. Coffee didn't work, the newspaper didn't distract her, and she didn't really feel up to a conversation with Elouise about her dinner with George. Finally, she decided on Elouise's offer to join an American group on a sightseeing tour of Delhi. Elouise had arranged for Carla to join the group through one of the organizations she belonged to. The tour guides, former university professors, delighted in imparting their expert knowledge. Carla had a keen interest in British Colonial architecture and thought the outing would be the perfect distraction for a few hours. She would at least be prevented from over-analyzing her situation.

But she only became interested when the professor of architecture shared his opinions on Lutyen's Delhi. He smugly pointed to Lutyen's one flaw, the splendid Rashtrapati Bhavan, built for the former viceroy, now the home of the president of India. The palace was meant to be visible in all its splendor when approached from the top of the hill. Unfortunately, this was not the case, as the gradient was too steep and the only visible part, the dome, now dominated the Delhi skyline.

A cosmetic surgeon from San Diego and his wife, who resembled a shrine with a beatific expression frozen in celestial joy, started chatting to Carla, or rather, quizzing her about her life. They weren't satisfied with the broader outline but relentlessly extracted as much detail as possible. Carla felt like a witness in a murder trial. The thought of being interrogated by Elouise about George seemed more preferable to this "American Inquisition."

When the tour leader asked them to return to the bus, Carla hung back, trying to avoid the enthusiastic couple's company on the bus. A handsome young Indian boy, not much older than sixteen, watched her intently, smiling fervently when she glanced in his direction. She gave him an inhibited smile, and as if invited, he rushed to her side and said, "Madam, you like verri, verri old drawing make by your fellowman Lutyen?"

Carla was intrigued. "What type of drawings?"

"Beeootiful bungalows, big palace, one hundred percent original. I, my name is Manan, will show you this thing." He leaned conspiratorially toward her and said, "But verri secret, not too many drawing, get good price if not too many rich American see, too."

Original architectural drawings by Lutyen, what a find, Carla thought. "Where will I find this place?"

"No problem, Madam, I take you, look my bhai." He pointed to a man who was sitting in a three-wheeler scooter. He was chewing betel nut and spat the red juice and saliva in an accurate arch against the sandstone pavement.

"He takes you me in tuk-tuk, not cost too much money, no worry, come, come let's go."

Carla looked at the bhai's red-stained teeth and was undecided, but changed her mind quickly when she saw the surgeon's wife waving and pointing in triumph at the empty seat on the bus next to them.

With a wave and a "thank you" mouthed at the tour leader, Carla jumped into the tuk-tuk. Manan got in beside her. As the scooter bhai drove noisily away, Carla could almost make out an expression of dismay on the Californian's face.

They drove for about half an hour, and the traffic started becoming more congested. Manan kept reassuring her that they were about to reach their destination, but Carla couldn't suppress the wave of nausea and panic.

"I think it is late, and it's better if we turn back."

Manan laughed and insisted that they would reach the place in less than five minutes. The tuk-tuk was now almost motionless in the traffic, as people rushed alongside them or darted into the road, weaving in and out of rickshaws, motorbikes, and donkey carts pulling huge bales.

From one of the many alleys leading into the market, Manan waved to a man in his midthirties with long, wavy hair worn like the heroes in Bollywood films. He smiled broadly as Manan told Carla to get off the tuk-tuk—it would be faster to walk the last bit, he told her.

Carla struggled to find space for her feet on the road, but Manan pushed her through the heaving throng of human traffic. The Bollywood hero and Manan embraced; then he turned around and introduced Carla to Rohit.

With a friendly smile, Rohit took her arm and lead her deeper into the alley.

They walked fast, dodging rickshaws and motorbikes. Carla tried desperately to memorize the route they were taking, but after the third or fourth turn into another alley that looked exactly like the others, she realized she would not be able to get out of this labyrinth.

Hundreds of small fabric shops looked identical, their barefooted shoppers and sales assistants sitting on the sheet-covered floors. Shoes spilled into the walkway, which was trickling with old tea, water, mud, and foul-smelling ooze. They walked past the hundreds of sweets and snack shacks frying up their ware in huge, black, iron woks. The aroma of old oil coated the stench that permeated the air.

Carla stopped and ignored Manan and Rohit, who were urging her to continue. She took out her cell phone to advise Elouise of her whereabouts, but as she held the phone to her ear, Manan fell against her. He tried to steady himself, but in the process knocked the phone out of her hands, onto the sullied passage. He made as if to retrieve it, but Rohit stepped onto it and crushed it under his black Western-style cowboy boots. They exchanged a look, and Carla realized with a strange tingling sensation that started in her toes that she was in deep trouble.

Rohit took Carla's purse roughly from her, while Manan interlocked his arm in hers, and with his other hand he pointed to a small dagger stuffed into the waistband of his Levi's. They marched her through the congested alleys. Carla realized it was futile trying to talk to them. She had no idea where they were taking her or what their intentions were.

She looked around her, desperately trying to make eye contact with someone. Those who gave her a customary glance quickly averted their eyes.

After about ten minutes, they stopped in front of an

old carved wooden door. A bulky man with a pockmarked face looked at them dourly; then he opened the heavy door and waved them toward the dark, narrow staircase. The air was damp and surprisingly cool as they descended the worn gray-white marble staircase.

Rohit knocked on the door at the bottom of the stairs, and they entered a well-lit room, sparsely furnished, a large desk in the center. The wood-paneled walls were cracked and in disrepair. A wooden bookshelf filled with old, musty books leaned against one wall.

Sitting in an office chair behind the desk, a slightly built man with a large, shiny baldhead and wearing enormous black-rimmed glasses looked up and smiled tauntingly at Carla.

"Well, well, what a pleasure to meet you, Miss…?"

Carla frowned and asked in a haughty tone, "How long do you propose to keep me here? I'm staying in India with friends who are well connected, and it is only a matter of time before I'm found, and I suspect you'll be in a great deal of trouble."

The man threw back his head and laughed loudly, snorting with derision. "Thousands of girls and women disappear in India yearly, trying to find themselves. They disperse into the cult-like-ashrams, never to be heard of again, bar the one letter written to their families explaining their newfound self."

He spoke with a perfect English accent, except for the slight lilt, which betrayed his South Asian roots. This was common among well-to-do Indians who liked to send their children to exclusive British boarding schools. With a wry smile, he took Carla's purse from Rohit. He then unceremoniously turned it upside down, and shook out its contents on top of the vast desk, already littered with papers and paraphernalia. He picked up her passport and, with a look of contempt, which changed rapidly into annoyance, flicked through it. He roared, "South African! This is a South African passport."

He hurled it at the terror-stricken Rohit. "You fools, I need American identities." And, as though having to emphasize every syllable to the very young or dumb-witted, he shrieked, "Ammmeerriccan!" throwing Carla's purse angrily on the floor.

Rohit swallowed hard, sighed, and bravely tried to defend himself, explaining how the tour from which he had abducted Carla was only for Americans—his contact in the United States embassy had confirmed this.

"Not interested! You moron. I needed an American identity fitting this description—" he pointed at Carla—"by tomorrow. How do you propose we do it now? I have assured our buyers, and I don't want to be accused of double-crossing them. You have seen what they are capable of."

With a menacing glare, he sat down, spreading out his hands on the desk in front of him, as if awaiting a manicure.

Grasping her predicament, in a tremulous voice Carla addressed the bald man. "I promise, if you let me go I will not breathe a word of this to anyone. I promise; please trust me. Just let me go." Her eyes started stinging, and warm, salty tears flowed down the gentle curve of her cheeks. He looked at her with contempt and called the pockmarked man at the door. He spoke rapidly in Hindi and then dismissed the man.

Turning to Rohit and Manan, he ordered them to take Carla to Ghulam Baazaar. Manan looked alarmed and started to protest, but the bald man silenced him and said, "Bir has gone ahead to prepare them for her arrival."

The incredulous Manan and Rohit tightened their grip on Carla's arms and started dragging her up the marble stairs. She decided not to offer resistance, waiting instead for a good opportunity to escape when her captors were at ease and least expected it.

As they led her through the maze of alleys again, Carla asked about her whereabouts. But her query was met with silence. "If you let me go, I will reward you very well," she pleaded. "Lots of money. I promise you, no one will know anything."

Rohit looked at her and in a calm voice he told her that no amount of money could possibly keep them safe from Bharra Bhai—they had seen what happened to men who had been stupid enough to disobey.

As they walked through the narrow, stinking passages, each new turn or descent into yet another darker, foul-smelling course suffocated Carla. She was beginning to apprehend the futility of attempting any escape. Her body, now drained of adrenalin, was weak and heavy, each step a grueling effort. Aware of her deterioration, Rohit barked an order to Manan. Changing their grip, they now supported her under the elbows. Carla was dragged along with her head slumped on her chest, her toes barely scraping the ground. Eyes tightly shut, she tried to still her fear, breathing as deeply as the stench allowed. "I must remain calm, must remain calm. I will be OK as long as I remain calm," she muttered.

She opened her eyes when they stopped in front of a dilapidated building. The door was in shards of decay through years of neglect. The carving of a bird in a cage on the jutting frame proffered the only hint of former beauty. Rohit knocked in rhythmic sequence and Carla thought: *How original.*

A small, window-size panel in the door was opened. Rohit leaned forward in rapid exchange with the person on the inside. Creaking and groaning like an old woman under its own weight, the door swung open, allowing Rohit and Manan just enough space to propel her through. The rusted ironwork on the door scraped her shoulder, but she controlled the urge to cry out as rough hands pulled and pushed her along the dark shadows of the entrance. She looked back, but Rohit and Manan were no longer there. Carla experienced a weird sense of loss.

They passed a door leading to the outside, which looked like a courtyard. In the fading light, she stared at her captors. She was surprised to see that they were two women dressed in traditional salwar kameezes. With dupattas draped over their heads, their features were hidden from view. They climbed up two flights of narrow stairs, pungent with the unmistakable ammonia odor of urine, filtered by sandalwood incense and curried vegetables soured in the heat of the day. At the top of the staircase, they turned left into a passage and stopped in front of a heavy iron gate with an enormous brass padlock. The woman in the lead took out a bunch of keys attached to an undergarment of some sort and unlocked the gate.

The three entered the dark room. A single bulb hung from the center of the ceiling, bravely casting its light, swinging yellow beams between the shadows. The shadows were human. Her eyes now growing more accustomed to the gloom, Carla was horrified to see about a dozen girls sitting or lying crumpled against the wall and along the stained and tattered marble floor. Unnerved by the thought that the girls might all be dead, Carla gasped with fright as the iron gates clanged shut behind her. The two women removed their dupattas. The dark shadow of an unshaven beard only confirmed what Carla had suspected: her two captors were eunuchs, their movements and carriage convincingly feminine. With dissonant, deep voices the eunuchs started shouting something in Hindi to the girls, who then began to show signs of life.

A young, frail-looking girl with disheveled, long black hair approached the eunuchs and knelt in front of them as they handed her a candle and a tin spoon. The taller eunuch took out a small plastic bag, again from somewhere under the folds of his salwar. He sprinkled some of its contents onto the tin spoon that the young girl held over the flame of the candle.

Sitting on the floor with her back against the wall, Carla watched the drug melting on the spoon. With dread she observed the eunuchs administering the heroin intravenously to the girls. Some seemed shy, offering no resistance as the eunuchs injected them in the soft folds of their inner forearms. The silence was almost as tangible as the rancid odor of fear.

A young girl in her early teens, bright pink, heart-shaped pins fixing two braids to the top of her head, started crying softly when the fat eunuch approached her. He tested the syringe, and some of the golden liquid squirted out of the needle. She started screaming, biting his arm, and trying to scratch him in his face. Urine seeped from under her fuchsia salwar, wetting the marble floor. The eunuch slipped, but managed to retain his balance. Two older girls with fierce expressions jumped up and onto his back. Screaming in anguish, they clawed at his eyes.

From the opposite side of the room, two girls ran for the gate. The tall eunuch stopped them. He twisted their arms behind their backs and tied them up with his dupatta. Shaking with fear and defeat, they acquiesced. The girls on the back of the fat eunuch were thrown clear with such force that they were winded, lying in a heap, gasping for air. The brave young girl, now in a vicelike grip, was injected with cruel intent. The flustered fat eunuch wiped the perspiration from his face with the corner of his kameez. The taller one whispered something to him. He nodded and moved to the opposite side of the room, where he scrutinized the girls, slapping them lightly on their cheeks.

Hypnotized, Carla watched the surreal scene unfold in front of her. The reality of the eunuch's intention hit her like a physical blow to her stomach. She was to be drugged. She was next. Her heart raced, pounding uncomfortably in her chest. She breathed deeply; the air felt hot and tasted foul, but she was determined to find a way to elude her captors.

The tall eunuch was now speaking softly to the girl next to Carla. His voice was calm and almost intimate. The girl looked up at him. Her eyes were large, shining with unshed tears. The slight blinking of her small rhinestone earrings reminded Carla of the stars. An idea took shape. *Of course, it could work...*

Carla removed her pearl stud from her left ear. With the sharp pin of the stud, she pierced the vein on the inside of her left arm, biting the lining of her cheek as some blood trickled down her arm. She flopped her head forward, turning her arm out, the blood noticeable. She remained as still as possible. As the taller eunuch approached she closed her eyes, slackened her mouth, and dribbled saliva onto her chin.

Every muscle was as tense as a predator about to strike its prey in the wild, but she forced herself to relax her body. The sandaled foot of the eunuch kicked her on her shin, but Carla remained motionless with a will she didn't know she had. Her head swung when jolted by the eunuch. Slapping her cheek, he stared at her for a few seconds, and then moved to the girl who was crying loudly into her dupatta on the other side of Carla.

Too afraid to open her eyes, Carla listened intently to every sound, trying to gauge the situation. Her mind was racing; her heart was beating so loudly that she was almost sure it could be heard in the room. Then she heard the loud clang of the gate as it was closed, and the brass lock clicked into place.

Lifting her head as slowly as possible and peering through half-closed lids, she scanned the room thoroughly. The eunuchs had left, and no one had taken their place to guard them. The heroin had become their silent jailer instead.

Feeling a little calmer, Carla tried to clear her mind, to think logically and to take stock of the predicament she had landed herself in. The room was unfurnished, with only a few dirty blankets scattered on the floor, unused in the oppressive heat. The stench of sweat, vomit, and fear clung to Carla.

Moving as stealthily as possible, she tried to get to the window that had been boarded up. She was hoping to get a glimpse of what was on the other side through the cracks between the boards.

The girls were still heavily drugged and made no reaction to Carla's stealthy movements as she crept toward the window. When she reached it, she had to push a girl out of the way. The girl was almost weightless, and with a shock Carla realized that she was only about ten years old, her body still childlike and shapeless, eyes empty and glazed over. Carla was horrified. Despondency whittled at her resolve to find a way out. Biting hard on her lips, she heaved herself up and managed to peer through a crack in the board, no wider than a matchstick.

The window had a view of what resembled a courtyard, badly lit, with lanterns hanging from iron chains along the walls. Indistinct figures stood in groups; they looked like men and filled most of the courtyard. The sound of Eastern music drifted through the sultry night air; it was strangely comforting to Carla.

A young boy darted in between the men, carrying a tray with glasses and a bottle of liquor; the men were pouring their own drinks. The conversation seemed to be getting more animated, and the atmosphere became charged with anticipation. Impatient to improve her view, Carla managed to enlarge the crack with her nails.

Eager to try and locate herself, she scrutinized the courtyard for any clues of her whereabouts: a sign or landmark. But her effort was in vain. There was nothing recognizable or distinguishable. Where was she?

As she was contemplating whether she should try to attract someone's attention, a bright spotlight suddenly lit up what looked like a podium. The audience faced it expectantly as the music blared disturbingly loud and distorted. And then, like a David Copperfield illusion, a young woman was standing on the platform. She had an unworldly aura about her: diaphanous robes, hinting at her nakedness underneath and her ethereal beauty, all framed in the harsh light.

A man in tight blue jeans and a dark-fitted shirt stepped onto the podium next to her and in a deep baritone started the bidding in English.

CHAPTER 6

Drained of all strength, Carla sank back against the stained wall. She felt numb. Her mind was strangely empty, yet she was somehow cognizant of the hopelessness of her situation. She tried desperately to recall every detail, path, or landmark. What were they going to do with her? Who were they? Unable to find a single answer to her questions, she closed her eyes and succumbed to immense fatigue, sinking into a deep, but fitful sleep.

She awoke stiff and sore to the grating of the iron gate and was surprised to see sunlight filtering through the jali windows. Some of the girls in the room started moving limbs and heads, groaning. Two women dressed in filthy saris, carrying a metal pitcher and cups, spilled water as they impatiently offered it to their captives.

The water was tepid and smelled faintly of chlorine or bleach. Encouraged by this, Carla broke the golden rule of drinking the water in India. Too thirsty to care about dysentery, she drank deeply from the metal cup.

From a round plastic tray, the women produced chapattis and heaped a couple into the hands of those who had the strength to lift them. An ironic thought crossed Carla's mind: the girls looked as if they were receiving Holy Communion. For the weaker or comatose girls, the women simply dumped the bread on the dirty floor next to them.

Carla bit cautiously into the bread but found the smoky, earthy-flavor palatable. Wolfing down the two chapattis, she looked up expectantly, hoping for another one. With a jeering "Bas" to Carla, the women continued tossing the chapattis at their lethargic recipients.

A sudden, shrill scream brought all activity to a sudden halt. A terror-stricken young girl was holding a limp, elfin-like waif in her arms. The young girl started sobbing, shaking and shouting to the girl in her lap. As her tiny head lolled to the side, Carla saw that her face was covered in vomit, dry in patches, the acidity staining sections of her sweet face purple. Carla registered with horror that the girl appeared dead. Was it a reaction to the heroin, or simply a mistaken overdose?

Some mild commotion broke out, but within minutes the tall eunuch from the previous night appeared in the doorway and walked to the sobbing girl. Speaking quietly to her, he released her grip on the dead girl. He picked her up with ease and carried her out through the doorway, like a young bride.

Carla stared at the inconceivable scene, dry-eyed and feeling strangely detached. She hoped, even while knowing that it was impossible, that this was a dream from which she would soon wake.

Satisfied that all had been fed, the two women left through the gate and were replaced by the two eunuchs. They stood in front of the gate, chatting loudly in their strange boy-man voices. Eyeing the captives with open curiosity, they walked closer to inspect certain features. They ran their hands through the incredibly long, silky-black hair of a girl in the traditional clothing of the Punjab and even forced open the mouth of a slightly older girl, counting and inspecting her teeth.

They became more and more animated and kept glancing over at Carla. At first they seemed slightly reserved, but gained confidence as Carla forced herself to appear listless and indifferent to her surroundings. Unable to contain their inquisitiveness a minute longer, they approached and barked out an order in Hindi. Carla looked up at them and ignored the order by looking the other way. Suddenly they bent down; one grabbed her legs, the other her arms. Without thinking, she tried to fight them off, but their grip was strong and she found herself powerless as they pulled down her khaki pants. The button popped off, and then they tugged at her white cotton briefs.

"Stop! Please. What are you doing? What do you want?" Carla sobbed as they managed to pull her briefs down to her knees. Kicking fiercely, she managed to wrestle one leg free, but for a split second only. Then she registered the look of absorption as the eunuchs stared at her pubic hair, inspecting it with open curiosity, making obvious comparisons with her hair, which was disheveled and dirty. Satisfied, they pulled up her pants and briefs, chatting and guffawing as they made lewd movements back to their guarding post at the door.

Humiliated, exhausted, and terrified, with sweat pouring down her face, Carla started crying for the first time since this nightmare had begun. She cried quietly and only stopped when her stress had dissipated in the raw energy of her emotions. Spent, she fell asleep in a fetal position, knees under her chin.

The cool water of the Mediterranean washed over her face as she lay in the soft golden sand. She smiled at Andrew in his ridiculous swimming trunks, sporting baby hippos in lime green. He leaned over her, and as he kissed her, she opened her eyes. She was looking into the dark, laughing eyes of George. Confused, she tried to sit up, but he held her down and the water covered her face. She fought for air as the water filled her mouth and nose. She screamed, but made no sound...

Carla felt something scratch her on the side of her neck and awoke suddenly from her dream. It was one of the eunuchs; he threw a bucketful of water in her face. As Carla began to focus, she realized that the rusty rim of the bucket had scratched her. Scanning the room, she was surprised to find herself alone.

"Get up. Jaldi, jaldi," the eunuch said loudly as he tried to pull Carla by her arm. She got up as fast as her body would allow her to move, but she felt achy and heavy. The eunuch scowled at her white cotton shirt, transparent from the water. Throwing a dirty pink dupatta at her, he gestured that she should cover her torso and head.

Her legs were unsteady as she rose. The younger of the two eunuchs held her at the elbow, as though escorting her to a ball. He took her down the same dirty staircase she had ascended the day before.

They passed the large wooden door and down a passage until it made a sharp turn. She found herself in front of a small door with an iron grate. The eunuch knocked rhythmically. After a while, a woman wearing a pale green washed-out sari unlocked the door. She and the eunuch exchanged a few rapid words, and then Carla was handed over to the woman, who gave her a benign smile.

Taking her by the arm, the woman guided Carla through a very narrow passage resembling a tunnel. After several twists and turns they arrived at another door, beautifully carved with figures of bathing women, the heavy wooden frame set in stone pillars. The woman pushed open the door to a pervasive humidity and exotic fragrance. Carla stared in wonder. The high-domed roof was of a glasslike structure. Bright light created a soft rainbow effect through the steam. In the middle of the large room was a massive stone platform of white marble veined with green.

Three girls were being scrubbed and massaged on the stone platform by women dressed in saris, worn without blouses, and hitched to their knees. The girls were stark naked, their skin glowing like burnished copper. The sound of running water came from fountains against the walls, which were beautifully embellished with pietra dura in a typically floral Mughal-pattern. Some older girls were being rinsed in the steaming water.

A Mughal hammam. Carla was amazed to see this ancient relic of the Mughal Empire still intact and in use. In a book on the Moghul Empire at Elouise's house Carla had read that many wealthy Mughals and Nawabs had built them into their havelis, as they found the dust of India so unbearable. With the fall of the Mughal period, many of these hammams were destroyed, and now only fragments could be found in a few small shops selling spices or nylon rope. Despite her situation, Carla found herself in a fascinated recall of the intelligent engineering of the Mughal period: to create the steam or hot rooms, water was heated by wood fires, pumped through copper pipes, creating heat and steam, and then finally through the steaming, hot fountains. For a fleeting moment Carla found herself comforted by something familiar in a terrifyingly foreign atmosphere.

The attendant steered Carla to a corner of the room to a marble bench, where she started undressing her. Carla pushed her hands away and indicated that she would undress herself. Feeling strangely uninhibited, Carla stripped and was then lead to the large stone slab at the center of the room. She lay down on her back while a warm, wet muslin cloth was placed over the lower half of her torso. The attendant started scrubbing her down with coarse salt, smelling of sandalwood. Carla closed her eyes: a part of her enjoyed the rough scrubbing, as if the mental filth of the past day was being scoured away; another part of her, a part she didn't want to listen to, was wondering what this cleaning ritual could be preparing her for.

Afterward, her skin was tingling and quite pink. She was led to one of the fountains, where she was rinsed off in the hot, steaming water. As they led her back to the stone slab she tried to peer through the steamy haze. She recognized many of the girls who had been held captive with her the day before. The attendant then indicated to Carla that she should lie facedown on the hard marble surface with her hands under her chin. Hot fragrant oil was massaged expertly into her skin, and although it was physically relaxing, the reality of the ritual began to dawn on Carla.

Carla was pummeled, pounded, and kneaded. With her eyes tightly shut, she drifted in and out of a trance-like slumber. When she opened her eyes, she found a pair of light brown eyes with specks of honey staring at her with open curiosity. Carla guessed the young girl to be in her late teens. Her breasts were small and firm, as was the rest of her golden, youthful body. Her sable hair was spread over her shoulders and onto the marble slab. She was lying on her back next to Carla while being massaged with perfumed oil. She smiled shyly and said, "Hello, my name is Nazeema."

Surprised that they were allowed to talk to each other, and shocked to find someone speaking familiar words to her, Carla quietly replied, "Oh. Hi. My name is Carla. You speak English."

"Yes, I studied in school, but..." As Nazeema's voice broke, huge glistening tears rolled down her young face. Devastated by the reality of what was to become of the young girl, and herself, Carla tried desperately to think of a way out, but the entire experience had somehow dulled her senses.

Looking over at the young girl's perfect youthful features, she asked, "Nazeema, how did you get here?"

With wide eyes Nazeema said, "Like everyone else. How did you get here?"

"I was kidnapped for my passport and identity, I think. They brought me here only because they don't know what else to do with me."

Nazeema studied her intently and then smiled shyly. "Yes, you are quite old, but you have beautiful skin, so golden. Good hips, not too late for children, I hope…"

The simple words, spoken so matter-of-factly, cut through Carla's entire being. A blend of hot tears, scented oil, and steam stung her eyes. *Pull yourself together, Carla,* she admonished herself. If she had any hope of getting out of there, she had to keep her wits about her.

Nazeema had closed her eyes. She seemed to have drifted off to sleep. Carla whispered loudly, "Nazeema. What happened to you and the other girls?" Not sure that she had heard, Carla poked her gently on the arm. Nazeema opened her eyes lethargically.

"I was betrayed by my family, sold, used, and then I decided to run away instead of them throwing me out." She sighed. Then, turning her head, she looked intently at Carla. "I have nothing left to live for, except for that wonderful gold liquid my body craves, the floating nothingness, and then the hope that one day too much will enter my bloodstream and I will remain in that lovely place forever…"

CHAPTER 7

Slapping Carla on the thigh, the attendant indicated the end of the massage. Nazeema sat up, smiled sadly at Carla, and walked with the attendant to another room. Carla watched as the hot steam swallowed her small frame, and then, getting up slowly, she followed.

She found herself in a room with similar marble floors, where about a dozen girls were being draped in saris without blouse or petticoat, their young bodies displayed seductively through the sheer fabric. Some of the girls giggled as they pointed to each other in mock horror, while others looked on with dull eyes. Carla was surprised to see a woman dressed in trendy jeans with a short kurti and silver sneakers sitting on a small stool applying makeup expertly, a toolbox next to her.

Carla couldn't help smiling at the irony. It all seemed like a Bollywood movie set. *I suppose my experience at the Kapoors' party should come in handy,* she thought sardonically. But all traces of humor left her instantly when she saw the tall eunuch, who had administered the heroin the previous night, enter through the solid wooden door, his expression solemn.

Oh no, he's here to subdue us again, Carla thought, her heart beating faster. Her throat felt tight, making her swallow hard, forcing the hot, humid air through the narrowed passage. Carla was led to a bench, where her hair was brushed into a damp, oily braid. The attendant removed the excess oil from her skin with a muslin cloth and proceeded to dress her like the others. A pale turquoise, sheer silk sari with a small paisley pattern embroidered in silver along the border was chosen for her. Carla was so engrossed by the eunuch's every move that she was quite unaware of how beguiling she might look in the folds of the sari.

The trendy woman in the jeans fussed around Carla, pointing to her freckles in dismay and saying in English that she did not have the right shade of foundation to cover those spots. Suddenly, quite irritated at the triviality of her freckles causing so much dismay, Carla said curtly, "Use the blush; it should cover my freckles just fine."

The makeup artist was taken aback by the outburst and quickly applied kohl and mascara to Carla's eyes, brushing a pink powder over her cheeks and nose. She used a light pink lipstick, leaned back to examine Carla from a slight distance, and then, murmuring approval, asked Carla to move to the end of the room to join the other girls.

Carla couldn't help but recognize how lovely Nazeema looked as she moved toward Carla and took her hand in hers, small, warm, and comforting. Her eyes were bright with unshed tears.

Just then a ruckus erupted at the other end of the room. The eunuch had patiently started the dreaded administering of the drug once again. *I will not be able to prevent it this time.* Carla felt defeated. She sat down on the hard stone bench, and holding her hands together in a childlike pose, she prayed.

She opened her eyes as the wide sleeve of the eunuch's kameez brushed her face. He looked at her dispassionately and reached out for her left arm. He studied it for a moment, and then tied the rubber belt firmly above her elbow; the rubber pinched the soft skin of her upper arm.

Carla tried to make eye contact—maybe she could assure him of her cooperation—but he was looking intently at the syringe filled with the yellow, toxic liquid, tapping it gently, expelling air bubbles. Carla's fingers started tingling, and she closed her eyes. She felt the sting of the needle on her arm, and a warm sensation flooded through her veins. She could almost track the rush of the drug through her body. Her heart beat violently in her chest. Looking down at her lifeless, heavy limbs, she became confused. And then, suddenly, the heroin-laden blood rushed to her brain.

The sari unwrapped around her body and was transformed into large gossamer wings. Delicate yet strong, they lifted her into the bright blue sky. It felt wonderful to soar so high. But now the light was becoming uncomfortably bright and hot, stinging her eyes as tears rolled down her cheeks. She dipped her head and found herself flying lower. The sky was darker now—the birds flying with her were laughing and pointing at her. Beak-like noses prevented her from identifying the flying bird-human creatures.

The sky was blue and purple like an angry bruise. Suddenly the wings disintegrated, and the sari wrapped itself around Carla. She tried to lift her arms, wanting to flap like a bird, but they were too heavy. Someone had tied a rope around her hands and feet, and they were pulling her down—it was dark and cold, and she was thirsty; maybe she could drink from the large, black lake…

Although not fully conscious, Carla sensed someone pushing or maybe carrying her. Just trying to grasp what was happening was exhausting, and she drifted off again. She barely touched the ground, yet she was unable to lift herself off the ground.

The sound of loud music brought her out of her stupor. She had to shade her eyes from the bright, blinding light. A man was talking loudly next to her, his voice echoing hollowly in her ears. She tried to understand what he was saying; he wasn't speaking English.

Some movement beyond the pool of light caught her attention. Feeling strangely alert, she squinted through the gloom and saw men standing in groups or alone. Some were talking animatedly; others were drinking, with seeming disinterest in what was happening. A vague recollection was tugging at Carla's consciousness. *I know what they're doing; I've seen it before.* Carla desperately tried to stay alert, but the powerful drug kept dragging her down into the fog, the nightmare. *I'm so tired; if only I could lie down for a moment.*

She closed her eyes and started swaying. Her brain was spinning around and around to the cacophony of loud music. She could feel the dampness of the evening grass of childhood between her toes. They played their spinning game, falling down, laughing; last kid standing was the winner.

The droning voice suddenly made sense as she opened her eyes again. She looked at his mouth with its full lips and perfect white teeth; the mouth was moving fast, the tip of the velvety pink tongue licking the dryness from the lips, like a snake tasting the air.

"I have ten lacs, ten lacs for this beautiful, intelligent, mature woman. A sure prize—any more bids, gentlemen? Yes, we have eleven lacs, eleven lacs.

"Any more bids, gentlemen? Yes, we have eleven lacs, eleven lacs."

Oh my God, I'm being sold. The dawning realization shook

Carla out of her drugged haze.

The bidding was heating up between two men. One looked Middle Eastern; he wore a dark Western suit and had a slight build. The other was tall, wearing traditional Afghani clothes. He was standing in the shadows, casually raising his hand to counter bid on Carla.

Her heart was beating impossibly fast, yet she managed to stay focused, watching the bidding with morbid curiosity. A young boy was carrying a lamp past the Afghan, and as his face lit for a moment, Carla recognized the unusual light gray of his eyes. *I know him from somewhere...* With desperation she tried to recall where she knew him from, but the heroin impeded all lucid thought. Then, again, she sank into oblivion, deeper into the vortex of her incubus.

The auctioneer nodded as the bidding ended, and Carla was carried out to an adjoining room where she was dressed in a large black burqa that covered her body and most of her face. A pair of cheap imitation Dior sunglasses were placed over her eyes. Two men carried her to the waiting jeep and lay her down on the back seat.

Carla felt hot and thirsty as she regained consciousness, but her moaning went unheard as the jeep's engine roared into life and, with a jolt, pulled away.

Lying on the back seat of the jeep, Carla listened intently to the sounds. Again she tried to gauge her whereabouts. A dull headache threatened her concentration, but she was determined, and to her surprise, she found herself reliving an unmistakable street scenario: the sound of vehicles; hooting; the loud cries of pedestrians; sidewalk traders. The jeep was moving slowly through the traffic. The men in the front seats were silent, except for the occasional expletive uttered in Hindi by the driver.

We must be leaving Old Delhi, Carla thought, as the jeep started traveling faster and the roads seemed less congested. *What if we are heading for the airport? Oh God, what am I going to do?* She began to panic. *I must stay calm.* Her only hope was to think and behave rationally.

The situation worsened with the jeep accelerating, making Carla nauseous, bitter gall welling up in the back of her throat.

Then, the jeep suddenly stopped. The driver and passenger got out, and as Carla tried to sit up, her door was opened and strong arms lifted her out of the car and bundled her into the back of another car. She tried to stay upright, but someone got in beside her and pushed her down on the seat. She had no strength in her body, and with a sigh she surrendered wearily. Closing her eyes, she drifted into a shadowy state of sleep and wakefulness. The sounds from outside mingled with her dreams. She was confused, unable to discern reality.

She laughed as Andrew insisted on carrying her over the threshold of their front door after their weeklong honeymoon on the idyllic islands of the Seychelles.

"You'll break your back—I'm at least four kilos heavier from all those pina coladas on the beach!"

Andrew smiled as his face turned red with the effort of lifting Carla. "What are you talking about? You're as light as a feather!"

He stumbled over the mail on the floor at the entrance, and the two of them fell down clumsily, laughing and moaning as they crashed to the wooden floor.

"Wow! What a smashing start to our marriage," Andrew said, laughter lines accentuated by his glorious tropical suntan.

Carla remained motionless on her back, too winded to move. Andrew leaned over her; he stopped smiling, and his eyes were filled with concern. "Are you OK? Carla, can you hear me?"

Mustering a smile, she gasped: "I'll be OK, Andrew, stop fussing!"

"No, Carla, it's me, George. Do you know where you are? Do you remember what happened? Come. Sit up. Drink something." George lifted Carla and gave her some water from a plastic bottle. It tasted strange and made her gag. "It's OK. I've added some electrolytes and paracetamol. Drink as much as you can. You'll feel better, I promise."

After a few sips, Carla sank back into George's arms.

"I don't understand. How did you find me?" Carla asked.

"We'll discuss that later, but right now you must try and sleep. But you're going to feel very unwell for the next twenty-four hours." He stroked her face gently and continued, "I won't leave you. You have nothing to worry about now. You're going to be safe. OK?"

She nodded, the effort sapping her of every bit of energy. Watching the ceiling fan spinning hypnotically, round and round, Carla closed her eyes and fell asleep.

❦

"Sunil, is the room ready?" George called out.

His bearer hurried to his side and said, "Anjee, Sahib. I can help you with the madam?"

"No, thanks, it's fine. I can manage."

The slightly built Sunil moved nimbly, quite youthfully despite the round potbelly that betrayed his age. He led the way as George lifted Carla effortlessly and carried her through to a bedroom, where he lay her down on a large bed. On the bedside table were a pile of clean white towels and a bowl of water. An empty bucket was on the floor next to the bed.

When Sunil left the room, George undressed Carla, throwing the clothes on the floor. Wetting a towel, he wiped her down, and then he covered her with a white cotton quilt embroidered with a tree-of-life motif. He carefully brushed a few strands of hair off her face and, with a sigh, sank into a large rattan armchair next to the bed. He looked at her face relaxed in sleep, but her skin was pale, the freckles over the bridge of her nose pronounced, making her look very young. He felt a pang of regret and held her clammy hand in his.

He let go of her hand as Sunil knocked softly on the door and entered carrying a tray with a cup of tea and a small plate of biscuits. "Thank you, Sunil. You can go to bed. I'll call you if I need you."

"Good night, Sahib."

Taking a sip of his tea, George quickly called Sunil back. "Don't mention tonight to anyone, especially that gossiper Saroj. You understand?"

"Of course, Sahib." Sunil mimicked locking up his mouth and tossing the key away with an exaggerated cricket-bowling move. George smiled, despite himself.

Throughout the night George watched Carla as she broke out in cold sweats, running high fevers and vomiting. He was worn out, but resisted sleep. Finally, as Carla was resting peacefully and only when the first rays of the dawn broke through the blinds, George surrendered to sleep.

The incessant chirping of the mynahs nettled Carla. Her nerves were frayed. Her head pounded terribly. She tried standing, but her legs buckled, and she felt herself falling.

"I've got you. You're still weak. If you're in a hurry to go somewhere, just ask, OK?" George smiled a little roguishly and said, "Plus, you're stark naked!"

Carla grabbed the sheet from the bed and covered herself hurriedly. George handed her an oxford blue men's shirt, which she put on very quickly, her eyes on George, confused and accusing.

"You had a bad night, Carla. You were running a high temperature, seizures and vomiting. It was easier to manage you without clothes. Do you remember anything at all?"

Feeling totally drained, Carla tried to recall the events

of the previous day. Her mind was a hotchpotch of images, smells, emotions. "Can I have something to drink, please?"

"Of course." George handed her a glass of salted nimbu pani. She drank it with a grimace, but regaining a little of her sparkle, she held up her hand and said, "I know—it's good for me."

George laughed. "I'm glad you're feeling better. Sunil has made you some chicken broth. Try to have some, but if you can't, don't worry. You'll slowly regain your appetite."

Sitting back against the pillows, Carla said softly and with deliberation, "I can remember everything, well—almost."

With a start, she suddenly sat up, frowning. "Elouise must be frantic! I have to call her right away. Do you have her number? I don't have my phone."

"It's OK. I spoke to her, and she knows you are with me. But, Carla, we have to talk. Not now, though, you must first get better completely."

Carla nodded obediently and tried the broth.

"I'll do as you say for now, George, but you have a lot of explaining to do."

George smiled and said, "I promise, but believe it or not, I'm going to insist you sleep some more. Here, take this; it is an Ayurvedic remedy that will relax you, and hopefully it will make you sleep. It is also known as a detox." He handed her two large green capsules with a glass of water. After taking the capsules, Carla asked George to help her to the bathroom. As he was helping her up, there was a knock on the door, and Sunil entered with some folded garments that he gave to George.

"Those are my things!" Carla noted with surprise.

"Elouise sent them over. You can change in the bathroom; if you need my help I will be outside the door."

"Thanks." Carla changed into the navy tracksuit. When she saw her reflection in the mirror, she held her breath in dismay. She was pale and pasty with dark blotchy patches under her eyes. Her hair was lank and oily, and as she tucked some strands behind her ear, the fragrance of the oil reminded her of her nightmare experience.

Her large blue eyes stared back at her, and then, whether feeling sorry for herself or simply relieved, she started crying, silently, at first, tears rolling down her cheeks. But as she found release, she began sobbing uncontrollably. The bathroom door opened, revealing George's face full of concern. He held her in his arms and waited for her crying to subside.

Leading her back to bed, he said, "It's OK. Remember, Carla, you're safe now." Finally spent, she fell into a peaceful sleep.

George made her comfortable, adjusted the air-conditioner and left, closing the door softly behind him. He spent the day at home. Looking at her, restful in her sleep, he realized with much relief that the heroin dosage had been relatively light. He kissed her gently on the forehead, her skin cool against his lips. *It was close, too close.* The thought gripped George with horror and even remorse.

As the stretching shadows of the peepal trees in the garden indicated the cool onset of evening, Sunil entered the room and said, "They are waiting in your study, Sahib. Shall I bring some tea?"

"No thanks, Sunil. I want you to wait outside Madam Carla's room, and don't allow her to leave the room. She is sleeping, but I still want you to wait there."

"Anjee, Sahib," he replied dutifully.

As George entered his study, his driver, Kamal, was standing at the window. George smiled and greeted him politely. A man wearing a Pathani suit was seated on the leather armchair opposite the leather-bound desk, scattered with papers and document folders. George approached him, and as he stood up, they hugged each other warmly.

"Good to see you, my friend!" George said amiably. The man slapped him heartily on the back and laughed, his remarkable, light gray eyes alight with joviality.

CHAPTER 8

It was the sudden silence that roused Carla out of her deep sleep. India was never quiet. Whatever the time of day or night, whirling fans, the drone of air-conditioners, and the constant sound of a billion-plus population going about their business were the constant.

The darkness was intense when she opened her eyes. She sat motionless for a while in order to adjust her vision.

The room was hot and stuffy. She realized that this must be one of Delhi's infamous power cuts. She got up gingerly and with shaky legs made her way to the window. She opened it with difficulty, making sure that the mosquito netting stayed in place.

But even the outside air was still and felt hotter than ever. She decided to close the window again but stopped as a movement near the gate caught her attention. *It must be the chowkidar.* Somehow, she wasn't convinced and remained motionless, her hand on the window latch. She heard some muted tones but was unable to catch what was being said. Then she heard the grating of the gate, opening and shutting. Carla was taken aback by how nervous she was. *Why should someone driving out a gate worry me?* If she continued this way, she would go crazy. She took a deep breath: *I have to be strong.*

A sudden, hot breeze rustled the leaves on the driveway, and a waft of perfume reached Carla just as she was about to shut the window. The scent was soothing, familiar, and as she walked back to the bed she realized it was the unmistakable fragrance of the special edition Chanel perfume she had bought the day she arrived in Delhi. Now suddenly filled with suspicion, Carla thought that whoever had left through the gate minutes before was certainly not a maidservant: a friend of George's? A girlfriend, perhaps? *Why am I thinking this? Why this jealousy?*

Carla tried to get a grip on her feelings and got back into bed. But sleep evaded her. On discovering a battery-operated flashlight in the bedside drawer and resigned to her nervous energy, Carla left the room to explore the rest of the house. The granite floors felt refreshingly cool and smooth under her bare feet. She stood at the door to the living room. It was large and spacious. At the opposite end, French doors in Burmese teak led out to a wide veranda overlooking a small, compact garden. She then walked past what seemed to be George's study. Taking a few steps forward, she stopped. Despite the feeling that she was intruding, Carla turned back to the study and opened the door.

A Persian carpet covered most of the floor, and on it stood two large leather armchairs and a carved wooden and leather-bound desk. A large, antique-looking bookshelf dominated one wall in the room. It was half lined with books, interesting-looking travel memorabilia, and some silver-framed photographs. Carla peered at the photos with interest. An elderly couple smiled warmly at the camera, sitting at a dining table laden with all the delectable trappings of Thanksgiving. The elderly man was handsome, in a scholarly way, wearing black-rimmed spectacles, with thinning white-gray hair. The woman beside him was attractive and evidently George's mother. Her hair was steel gray, worn in a short bob with the same Mediterranean complexion as George's.

In another photo a very young-looking George, smiling cheerfully, stood with a group of men dressed in Harvard football gear. The last photo was taken from a distance: a young, dark-haired woman, somewhat familiar, was sitting on a camel, wearing khaki trousers and a large hat that cast a dark shadow over her face. George was tethering the camel, laughing merrily and looking up at her.

Carla stepped back, suddenly feeling uncomfortable looking at George's private memories. She now wanted to leave the room as quickly as possible. Just as she turned toward the door, the power came back on, lighting up the passage. She gasped: there was George, standing in boxer shorts and arms folded across his chest in the doorway. He was frowning.

"Do you need something, Carla?"

Blushing furiously, she replied, "No. No, thank you. I was just looking for the, um, kitchen." She looked at him and smiled guiltily.

"Are you hungry?"

She nodded, and George held out his hand. Her hand in his, Carla was led to the kitchen.

With Carla seated on a wooden bench next to the granite counter, George busied himself taking out ingredients from the large refrigerator.

"I'm glad you're feeling better; regaining your appetite is a good sign."

Carla smiled feebly. She wasn't actually hungry, but she made up her mind to eat whatever George offered.

"Chicken sandwich?" he asked, cutting a thick slice of

ciabatta.

"Thanks, that's great, just go slow on the mayo."

He smiled and with obvious concentration and pleasure prepared a snack for Carla.

She watched him as unobtrusively as possible. He was lean and broad shouldered, with the well-defined torso and arm muscles of a natural athlete. His skin was smooth and tanned with remarkably little chest hair. Suddenly self-conscious, Carla smoothed her hair and tugged at her T-shirt, a fleeting glance confirming that it was much too tight over her breasts.

He cut the sandwich in half, put one half on her plate and kept the other half for himself. "Bon appetit!" he said and took a large bite.

"Thanks, this looks delicious." Carla chewed slowly, enjoying the simple sandwich. They ate in silence. Then she asked, "Do your servants live on the property?"

"Yes, why?"

"Just wondering." She smiled and continued eating. "And their wives?"

George looked at her quizzically. He wiped his mouth and hands with a paper napkin and said, "Yes, some of them."

He poured two glasses of cranberry juice and moved to her side on the wooden bench. She put her half-eaten sandwich down and said apologetically, "I shouldn't eat too much—my stomach is still a little queasy."

Taking her left hand into his, he stroked it almost absentmindedly. He looked at her with an intensity that lit up the amber in his eyes. Carla's heart literally skipped a beat. Conscious of her uneven breathing, she sipped the juice, keeping her eyes on his hands. They were deeply tanned, square and large. He curled his fingers around and in between her long, elegant fingers, massaging them gently. She bit her lip. How could she possibly feel so aroused after everything that had happened to her? She was obviously going mad! Admonishing herself, she pulled her hands away and folded them in her lap. She didn't care if she looked like a prude to George—he should've known better than to touch her like that.

Laughing softly, he picked up her plate and took it to the sink. Feeling like a naïve, blushing teenager, she followed with the empty glasses. His fingers brushed against hers as he took the glasses from her. The light feathery touch unleashed a longing, a physical need to be touched, held, kissed. Carla turned around abruptly, afraid of George reading her thoughts.

He followed her out of the kitchen, saying, "I think you should try to get a little more sleep."

Carla nodded and smiled. "Thanks for the sandwich. I didn't mean to wake you."

"It's OK; I wasn't sleeping."

As they reached the bedroom door, she turned and said, "George, I don't know how to thank you—"

"Stop. There's really no need." In his forced reply, George's voice was slightly gruff. She stared at him, sensing danger, her emotions roused and her heart hammering in her chest in quick uneven beats. He moved closer to her, his dark eyes boring into hers; she was hypnotized. Time was of no consequence as she started drowning in the pool of her desire. His masculine scent, his presence, was so commanding, so intense, filling up her personal spaces, so jealously guarded. He cupped her burning face in his hands, and she looked up. Her mouth was quivering as she watched his full, beautiful lips smiling ever so slightly. Then she felt them, hot and fervent on her mouth. As his tongue parted her mouth and ardently explored its inner depths, she felt her legs buckling, but George steadied her against the door, his body lithe and strong against her melting frame.

George whispered throatily into her ear, "Are you OK, Carla?"

She opened her eyes languidly and nodded. As he swept her into his arms, an image of Andrew drifted briefly into her mind. She banished it brusquely; he was not going to come between her and George, not tonight.

George lowered her gently onto the bed and switched on the small table lamp, its rattan shade diffusing a soft, textured glow. Carla lay back against the pillows; her mind had emptied. She was aware only of her body—it was molten gold, hot and liquid. Raising her arms, she surrendered to him taking the T-shirt off over her head. In the slight struggle, she laughed self-consciously, but George's expression was intent as he touched her breasts lightly, almost shyly. She arched her back, and with a groan George buried his head in between her breasts, kissing them passionately, his fingers teasing her nipples. Carla cried out, throbbing with pleasure. George gazed at her, his eyes soft and caring. He covered her neck with kisses, her chin, nose, and eyes. Carla ran her fingers through his short, thick hair, and pulling his head closer she kissed his face with light, dancing butterfly kisses.

Suddenly Carla stopped kissing him. *It's the perfume, the Chanel perfume,* she thought, and pulled away. The fragrance faded away into the night air. But, resting again in his arms, her face in his neck, she smelled it again. She lifted her head and looked at him. His eyes were enquiring, hers disillusioned.

"I'm sorry, George; this a mistake."

"Are you sure?" He looked at her intently.

She nodded and looked away as he got up from the bed. She grabbed a pillow and tried to cover her naked body.

Up against the bed, he watched her for a few moments, a slight frown creasing his brow. He opened his mouth to say something, but instead left the room wordlessly, closing the door softly behind him.

Carla lay still, listening intently to George's retreating footsteps. A sense of loss—no, betrayal—enveloped her. She thought of Andrew, but there was no guilt. It was she who couldn't trust anymore. Sleep eluded her; her brain refused to shut down. Closing her eyes, she replayed every conversation, look, and touch she had shared with George. Finally, as a blushing dawn warily announced its arrival through the blinds, Carla fell into an unsettled sleep.

✦✦✦

Carla awoke ravenous. As she opened her eyes, she was greeted by the smell of frying onions, garlic, and coriander. She jumped up and had a quick shower, washing her hair with almond-smelling shampoo, which only increased her appetite. When she came out the shower, she was surprised to see a clean white linen blouse, khaki pants, and underwear neatly displayed on the rattan armchair next to her bed. Smiling at the generosity of this gesture, she dressed and left her room to look for the kitchen.

She had decided to simply forget the events of the night before and pretend nothing had happened, nothing mattered. She was alive; she was free, and she was going home. After all, she had done pretty well so far in not thinking about Andrew and Leila—she could just add the kidnapping and George to the list of denial, but as she thought this, she realized that, even if she weren't consciously acknowledging the traumatic events of the past week, they would still be there—an undeniable part of her history she could never erase.

Sunil was at the gas stove in the kitchen. On the counter next to the stove Carla saw a large, stainless-steel bowl in which rested smaller bowls of pungent-smelling spices. Sunil's artistic, nut-brown fingers were deftly sprinkling the ground spices into the black wok on the flame. His work of art was nearing its completion, and Carla was quite ready to devour it.

Sunil turned around when he heard Carla pulling out the wooden bench to sit down. He gave her a wide, apologetic grin and said, "Oh no, Madam, you should call Sunil to bring good cup of Indian chai to you while stay in bed."

"Thanks, Sunil, but I am starving. What are you cooking?"

"I am making dhal; you wish to eat something now?"

'Yes, please, whatever is ready. What's the time, by the way?"

Sunil looked at his large Titan watch with its black Roman numerals, squinting slightly; then, as if making an announcement of grave importance, he said, "Four minutes to one o'clock. Lunch ready at two o'clock."

Seeing the dismay on Carla's face, he said quickly, "No worry, Madam, you sit on veranda, and I bring some chai and paratha in two ticks."

Hurrying her out, he shouted for someone called Asha. Carla walked out onto the veranda and sat down in a comfortable reclining chair next to a small, round, marble table. A slight, dark-skinned woman of undetermined age hurried toward her with a huge feather duster. She dusted the furniture around Carla with gusto, smiling happily as Carla started to sneeze from the dusty onslaught.

With her eyes streaming and her hand clasped over her nose, Carla saw George drive through the gate and wondered what she must have looked like to him. He got out of the jeep and walked quickly to the veranda. He was wearing khaki chinos with a navy Polo shirt and polished tan Sebago loafers. He smiled warmly. "Hi, you look well rested."

"Hi. Yes, I'm feeling OK. I think I've pretty much recovered."

Sitting down on the recliner next to her, he asked Asha

to call Sunil. Carla watched him, and suddenly she wasn't so sure about the little speech she had prepared for him. She decided to keep it simple. "I want to go back…home… I mean, I'm grateful to you for saving me from who-knows-what, but I think I should go home."

He looked at her questioningly but remained silent.

Sunil broke the uncomfortable silence by announcing, "One very hot, tasty paratha for Madam coming up." Relieved, Carla thanked him and asked George politely if he'd like some.

"No, thanks, please go ahead—it's getting cold."

Biting into it, she felt a bit self-conscious, but luckily George got up and said, "I'll be in my study. We need to talk."

The words chilled Carla, almost taking away her appetite, but she continued eating slowly, postponing the inevitable chat.

She finished her last sip of fragrant chai, got up slowly, as if in pain, then walked toward George's study. The door was shut so she knocked softly. George called out, "Come in."

She entered. He was sitting behind his large desk, a folder open in front of him, the computer screen blank and silent. Feeling like a schoolgirl called in to see the headmaster, Carla sat down on the leather chair facing George across the desk.

"I suppose you need some questions answered," George said, looking at Carla with guarded eyes.

"Yes, of course and…about last night—"

But with a wave of his hand, he interrupted her and said, "Forget it, I don't need explanations; it's OK. You've been through a tough time, and I'm sorry, I shouldn't have kissed you."

Carla flushed and said, "Good, so that's behind us. What now?"

"Well, I guess you need to know how I found you, right?"

"Yes, something like that."

"Do you remember everything?"

"Pretty much. After the heroin my memories get a bit fuzzy, but I think I can recall most of it."

George sat back in his chair and stared out of the window for a few seconds; then he looked at Carla and said, "You have no idea how lucky you are that we found you. The person running this trafficking ring is an evil, unscrupulous bastard."

"How do you know?" Carla asked, frowning deeply.

George smiled at the petulance in her voice and continued, "A few years ago I was introduced to an Italian woman, Valentina Nesi. She works for UNODC, you know, United Nations Office on Drugs and Crime?"

Carla nodded. "Yes, of course."

"Well, she was instrumental in the signing of the Trafficking Protocol in Palermo in 2000. It was adopted by the General Assembly and implemented on Christmas Day 2003. It is the first clearly defined and global legally binding indictment on human-trafficking."

"You're joking. You mean to tell me that there has been no recourse until a few years ago?" Carla was shocked.

"I'm afraid so. Valentina was passionate about bringing the perpetrators to book, but she felt that they were fighting a losing battle. As we know, certain governments tend to turn a blind eye to something that has been going on for decades, even centuries, only signing the convention to score brownie points with the international community.

"Anyway, I was attached to the Embassy in Kabul at the time when one of our Afghani informers told us about this Italian who was asking too many questions and meeting too many nasty characters. I was asked to keep an eye on her. At that time Afghanistan was not and still isn't party to the 2000 Trafficking Protocol." George paused for a few seconds and said, "I'm not boring you, am I?"

"No, of course not—please go on."

"The embassy tried to contact her, but she didn't return calls and refused to come in. I was asked to befriend her, glean something from her—for her own protection, of course. She made use of the gym at the Serena hotel, the only five-star hotel in Kabul where expats would gather to escape the dust and Kalashnikovs, literally an oasis in the middle of the city.

"It wasn't difficult spotting an Italian woman in the middle of Kabul. She was doing laps in the pool, so I just waited at the coffee shop where, as I was told, she usually had a coffee after her workout. We got chatting on how bad the coffee was, and I invited her for dinner the following evening."

Carla laughed and said teasingly, "And of course, she said yes."

To her surprise, George flushed ever so slightly, causing a slight flutter in her stomach.

"Well, you know how it is—it can get lonely in Afghanistan, I guess, especially if you're Italian and female."

Smiling, Carla continued teasing, "Yeah, yeah…"

George laughed. "Do you want to hear the rest of it or are you having too much fun at my expense?"

"I'm sorry. Please carry on. This is turning into a very good story."

"Valentina confided in me that she wasn't comfortable working with the authorities. She believed there were informers in most of the departments and asked me if I could help her, unofficially, that is. I couldn't refuse. Human trafficking is possibly the most lucrative illegal activity in the world today. Besides, it's just plain evil.

"She asked me to help her find a certain character, Abbas Zahid, a big shot in the Taliban. A young Afghani girl was rescued from a brothel in Teheran, and she described her abduction at the hands of this man. Hectic stuff. It haunts one—for a lifetime. You're sure you want to hear more?"

"Yes, although it scares the hell out of me." Carla was listening with journalistic curiosity and intent to everything George was saying, but at the same time, she knew that she could just as easily have been a statistic. She felt blessed, lucky, but with a sense of guilt. Nazeema's young face flashed before her eyes—why had Carla been saved and not her? But she realized that there was simply no answer—no point in mulling over the harsh reality. Her very brief introspection was broken as George resumed his story.

"One of our Afghani informers came from the same district in the province of Ghazni. His sister was murdered by her husband for being disrespectful—with the approval of the local Taliban, of course. He hated the Taliban, and it was his mission to see them defeated in his lifetime. When I asked him to help me find Abbas Zahid, he agreed, and along with his informers we came pretty close, but I'm afraid we lost Zahid when he crossed into Pakistan."

"Is he still at large?"

"Yes, and more powerful than ever."

"So you are still trying to find him?"

"Of course, but it's amazing how it has opened a can of worms."

"What do you mean?"

"Human trafficking isn't the only activity the Taliban is involved in. Identity theft has become a big one."

"I think that's why I was kidnapped."

"Yes, I know."

Carla looked at him in surprise. "How do you know? I haven't told you anything."

"Carla, I had you followed." George's expression was grim.

The air was suddenly stifling hot, as if the air-conditioners were no longer working.

Carla wiped away the beads of perspiration on her forehead as her heart started racing. Feeling ill, she looked at him and said calmly, "Why, George? Please explain to me why in heaven's name you had me followed on a perfectly normal tourist outing?"

CHAPTER 9

George looked at Carla for a few moments, dropped his gaze, and started rummaging through some files on his desk. Where the air had been too hot a few moments earlier, the air-conditioning now felt too cold, and Carla shivered slightly. The silence was unbearable. Biting her lip, she wondered if she should just leave. Was it possible that George actually had something to do with her kidnapping? She decided to ask him directly.

"George, did you have something to do with this?" Her voice was soft, but her tone was firm.

"Yes, and no. Well, indirectly, yes." He sighed and looked her. "I don't know how to describe my involvement. It's complicated."

"Just try me. Any explanation will help—I can promise you that." Carla leaned forward, her expression grave and expectant.

Just then a knock interrupted the drawn-out silence. Sunil entered, carrying a tray with a cup of tea for George.

"Some more chai, Madam?"

"No thanks, Sunil."

He turned to George and asked if he should still serve the lunch at two. On George's instruction to keep to the plan, Sunil left, closing the door behind him.

"I believe we have an informer in the Embassy. In fact, I think he works in my section." George took out a photo from a file on his desk and showed Carla. The image was an enlarged version of a passport photo. The young, dark-haired woman wasn't smiling, but Carla couldn't help but notice the humor in her eyes. George put the photo back in the file and continued. "I was contacted by the parents of a young American woman of Asian descent at the beginning of this year. They were distraught because their daughter had decided to stay on indefinitely in India. They thought this was out of character and asked me if we could investigate.

"I was rather surprised to see that this young woman had come into the Embassy to ask our advice in helping her obtain a visa for Tibet. Her address and contact number in India were left with us. I became even more suspicious when we checked the guesthouse she was staying at and was told that her boyfriend had checked her out. He told the owner that she had gone to Tibet and then had decided to go on to China from there. I could imagine that it doesn't mean much to someone not familiar with the politics between China and Tibet, but in reality it's virtually impossible to enter China from Tibet. Even from a different port. If the Chinese authorities know that you've just been to Tibet, they tend to deny access."

"Did you find her?"

"No, and we couldn't find any evidence that she had left India."

"How did her parents know she wanted to stay?"

George smiled at Carla's impatience and said, "I'm getting there, OK?"

"Sorry."

"Her parents sent us a copy of the letter she had sent them. They confirmed it was in her handwriting."

Carla's heart was hammering against her chest. "What did it say?"

"Basically, she said she was tired of her futile life in the West, something along the lines of her having started 'her divine life.'" He looked through some of the papers in the file and pulled out a photocopy of the handwritten letter. "Hmm, yes, here we are, she says her life 'only has meaning if she follows the ethos of the ashram, which is to serve, love, give, purify, meditate, and realize.'"

"I don't suppose there is a return address?" Carla asked in a wry tone.

George shook his head. "The postmark shows that it was posted in Delhi."

"Did you go to the police?"

"Of course, but they were apathetic, said there was nothing out of the ordinary here. India was the answer to many Westerners' 'search for spirituality.'"

"Oh my God. That's exactly what he said."

George looked at her with a puzzled expression. "Who?"

"The small, bald guy, the identity thief."

"Do you think you could identify him?"

"Yes, of course. But how? He won't know it's me, will he?"

"Don't worry, you'll be protected. I promise."

"But, George, I want to go home. I'm scared. You should've seen how fearful the young guys who kidnapped me were of Barra Bhai."

"Is that what they called him?"

Carla nodded.

George sighed, got up, and walked around the desk toward Carla. He knelt, his face level with hers.

"Carla, I know this is difficult, but we need you. Those girls need you. As you can imagine, it is extremely rare for anyone to escape."

She turned her face away from his intent gaze. "You still haven't told me how you found me."

He smiled warmly, stood up, and held out his hand to her. "Come, I'll explain during lunch."

❦❦❦

George sat down at the head of the dining table as Sunil pulled out a chair for Carla on George's right. Sunil served them a chicken curry in spinach gravy, yellow dhal, steamed basmati rice, and a platter of sliced onion, carrots, and cucumber. Carla didn't have much appetite but sat silently, watching George eat. Finally, when he had almost finished his lunch, he told Carla about the events surrounding her rescue.

George had had an agent follow the tour Carla was on. On the day of the tour a young American woman who was traveling alone in India had requested the embassy's assistance in finding a certain yoga ashram somewhere in the foothills of the Himalayas. They obliged, and somehow she was invited to join the tour group. George had a hunch that the group suspected of kidnapping the other American girl could have been tipped off again by the informer. When the agent saw Carla leaving in the tuk-tuk, he followed her in one, too. Unfortunately, he lost sight of her when she got off the scooter in the middle of the road. He tried to find her, but he was already too late. Carla had disappeared in the bedlam of Old Delhi's mazes.

George was notified, and a team was deployed to search for her. When Elouise called the embassy to find out what time they were expecting the group's return, George told her that he had persuaded Carla to join him on a short trip to Jaipur in Rajasthan. The search continued, but the trail had gone cold.

Then George received a call from Asef, his informer from the Ghazni province in Afghanistan. He had recognized Carla on the night of the sale.

"How did he know it was me—do I know him?" Carla asked.

"I pointed you out to him. You were in Lodhi Garden."

Carla looked at him in confusion and said, "I don't remember seeing you there?"

"You didn't see me, and I didn't want to interrupt you; you looked like you were having fun." George seemed uneasy and evaded her next question by continuing his narrative. "Asef was working undercover, impersonating a Taliban commander. He asked what he should do, and I suggested he bid for you."

Carla's face drained of all color as she gaped at George.

He smiled. "You were pretty expensive. Asef was getting very nervous, but luckily the other guy who was bidding furiously for you, an Arab from Oman, gave up, and we managed to get you out of there."

Sunil entered with sliced mango and vanilla ice cream for dessert. They ate in silence. Carla was afraid and wanted to leave India as soon as possible, but something was holding her back. Was it Nazeema and the other young girls? Or did George have something to do with her halfhearted desire to leave? Carla watched George eating the ice cream slowly. *I owe him, I owe Nazeema.* "OK, George, I want to help. What do you want me to do?"

George wiped his mouth with the linen napkin, folded it carefully, and put it next to the bowl. "Carla, I need you to return to the Singhs' bungalow. You can't tell Elouise about any of this."

"But why?" Carla interrupted.

"Please trust me on this. We will continue seeing each

other, and it's up to you what you want Elouise to think about our relationship."

She looked away, embarrassed, but urged George to continue.

"Carry on as usual, but I don't want you leaving Delhi, and don't go to Old Delhi."

"Is that it?"

George laughed and said, "Wish it was, but I'm afraid not. I need you to keep an eye on Harry."

"What? Elouise's husband?"

George's expression was serious. "Yes, this may come as a shock to you, but we have intel that he might be somehow involved."

A look of total disbelief swept over her face; she was speechless.

"I will guide you day by day, as long as you can keep tabs of his comings and goings. Are you OK?"

Carla found her voice, which was thick with emotion. "Does Elouise know about this, I mean, about Harry's involvement?"

"I'm not sure, but under no circumstances whatsoever can you talk about this to her or anyone. Please, it is for your own safety."

Something in his eyes almost scared Carla as he said these words.

"Do I have to follow him?"

George laughed. "No, of course not, but I do want to know when he's traveling, possibly where to and so on. You're a journalist; you guys are good at extracting all kinds of information."

Carla smiled.

He leaned forward, his face once again serious. "I need you to get into his study. We need to see his computer files."

"What? I can't get in there. I don't even know where it is. And how will I get the files?"

George took out a small flash drive from his pocket and handed it to her. It was in the shape of a heart, covered in Swarovski crystals. It had a neck chain attached to it.

"A bit too much bling, don't you think?"

He shook his head and laughed softly. "It's perfect. Custom made and very fast. You can transfer over 250 megabytes per second."

"And that's the absolute fastest?"

George gave her a look of mild amusement while nodding his head.

"We'll obviously be in touch, talking or meeting daily. Here, you can use this phone; it's safe to talk on it." He gave her a new looking iPhone. "I'll guide you. Now I want you to call Elouise and return to the bungalow today. OK?"

Carla nodded, "George, please find out what's happened to Nazeema. Maybe you guys can try and buy her. I have some money."

"Of course, we will try, but you must understand we have to be very careful. It's pointless saving a few girls and then exposing ourselves before we get to the group's leader." Carla nodded, feeling extremely sad for the unfortunate girl. George dialed Elouise's number. He listened intently for a few seconds, then passed the handset to her.

Elouise seemed irritated with Carla when she described how she had decided to go away with George on the spur of the moment. She wanted to know why Carla hadn't called herself. Carla explained that her cell phone, which was in her pocket, had fallen into the toilet. This broke the slight tension, as Elouise started laughing. "Oh, you're such a klutz. Come home; I've missed you. Must I send the car?"

"No thanks, George will drop me."

They said their good-byes, and as Carla got up, she felt a pang of regret. Walking to the bedroom to collect her things, she wondered whether recruiting her to spy on Harry was George's only reason to rescue her. *Surely not,* she thought, and tried to push the preposterous idea out of her mind.

Elouise beamed when she saw Carla. She embraced her and invited George to stay for tea. He accepted graciously and followed Elouise to the veranda. Kishan was showing Seema how to plump up the Sanderson print cushions on the plantation chairs. He greeted Carla warmly and on Elouise's cue hurried to the kitchen to prepare the tea.

It was a hot afternoon. The overhead fan was whirling noisily but not giving much respite from the heat. The emerald green parrots were particularly loud, frolicking in the massive mango tree in the corner of the garden.

Elouise called the mali and asked him to switch on the large air cooler out on the lawn. Carla was fascinated. The large box held a fan that sprayed a fine, cool mist smelling of jasmine into the air.

"I've never seen anything like this—where does the moisture come from?"

"A water tank is connected to it. But we have to be very careful. If the mali doesn't empty the tank daily, the water becomes stagnant."

"Why?" Carla asked.

"Dengue. It has become quite a problem in the past few years. Malaria in Delhi is almost unheard of these days, but now we deal with dengue, also a mosquito-carried disease. It is, in many ways, more dangerous, as no preventive drugs are available such as those for malaria."

Kishan returned with the tea and a platter of hot pakoras, dainty cucumber sandwiches, and slices of buttered banana bread. During tea they made small talk about the weather. And then, Elouise asked the dreaded question: "So how was your trip?"

George smiled, as smooth as ever, Carla thought, and said, "Fantastic. I had a great time. What about you, Carla?"

"Uh! Great." Carla coughed and dabbed at her mouth with the embroidered napkin bought from the Mother Theresa's order in Calcutta.

"So where did you guys go?"

Carla took a huge bite from the pakora on her plate. Holding her hand over her mouth, she gestured with the other to George for a response to Elouise.

Amused by Carla's discomfort and with a mischievous flicker in his eyes, he related their itinerary to Elouise. "We had dinner at home and then decided to drive through to Jaipur so that we could spend the following day there and return the same evening. There was a group of Italians also staying at the Rambagh Palace, and they joined us on our elephant-back tour of the amber fort. They had just returned from Udaipur, and it didn't take much for them to convince us to include it in our itinerary. The next morning we took the early flight to Udaipur. Kamal, my driver, drove through the night, and he was at the airport the next morning to pick us up."

"Did you stay at the Lake Palace?" Elouise asked.

Narrowing his eyes discernibly, George hesitated before replying, "No, actually we decided to stay at the new Leela Hotel. It's also on Lake Pichola."

"Oh no, I love the Lake Palace; we spent part of our honeymoon there." Elouise smiled, wistfully it seemed to Carla.

Clever George, Carla thought, *choosing a new hotel, guessing that Elouise would have stayed at the world-famous Lake Palace Hotel.* Elouise had always been a comfort creature, right from their days at college when she had to have her special thread-count sheets and cookies from home.

"So, what did you think of it?" Elouise asked Carla.

"I loved it, so beautiful. The sun setting over the lake,

turning the marble palace pink, it was awesome."

She remembered reading something like this and was about to continue her narrative when George interrupted her somewhat abruptly by saying, "Look at the time; I must get going. I have a meeting at six." He got up and kissed Elouise on her cheeks, thanking her for the tea. Then he turned toward Carla, and with his back to Elouise, grinned broadly at her as he pulled her up. She understood the questioning look. It was the moment where she had to decide how she wanted Elouise to perceive her relationship with George. She hesitated for a second. Then she kissed him, on the lips. A searing desire made her legs feel like liquid, and she had to sit down quickly. George left with a promise to call her later.

Elouise sat back in her chair and sighed. "Carla, I'm glad you had a good time, but I was really worried. George phones to tell me you were going on this trip, and then his driver, Kamal, rocks up here and asks for an overnight bag with your clothes. Kind of weird. And still no phone call from you…"

"I'm so sorry, Elouise. I know it was irresponsible of me, but I was so caught up in the moment, the adventure. It was exactly what I needed. George is a great guy. He made me forget." Annoyed with herself, Carla could feel herself blushing.

Elouise stared at her with unnerving concentration. Then she relaxed and said, "You're right. Life is short, and we need to live it in any way we can. Go rest a little; tonight we're going to a sangeet."

"What's that?"

"It's one of the many Indian wedding functions. It's meant to be a singing and dancing party."

"So how many functions are there in total?"

"It depends on the family, but on average about four."

"I'm not sure, would love to go, but I'm bushed. An early night with a book sounds like bliss to me. Do you mind?"

"Of course not."

With a relieved smile, Carla got up and said, "You haven't shown me the rest of the house. Do you mind?"

Elouise smiled with pleasure. Carla knew she was proud of her beautiful home. "No, of course not. Come."

An open courtyard divided the bungalow. To the right were the guest wing and an informal sitting room. Harry and Elouise's bedroom was on the left next to their children's rooms. The rooms were large and spacious with a study leading off of each. Harry's study was locked with an antique-looking brass lock. The children's study was identical to Harry's. Carla noted with relief that Harry's study also had an exit to the back courtyard.

After expressing her admiration and thanks to Elouise, Carla went to her room. She lay down on the bed, but instead of relaxing, her heart started pounding in anticipation of what George had asked of her.

CHAPTER 10

Elouise was dressed and eating her breakfast of fruit and yogurt when Carla joined her on the veranda carrying the cup of tea Kishan had brought her in bed. She had switched off the air-conditioning during the night and had woken up hot and sticky, and so had decided to drink her tea on the veranda, where a faint morning breeze was just beginning to stir, rustling the leaves of the large mango tree.

"Good morning! You're up early!" she said to her friend.

Elouise smiled and blew her a kiss. "Yup, have to be at school today. We're discussing the summer fair. You know me, always the sucker to get nominated as fundraiser."

"I'm sure you have loads of fun bossing all those other moms around."

"I guess. What are your plans today, meeting George?"

"Not sure; we'll chat later and decide." Kishan brought her a glass of watermelon juice and asked her if she'd like something to eat. "I'd love some scrambled eggs on toast.

Thanks, Kishan." Carla took a sip of the sweet, refreshing juice and asked Elouise, "Is Harry back yet?"

"He got back yesterday morning."

"Has he had his breakfast?"

"Yes, he eats pretty early, normally in bed."

"Then he goes to the office, I suppose."

Elouise looked at Carla for a second and said, "Yes, I suppose he does, but why all these questions?"

Carla laughed a little self-consciously and said, "No reason, I guess I'm just curious about day-to-day living in Delhi."

"Are you thinking of settling down here by any chance?"

"Don't be ridiculous, of course not."

"Just checking." Elouise smiled. "I hope you don't mind, but I'm taking Om Prakash with me. Parking is a real nightmare near the school. The taxi stand is on Lodhi Road on the other side of the park. It's not far, so if you need a car, Kishan will send one of the chowkidars to fetch one for you. We know all the drivers, and they know who we are, so you don't have to worry about being ripped off."

"Thanks, that's great to know. I think I'll try to contact my dad's aunt; she's the most senior member of the family and always had a soft spot for my dad. Let's see, maybe she'll invite me for tea. Will you be back for lunch?"

"I don't think so. These meetings often run into long lunches."

"And Harry, will he be back for lunch?"

"Not usually, but who knows. You shouldn't worry about us; Kishan has lunch ready every day, whether we're here or not."

"Great, maybe I'll eat at home then."

Elouise looked at her watch and said, "Got to dash. Will I see you for drinks this evening?"

"Yes, of course. Have a nice day."

Elouise hurried to the car and waved to Carla as Om

Prakash drove off in the white Ambassador.

Right. My first day as an official spy, Carla thought, a sardonic grin twisting the corners of her mouth. *What now?* Kishan brought her breakfast and asked if she wanted tea. She nodded. *I suppose I should start after breakfast.* When she had finished eating, Kishan brought her tea, Carla asked, "Kishan, how many staff are you altogether in the Singh household?"

Smiling coyly he replied, "Many, many servant, Madam."

"I see, but how many? Five or fifty?"

He laughed loudly and said, "No, no, Madam, not so many, maybe ten together."

"Do they all stay on the property?"

"No, Madam. Only two driver, ayah, cook, houseboy and housemaid stay in servant quarter. The chowkidar come for day or night shift only. The mali come in morning and leave evening, and Harry Sahib peon come morning and sometime stay all day here or sometime go with Sahib."

"What is a peon?"

Kishan frowned. "Madam not know this?"

Carla shook her head. "No, I've never heard that word before."

"Oh, I see. Umm, he is helping Harry Sahib in study. Sometimes he going post office or making typing."

"OK, like a secretary?"

Kishan was relieved and said, "Yes, Madam. Like this."

That could be a bit of a problem, thought Carla. She had hoped to have access to Harry's study when he was at work. A secretary occupying the same space would complicate things.

"What about your family, Kishan? Do you have children?"

"Yes, Madam. I have one girl and one boy."

'Do they live here with you?"

"No, they are in my village with wife and family. My son

is in eleventh standard, and he is very good boy. Next year Madam Elouise is paying for him to study in college here in Delhi."

"That's wonderful, what does he want to study?"

"Computers." Kishan lifted his head slightly and Carla detected the pride in his eyes.

"What about your daughter?"

Looking down at his feet he replied, "Big problem, Madam, big problem."

"Why, is she sick?" Carla asked, alarmed.

"No, but she is very ugly. Very dark. Even with big dowry I can't find husband for her."

Carla's mouth opened in shock and surprise. *Was he serious?* "I'm sure that's not true. And in any case, she doesn't have to be married, she could study and get a job somewhere."

Kishan shifted his feet and said, "My daughter she stop school when she is fourteen. She must help her mother in the field. In my village if boy studies it is very good."

Memories of Nazeema's story flashed through her mind. Carla felt quite ill. She looked at Kishan and noticed the serenity and kindness in his face. He must love his daughter, yet these circumstances, socially accepted by millions of poor Indians, made him inhumane. Is it cruelty or just a fact of life in their arduous existence?"

"Do you have a photo of your daughter, Kishan?"

He laughed and took out a tatty wallet from his trousers' back pocket. He pulled out a few photos and showed Carla a formal looking family portrait. Carla looked at it and smiled. A proud looking Kishan stood next to his wife, a tiny pretty woman, not smiling. His son, almost the same height as his father, suppressed a smile. Next to him stood his sister, She was beaming. Her face was round and sweet and her smooth complexion looked like polished walnut, eyes bright with mirth. Unfortunately her teeth spoiled her beautiful smile. Her front teeth looked like they were jutting out of the top half of her gum and the incisors climbed over the canines. "She's not ugly at all! All she needs is a good orthodontist." Carla was smiling and handed it back to Kishan.

Kishan asked, "What is that?"

"A doctor, dentist? It's someone who can fix teeth. It is easy and not very painful."

Regarding her for a few moments he replied, "Madam, my village is very small and even doctor is far away. Where I must find this man?"

Embarrassed by her insensitivity, she should have known an orthodontist was hardly accessible to the majority of rural Indians, barely scraping a living together.

She stood up and said, " Kishan, I will talk to Madam Elouise about this. I would like to help your daughter, if that's all right with you?" With a shy nod and smile he took her empty cup and returned to the kitchen.

Carla returned to her bedroom for a shower and decided to speak to Elouise about the possibility of helping this girl at the earliest opportunity.

Dressed in a pair of khaki pants and a white linen shirt, she thought it might be a good idea to see Harry's study from the back courtyard. Carla remembered that Elouise had mentioned a vegetable garden in the back. Feigning interest, she asked the mali to show it to her. He smiled with obvious pleasure, leading her to the garden. They passed the back courtyard and crossed the immaculate lawn. The vegetable garden was much larger than Carla had expected. It stretched from the back courtyard along the fence bordering the adjacent Lodhi Garden.

The mali pointed out the neat little rows of his verdant pride, chatting happily in Hindi, oblivious to the fact that Carla could not understand a word. A high wall separated the servants' quarters from the vegetable garden. Carla looked back and saw a wooden swing in the back courtyard. She thanked the mali and walked toward the large Indian jula, with its ornate carvings, hanging on thick brass chains tarnished black. She smiled and sat on it, swinging herself backward and forward, enjoying the motion.

Her view of Harry's study was perfect. She scrutinized it as unobtrusively as possible. It had a teak double door with a brass bolt and lock, much like the doors in the rest of the house. The door was open, the brass lock hanging loosely in the bolt. She could see movement through the cane blinds inside both windows. She sat watching patiently to see who was inside. After about twenty minutes, the houseboy came through the door with a broom and bucket. He then closed, bolted, and locked the door with the large brass padlock. Seeing Carla on the swing, he greeted her politely and walked past her toward the kitchen. The study seemed quiet and dark, as if the lights had been switched off. Carla sat on the swing for a few more minutes and then decided that there was no one in the study.

She returned to her room and studied the make of the brass lock on her door. It was a Godrej lock, made from solid brass and not particularly old. With a plan beginning to formulate in her mind, she called Kishan and asked him to call a taxi.

She grabbed her purse as a black-and-yellow Ambassador taxi pulled into the driveway. An elderly Sikh driver opened the door for her, introducing himself as Harjeet Singh.

"Khan Market, please."

Carla was dropped outside a fabric store, where she asked to see the tailor. She was led to the end of the narrow shop, where a young, good-looking man greeted her politely. She introduced herself and told him she was Elouise Singh's friend.

"How do you do, Madam? I am Sanjay. I've been tailor

to Madam Elouise and her family for a long time. Please, how can I assist you?"

"I have a linen dress I would love you to copy for me. It's quite simple. How much do you charge?"

"You have the dress here?" he asked.

"No, I can send it with the driver after I have selected the fabrics."

Sanjay frowned and said, "I need to see the dress to give a price."

"Of course, I will bring it later. Where will I find a hardware store?"

"What are you looking for?"

"I wanted to buy a lock for my suitcase—it was damaged coming over."

Sanjay thought for a second; then he said, "You'll find this shop in Prithviraj Market. It is next to Khan Market."

Promising to return with her dress, she said goodbye and left. She found the market and the hardware store with ease. The shop was small, and every inch of it was filled with hardware. The padlocks were displayed in a large wooden box. As she was about to start rummaging through them, a teenage boy with acne stopped her and said, "Madam, I help you?"

"Yes, please, I'm looking for a large Godrej brass lock."

Shaking his head in the quaint Indian "yes," he took out four locks in different sizes and displayed them proudly on the dirty counter.

"Yes, exactly what I am looking for." Carla took the largest lock and said, "This one, please. How much is it?"

Smiling, he said, "No problem, Madam, I make special price for you. Only four hundred rupees."

Carla smiled. "Thanks." She paid and left, walking back to Khan Market. Her large Louis Vuitton purse felt weighed down with the brass lock in it. Passing a magazine stand, she stopped to buy the latest *Time*. The cover of an Indian *Hello* magazine caught her attention. Picking it up, she recognized Ronnie and Preeti Kapoor, glamorous in their traditional dress. She paged through it to find the related article when someone touched her shoulder, and with a fright she turned around and saw Harry, smiling at her.

"Sorry, I didn't mean to startle you," he said.

"Oh, don't worry. I was just getting acquainted with Delhi's gossip. Aren't you at work?"

"Just a quick coffee break. Would you like to join me?"

Carla was unsure, but thought it might seem strange if she refused him. She followed him to the same coffee shop Elouise had taken her to on her first day in Delhi. Harry was wearing dark jeans and a Lacoste striped shirt with his sleeves rolled up. He ordered an iced coffee, and Carla ordered the same. Then he sat back and said, "So how are you enjoying India so far?"

"It's great, thanks."

"I believed you went to Rajasthan with George."

She felt herself blushing and said, "He was kind to take me—he's quite the expert, you know."

"Is that so? I didn't know he was so familiar with Rajasthan."

Carla thought it best to change the subject as quickly as possible and said, "Where are your offices, Harry?"

"I work quite a bit from home and at a government office in Lodhi Colony. The nuclear research center is in Mumbai, so I have to go there every other week."

"Wouldn't it be better to live in Mumbai then?"

"Elouise doesn't like it; plus we are lucky to have my family home here in Delhi. Properties like ours are almost impossible to come by in Mumbai, and besides, they're unbelievably expensive."

Carla thought she saw a peculiar expression in Harry's eyes as he spoke of his family home, but she brushed it aside, thinking she was reading too much into everything now that she was George's spy.

As they finished their drinks, Harry said, "Any news from Andrew?"

"No, nothing at all."

"Don't be hasty, Carla. Things aren't always what they seem."

The waitress brought the bill, and Carla reached for her purse. As she pulled it toward her, the padlock fell out. Luckily it was in a paper packet. Harry picked it up and handed it to her, looking somewhat surprised. She thanked him, stuffing it back in her purse.

Insisting on paying the bill, he said, "See you for dinner," and left.

The iPhone George had given her rang. It was George. "What are you up to?" he asked.

"I'm at Khan Market. You?"

"At work. Do you have any plans for dinner?"

"I think I should have dinner at home."

"Will Harry be home?"

"I think so; we just had coffee together."

"Good, then I'm also coming for dinner. Make sure I'm invited."

Carla was about to protest, but the finality in George's tone prevented her. They said good-bye, and Carla promised to call him later to confirm dinner.

Carla went back to the bungalow to fetch her dress and dropped it at the tailor after selecting some fabrics. Sanjay promised to have them delivered in a few days.

Harry wasn't home for lunch, so Carla ate alone on the veranda. After lunch she called her dad's aunt but was told that she was out playing cards at the gymkhana club. Carla decided not to leave a message and said she'd call back later.

She moved to a recliner on the lawn, where she reveled in the misty spray from the cooler. After briefly reflecting on the hazardous past couple of days and her amazing escape, Carla sighed with pure relief and joy. Her whole life, once so taken for granted, had now acquired a whole new meaning. She closed her eyes as the humming from the fan and the chatter of the birds in the lush garden lulled her into slumber.

"You're getting soaked."

Carla woke up with a jolt, seeing Elouise smiling down at her. "Hi. I had a lovely sleep." Her clothes and hair were damp from the air cooler.

"How about a cup of tea?" Elouise asked, sitting down.

"Thanks, sounds great. How was your meeting?"

"Good. We're going to host a fashion show. Some of the moms are friendly with a few Indian designers who are keen to show off their Western designs to a more international audience. Hopefully you'll still be here. You should come."

"When will it be?"

"Next week. We were thinking of hosting it the week when the American First Lady is in town on an awareness campaign for human trafficking."

Carla had to hide the surprise in her face by saying, "Oh, by the way, I invited George for dinner. Is that OK with you?"

"Sure, what time did you tell him?"

"I didn't. What time should I tell him to come over?"

"He can join us for drinks at about eight; then I'll serve the dinner about nine."

"Great, I'll give him a call later."

Kishan served them their tea, which they drank while discussing Elouise's plans for the fashion show. When they had finished, Carla excused herself and returned to her bedroom to call George.

CHAPTER 11

George had already arrived by the time Carla joined Elouise and Harry on the veranda for drinks. He kissed her lightly on both cheeks. To her relief it wasn't her lips, as a display of affection in front of Harry and Elouise would have embarrassed her. George was wearing his usual khaki chinos with a Brooks Brothers pink-and-white-striped cotton shirt, casually rolled up to his elbows. He looked tanned and relaxed with a scotch and soda in his right hand. Elouise looked glamorous in a fitted short embroidered kurti worn over jeans.

She smiled at Carla and said, "Hey, I was just about to call you." Harry, dressed in a comfortable white Pathani suit, greeted Carla amiably, sipping a mango lassi. Carla thought how cool and comfortable that must be. Her cream silk blouse was definitely too hot for a Delhi summer. Kishan, without asking, brought Carla an icy gin fizz brimming with fresh mint.

George was telling them a story about an incident at the

US Embassy in Kabul, where the brother of a young bride was trying to get asylum for himself and his sister, who had her nose and ears cut off by the Taliban-led village court, after he had rescued her from her husband's family.

"How old was she?" Elouise asked.

"Not quite eighteen. She must've been a beauty. But you can imagine what the poor girl looked like without a nose, which was literally hacked off with an Afghan choora."

"Oh my God, that's terrible." Carla was shocked. "What was her crime?"

"She tried to run away from her husband and in-laws. They used to beat her daily, and who knows what else? She could've been sexually abused, too, but too ashamed to tell us or her brother."

"So what happened—did you get her out?" Elouise asked.

"We contacted the NGO, Women for Afghan Women, and they took her to a safe house somewhere in Afghanistan. It would have been too dangerous for her, and we couldn't exactly take her into the American compound, as her in-laws could've laid kidnapping charges."

"And her brother?" Elouise asked.

"We managed to get him asylum in the US, but he preferred to stay in Afghanistan and went undercover or something. We never heard from him again."

Harry got up and, as he started moving toward the dining room, said, "I suppose stories like these help the Americans justify their presence in Afghanistan even more." As he said this, he turned his back on them, not expecting an answer.

George looked at him, his eyes piercing. "We have been there longer than the Soviets, and it looks as though we are going to beat their record by four years."

Elouise got up and said, "Come, let's move inside where it's cooler. I'll tell Kishan to serve dinner." She disappeared into the kitchen while Harry showed Carla and George where to sit at the large, oval, Rosewood dining table. It was attractively laid with a white, starched, embroidered, cotton tablecloth and matching napkins. Wedgwood white dinner plates and antique-looking silver cutlery were carefully laid next to crystal water tumblers and wine glasses. Carla noticed that no wine glass was at Harry's table setting. He sat at the head with Elouise opposite him. A large oil painting of a fierce-looking Sikh man in a blue turban was hanging directly behind Harry on the wall. He reminded Carla of her grandfather.

Kishan came in with a bottle of wine and poured the South African Merlot for everyone except Harry. Kishan and the houseboy, who was serving the starter of masala-fried pomfret, were impeccably dressed in crisp white pants and matching shirts. Carla smiled as she noticed their bare feet.

"This is great, thanks, Elouise, Harry," George said raising his glass to both of them.

"It's our pleasure. Bon appetit," Elouise said, raising her glass in a toast.

Harry, who didn't join in the toast, addressed George. "Are you sure the US is going to pull out of Afghanistan by 2014?" Before George could respond, he continued, "It seems to me, and others I'm sure, that the US has carved out a nice little military base for themselves flat bang in the middle of the Middle East and South Asia. And conveniently close to Russia, too, who has been flexing its military muscle lately."

George laughed and said, "Wow, what have you been reading?"

Harry flushed slightly with a tight smile, cold accusation in his eyes.

"The US has everything in place for a 2014 withdrawal. We are pretty sure that by then we would have proved to the Afghans that we're not just abandoning them, and hopefully they will throw themselves in with us," George continued.

"And do you really think the Taliban is just going to sit back and watch?" Harry asked mockingly.

"No, of course not, but we are hoping that the majority of Afghans want to be rid of the Taliban and bring an end to it all," George returned with a serious expression.

Harry took a sip of the water in his crystal tumbler. In a tone so soft that Carla had to strain her ears, he said with great emphasis and conviction: "You must have heard the much-quoted saying of the Taliban, regardless of the US end date: 'You may have all the watches, but we have all the time.'"

There was an awkward silence for a few minutes, broken by Kishan and the houseboy as they entered with trays of mouthwatering curries and fragrant basmati rice. The houseboy started serving the curries, dishing directly onto their plates. Kishan was back in the kitchen making hot chapattis, which were then brought to the table still puffed up and hot, to be served by the houseboy.

They ate in silence, and when Carla couldn't bear it any longer she said, "Harry, is that your father in the portrait behind you?"

"Yes it is."

"He was quite dashing, not unlike yourself." She studied it for a few seconds. "Yes, I can definitely see the resemblance. It is pretty strong. Don't you agree?"

With clenched jaw Harry replied, "He's dead now; what does it matter?"

"Harry!" Elouise was angry. "What a terrible thing to say. I'm sorry, Carla, Harry was very close to his father. I don't understand this insensitivity—"

Harry forced an apologetic smile and said, "OK, I'm sorry. I didn't mean anything by it. It's just he's gone, and I don't like talking about it."

George was watching them all closely. "Elouise, you have a marvelous cook. He is almost as good as my Sunil. I think we should have a cook-off." He laughed heartily at this, and Elouise and Carla joined him, laughing with relief as much as at his timely gusto.

Making an effort, Harry smiled, but Carla noticed the strain in his eyes.

From then on the conversation became more formal. Discussions revolved around the friends they had in common from Boston. They also spoke about the economic future of the US. Harry was quiet and didn't participate in much of the conversation.

After a delicious dessert of hot jalebis and vanilla ice cream, George stood up and said, "Thanks so much, Elouise, Harry, for a great evening, but I have an early meeting tomorrow, so it's best I get going. Perhaps we could have dinner next week at my place?"

Elouise got up and said, "Sure, we'll chat about it. Thanks for coming, and thank you for the lovely flowers." She glanced in the direction of a crystal vase on a side table filled with crimson roses and sprigs of white jasmine.

Carla felt a stab of jealousy and admonished herself for it. She stood up from the table and watched Harry shake George's hand and say, "See you around, George. Thanks for coming."

George looked at Carla. "See me out?"

"Of course." She kissed Elouise on the cheeks and said, "Good night and thanks for a lovely dinner." Harry had already gone inside.

The heavy fragrance of jasmine and overripe fruit filled the sultry night air. George had parked his car in the street, and as soon as they were out of earshot, he said, "Well done, Carla. That wasn't so hard, was it?"

Carla laughed. "No, I guess it wasn't. But getting into

Harry's study is giving me sleepless nights."

"Any plans?"

"Yes, I'm working on something, I'll keep you posted."

They reached his jeep, and he went to the driver's door. "Where's Kamal?" Carla asked.

"I gave him the night off—a relative of his from Kashmir is in town." George kissed her lightly on her cheeks. "Good night, Carla." His eyes were gentle as he looked at her for a few seconds without speaking. His masculine scent of leather and green tea was intense, and Carla felt slightly giddy. She had a powerful urge to lean close to him, to feel his body against her own, but was luckily thwarted by the curious eyes of the chowkidars watching them from the entrance of the bungalow.

George got into the jeep, made a U-turn, and drove away. Carla walked back to her room. She was physically lethargic but mentally wide-awake. She didn't realize she had been smiling until she looked in the mirror while washing her face before bed.

Her phone rang as she was creaming her face. It was George. This only made her grin even broader. "Hi, George, something wrong?"

"You'll have dinner with me tomorrow night. OK?"

"Yes, Commander, whatever you say." She laughed.

George was quiet for a moment. Then he said, "I miss you," and hung up.

Carla stared at her phone for a few seconds. With a groan she fell into bed and thought, *What is wrong with me? I feel like a stupid teenager with a crush on the biology teacher.* She closed her eyes, convinced that tonight she would have good dreams about a broad-shouldered embassy official from America.

Carla was hoping to be alone in the morning for a blitz on Harry's study, but Elouise insisted that they spend the day together. "I've been a terrible host. You've been here for over a week, and I've hardly seen you."

"Don't stress; I'm fine. I love finding my own way around."

"Well, today I'm taking you out. I was thinking of taking you to a jewelry exhibition, lunch at the Oberoi, and then some Ayurvedic treatments at a center in Janak Puri."

"Are you sure? What about the kids?"

"All sorted. They're going to friends after school, and then Harry will pick them up later."

Carla felt frustrated, but putting on a bright smile said, "OK, sounds great. What time will we be home? I'm having dinner with George tonight."

Elouise frowned and said, "We'll be back early evening."

Carla knew not to address Elouise's issue with George. It wasn't like she was actually in a relationship with him, anyway, she thought. "Great, let me get my purse."

The jewelry exhibition was held in the ballroom at the Oberoi hotel next to the Delhi Golf Club. The architecture of the hotel was typical of the sixties, Carla thought, but the interiors were a stunning mélange of modern and classical Indian decor.

As they made their way across the lobby to the ballroom, Elouise explained to Carla that a cousin of Harry's held the exhibition. She'd studied fashion at Parsons in New York and then came back to Delhi to get married. She wasn't happy with her wedding jewelry, so she redesigned the lot. It was a hit with Delhi society. She then started designing her own range, which she sold at exhibitions. "You'll be shocked at how much money is spent on wedding jewelry. In fact, I've started buying pieces for my daughters so that I'm not bankrupt by the time they get married."

"You're kidding."

Elouise laughed and greeted an elderly Indian woman, elegantly dressed, wearing the largest diamond earrings Carla had ever seen. There were quite a few women in the ballroom already, which was decorated as though an Indian wedding were taking place. Stunning models were drifting through wearing simple, vermilion silk saris and the magnificent jewelry. The effect was quite spectacular.

A model stopped in front of Carla, showing off a necklace that made Carla gasp. Diamonds the size of her pinky nail were set in chunky yellow gold from which hung grape-sized South Sea pearls and, in between every two pearls, a pear-shaped polished Columbian emerald the size of a pigeon's egg.

A young woman wearing a fitted Hervé Léger dress rushed up to Elouise and touched her feet briefly, greeting her in the traditional Sikh custom. "Sastrikal chacchi, I'm so glad you could make it. Do you like it?"

"Anni, I love it. Let me introduce you to my college friend, Carla."

They shook hands, and Carla said, "Congratulations, your designs are amazing."

Anni smiled. "Thank you so much. Please have some champagne. It's French, Moet & Chandon. They are sponsoring. It wasn't difficult to persuade them after they saw my guest list. Anyway, let me mingle, and if you see anything you like, let me know quickly so that I can reserve it for you. I sold out within two hours at my last exhibition."

With a smile she rushed off toward a group of women who were admiring a Burmese ruby necklace.

"Wow, she has quite a business," Carla said.

Elouise smiled knowingly and looked around. Carla followed her gaze and watched the fellow guests with amusement: they looked like magpies, gasping and gaping at all the shiny stones. "Too much money is spent on Indian weddings," Elouise whispered to Carla. "I'm not prepared to spend so much on my daughters—I could buy them an apartment in Manhattan instead."

The ballroom was getting crowded, and Carla noticed a few men, too. They were mostly middle-aged or older. "Fathers and grandfathers," Elouise said when she noticed Carla looking surprised. "The men in the family have quite a bit to say about the wedding jewelry for either their future daughters-in-law or daughters."

Elouise was suddenly ambushed by a group of loud women, so Carla wandered toward the refreshments table. She helped herself to sushi. As she was pouring soy sauce into a small bowl, she heard the voice of a man chatting to someone on the other side of the Indian goddess ice sculpture. Carla's heart started hammering in her ears. *I'm imagining it,* she thought to herself, but the deep baritone voice was unmistakable. She peered through the foliage of the huge flower display: there was the auctioneer from Ghulam Bazaar. She dropped her plate on the thick, dark blue carpet.

CHAPTER 12

Carla quickly turned her back to the man. It felt like a million fingers were gripping and squeezing her heart. She was having trouble breathing, and the thought that she might be having a heart attack or stroke briefly crossed her mind. Swallowing hard, she dismissed the notion and walked as fast as she could toward the exit. Her legs felt like lead, and she had to control the urge to look back over her shoulder. Once she was back in the lobby, her breathing became easier. Seeing the sign for the powder room, with an audible sigh of relief she crossed the lobby and, once inside, locked herself inside the small toilet cubicle.

Sitting on the toilet lid, she rummaged through her purse and found the herbal drops she had bought at the Ayurvedic pharmacy in Khan Market. She had pretended that she was a fearful flyer. The pharmacist had told her that the drops would keep her as "calm as a baby who has just made potty." She smiled despite the bitterness on her tongue. *I need to get out of India. What am I thinking, trying to help George spy on my best friend's husband?*

Within a couple of minutes, Carla felt better. *The unbelievable power of the mind.* She took out her phone and texted Elouise, saying that she wasn't feeling well and had taken a taxi back to the house. As she waited for the taxi in the hotel foyer, the Ayurvedic euphoria began to wear off. She extricated her crumpled safari hat out of her purse and tucked in as much of her hair as she could. Her large red Marc Jacobs sunglasses completed her disguise, but the possibility of being recognized was almost unbearable.

Elouise called her as she sat in the back of the black Ambassador taxi. "What's wrong?" Elouise asked, concerned.

"Just feeling a bit queasy."

"Do you want me to come home?"

"No, please don't. I'll be fine, really. Stay and tell me all about it later, OK?"

"Well, if you're sure. In the meantime I'll call Kishan and ask him to make you something light for lunch."

"Don't worry, I'll be fine. I'll eat something later when you get home."

"OK, but call me if you need anything, OK?"

"Sure. Bye."

Carla's fingers were tingling with the release of adrenalin. It wasn't very long before they drove through the gate. As they approached the house, Carla saw Harry and his peon, a young man dressed in white trousers and short-sleeved shirt, get into his car. He was carrying a black leather briefcase. Harry saw Carla and waved absentmindedly. The day before she would have seen this as a golden opportunity to get into Harry's study, but Carla's encounter at the hotel left her feeling completely vulnerable. *Don't be spineless! You made a promise to George. You have to keep it, and then you can get out of here.*

Kishan hurried out to greet Carla. Elouise had obviously phoned to tell him that she wasn't feeling well.

"Chai, Madam?"

"Thanks, Kishan, I'll just wash up; then I'll have it on the swing. I need some fresh air."

Kishan looked at her with a dubious expression. "It is too hot, Madam."

She laughed and said, "Just for a little while, OK?"

Shaking his head, he ran to the kitchen to prepare her tea. With renewed courage Carla went to her room and took out the large brass lock, which she had locked inside her suitcase. *I hope they haven't finished cleaning his study.*

Hiding the padlock in her pocket, she went to the patch of lawn outside Harry's study. She sat on the swing facing the study and almost smiled with relief when she saw the opened padlock hanging in the hook. A metal bucket with a mop was outside the door. She walked calmly to the door and casually swapped the lock with the one in her pocket. Then she walked back toward her room, and as she met Kishan, she said, "You're right; it is far too hot outside."

Kishan smiled and said, "Good. Madam drink chai in bedroom now." Following him to her room, she told him she wanted to have a little nap. As soon as he had closed the door, she studied the padlock and was excited to see that it was indeed identical with the one she had bought. Taking care not to lock it, she placed it back inside her suitcase.

Carla tried to read, but she couldn't concentrate. *When should I go back to the study?* She realized that it would have to be before Harry tried to unlock the back door. The realization that he might come back with the peon and try to unlock it made her feel quite ill. *I have to go in soon,* she decided, and got up, but as she was about to leave her room, Elouise knocked gently on her door. Carla jumped back onto the bed and lay down.

"Hey, how are you feeling?"

"Much better, thanks."

"Should I call the doctor?"

"There's really no need. I'll be OK."

Elouise smiled and said, "Good, try to get some rest. Kishan will bring you some kichry for lunch. Not the tastiest of meals, but the best thing for Delhi belly."

"Thanks. What are your plans for the rest of the day?"

"I called one of the moms on the fundraising committee to come for tea to discuss the fashion show. This evening, Harry and I are going to the Habitat Centre for a piano recital—you're still having dinner with George?"

"Let's see how I feel; probably better if I stay home."

"OK, but shout if you need anything. I'll check on you later." Elouise left, and Carla lay back against the cushions breathing with slow deliberation.

The shrill ring of the phone made her jump. It was George. "Hello, Carla."

"Hi, George, all OK?"

"Yeah, where are you?"

"I'm home. I was about to call you; I can't have dinner with you tonight."

George's voice was guarded. "Is everything OK?"

"I'm a little under the weather, but I think an early night will do the trick. Elouise and Harry are out, so I'll just have an early supper in bed."

"Yes of course, I understand. If you're better in the morning then maybe we could take a walk in Lodhi Garden?"

Carla realized that George had understood exactly what she had meant, which gave her an odd thrill.

"Sure, at about eight?"

"Looking forward to seeing you. And, Carla, take care." George hung up.

Carla spent the rest of the day corresponding with friends, but when some of them started asking too many questions about Andrew, she stopped. She had too much to think about right now; Andrew, it surprised her to realize, was the least of her worries. Kishan brought the kichry, a bland rice and lentil dish. She asked him casually whether Harry was coming back for lunch.

"No, Madam. Sahib take tiffin lunch to office."

After lunch she walked around the back garden, but the mali was working in his vegetable patch with a good view of Harry's study. The dhobi was also scuttling back and forth with the family's washing. Realizing that it was impossible to enter the study undetected with the army of staff on the property, Carla went back to her room, where she tried to read. The advocate returned her call, and after she explained who she was, he said he'd meet her on his return the following week from Calcutta. Carla wondered whether she'd still be there and realized her trip to India had not been very successful.

Elouise brought her a cup of tea in the late afternoon. "Feeling better?"

Carla took the tea and smiled. "Yes, thank you. This tea smells divine. What is it?"

"It's Darjeeling, but with added secret spices. It's supposed to take away nausea. Harry told me that it was his ayah's recipe, and he swears by it. Made me promise not to ever give it away." She laughed.

"How did your meeting go?"

"Good, I think we're almost set. We need to find a few more models. We're using some of the moms. They have great figures. Hey—what about you? You'd be perfect, and it's all for a good cause."

"No way. You must be mad."

"Come on, it will be fun. You'll still be here. Go on, do me a favor?"

Laughing, Carla said, "I can't, really; I might not even be here." She was trying her best to feign embarrassment. She knew she couldn't model in front of a crowd of strangers—what if someone from the auction attended?

The Delhi Deception

Elouise gave her a kiss and said, "OK, I'll let you off. Are you fine staying in tonight?"

"Absolutely. I'm going to watch the History Channel and get some beauty sleep."

⁂

Harry returned just before seven, and Carla was so nervous that she thought she was going to gag—terrified that he would discover the changed padlock. She had left her door ajar so that she could hear the goings-on of the household. It sounded like they were running late for the recital, Elouise fussing and hurrying Harry and the kids. At last the house was still. Carla's heart was pounding violently, throbbing in her ears—cutting through the palpable silence. After a light dinner of bland chicken soup, she dismissed Kishan, and to her relief he retired to the servant quarters.

Carla walked around to the front veranda and pretended to select some magazines from the rack while her eyes were scouring for the whereabouts of the chowkidar. He was standing at the front gate chatting loudly to a passerby on a bicycle. The back garden and veranda were quiet. The outside light was off—*Hopefully fused*, Carla thought, pleased with the semidarkness outside Harry's study. She went back to her room to retrieve the lock and USB flash drive George had given her. Turning up the volume on the television, Carla closed her door and hoped that she had succeeded in giving the impression that she was in her room.

Her hands were clammy. With slow, deliberate steps she made her way back to Harry's study. Holding the small flashlight in her mouth, she unlocked her brass padlock on the door and swapped it with the original one, which she left open. She pushed open the double door, and it creaked loudly. Glued to the spot, she listened, but nobody else seemed to have heard, as laughter and chatter continued to filter through faintly from the servant quarters. Hunching her shoulders, Carla crept into the room.

It was dark, and after placing her padlock in her trouser pocket she used the flashlight to look around. Dark wooden bookshelves, overcrowded with books, covered the walls. Piles of books were even stacked on the floor. She inspected them briefly, but they were mostly textbooks ranging from quantum physics to algebraic topology. A large wooden desk, also covered in books and files, took up most of the space in the room. She couldn't find a laptop, but three separate monitors sat buzzing on the desk. The computer was in a glass and steel cabinet with a couple of routers; it looked as if it was locked. Carla felt like crying but tried to open it anyway. To her surprise, it opened, and she almost shrieked with joy.

It wasn't a standard computer, and Carla remembered Elouise telling her that Harry always built his own computers. It didn't take her long to find the USB slot. She removed the bejeweled flash drive, hanging on a chain from her neck, and slotted it in. The middle monitor lit up, and to her relief no password was required. Using the keyboard on the desk, she started the cloning process. With a groan she saw that it would take about twenty minutes. She clicked continue and opened the drawers on the left-hand side of the desk. They were messy and filled with stationery and papers. The bottom drawer was locked. There was a bunch of keys in the top drawer, but none of them unlocked the drawer. Remembering a movie where a key was stuck to the underside of a desk, she went down onto her hands and knees. With the flashlight she examined the underside of the desk but found nothing. Irritated, she bumped her head as she started crawling out from under the desk. The dust made her nose tickle.

Halfway out, she froze on hearing Elouise's daughters

screaming at each other in an obvious childish argument. *They're back. So soon!* She had to clamp her nose and mouth closed, as her eyes had started streaming and she had the urge to sneeze. The light was switched on in the children's bedroom, and then, the stiletto rays of light coming through the blinds on the glass door dividing the study from the master bedroom cast menacing beams on Carla's body. She could see movements in the bedroom and guessed it to be Harry, as she could hear Elouise's raised voice coming from the girls' bedroom, admonishing them for not getting to bed.

She jumped up from under the desk and saw that there were four remaining minutes on the cloning process. *What do I do now?* With an iron will that surprised her, she controlled her reflexes to run. There was no movement in the room. Her hand poised at the USB slot, she whispered softly, "C'mon, c'mon." She sensed rather than saw the shadow in the doorway. The door was opening. As Harry's head poked through, Carla ducked behind the desk. *Oh no, oh no, I'm going to be caught.* The perspiration was cold against her skin. Closing her eyes, she waited for the light to be turned on.

Then Elouise said something to Harry. Carla could only make out the last words, "They're not listening to me; please do something."

Carla opened her eyes and heard Harry retreating to the bedroom. "Thank you, God, thank you," she prayed silently. As if hypnotized, she watched the final seconds of the cloning, yanked out the USB, and cleared the screen. She hurried outside, closed the door, and latched the brass padlock, which clanked uncomfortably loud. As she crossed over from the back veranda, she ran into Kishan who, surprised by Carla, breathed something in Hindi. She smiled and said, "There you are, Kishan. I was just looking for you. I am desperate for a cup of Horlicks. I can't sleep."

Kishan looked at her for a split second, his expression puzzled, but then to Carla's relief he smiled broadly and said, "No problem, Madam. I bring to your room."

Once inside her room, Carla washed her face with cold water and, after staring at herself in the mirror for a minute, started laughing quietly. "I did it," and then, with obvious triumph in her voice: "I did it!"

Kishan knocked and placed the cup of steaming Horlicks next to her bed on the pedestal. "Something else you need, Madam?"

"No thanks, Kishan. This is wonderful. I'm sure I'll sleep like a baby now."

"Good night Madam."

"Good night, Kishan, and thank you."

Carla sat on her bed, wanting to phone George and tell him about her victory, but she decided to wait until morning. Elouise called out softly to her as she knocked gently on her door. "Are you still awake?"

"Yes, come in—it's unlocked."

Elouise looked tired as she sat down at the foot of the bed. "Kishan said you couldn't sleep?"

"I guess I slept too much this afternoon. How was the recital?"

With a sigh Elouise replied, "It was OK, but the kids were bored and started acting up. Harry was so annoyed that he insisted we come home at intermission." A despondent look flitted across her face.

Suddenly, Carla felt desperately sorry for her friend and asked, "Is everything all right between you and Harry, Elouise?"

Elouise's eyes glistened with unshed tears. "Oh, Carla, I wish I knew. I love him so much, but it is as if he wants to push me and the girls away. He has even suggested that we go back to the States without him."

"Do you have any idea why?"

"No, I wish I did. He changed after we came back to India. The first few months were fine. It was like a great adventure for all of us, but then he just changed. He never has time for us anymore; he never stops working."

Carla reached for her friend's hand and held it tight. "Have you tried talking to him?"

Elouise grimaced. "And how. He's not interested in talking. A couple of weeks ago he presented me and the girls with first class tickets back to the States. He said I should visit my parents and check out the schools for the girls."

"What did you say?"

"We had a huge fight, and I told him that I was not going without him. We haven't spoken about it again." Elouise suddenly stood up and said, "I'm keeping you from your sleep. We'll chat tomorrow, OK? Good night, my friend."

She kissed Carla lightly on the cheeks and left.

An uneasy feeling of guilt and disquiet clutched Carla. She picked up her phone and sent a text message to George that she wouldn't meet him the next day in Lodhi Garden. "I can't do this," she whispered softy to herself.

The idea of betraying Elouise became unbearable. If it hadn't been for her support, years ago, Carla wouldn't have had the guts to get to know her grandfather.

Carla shared a last name with a set of Indian twin girls in her economics class. They were curious to get to know Carla, as her appearance wasn't obviously Indian. Delighted that her father was from Delhi, they introduced Carla to their parents, both medical doctors from India. Carla was often invited to their family dinners. At one of these dinners, she met a relative visiting from India. The middle-aged woman questioned Carla about her father and realized that they were related. She must have told Carla's grandfather, because not long after this meeting, Carla received a rather formal introductory letter from him. Carla responded and a month later he flew over to meet his granddaughter. After their first meeting, Carla was confused and racked with guilt for not telling her father. Elouise advised her to continue meeting him and told her that an opportune time for telling her family would come later. Her grandfather, whose second wife had family in the States, visited her every year. Unfortunately, her paternal grandmother had passed away shortly after her parents got married. Her grandfather had remarried a year before Carla started college. His wife had accompanied him on his second visit. She was much younger than Carla's grandfather and seemed sweet on the surface. It was Elouise who noticed the jealousy and the control she had over Carla's grandfather. So when Carla suggested they join her in South Africa for the Christmas holidays and surprise her dad, her grandfather was, at first, excited, but then suddenly changed his mind after having discussed it with his new wife.

Carla and Elouise used to make fun of her and called her "the Enchantress," as she had the skills and demeanor of a seventeenth-century Mughal courtesan. But it was not a laughing matter, as she managed to keep father and son apart. She also tried her best to discredit Carla in the old man's eyes and often made it difficult for Carla to spend time alone with him.

Elouise was ingenious in entertaining the Enchantress, which gave Carla precious moments between grandfather and granddaughter. These memories brought Carla to the realization that she had to protect Elouise as Elouise had so fiercely protected her. And that meant protecting Harry.

George could be barking up the wrong tree. Maybe there was no connection whatsoever. Just because Harry was working for the Indian Nuclear Program—Americans could be so paranoid. She decided she would examine Harry's computer files herself and not mention anything to George, not yet. This much, at least, she owed Elouise.

CHAPTER 13

Carla listened closely to the sounds of the house as it started to quiet down. She felt acutely alert, probably, she thought, as a result of the day's activities. Locking her door, she dimmed the lights and opened her laptop. Afraid of using her host's network, she connected to her mobile phone instead.

She couldn't concentrate. She couldn't believe that she was actually going to read the private files of her best friend's husband. But, opening the files, she was surprised and relieved to find that they contained nothing unusual. She went through most of them carefully. With only a few more remaining, she thought she'd tackle them the next day, as it was past three in the morning. She was about to close her computer when she saw a file named "Soraya." Her curiosity roused, she opened it, but was blocked—she'd have to have a password to open the file. Her skin prickled; she knew this was the file she had to see. It was the only one that had been given a password. Why such an elusive name? The file must be highly secretive. Carla tried a few obvious passwords, like the names of Harry's daughters and anniversary dates, but was unsuccessful. With a groan, she closed her laptop and locked it in her suitcase.

The following morning Carla woke up late. Kishan must have tried waking her, knocking on her door as he did every morning, but she slept soundly. When she awoke, he brought her tea and fruit in bed, explaining that it was too hot on the veranda. Elouise and Harry had already left, and Elouise had instructed him to get Carla to call her when she woke up.

George rang as she finished her breakfast. "Good morning. Did you sleep well?"

"Yes, thanks, I did."

"How about your hosts?"

"Oh, of course. They were out, but came back early as the kids weren't behaving."

George replied quietly, "I see. What are your plans for the day?"

"I was thinking of going to Santushti for some shopping. Preeti Kapoor suggested it. Apparently it's like a garden surrounded by high-end boutiques."

"I know it well. The land actually belongs to the Indian Air Force. Their barracks are adjacent it. It's not cheap, but the shops carry good quality stuff. There's a nice little continental restaurant—do you want to meet for lunch?"

Carla hesitated before replying, "OK, what time?"

"Why don't you give me a call when you're done shopping and ready for lunch? The embassy is only ten minutes away."

"Sure, see you later."

"Carla, I almost forgot. The embassy is hosting a pool party tonight at some farmhouse outside Delhi. These parties are normally great fun. Do you want to go?"

"As long as I don't have to wear a bikini." Carla laughed.

"With a body like yours, you should go naked." George chuckled, and Carla blushed.

In a somewhat haughty tone, she said, "Good-bye, George. I'll see you at lunch."

Carla phoned Elouise, who was visiting a relative of Harry's in the hospital and told her that she was meeting George for lunch and dinner.

"That's fine, thanks for letting me know. I might be stuck here for some time. It's customary for relatives to hang out at the hospital in moral support of sick family members. You are so busy with George these days, but I'm going to demand a few days soon so that we can get out of town, OK?"

"Of course, I'd like that. We'll chat later, and good luck with the sick relative."

Carla dressed in a hurry, taking care to remember her hat and large sunglasses. She couldn't risk being recognized. It was only the previous day that she had seen the auctioneer. But she wasn't one to be easily cowed either. She no longer felt so vulnerable. She wouldn't let the possibility of being seen keep her at home while she was in such a fascinating city.

Then, for an instant, Carla's resolve crumbled. The little girl who had died just days before of a heroin overdose flashed before her eyes. *I can't go back there. I won't make it out alive the second time around.* Thinking rationally again, she figured the chance was pretty slim of someone being there who could possibly recognize her. And besides, giving in to the crippling fear of "what if" would only drive her into a life of seclusion—a hermit haunted by disturbing memories.

Santushti was a charming garden shopping center. It reminded Carla of the Koi Samui Airport's open-air, duty-free complex. There was a good balance between fashion and home-ware stores. Carla found herself engrossed by one specializing in ethnic techniques like tie-dye and handwoven embroidered quilts and bedspreads. She was so tempted to buy something, but the thought that she might not be moving back into her flat in Harley Street stopped her. As consolation she bought a couple of magnificent tie-dyed scarves in vibrant colors.

Carla continued browsing, making her way to the restaurant, where she looked at her watch for the first time. It was past two. She phoned George, but he did not answer. As she was about to leave a voice message, he phoned back. His voice was strained. "Hey, I'm afraid something's come up. I won't be able to make lunch. I'm really sorry."

She was disappointed but replied, "No problem. I'll see you later. Are we still on for tonight?"

"Yes of course, I'll pick you up at eight." He hesitated for a second, his voice gentle when he said, "Carla, I'm really looking forward to seeing you tonight. Don't cancel on me, OK?"

Carla went limp at the longing in his voice. "I won't, I promise."

She asked for a table and once seated, she studied the menu. Realizing that she had lost her appetite, she ordered a small salad and nimbu pani. She then scanned her phone for messages or missed calls. She was relieved to see nothing from her husband. *What am I doing? Why am I so attracted to George?* I'm still married to Andrew. Carla sighed and realized that she couldn't keep sweeping the fact under the table. She'd have to face things sooner or later, but right now it was so convenient. *Really, is that all it is? Convenient?* Groaning softly, she dug her fork into an olive, and covered her mouth in embarrassment when it sped off her plate, and landed in an expensive looking purse next to a woman at the next table. Luckily no one noticed and Carla called for the bill.

After lunch she picked up chocolates she had ordered for Elouise and the girls from the chocolatier at the Hyatt Hotel and then went home to nap. When, at seven, she started getting ready for the party, she realized she didn't have a clue on what to wear. She went looking for Elouise, who was doing homework with Chanda in the girls' study.

"I'm going to a pool party with George tonight. Any suggestions what I should wear?"

"A bathing suit," Chanda said, smiling broadly. "It's a 'pool' party, get it?"

Carla laughed and hugged her. "You're so cute, I could eat you."

Chanda screamed in mock fear, and Elouise told her, "Not so loud, Chanda. Finish your math and I'll be back in a sec to check it. I'm going to show Auntie Carla what to wear." Elouise led the way to her bedroom and then onto the spacious dressing room. An upholstered bench was in the middle of the room. Carla sat on it while Elouise opened her cupboards. "You could wear just about anything, but most women wear a bathing suit with a sarong or kaftan. Full makeup and jewelry are a must, as well as Jimmy Choos. The glitzier the better."

"I suppose you are going to loan me everything, as I most certainly have none of this."

Elouise smiled. "That's what friends are for."

Carla loved a turquoise full-piece bathing suit with golden shells beaded on the straps. Elouise took out a matching floral-patterned kaftan in sheer silk. "That is gorgeous, let me try it on." The bathing suit was a little small for Carla's bust, but Elouise convinced her that she looked great and was wearing the kaftan over it anyway. Carla wore her hair loose over her shoulders, with a yellow hibiscus behind her ear. Her gold-plaited sandals matched the beading, and she felt beautiful.

George arrived promptly at eight. He whistled when he saw her. Suddenly quite self-conscious, she wished she hadn't decided to be so daring. Kamal opened the door for her but avoided looking at her in the slightly transparent kaftan. *Is he just being respectful or is he disgusted?* Carla wondered. George got in beside her, and his loud Hawaiian shirt made her laugh. She realized that with such a garish print next to her, she wouldn't be the one people would be staring at. "Where did you find that?"

"A treasured memory from Hawaii, Spring break, many years ago…"

"I see. That must've been fun."

"It was."

Kamal followed George's directions to the venue, and after forty minutes the jeep turned off the congested road, where it was stopped at a large steel gate. Private armed guards checked credentials, while US military police watched from a distance. They were all well armed, and Carla was surprised to notice the stacked sandbags near the security checkpoint.

"I don't have any ID," Carla said, concerned.

"It's OK; you're with me—I'll vouch for you." The way George said this—humbly but with authority—excited Carla.

The checkpoint guards scrutinized both George and Kamal's IDs and then handed them back, asking for Carla's. George got out of the vehicle and approached a US military policeman. They talked for half a minute. The policeman walked toward the security guard and said something to him, pointing to Carla. The guard then smiled and saluted both George and the policeman. George got back into the car as Kamal was waved through.

They drove down a long driveway framed by enormous palm trees. Fairy lights encircled the tall, slender trunks.

The villa was a spreading single-story building on an expanse of manicured lawn. At the entrance to the villa, uniformed men ushered George and Carla inside. Music and laughter drifted in from outside. They walked through the large glass sliding doors onto a sandstone deck with an exquisite swimming pool. "Oh my God, it looks like an exclusive resort," Carla said, enthralled.

With an indulgent smile, George took her by the arm, and they walked toward a group of Western guests dressed much like themselves. A stocky man in his late fifties smiled warmly as he greeted George, slapping him on his back. "Hey, my man, how're you doing?"

George slapped him back and said, "I'm good. How are you guys?"

A tall, dark-haired woman standing next to him smiled and said, intoned with the distinctive mark of the American privileged, "We are fine, thank you, George."

Turning to Carla, George said, "Let me introduce you: our ambassador, Richard Summers, and Anne, his better and ever patient other half."

Richard shook her hand in a firm grip and said, "It's nice to meet you."

Anne shook her hand limply. Her hands were cold. "Are you from Delhi?" she asked.

"No, just on vacation." Carla was distracted by a waiter offering her a tall, ocean-blue drink with a cherry and pink cocktail umbrella hanging off the side of the glass.

"Those are lethal," Richard warned with a smile.

"What's in it?" Carla asked, taking one from the tray.

"No idea, and I don't care. They are delicious," Anne said, taking one from the waiter. Carla smiled, her glass to her lips. She had the distinct impression that Anne was baiting, or competing with her in some way.

Detecting the tension between the two women, George steered Carla to another group of people and introduced her to some of his embassy colleagues as well as English diplomats and attaches from the British High Commission.

Carla recognized the band, playing on a small island in the middle of the meandering swimming pool, from the party at the Kapoor's. Guests were dancing in the shallow side of the pool, and the atmosphere was unlike anything Carla had ever experienced.

The Americans were discussing the First Lady's visit to Delhi, and some concerns were raised for her security.

"She keeps changing her itinerary, and she's accepting way too many invitations," a man with a crew cut said.

"She's here on a charity mission—it's apolitical," said an elderly woman.

"Oh come on, the First Lady of the United States? It's never apolitical. I bet there's a team of political strategists in Washington who have analyzed and proposed every step she takes and every word she utters, all for the benefit of the commander in chief."

George laughed and said, "We are boring my charming date. Who's going to beat me to the other end of the pool?" He stripped down to his swimming trunks as he started running to the pool, leaving a careless trail of clothes behind him on the lawn. He was followed by a couple of men who dived in after him.

Carla collected George's shirt and walked along the edge of the pool, watching the race. The other two swimmers were obviously British, as two distinct cheering crowds formed at the end of the pool, one with British accents and the other obviously American. George swam with the strong, regular strokes of a professional swimmer. An Englishman was catching up, and Carla found herself cheering loudly. George won by a second, and the Americans cheered as if they had just won gold at the Olympics. *Typical*, Carla thought with a smirk.

A waiter gave Carla a towel, which she offered George, who was still laughing in triumph. He held out his hand, and she took it to help pull him out, but he yanked her into the water, head first. The water was warm, and after her initial shock, Carla delighted in the sensuous pleasure. George had his hands firmly around her waist as he pulled her toward him. Their bodies touched lightly.

George smiled roguishly. "Am I going to get a kiss for my victory?"

Carla glanced furtively around her, but the other revelers were partying on the other side of the swimming pool. She looked at George intently. His handsome face was expectant. An uncontrollable desire took root as Carla held his face in both her hands and without a moment's hesitation kissed him fully on his lips. They were wet and tasted of chlorine.

George held her closer, and they drifted toward deeper water, still locked in the kiss. Opening her eyes, Carla exhaled, air bubbles racing them to the surface. They treaded water in each other's embrace. Then, as Carla tired, they swam slowly to the edge of the pool.

They got out and found a couple of towels strewn on a double rattan lounger. "Oh no, I hope haven't ruined Elouise's kaftan," Carla said.

"I'll ask Anne to take it to her Chinese drycleaner's. She's always boasting about him."

"Thanks, George, that's sweet of you, but I think Anne would sooner shred any garment of mine. She seems to be sweet on you." Carla winked at George, whose cheeks quickly reddened in embarrassment.

Carla saw a waiter with a tray of corn dogs and asked George to call him over. They sat back on the lounger, enveloped in a sense of calm. With a sigh, George leaned back against the cushions, drawing Carla close to him. Leaning against his chest, she listened to his heart beating rhythmically. She felt completely at peace and closed her eyes.

George kissed the top of her head. "Are you cold?"

"Not really, but I think I should change." Luckily she had heeded Elouise's advice and had packed underwear and a linen dress in a basket, left in the jeep. George called Kamal and asked him to bring the basket. Carla changed in a cabaña. While she was brushing her hair, Preeti came up to her and said, "Hi, Carla, I thought I recognized you with George."

Carla blushed. "Hi, yes, it's such a fun party. I didn't think I'd land up in the pool, though."

Preeti laughed and then, leaning forward, whispered in Carla's ear, "I know George is irresistible, but be careful." With a knowing smile she walked out.

Watching her leave, Carla thought, *What is it with everyone, warning me all the time? No one warned me about Andrew. I deserve to have some fun, and George certainly knows how to make me do just that.*

Carla walked resolutely toward George; he had changed into a T-shirt and Bermuda shorts. She flung her arms around his neck and whispered throatily, "George, let's go home." His eyes bore into hers with hunger. He smiled and answered her with a long, sensual kiss. Without greeting anyone, they left. They sat close in the jeep, their bodies touching. Carla's skin was tingling, and to her surprise she noticed gooseflesh on her arms.

The drive to George's place was much quicker, as traffic had eased up considerably. George dismissed Kamal and unlocked the front door, saying good night to the chowkidar. They were completely alone.

A couple of lights burned in the passage and the kitchen. George led Carla to the lounge, and she sat down on the couch while he walked toward the butler's tray with a couple of crystal decanters and glasses on it. "Can I pour you a single malt?" he asked, holding one of the decanters in his right hand. Carla nodded shyly. He poured the drinks and sat down beside her. "To us," he said, raising his glass to his lips.

Carla smiled and took a sip. George drank half of his and placed the glass on the wooden table. He took her hand and kissed it. "Carla, are you going to spend the night?"

She nodded simply. He took the glass from her and put it beside his on the coffee table. A happy smile lit up his eyes as he took her face in both his hands and kissed her passionately. Carla's mind emptied; she was no longer in control of anything. Aware only of George's soft lips and searching tongue, she felt release deep inside. The will to control how she felt, how she should behave, was lost in the vastness of her longing and desire.

To Carla it felt as if their bodies were defying gravity as they floated entwined in each other's arms. George's bedroom was dark except for the glow of the full moon on the white linen of his antique four-poster bed. As Carla fell back against the silky pillows and cushions, she smelled the delicate fragrance of lilies. George undressed her slowly; but she was impatient, and pushing his hands away, she pulled the dress over her head. She undid her bra, but he stopped her from removing it, allowing himself the pleasure of cupping her breasts in his hands as he removed it. George took off his T-shirt while Carla undid his brown leather belt. He watched her, but suddenly shy, she stopped herself from unzipping his shorts. With a faint smile he unzipped and pulled off his Bermuda shorts and, in quick succession, his boxers. Carla's sharp intake of breath was audible as her eyes glanced over his erect penis. She looked at his statuesque outline in the moonlight and knew that she wanted him more than anything. Nothing else mattered.

George was kissing her toned belly. His mouth was playful as he searched for her. He removed her panties, and as she felt his hot breath on her inner thigh she reached for him. He levered his body over hers, his weight and the texture of his taut skin making her gasp. Then he was inside her. They were still, adjusting to one another and the satisfying feeling of physical unity. Carla and George's eyes locked. Then as one they started moving, slow and languid; the pure, naked pleasure made Carla cry out as George brought her close to climax, and then with a moaning sigh he changed his rhythm, thrusting fast and precise. Carla bit her lip—she could no longer control her body, a searing light of indulgent relish tearing her body apart. George called her name as he shuddered, and then, spent, he lay down next to her, his hand searching for hers as he gently squeezed it.

Carla opened her eyes; it took her a moment to recall the evening's events. A happy smile tugged at the corners of her lips. George was still sleeping. He lay on his stomach with his arm across her chest. The cotton sheets were in total disarray, and unabashedly she studied his strapping build. She knew in some part of her that she should feel guilty—what she had done was essentially adultery—but she also felt strangely comfortable in that knowledge. Andrew hadn't tried to contact her again. In a way, she felt that George had almost shared more with her in this last week than she had shared with Andrew in their entire marriage.

"Hey, how long have you been awake?" George asked with one open eye.

Carla smiled and kissed George on his cheek. "Long enough to study you, I suppose."

He turned onto his back and pulled her to him, kissing her gently on the mouth. Then, sitting up, he slapped her playfully on her buttocks and said, "We'd better get dressed—Sunil will be mortified if he finds us like this."

"Oh my goodness, he doesn't knock?"

George smiled ruefully. "He knocks, but he doesn't wait to be invited in."

Carla jumped out of bed, grabbed her dress and underwear on the floor, and went to the bathroom. It took her less than five minutes to shower and dress. When she came out of the bathroom, George laughed and said that was the fastest he had ever witnessed.

"Boarding school, darling, it equips one with some important skills," she replied with a grin.

George laughed and went to the bathroom while Carla went to the kitchen to make tea. She was searching for the matches when Sunil appeared wearing only a dhoti. "Oh, Madam Carla, what good surprise to meet you so early in my kitchen. What can Sunil make for you?"

Carla blushed and said, "Good morning, Sunil, I'd love a cup of tea."

"No problem, no problem, Sunil make special chai for special guest of Sahib."

Carla was blushing furiously, so she left and asked Sunil to bring her tea to the veranda.

George, smelling fresh and dressed in chinos and an Oxford blue shirt, joined her on the veranda. The chowkidar ran toward him with the *Indian Times*. Carla glanced at her watch and realized she had left it in the bathroom.

"What's the time?" she asked.

George looked at his stainless-steel Rolex. "Almost nine."

"I should go. I didn't tell Elouise I'd stay out all night."

"I don't think it's a problem. Have some breakfast with me, and then I'll drop you on my way to work."

"OK, sounds good."

After a quick breakfast of fruit and poached egg on toast, George drove Carla back to Elouise's bungalow. "Do you mind if I drop you at the gate? I'm a bit late for work."

"Of course not."

She kissed him on the cheek, and as she got out George said, "Thanks for last night, Carla."

She smiled and walked toward the gate, which the chowkidar was holding open for her. Elouise was having breakfast with someone on the veranda. She looked up and, seeing Carla, waved her over. Carla didn't feel like chatting to Elouise or greeting her visitor, but not wanting to appear rude, she walked toward them. As she approached the marble steps, which lead up to the veranda, the man sitting with Elouise turned around and smiled. It was Andrew.

CHAPTER 14

Harry Singh was eating breakfast in his study when Kishan called Elouise to inform them of their visitor. He looked at his watch and was surprised to see the hour. In Delhi no one made house calls before noon. It was 8:35.

Elouise hurried out in the cream tracksuit she usually wore when dropping the girls at school. Harry continued eating his melon, chewing slowly while scanning his e-mails. Not usually a curious man, he drank his tea in one long gulp and walked toward the veranda through the kitchen. He could see Elouise sitting opposite a man in a light blue shirt. It was Andrew, Carla's husband. They had met on a number of occasions and though not close were comfortable in each other's company.

Andrew stood up as Harry slapped him on the back, saying, "Hey, Andrew. Welcome to India."

"Thanks, Harry. How are you?"

"I'm fine thanks, but what brings you to Delhi?"

Andrew glanced briefly in Elouise's direction and said,

"I wanted to see Carla actually. I believe you know what happened…"

"Oh yes, that." He sat down, nodding his head in what seemed to be mild amusement. "Where is our lovely guest, still sleeping?" he asked, looking at Elouise.

She gave him a look that could've turned him to stone. "Carla is out; she'll be back soon."

Seeming to enjoy the awkwardness of the situation, Harry rejoined, "I see. Where did she go?"

Elouise said with a tight little smile, "She went out with George."

"Ah, George. Charming George?"

"Yes, Harry, George Alexander from the US Embassy."

"The same George you had a 'thing' for?" Harry taunted but his eyes were wary.

With flushed cheeks Elouise said, "I've never had a 'thing' for him, as you put it."

She seemed immensely annoyed and Harry decided to stop teasing. Turning toward Andrew he said, "You must join me for a game of golf before you leave. I have an extra set of clubs."

"Thanks, I'd like that." The dark circles under Andrew's eyes accentuated his pallor.

"I'm off to work. Do we have any dinner plans tonight?" Harry asked Elouise.

"No. Nothing. Do you want to go out?"

"Not really, we can eat at home. I have a lunch meeting so I'd like a light supper. See you later." He kissed Elouise on the top of her head, shook Andrew's hand, and then drove off in his jeep.

It didn't take him long to reach his office in Lodhi Colony. His secretary, a young man wearing black pants and a white shirt, greeted him and ran off to get him a cup of tea. The office was in a separate part of a large residential bungalow complex. It had a small reception leading to a room with a large desk, computer, and steel filing cabinets. Harry sat down, sighing as he switched on the computer. He opened the top drawer of the desk and took out a file, opening it.

Knocking softly, and then opening the door, the secretary came in. He carried a white porcelain cup that he put on a carved wooden coaster to the right of the computer.

"Thanks. Any messages?" Harry asked without looking at the young man.

Clearing his throat his secretary said, "The office of the Ministry of Defense called late yesterday afternoon when you had left. They didn't leave a message, asking only if you'd be in today." Harry looked up briefly from the computer screen. The young man continued, "Dr. Goyal called from BARC earlier this morning and asked you to call him back on his mobile number."

"That's it?" Harry asked.

The secretary nodded and asked if he would like anything else.

"No thanks, Tahir. And by the way, I'll be having lunch with a friend today so cancel the meeting with the young Caltech graduate. What's his name?"

"Ali Mussafir, sir."

"That's right, reschedule for later this week."

Tahir returned to his post in reception, closing the office door on his way out.

Harry watched the door closing, a feeling of angst overwhelming him. He dug deep into the bottom desk drawer and brought out a container of tablets. Gulping down two with the very hot tea, he burned his throat. Wincing, he closed his eyes for a few seconds. And then, with a groan and a fixed stare at the computer screen, he started typing.

An hour later, the secretary brought Harry another cup of tea. Highly irritated at the sudden break in his concentration, Harry waved him away with "I did not ask for tea.

Don't interrupt me again, do you understand?" The perplexed young man quickly stepped back and emptied the tea into the sorry-looking pot plant on the desk.

At twelve thirty, Harry switched off his computer and locked away the file he was working on. As he walked past his secretary's desk, Harry muttered something inaudible. The young man smiled and nodded.

Harry cursed the traffic under his breath. It was inordinately heavy for that time of day. A line of devotees was eating prashad in bowls made from leaves in front of a temple on the right side of the road. After a few minutes, he turned into a residential area where the large houses stood close to each other. Finding a parking space in front of a shop selling perfumes and crystal decanters, he asked a young boy to watch his jeep. He paid him ten rupees with the promise of another ten on his return, then walked away.

The street narrowed. Groups of merchants and moneychangers lined the sides. Wooden carts on bicycle wheels were either loaded with fruit or fridges of ice cream and popsicles. Litter was piled high everywhere. All the men wore kufi skullcaps. There were a few women—all wearing the hijab. Harry walked past a restaurant. There were chefs cooking out on the pavement. A young boy sat lethargically swatting flies away from the skewers hanging on a metal rail next to the tandoor oven.

Harry hurried on. His head was uncovered, but no one seemed to notice. An American woman asked a merchant selling dates and dried fruit if she could take a photo, but with a scowl he wagged his index finger at her. She apologized, but the flash of light from the camera indicated that she had taken the photo anyway. This irked Harry.

A large gray concrete building of arches and cement jali windows dwarfed the end of the lane, and Harry couldn't help thinking that this was what a mosque would have looked like if it had been built in Communist Russia.

The lane became a corridor of narrower stalls of Quran and prayer bead sellers on either side. Harry had overtaken the American, and as he approached a restaurant called Karim's, he heard a commotion behind him. The angry American was remonstrating loudly, pointing to a youth who had apparently fondled her bottom. The crowd around the woman was growing, and Harry had to fight the urge to beckon her into the safety of the restaurant. With a contrite clenching of the jaw, he turned his back on the ensuing mayhem.

The dirty white lace curtains on the aluminum doors belied the elegant interior of this Kashmiri restaurant established in the early nineteen hundreds. The carved, walnut-paneled interior created the famous Kashmiri houseboat effect. Booth tables with leatherette upholstery lined the sides, with a few square tables in the center of the restaurant. Two exquisite silk carpets framed in gold hung against the wall. The tables were laid with yellow tablecloths and maroon overlays.

A team of pathani-dressed waiters hovered at the entrance, smiling broadly as they showed Harry to the booth table in the far right corner. The restaurant was empty, but within minutes a couple with two children entered and sat at a table at the other end of the room. The man looked Iranian and was dressed in gray flannel trousers with a navy blazer. His wife, wearing jeans and a black hijab, scolded the round-faced little boy, who had scattered toothpicks on the floor.

Feeling hot and bothered, Harry ordered sweet nimbu and soda. A menu was brought to the table, but he was preoccupied with his iPhone. He didn't notice the woman, in full burqa, enter and walk toward his table. She stood quietly for a while and then cleared her throat, startling Harry. Slightly embarrassed, he asked her to sit down. Clearly uncomfortable, she pushed the table rather clumsily toward

Harry and then planted herself heavily on the seat.

Harry bowed his head slightly and said, "Salaam aleikum."

His companion responded, "Man, it's hot under this thing." The voice was that of an African man.

Harry smiled and said, "Sorry, but I can't be seen with you. Have a cold drink."

The man grunted and said, "I suppose an ice-cold beer is out of the question."

The image of a burqa-clad "woman" drinking a beer amused Harry, eliciting a stifled chuckle. But his meeting with the man was no lighthearted matter. He ordered another nimbu soda and asked, "Are you ready for lunch?"

"Sure, I just don't know how I'm going to eat under this thing." Ignoring him, Harry ordered tandoori murgh, rogan josh, naan, and roomali roti. As soon as the waiter was out of earshot, Harry looked at the African, whose eyes were dark and unfathomable, but strangely feminine peering through the narrow slit in the burqa. "So, I believe you have something to sell?" Harry asked, hiding his hands under the table. They were trembling.

For a fleeting moment the African's eyes flashed with apprehension; it could have been anger. He sat back against the seat and drew himself up to his full height. Harry realized he had forgotten to use the agreed passphrase. "Uh, I meant to say the temperature in Delhi this year is said to reach forty-eight degrees Celsius." Harry was sweating, even though the air-conditioners were humming, cooling the interior to a comfortable twenty-two degrees.

After what seemed like an age, the African slumped forward and replied, "I was told that an unseasonable heat wave could strike as early as next week."

Harry continued, "The price has been agreed on. The transfer will be made on receipt of the goods. You are to give me the address."

"It's at the container depot in Tughlaqabad." The man slipped his hands into his robes and took out a document that he handed to Harry. "The bill of lading—you must give it to a Mr. Ramesh Gupta. He's been well paid to allow you access and total privacy with your people."

Harry glanced at the papers and said, "Is that it?"

With a puzzled look the African replied, "That's it from my side. I'm out of here this evening back to Cape Town via Dubai. The transfer into our Mauritian account has to be made within the next twenty-four hours." He paused, drank half of his nimbu soda, grimaced slightly, and said, "Only then will our 'guarantee' be released into safe custody."

Harry nodded. He looked at the air-conditioners again. Beads of perspiration were dripping down the side of his face. He used the maroon napkin to wipe them away.

With a flourish, two waiters placed the aromatic dishes on the table. The African murmured with pleasure and broke off a piece of naan, stuffing it uncomfortably into his mouth under the cloth. Harry had no appetite. The rogan josh looked oily.

The African looked at him curiously, chewing loudly under his disguise. Harry broke off a piece of the bread and ate it slowly, dipping it carefully into the gravy. After what felt like an unbearable hour, the African washed his hands in a stainless-steel finger bowl, burped, and, greeting Harry, left.

Harry sat still for a few seconds, his face drawn. Then he stood up quickly, leaving cash in the bill folder. The waiter hurried after him with the change, but Harry waved him away. His tip was more than generous, and the waiter stood staring after him, a broad grin spreading across his face.

As Harry entered the lane, he patted his pocket where he had put the folded documents to make sure they were secure. It was more congested than earlier, and Harry had to walk slowly, almost in bodily contact with the crowd. A woman carrying a baby with a severe cleft palate tried to push the baby onto Harry. She was wailing, begging him to take the child. She pretended to drop the baby, and instinctively Harry caught the howling child. The crowd blocked the woman as she was trying to hurry away. Harry called her back angrily, the hysterical child struggling in his arms. Some men dressed in long white robes noticed his dilemma and ran after the woman. She was caught by the hair, having lost her hijab in her hurry to get away. She kicked and tried to bite the man's hand, but another was dragging her by the arm. When they reached Harry, another woman, wearing a floral hijab, had taken the baby roughly from him. She was saying something to Harry, but in the deafening commotion he couldn't hear her. More women had appeared, and arguments ensued. Harry slipped away unnoticed.

Reaching the jeep, he paid the young boy, scolding him for sitting on the bonnet. Shamefaced, the boy ran away. Harry's hands were shaking on the steering wheel as he approached the Oberoi hotel and stopped at the drive-through entrance. A valet took the car keys from Harry, who then headed for the security check. He walked past the bookshop and the Louis Vuitton boutique in the foyer and headed toward the "Threesixty" restaurant. Explaining to the hostess that he was waiting for someone, he sat down on the tan leather couch.

"Would you like a drink?" the young woman asked.

"A Kingfisher beer, thanks." Harry smiled and thought, *What the hell, a beer in these circumstances won't hurt.*

He scanned the restaurant as memories of his childhood flooded his mind. He knew this building well. He had once been a pupil at the Delhi Public School, a private co-ed school opposite the Oberoi. Although there were more than 350 pupils per grade, the school was, at the time, one of the better institutions in Delhi. Some parents were willing to pay well over the required fees in order to gain admission for their children. Most of the students were from wealthy families, and some would spend their lunch money at the internationally famous coffee shop of the five star–rated Oberoi.

It was during a rather long and illicit lunch at the Oberoi that Harry fell in love for the first time. It was 1988, his final school year. His friends had ordered French onion soup and two club sandwiches to share when he saw the most beautiful girl in the world. Two women dressed in fashionable clothes, obviously from abroad, accompanied her. The girl wore a white skirt and shirt with a bottle-green belt, the official uniform of D.P.S. She looked over her menu at Harry, and he found himself mesmerized by her crystal-clear green eyes, demurely framed by thick, dark lashes. He could not take his eyes off her. Taking full advantage of the moment, his hungry friends wolfed down his share of the sandwiches.

Harry knew that he had to find out who she was—not an easy task at his mammoth school. The girl left with the women, and as she reached the exit she looked back over her shoulder at Harry. He could happily have died on that day, having found true love.

The quest to find her was much easier than anticipated. The school was hosting a *Flashdance*-style competition. Harry had no interest in song and dance; even the Bollywood films his parents so enjoyed to watch annoyed him. It was a hot afternoon in May, and the driver sent to pick him up was late. He stood around for about ten minutes and then, unable to stand the heat any longer, went inside in search of a room with a fan. The classrooms had been locked, so he went into the school hall. Auditions for the competition were in full swing. Feeling awkward but determined to enjoy the cooler air from the ceiling fans, he sat down on a chair in the back row. A group of girls wearing leotards and knitted ankle warmers left the stage.

And then she walked on. It was the face that had haunted his every waking moment. Dressed in a simple, sleeveless gown in dark emerald reaching her ankles, she sang. To Harry her sweet voice sounded like heaven. After her song she curtsied. Harry was clapping and cheering loudly. Miss Rathore, the drama teacher, turned around—he was the only one applauding.

Mr. Tandon from the music department said, "That was a good performance, Miss—?"

She smiled with pleasure and said, "It's Miriam. Miriam Waseer."

"Congratulations, you're in the show. See Miss Rathore after school tomorrow; she'll give you the rehearsal schedule."

Miriam ran off the stage, and as she was about to pass Harry, she stopped in recognition. Harry stood up slowly and then, holding out his hand said, "Hi. I'm Harry." She blushed as he shook her hand. Together they left the hall.

They were inseparable after that. Her father worked for the Indian Foreign Service back in Delhi, waiting for a new posting abroad. Their affair was common knowledge among the students, but parents and teachers were kept in the dark. After three months Miriam told him that her father had been posted to the Hague, but she would stay on with her aunt in Delhi to complete her final year. They made their plans to attend the same college in the United States. Harry was accepted at MIT in Massachusetts. Miriam's application was unsuccessful. UCLA in Los Angeles, however, offered her a place.

After much deliberation, Harry decided to tell his parents and ask for their blessing on his marriage to Miriam. It was to be the first unfortunate step in an unfolding disaster. Harry's parents contacted Miriam's parents. Her father flew from Europe to stop the idiotic liaison: idiotic, not because they were too young to marry, but because Harry was a Sikh, and Miriam, a Muslim. Miriam was taken to Europe, and Harry never saw her again . . .

"Mr. Singh?" a deep voice pressed politely. A man stood over Harry, his hand extended. Shocked out of his reverie, Harry looked up, blinking furiously. He had to compose himself. This was serious business. The man repeated Harry's name.

What a rich baritone; if the man could sing he would surely be an opera singer. It was this thought, absurd as it seemed, that allowed Harry to regain his sense of purpose and composure.

CHAPTER 15

Andrew was saying something, but Carla couldn't hear him. *Has he had his teeth whitened?* She felt him touching her shoulders, and then he was kissing her on both cheeks. His lips were warm, but her cheeks felt cold from the fan blowing on the slight wetness of his kisses.

Carla followed Andrew back onto the veranda in a daze. She sat down, and Elouise looked at her with a solicitous expression. The buoyant face of Kishan asking her if she would like some tea shook her out of her stupor. She smiled a thank-you at him.

An uncomfortable silence followed, interrupted only by the chirping of the parrots in the mango trees. Carla swallowed hard, looked at Andrew, and said, "When did you arrive?"

"This morning. My flight came in at seven."

"From where?"

"London."

"Oh, I see. Who told you where to find me?"

Andrew hesitated before replying, "A colleague told me, and of course, I knew if you were in Delhi you'd be staying with Elouise."

Elouise looked ill at ease. "Maybe I should leave the two of you alone. I have to meet someone. Andrew, please make yourself at home, and if you need anything Kishan will be happy to oblige."

Andrew stood up as Elouise got up from the breakfast table. He kissed her on her cheeks and said, "Thanks, would you and Harry like to join me for dinner tomorrow night?"

Elouise glanced at Carla, her expression guarded. "Let's see; we'll chat about it later. Carla, give me a call when you're free, OK?"

"Sure."

Andrew sat down and asked Kishan for another cup of tea when Carla received hers. "Be a good chap and make it plain without those added spices, thanks."

Carla inwardly groaned at this request. "Where are you staying?" she asked.

"At Claridge's. It's literally down the road from here."

"Yes, I know; the driver has pointed it out to me. Apparently the best paan wallah in Delhi operates on its sidewalk."

"Have you tried it? It's dreadful. Some of my Pakistani colleagues were addicted to the stuff in Peshawar."

At the mention of Peshawar, Carla's face drained of color. Andrew noticed and took her hand, squeezing it a little too hard. Carla flinched.

"I'm sorry, Carla, but we have to talk."

"You're damn right we have to talk."

"Can we go somewhere private? You could come to the hotel."

"No! You can tell me right here, and right now what the hell you were doing in bed with that colleague of yours? Andrew shifted uncomfortably. His eyes were downturned.

Carla continued, two pink spots had formed on her cheeks. "And then you didn't bother to come after me, you just left me to process all this shit all by myself." She tried not to cry, but her eyes were stinging as they welled up. Carla stood up abruptly and moved toward the window. Andrew, standing, tried to embrace her, but she pulled away.

"I don't know what to say. I'm so sorry." Andrew again tried to hold her, but Carla moved back to the sofa and sat down heavily. "The truth is," Andrew continued, "I'm a coward, and I am ashamed. Please forgive me." He knelt down and took her hand in his. " I love you, and I don't want to lose you."

Carla studied him and wondered if she really knew him, after all those years of marriage. Surely she did not marry a coward. A headache was threatening and suddenly she wanted to be alone. " Andrew, I have a dreadful migraine coming on. Can we meet later?"

"Yes, of course, I'll be at the hotel. My room number is 303."

"Give me an hour or two, OK?" Without saying goodbye she stood up and walked through the house back to her room. Reaching her bedroom, she burst into tears. After a minute, she started laughing hysterically. *I feel like I'm stuck in a really bad soap opera.* She took out her phone to call George but decided against it. Her heart was racing as she lay down on the bed, closing her eyes. Images of her night with George crept into her mind, and she realized she had no wish to banish them. They made her feel safe and loved. Shocked with her thoughts, she sat up and drank an aspirin.

Seema knocked gently on the door, entering without waiting for Carla's response with a package of clothes. "Sanjay tailor make delivery for Madam," she said, smiling.

"Oh, that's great. Thanks, Seema." Carla took the package from her and opened it. The Armani copied dresses were neatly folded. As Carla unfolded them, she gasped with pleasure—they were exact copies. She gave the navy one to Seema and asked her to press out the fold creases. Suddenly energized and wanting to look her best, Carla took another shower and applied makeup. The navy linen dress was flattering against her golden skin, and as she brushed her hair into a ponytail, she smiled and said softly, "OK, Andrew, it's time you and I decide what's next."

The chowkidar ran to fetch a taxi for Carla, as Elouise had taken the driver. After dropping her at Claridge's, the driver asked if he should wait, but Carla said no and told him she'd call him if needed.

Reaching Andrew's hotel room, she felt nervous, but drawing herself to her full height, she knocked on the door. Andrew opened the door quickly, his graying, sandy-blond hair wet. He had changed his clothing and was wearing a stone-colored cotton shirt with a pair of khaki chinos. His favorite tan Church's chukka boots in suede were scuffed, and Carla found herself making a mental note to replace the five-hundred-dollars shoes for his birthday.

"Hi, please come in." Andrew smiled and showed her to a couch. He sat down on an armchair upholstered in the same shade of champagne.

Carla looked around the room and said, "This is lovely, so spacious."

Andrew looked around as if he had just noticed and said, "Yes, I suppose you're right. Would you like to drink something? A cup of tea or coffee?"

"I'm OK, thanks, but please go ahead—order for yourself."

"No, it's fine—"
"Sure?"
"Sure."

A strained silence followed, which was broken by Andrew. "Carla, there's something else I want to discuss with you. It's about George…"

A drumming sound in Carla's ears threatened her subdued headache. She felt hot, beads of perspiration forming on her nose.

"George?" she asked, frowning. *How does he know? What about Peshawar?* Carla looked out of the window. She wished the hotels would open their windows. The air was so stuffy.

"Yes, Carla, George Alexander, attaché to the US embassy in Delhi." Andrew's tone was serious and almost businesslike.

Carla looked at Andrew accusingly. "Who told you about him?" Her voice was calm, belying her tumultuous emotions.

"George is not who he seems. Carla, I believe he's using you in some dangerous exploits."

Carla looked at Andrew with an expression of utter disbelief. "What the hell are you saying, Andrew? This is such nonsense. If it weren't for George, I could have been living in some brothel or harem as a junkie and a sex slave."

"This is exactly what George wants you to believe."

"What do you mean?"

Andrew took Carla's hand, but she pulled it away. She glared at him, angry and confused. He sighed, and then he said quietly, "George is a CIA operative. His position at the embassy is his official cover."

Carla's tone was defiant as she said, "So what? I'm sure half of all the embassies in the world today are full of spooks."

"Carla, George is using you. Your name has come up, through official channels, as an asset to the CIA."

"What does that mean?"

"Usually a foreigner who is recruited to assist a secret service, in this case the CIA."

Carla was having trouble breathing. She stood up abruptly and walked toward the window, trying to open it, but it was stuck. She pushed and tugged impatiently, but it wouldn't give. Andrew pushed her aside gently and opened it. The air was hot and loud with the sounds of birds and traffic. Tears were welling up in her eyes, and as they started overflowing, Carla wiped them away with an annoyed gesture. Andrew took her by the arm and led her back to the couch.

They sat in silence, and then Carla said, "How did you get this information?" Her voice was without emotion, the one she used for conducting interviews.

Andrew shifted slightly in his chair. His expression was anxious. "Carla, it may come as a surprise to you, but—" Just then there was a knock on the door, interrupting him. Excusing himself, he went to the door and opened it.

Carla stretched her neck to see past Andrew's tall frame. The moment froze. She was looking at the attractive, tanned features of Leila Canaan.

"Hello, Carla." Leila's tone was measured.

Looking at Andrew questioningly, Carla asked, "Is this just some strange coincidence, or did you know she was here?"

Andrew was about to reply, but Carla interrupted him, "Oh my God, you came together!"

"Please, Carla, we can explain."

Carla stood up; looking like she was about to flee, she inched toward the door. Leila walked toward Carla and said, "It's not what you think. Please, come sit down. We need to tell you something."

Carla was certain she felt her heart constricting. But instinct told her to listen, so she sat. She didn't trust herself to speak. Looking down at her hands, she folded them on her lap and with a sigh said, " Leila, please go ahead." Leila moved to Carla's side and sat down on the armrest, resting her hand lightly on Carla's shoulder. "It's about George."

"Oh please, give me a break." Carla was irate. "I suppose

you believe Andrew's story about me being a CIA asset recruited by George?"

Leila's face was inscrutable as she said, "It was me. I gave that classified information to Andrew. I had to—your life is in danger, and after what happened…it's the least I could do." A frown creased her forehead, but her dark eyes were compassionate. With a sigh, Leila sank into the armchair opposite Carla and said, "I can understand your confusion, but please hear me out."

Carla was feeling testy and had to control her urge to simply get up and run. With great effort she looked at Leila and said, "Fine, I'm listening."

"What happened in Peshawar is not relevant to what I have to tell you, Carla. Please believe me, what you saw was a mistake. It happened only that one time, and it was a foolish lack of judgment on both mine and Andrew's part."

" You bet." Carla said, her tone was bitter.

Andrew ran his hand through his hair, which was longer than usual. With what seemed like a huge effort, he looked at Carla and said, "I'm sorry, Carla. We have both made mistakes, and we should forgive each other—"

"What do you mean, 'both of us'?"

He shifted uncomfortably and looked at Leila. She leveled her gaze at Carla and said, "Andrew is aware of your affair with George."

The patronizing tone she was using irked Carla; she wanted to scream in frustration. Closing her eyes, she breathed in deeply through her mouth, expelling the air in a controlled yoga discipline she had learned many years ago. She opened her eyes and, feeling less emotional, said, "OK, what's going on?" With a faint grimace Leila said, "You're not going to like it, but here goes." She opened her leather satchel and took out some documents and large black-and-white photographs, placing them on the coffee table. In a rather dramatic gesture, she looked through the photos and placed one of George, dressed in a suit, on top of the pile.

"George Theodore Alexander." Carla frowned, but Leila continued unperturbed.

"Recruited by the NCS in one of their earlier Undergraduate Internship Programs while he was studying engineering at Harvard. His personal relationship with the daughter of a well-known political Pakistani family gave him the legitimate cover, and as he became more interested in this line of work, he switched to political studies. He is a gifted linguist, fluent in Greek, Italian, and French. On the urging of his handlers in Washington, he took up Arab, Farsi, and Urdu." Leila paused, studying Carla's face intently. Then she continued in the same professional voice.

"After graduation he was offered an overseas post as a junior attaché at the US Embassy in Islamabad. He was hugely successful, especially as he had the interpersonal skills of using his contacts well, particularly the ones made through his relationship with the Pakistani girl he had met at Harvard. He had access to people and places no one at the US Embassy had ever managed to procure. Needless to say, his career was jumpstarted, and he became the golden boy of Langley, reporting straight to the director of the CIA.'

Carla stood up rather abruptly and said, "Excuse me, may I use the bathroom, Andrew?"

"Of course, it's this way," he said, standing up.

Carla locked the door and sat on the edge of the bath, not even noticing the exquisite Italian marble. She rummaged through her purse, sighing with relief as she found two paracetamol capsules. The dull headache that had started earlier had developed into a throbbing pain behind her ears and neck. She swallowed the pills, drinking from a bottle of Himalayan mineral water. Sitting still, she waited for it to abate. *How the hell did I get myself into this mess?* she thought, standing up and opening the bathroom door.

"Are you all right?" Andrew asked; his eyes were concerned.

"I'm fine. So, is there more?"

With a somber expression Leila replied, "I'm afraid so. Please, come sit down. George remained in Pakistan until 2001. He befriended an Afghani by the name of Asef Ali Khan." Leila placed another black-and-white photo over George's.

"Oh my God, I've seen that face before," exclaimed Carla. The photo showed a turbaned man with light colored eyes and a graying beard.

"Here in Delhi?" Leila asked.

"Yes, I saw him in Lodhi Garden, and then I seem to remember him from somewhere else…"

"Try to remember. In the meantime I'll continue. George learned to speak Pashtun and spent some time in Asef's village. We were concerned at the time, but George assured us that Asef was just a friend, and it gave him the opportunity to get to know Afghanistan and its people."

"Just a minute," Carla interrupted. "What do you mean by 'we'?"

"Oh, I'm sorry—I should have explained myself. I went to Cambridge, as you know, majoring in Middle Eastern studies where I, too, was recruited by the CIA. My cover at the BBC is genuine. I met George in Pakistan while on a field mission."

Carla was staring at Leila in utter disbelief. Andrew noticed and cleared his throat before saying, "I know it is all rather confusing. I had no idea Leila was working for the Americans as a spy." His tone irritated Carla—she didn't need him to reassure her of anything anymore, she thought, and told Leila to continue.

"In October 2001, the war in Afghanistan started, and after a debriefing in Langley, George was sent to Kabul in

January 2002. His knowledge of Afghan languages made him extremely valuable, as well as his flair at recruiting assets. Asef Ali Khan became an asset, but on George's insistence remained under the radar. During the first elections of 2004, George provided some really useful intel.

"In February 2006, he was sent to Seoul in South Korea. His cover was that of a software specialist. It was only after North Korea tested a nuclear device in October of that same year that George's mission became obvious to most of us. There was much debate whether the explosion was indeed a nuclear detonation, but some radioactivity was measured and the conclusion made was that the test was a failure, a fizzle. Of course, wild speculation at the agency pointed to George being somehow involved. He remained in Korea for a few years, as relations between North Korea and the South were pretty tense, with war between them a real possibility.

"In 2008 he returned to Afghanistan for a year and in 2009 was appointed as attaché to the US Embassy in Delhi."

"So he's super spy, and how does this affect me?" Carla said with a hint of irritability. An annoyed expression crossed Leila's face, but she was silent, watching Andrew closely. He ran his fingers through his hair, looked at Carla, and said, "Please hear her out." He looked at Leila and nodded.

"We know George is involved in something top secret. Only a few personnel right at the top along with the director have access to the files. It was pure chance that I stumbled onto your file."

"I have a file?" Carla asked, her eyes wide with surprise.

"Yes, of course." Leila continued, "You are obviously very important to this mission, as your file was compiled shortly after you arrived in Delhi."

Carla realized that she was gaping. She closed her mouth and said, "I see, please continue."

"George is trying to get close to Harry Singh. There was some evidence of him trying to seduce Elouise Singh, but it didn't work out as he had hoped. He managed, without much difficulty I may add, to become part of the same social circle. I can only guess that Elouise might have said something about her best friend coming to India to meet her estranged Indian family or something. Either way, he became interested and requested your file. Now I get to the scary part—I believe your kidnapping was staged."

The silence in the room was palpable. Carla pressed her fingers deeply into the side of her head, massaging it in a small circular motion. *Why isn't the paracetemol working?*

"Carla, did you hear what I said?"

"I sure did."

"It was a ploy to gain your trust and confidence. He asked you to spy on Harry, didn't he?" Leila asked.

Carla nodded her head and sighed. Her mind felt numb, her body, disconnected, as she stared at her fingers as if they belonged to someone else. She forced herself to concentrate, to shake herself out of this surreal nightmare. Connect her body to her mind. Resolutely she looked at Leila and asked, "Are you sure? Absolutely sure?"

'Yes, I'm one hundred percent sure. Carla you have no idea what you're getting yourself into."

Andrew said, "Please Carla, don't do anything George asked you to do and keep this conversation confidential."

"He's right, give us some time to get you out of this, safely." Leila said.

"Should I avoid George?" Carla said, realizing immediately as she uttered the words how much she'd regret that.

"Yes, but don't make it obvious. Actually, you should tell him that Andrew has arrived, and you need time to figure things out. That should keep him quiet for a bit."

"And Elouise?"

"Tell her the same thing."

Carla would avoid George, but she couldn't keep this information to herself; she felt sure that Elouise would understand and couldn't wait to get home to confide in her. Looking sadly at Andrew, she said, "Is this the only reason you came, to warn me?"

"Yes. I mean no, not exactly. I was worried about you, Carla, and of course I'm deeply sorry."

Carla stood up and said, "I'll go now. This is a lot of stuff to process. I'll be able to reach you here at the hotel? Both of you?"

As Leila nodded, a sharp pang tore through Carla. Noticing her expression, Leila said, "We're not sharing a room."

Carla wanted to hit her, but instead she walked out and called the taxi driver.

CHAPTER 16

Elouise was pacing, down the corridor and back and forth from the garden, complaining to the mali about the condition of the spinach, or the flowerpots that were askew. He muttered under his breath as he addressed the spinach with his head cocked to the side.

She called Kishan for the umpteenth time to change the lunch menu. He listened patiently, removed the yellow lentils from the stove, and started preparing the black lentils, Moghul-style.

Finally settling down in her bedroom with a book, Elouise stared at the words and wondered impatiently what time Carla would get back. At last she heard Kishan asking Carla if she would like lunch. Rushing out, she collided into Carla as she was walking toward Elouise's bedroom.

"Oops, sorry. You're in a big hurry. Late for the kids?" Carla asked.

"No, I was waiting for you. Where were you?"

"I went to Andrew's hotel. We needed to chat." Carla

grimaced. "He was not alone."

Elouise widened her eyes and said, "What do you mean?"

"Let's go to my room. I'll tell you all about it."

Passing the kitchen, Elouise told Kishan not to disturb them. Carla's room was cool, and with a sigh they both fell down on the bed, kicking off their sandals.

"This feels good. It's so hot today," Carla said.

"Yep, I'm afraid the temperature is going to start climbing now until the rain cools it down slightly during the monsoons."

"When's that?"

"From the end of June. But enough about the weather. Who was with Andrew?"

Carla pulled herself up into a sitting position propped up against the cushions and said, "Leila Canaan, his work colleague. The *one* in his bed in Peshawar."

Elouise was shocked and sat up. "You're kidding! But why?"

"I thought they were here to tell me that they were serious about each other and I should give Andrew a divorce—"

"That's not what Andrew told me," Elouise interrupted.

"I know. I was wrong. It's probably worse." Elouise noticed the dejection in Carla's eyes and felt desperately sorry for her friend. Her resentment of Carla's relationship with George was forgotten.

"Do you want to tell me about it?" Elouise asked.

"It's about George."

"They know about him?"

"Yes, apparently Leila has known him for years. They both work for the CIA."

Elouise was dumbfounded. "I can't believe it. So I guess all those rumors are true."

"What rumors?"

"George unsettled quite a few Delhi husbands. He is an incorrigible flirt and, as you know from firsthand experience, quite the charmer."

Carla blushed and asked, "They suspected that he was a spy?"

"Well, no one actually said it, but you know how rumors are fueled. The ladies put it down to jealousy on behalf of some deceived husband, but instead of scaring them off, it intensified their interest. He was the most invited guest on the Delhi social calendar." Elouise paused and noticed how pale Carla was. "Are you OK?"

"Yes, please continue. Tell me everything you know about him." Carla's voice was quivering.

With a frown, Elouise continued, "I don't know any details, just some gossip here and there."

"What were the husbands like, anyone important?" Carla asked.

Elouise laughed. "Carla, I don't know. It's all hearsay."

"But still, you once said something about him flirting with the wives of powerful men."

Elouise was beginning to feel uncomfortable. "I suppose so. It's a high-profile type of circle he moves around in, but we're getting sidetracked. What did this revelation have to do with you?"

"They said, I mean Leila said, that I was being used by George to help him get closer to certain people."

A tightness in her chest made Elouise gasp. Carla asked, "Elouise, are you OK?"

"Yes, yes, I'm fine." She looked at Carla with a pensive expression. "Did they say who?"

Carla shook her head. Elouise smiled halfheartedly and said, "How long have we known each other?"

Carla laughed. "I know, I can't lie to you, can I?"

"No, you can't. Who was it?" Elouise was feeling strangely detached as she asked the question.

"Elouise, did George try anything with you?"

Taken aback by the unexpected question, Elouise stammered, "Uh, what do you mean?"

"You know…"

"Oh, I see." Elouise sighed and continued, "He was very attentive. I liked him. A lot. Oh, Carla, I'm so embarrassed by all of this." She looked around frantically for the tissue box; taking one, she wiped her eyes and continued, "The thing is, our marriage is in trouble. I told you the other day how Harry has changed. I felt neglected, insecure, and then I met George. It was all rather innocent at first. We played tennis, had coffee, and then I went over to his place for dinner when Harry was away in Pakistan for a conference." She paused. "Do you want a cup of tea?"

"Elouise, no. What happened?"

"I'm getting there; don't be so impatient." Elouise was undecided, wondering what the implication could be if she told Carla the whole truth. She realized that the only way Carla would open up to her is if she knew everything. Elouise had the distinct feeling that she knew something that had something to do with Elouise and her family. Looking at Carla, she saw the concern and realized that if their friendship could withstand anything, this had to be it. She continued, "George cooked. He's not the world's best, but it was edible. I didn't have much appetite. We drank a whole bottle of champagne and then we had cognacs. I knew I should have stopped, but—"

"Did you go to bed with him?" Carla interrupted her.

"Gosh, Carla, what happened to your polite listening skills?"

Smiling bashfully, Carla said, "Sorry, so what happened after the cognacs?"

"You realize, of course, that this is embarrassing, don't you?"

"Your choice. I wanted to go straight to the nitty-gritty, but you are preferring the long, romantic version."

Elouise started laughing, the tension lifting slightly. She

hugged Carla and said, "It happened. I felt guilty and horrible. Took a taxi home and refused to speak to George again. It was three or four months later when I bumped into him at the golf club that I decided to talk to him. Of course, by now the rumors of his prowess with the ladies had spread like wildfire. I was relieved. At least it got me off the hook."

"And you never told Harry?"

"Of course not. Harry still invited George to play golf now and then. I didn't see the point in complicating things further."

"So you think George was just trying to use you?"

"I don't know. I often wondered about it." Elouise smiled with a doleful expression. "I guess Harry works for the government, so possibly. But then again, I don't know anything. Harry doesn't discuss his work with me."

Carla took her hand and said gently, "I'm so sorry, Elouise."

With a rueful smile, Elouise looked at Carla knowingly and asked, "It's Harry George is after, isn't it?"

"I'm sorry," Carla murmured.

Elouise withdrew her hand from Carla's. The silence became weighted, threatening Elouise with suffocation. When she looked up, her eyes were glittering with tears. "Carla, you must tell me everything and don't hold back."

With a dismal sigh Carla pursed her lips and told Elouise everything. Elouise listened without interrupting. Only her eyes mirrored the emotion she felt as she heard the inconceivable account of the past week's events. When Carla told her that she hadn't given Harry's files to George, she grabbed Carla by the shoulders and told her fiercely, "Don't give them to him. Please." Her voice was tremulous. "I'll help you. We'll find out if Harry is involved and—" Her voice broke, thick with tears. "I'll do the right thing. I will turn him in if we're certain of his involvement."

A knock on the door made them both jump with fright. "Lunch is ready, Madam. I must serve in your room?" Kishan asked through the door.

Wiping her face with the tissue in her hand, Elouise replied, "Thanks, Kishan, we'll be there in a few minutes."

Then she looked at Carla and asked, "Are we on the same page?"

Carla stared at her for a moment, a deep frown creasing her usually smooth forehead. Then, with a heedful smile, she said, "Of course."

Reassured, Elouise hugged her and asked, "Ready for lunch?"

"Yes, I am."

Surprising themselves, they ate the vegetarian meal of black lentils, smoky eggplant, paneer, and spinach with real appetite while discussing their plan.

Carla returned to her room while Elouise collected her daughters from school. She was emotionally exhausted. The fact that Elouise had slept with George made her feel physically ill, the jealousy undeniable. Resisting the urge to lie down, she sat on the chaise longue and dialed George's mobile number. He picked up on the second ring. She felt a flutter in her stomach on hearing his cultivated voice.

"I was just going to call," George said, and continued smoothly, "Let's have dinner at home. Sunil can use the small tandoor oven in the back garden and make his famous chicken tikka with garlic naan. What do you think?"

Oh, why can't it be so simple? Carla thought desperately. Finding her voice, she surprised herself by answering in an even tone, "That sounds wonderful George, but I'm afraid I can't come to your place. It would be better if we met somewhere else."

"Is everything OK?" George asked, sounding bemused.
"We need to talk. It's important. Any suggestions?"
"I guess we could go to Claridges; it's close."
"No, not there. What about the Imperial Hotel's coffee shop?"
"Sure, I'll pick you up at eight?"
"That's perfect. Thanks George."

George arrived early, but Carla was ready for once, wearing a coral linen dress. They left straightaway on Carla's insistence, without seeing Elouise or Harry. Kamal was driving and greeted her politely. George sat quietly without touching her. He wore a contemplative expression as he looked at her. Carla studied her small mother of pearl and coral beaded purse with earnest. Acutely aware of his presence, she had to control the urge to lean against him and feel the warm comfort of his muscular chest. This feeling surprised her, considering the information she had received from Andrew and Leila. *What's my problem, I can't trust him and I shouldn't? And yet all I want is to be close to him. Pull yourself together, Carla,* she reminded herself.

Arriving at the hotel, George steered her gently toward the coffee shop, his hand lightly on her waist. The hostess smiled and flirted somewhat with him when he requested a table in a quiet section. Carla refused to smile at her as they were shown to their table. George noticed and said, "Don't you like this table?"

"It's fine, really."

George ordered single malt for himself, and Carla opted for mineral water. *I need a clear head,* she reasoned. They studied the menu for a few minutes. George closed his and said, "New Zealand lamb for me; what about you?"

Carla realized that she had no idea. She had looked at

the menu without reading a thing. Frowning, she skimmed it and decided on the Caesar salad.

"Not hungry?" George asked.

"I had a big lunch. Kishan is quite the chef."

His smile was tender as he took her hand in his. She tried to pull it away, but he held it firmly. "What's bothering you, Carla?"

Her eyes were stinging and a lump formed in her throat. Swallowing hard, she tried to dispel it, but it seemed to have grown even larger. She looked at George and said simply, "Andrew, my husband, is in Delhi. He arrived this morning."

George withdrew his hand from hers, picked up his whiskey, and took a long sip, almost finishing it. A small muscle twitched in his jaw, but his eyes and face didn't betray any emotion. It annoyed Carla.

"Have you seen him?" he asked finally.

"Yes. He's staying at Claridges. We met there."

George studied her face and then with narrowed eyes asked, "Did he ask you to forgive him?"

"Yes, I suppose, in a way, but I haven't exactly been an angel myself."

He laughed, reached for her hand, and squeezed it. "Oh, Carla, you are so wonderfully old-fashioned."

Carla pulled her hand out of his grip; her face was flushed as she said, "You are so insensitive. I am a married woman, after all. Cheating husband or not."

"I'm sorry. I didn't mean to be callous." There was a trace of remorse in his voice.

With a strained smile, she said, "I'm so confused George. I really enjoy being with you, but—"

"It's OK. You don't have to explain or apologize for anything. I just want you to be careful. Don't rush back into it until you're quite sure you want to."

"You're right. I'll take my time."

"Are you going back with him to London?"

"No, I'll stay for another week or so. I've hardly spent any time with Elouise."

"And Andrew?"

"I don't know. We haven't really discussed it. I'm going to continue staying with Elouise at the bungalow."

"I see. Have you thought about your little mission?"

Carla shifted uneasily in her chair. *That's all he cares about.* "Yes, of course. I'll try my best, but I'm not sure if I'll manage."

His eyes were serious when he said, "Please try, Carla. It is very important for us to get that information."

"Who's us?"

Seemingly taken aback by the abruptness of her question, George hesitated before replying, "Me, Valentina, and the rest of the group trying to get to the bottom of this trafficking ring. But you knew that." His eyes bored into hers.

"Yes, I was just wondering if there was a more 'official' interest."

George frowned and said, "No, it's exactly like I explained it to you."

"I see." Carla watched the waiter with relief as he served their dinner. They ate quietly. The salad was fresh and crispy, but Carla couldn't eat much. George's lamb looked and smelled delicious, but it appeared to her like he was struggling to finish it, too.

"Would you like to see the desert menu?" George asked her politely as the waiter cleared their plates.

"No, thanks. I'll have an espresso with milk on the side, please."

George ordered the same and then looked at Carla with an intense expression. "I'm going to miss you."

She felt a physical, nagging pain somewhere inside her. Carla gazed at him and said, "Me too."

"We'll stay in touch. And, Carla, please…" He took her

hand; holding it tightly he continued, "If you need me for anything, anything at all, you know you can depend on me. OK?"

"Thanks, George, I know." For some reason she didn't fully comprehend, Carla meant what she said.

On the drive home, George held her hand gently in his lap. It felt so natural Carla hardly noticed. It was only when they arrived at the bungalow that she pulled it away somewhat self-consciously.

George walked her to the door and said, "Good night, Carla. I really hope this is not the end of something special."

Tears were threatening Carla, so she kept her eyes downturned. After a second or two, she looked up at him, stood slightly on her tippy toes, and pecked him hastily on his cheek. It was smooth and cool, smelling of his aftershave. The familiar scent and texture of his skin caused a slight tremor to run through her. Fighting the urge to touch him again, she turned on her heels and hurried into the house, almost bumping the slight frame of Kishan in her rush. She apologized quickly and, refusing his offer of tea, locked herself in her bedroom.

She lay fully clothed on her bed for a long time, trying to clear her mind. When her eyes started to scratch from fatigue, she changed into her nightgown, falling asleep moments after her head touched the pillow. A large, flesh-colored gecko lost his footing while trying to catch a mosquito, and fell heavily onto Carla's pillow. Her nose twitched, but she slept on.

CHAPTER 17

Harry was still in his study working on his computer when Elouise heard Carla's return. She couldn't dispel the images of Carla's ordeal from her mind. Harry couldn't possibly be involved. He had two daughters. What kind of father could possibly condone the kidnapping and trafficking of young girls?

She tried once more to focus on the novel she was reading but to no avail: the words were scrambled with no resemblance to any language known to her. With a sigh, she switched off the table lamp and lay down, facing the adjoining study. She could see Harry through the blinds, working with a deep frown creasing his brow. Impulsively she got up and walked barefoot toward the study, not making a sound. Leaning against the frame of the door, she watched him as he placed a folder in the bottom drawer of his desk, locking the drawer. He opened a gray hardcover textbook and placed the key inside a small cut out compartment. Closing it, he pushed back his office chair, scraping the wooden floor loudly. With her heart skipping a couple of beats, Elouise dashed back to her bed, lying down on her side facing away from him.

Harry switched off the study lights and walked toward the bed. He asked softly, "Elouise. Are you sleeping?"

She closed her eyes tightly and tried to breathe slowly and evenly, not answering him. When she heard him in the bathroom, she opened her eyes and wondered what could possibly be in that bottom drawer.

Harry slept while Elouise struggled to fall asleep. Eventually, as the faint coral of the early dawn painted the walls of the white bungalow, she succumbed.

Harry volunteered to take the girls to school while Elouise complained of a headache and remained in bed. "Are you coming back or going straight to the office?" Elouise asked him.

"I'll go to the office. A young Caltech graduate is coming for an assessment this morning."

"And lunch?"

"Not sure, but please go ahead without me."

"Dad. Let's go. We'll be late," Sara shouted from the passage.

Harry kissed Elouise on the top of her head. "Get better," he said, rushing out.

Elouise called Kishan and asked him whether Carla had woken up. He replied, "Yes, Memsahibji. Madam Carla already drink tea and eat fruit. You want breakfast now?"

"No thanks, Kishan, just another cup of tea, and please ask Carla Madam to come here if she's dressed."

Elouise heard a knock on the half-open door soon after Kishan left, and Carla's voice asking, "Are you decent?"

"Of course, come in."

"I saw Harry taking the girls to school this morning."
"Yes, I pretended I had a headache."
"Why?"
"I want to poke around his study this morning."
"Don't get caught."
"He won't be home before lunch. In any event you'll be sitting on the front veranda as my lookout, OK?"
"Sure, when do you want to do it?"
"Now."

Carla widened her eyes in what seemed to Elouise to be surprise and said, "OK. I'll read the paper there. How will I alert you?"

"Put my phone number on speed dial, then let it ring once."

"I'll just get it from my room. Give me five minutes." She hurried out.

Drinking her tea, Elouise kept an eye on the Waterford crystal alarm clock on her bedside table. After precisely five minutes, she entered Harry's study. She couldn't see the hardcover book on the desk, so she turned toward the bookshelves behind it. Her heart sank as she saw hundreds of gray hardcover books lining the shelves. Resigning herself to the fact that she would have to open them all one by one, she started systematically on the far left-hand corner.

A fine layer of dust covered the first book she took out, making her sneeze. It had no compartment. Studying the top of the books, she noticed a dust layer on most of them. She quickly scanned the top shelf. On the second shelf, she found a gray hardcover with less dust on it. With trepidation, she removed and opened it. The small steel key lay on the bottom of the cut-out compartment. She smiled with relief as she placed the book on the desk, making a mental note of where its place on the bookshelf was. She went down on her haunches to unlock and open the bottom drawer of the desk. A blue cardboard file closed with an elastic band lay on top of a book. She removed both and, sitting down on Harry's, chair she looked at them. The book was an old-looking, leather-bound Koran in dark green. The gold-embossed Islamic pattern on its cover was dull and faded from use. Elouise frowned as she opened it and realized that she had opened it left from right as opposed to right from left. She opened it correctly and saw a faded name written on the first yellowed page of the holy book. It read:

Soraya Khan
1948

Elouise flipped through the pages, stained and brittle with age, but saw nothing else of interest. She opened the file. It contained Harry's birth certificate and letters written on cheap white stationary. Picking up the one on top of the pile, Elouise read the date in scrawled handwriting as July 2007. They had arrived back in Delhi that January. She skimmed the dates on the other letters and saw that they ranged from July 2007 to the latest, which was dated three months earlier. The handwriting was the same on all of them.

Picking up the latest one, she was about to start reading it when she heard her phone ring. In a panic she put the book and file back in the drawer, locking it and hiding the key back in its compartment. Then she placed it back on the self. Sprinting back to bed, she dived under the covers, feigning sleep. Beads of perspiration formed on her forehead, and her pulse was racing.

"Elouise?" Carla called out softly.

She sat up and said, "Carla, come in."

Carla entered quickly, walking toward Elouise and whispered, "Sorry, I pressed the speed dial by mistake."

"You idiot," Elouise said, laughing. "I almost had a heart

attack."

"Did you find anything?"

"Yes, some letters and a Koran."

"Let me see."

"I put them back; I thought Harry was here," Elouise said with an exasperated tone.

"Where did you find them?"

"They were locked in his desk's bottom drawer."

"And the key?"

Elouise smiled. "I happened to see Harry last night hiding it in a compartment of a book which he kept on his bookshelf."

Carla laughed softly. "Wow, good work."

"What should I do?"

"Scan them with your iPhone. You have that application, don't you?"

"Of course, good idea. Now go back to the veranda and don't dial by mistake again—my heart won't survive it."

Feeling more composed this time around, Elouise unlocked the drawer, scanned the letters, and wrote down the name inscribed in the Koran on a Post-it. She was careful to keep the letters in the same order. As she locked the drawer and returned the key to its hiding place, she sighed with audible relief. Hiding the phone in her pocket, she walked to the veranda where Carla was sitting in a plantation chair reading the *Indian Times*.

"Done?" Carla asked.

Elouise nodded. "Can we download it onto your computer? I don't want Harry to find it on my phone."

"Yes, let's go to my room."

Elouise was amused when Carla took out her laptop, which was locked into her suitcase. "You're not bad as an amateur spy."

Smiling, Carla said, "Don't give me any encouragement. I have no intention of giving up my cushy job at CNN for this."

"Did you lock the door?" Elouise asked, concerned.

"Yes. Should we read it here, or do you want to go somewhere else?"

"I think it's fine. Harry won't come in here." Looking at the letters on the screen, Elouise asked, "Should we read them from the earliest date?"

"OK," Carla replied, opening the scans and placing them in order.

The first letter was dated July 2, 2007. It read:

Salaam aleikum,

How happy I am on this day by God's grace to write to you. The weather is too hot, and the electricity is not enough to keep the air-conditioners running. Many of the patients are exhibiting short tempers and fits of rage. Your mother is her usual self, quiet and dignified. She is singing in her sweet voice to many of the really sick patients, and they are responding so well to her.

God willing you will be reunited soon.

Dr. Yunis Malik

Elouise looked at Carla and said, "I'm so confused. His mother and father died in 2006 in a car accident in Kashmir."

"Are we sure this is addressed to Harry? It only says 'salaam aleikum,' and I don't see any envelopes."

"You're right. Let's see what the others say." Elouise scanned through them. "No, the same 'salaam aleikum' on all of them."

"Go on, read them all. There must be some clue as to whom these letters are addressed to."

Elouise started reading aloud for Carla's benefit. Her

voice was quavering. They were all written by Dr. Malik and more or less identical except for small details. "The woman he refers to as the mother appears to be a patient, but not as sick as the others, as she is asked to help control some of the more infirm," Elouise explained.

"That's it?" Carla asked.

Elouise replied with a puzzled expression, "Yes, and of course the old Koran belonging to a Soraya Khan."

"Does any of this make any sense to you?" Carla asked, studying the letters on her laptop.

Elouise shook her head, lay down and sighed. "No, it doesn't make any sense."

Carla saved the scans and locked her computer back into her suitcase. "Now what?"

Elouise was staring at the ceiling fan whirling noisily. "I don't understand. If those letters are addressed to Harry, then it means he has another mother. As far as I know, the only mother he knew died in a car crash along with his father in 2006."

"Maybe those letters belong to some of the girls who were—" Carla stopped, looked guiltily at Elouise, and said, "Possibly...maybe?"

Elouise felt a sense of outrage, her face draining of color. Carla must have noticed this and said quickly, "Elouise, I understand." She leaned toward her friend and took her hand, stroking it gently. "We have to be objective. It's hard for me to imagine that George feels nothing for me and only used me to get close to Harry. My heart denies it, but facts are facts. I have to face it."

Tears streamed down Elouise's face, and then she started sobbing. Her hands covered her face as she cried. Carla held her tightly until her sobbing subsided.

Elouise smiled wanly and whispered, "Sorry." She went to the bathroom, where she blew her nose loudly and washed her face with cold water. She addressed her tragic face in the mirror, "C'mon girl. Let's get to the bottom of this. You owe it to Carla and all those other girls."

Carla smiled with relief when Elouise came back into the room. "Are you feeling better?"

"Thanks, I suppose I needed a good cry." Elouise sat down on the edge of the bed and said, "I have an idea. I'm going to visit an old relative of Harry's. She's pretty old and sickly, but hopefully she can give me some insight into Harry's family."

"Good idea. What should I do?"

"I think you should act normally. Spend some time with Andrew. Maybe you guys can work things out."

Elouise walked to the door as Carla asked, "Are you going now?"

"Yes. If you're still here when Harry returns, tell him I drove myself to the doctor and left the driver for you."

"OK, good luck." But Carla sounded concerned.

CHAPTER 18

The young Caltech graduate who had been sent for the post of assistant researcher at BABA smiled without a trace of embarrassment as he asked Harry for some scotch tape to fix his black-rimmed spectacles, which had cracked on the flight from Los Angeles. He was wearing a pair of aviator sunglasses on top of his spectacles when he arrived in the black and yellow Ambassador taxi. Harry was amused by the geekiness of this highly recommended academic.

Elouise used to tease Harry about his nerdy appearance and was met with very little resistance from his side when she insisted on the ultimate makeover. Contact lenses, sports jackets from Ralph Lauren, and Todd's loafers qualified him as the most stylish professor at Caltech. Harry smiled wistfully, remembering the makeover as he continued interviewing the candidate. When his phone rang, he ignored it until it stopped. But when it rang the second time, he glanced at it and picked it up, apologizing to the young man. He answered the call, got up, and walked toward the window, turning his back on the visitor.

"Salaam aleikum," said the voice on the crackled telephone line.

Breathing deeply, Harry replied in English, "Good morning, Doctor."

The doctor coughed and said, "I have some bad news. She had an attack. It is bad. I'm not sure she'll recover from this one."

Harry felt the color drain from his face; his legs were heavy. He needed to sit. "What can I do?"

"You need to come here. She wants to see you. There is a science conference in Lahore. It shouldn't be a problem to get access into the country. You still have your visa from last time?"

"Yes." Harry was beginning to sweat.

"We hope to see you soon. God be with you. Oh, I almost forgot, my wife would be so happy if you could pick up some green and white silk from Aabhas." He dropped the connection.

Sitting down at his desk, Harry said, "Sorry about that," and continued his interview, but he couldn't concentrate. After a few minutes he said, "I'm so sorry, but I have an emergency. I'll get my secretary to reschedule."

"No problem," the young man said, smiling happily in his scotch-tape-repaired spectacles. He got into the waiting taxi and waved. Harry laughed softly, shaking his head, and returned to his office, asking his secretary to meet him there. Pencil poised, Tahir sat down and looked up.

"I need you to book me a flight to Lahore this evening."

"On Emirates, sir?"

Harry sighed and said, "Yes, I don't have much choice. I have to go through the Middle East, as there are no direct flights between Pakistan and India."

"What about the train?" Tahir asked; his eyes were hopeful.

"I thought they stopped the Samjhauta Express between Delhi and Lahore after the bombing in 2007."

"Yes, but one can still take a train to the Indian border town of Attari and then change to a Pakistani train at Wagah."

"I suppose, but I'd rather just get there by air. What if the border post decides to strike or something? See if you can get me out on Emirates tonight on the 9:40 flight. I should have enough miles for an upgrade."

Harry watched Tahir hurry to his desk and phone the Emirates office.

When Harry got home, Kishan told him that Elouise had gone to the doctor. He called her at once, but her phone was switched off. In an irritated tone, he asked Kishan to pack an overnight bag for him. After packing, Kishan served Harry lunch in his study. Harry continued working for another hour, and then he called his driver to take him to Lajpat Nagar. He went into a ladies' fabric store and told the driver in the meantime to buy some traditional sweets from Haldirams; he'd wait for him at the fabric store.

Once inside he asked for Aabhas. The middle-aged shop owner walked toward him with a slight limp. He smiled warmly and said, "Mr. Singh, welcome to my shop. What can I help you with?"

"I am looking for some embroidered silk fabric."

"Any particular color?"

"Green. Green and white."

"I have many such lovely fabrics, but for you I have a special piece." Aabhas nodded his head at the young assistant, who scurried off to the back of the shop, returning with a dark, mottled green piece of silk fabric. Aabhas smiled and opened the fabric on the cotton sheeting that covered the floor. Intricate white embroidery filled most of it.

"That's perfect. How much do I owe you for this?" Harry said, taking out his wallet.

Suddenly looking coy, Aabhas said, "Many months of embroidery. The whole piece in hand embroidery, but I will only charge you two thousand rupees. A very special price for my good customer."

Harry counted out the cash and handed it to him. It disappeared into Aabhas's pocket, and within minutes the assistant presented the parcel to Harry, wrapped in gray paper and tied with faded red string.

Harry waited in between the parked cars and motorcycles on the side of the road, marveling at the fact that very few accidents actually occurred in the congested traffic. At last he saw his jeep inching forward on the opposite side of the road. He walked through the traffic and jumped into his car without the driver bringing it to a complete standstill. The sweets were stacked on the seat next to him in neat boxes. Harry told him to return home.

It took them almost an hour to reach home in the afternoon traffic. On the way, Elouise called, and he told her that he was leaving on business that same evening. She asked if he wanted a quick snack before leaving for the airport, which he refused.

Harry hurried inside while Kishan placed the overnight bag in the trunk. The fabric and sweets were left on the seat. Elouise kissed Harry on his cheeks and said, "I may go away with Carla to a spa in Bangalore tomorrow. Anu has kindly offered to take the kids for two days."

"Can't you wait for my return?" Harry frowned.

"No, not really, Carla is leaving next week, and we might not find the time again as I'll be hectic with the fundraiser."

"OK, but stay in touch with me." He kissed her again and hurried to the jeep.

The traffic was heavy, but luckily they reached the airport within an hour. Presenting his passport at the check-in, he sighed with relief—he had almost missed the deadline.

※ ※ ※

"Mr. Singh? We will be landing in Lahore shortly. Is this your jacket?"

Harry looked at the Emirates hostess, and it took him a few seconds to realize that he was on a plane. He had fallen into a deep sleep on the second leg of his journey. The sky was pink as the rising sun was threatening to break through the silver clouds.

Harry mused angrily over the unnecessary time spent in getting to Lahore when it was only a couple of hundred kilometers from Delhi. It was a two-and-a-half-hour flight to Dubai with a wait of four hours, and then another three-hour flight. He sighed and accepted some coffee, smiling at the attractive hostess.

As the aircraft started breaking through the thin layer of clouds, Lahore became visible. The second-largest city in Pakistan was sprawled along the Ravi River, which looked quite dry. Harry knew that in the monsoon, however, it would spill over its banks.

Harry fastened his seatbelt when he heard the landing gear descending, and a few minutes later they landed smoothly. The immigration officer chatted amiably to him about the cricket, surprising Harry with his open admiration of Sachin Tendulkar. "Best, best batsman ever," he said, winking at Harry. He stamped his passport and waved him through.

A driver and car were waiting for him. The driver, wearing a faded brown Pathani outfit, welcomed him in Punjabi. Harry understood it quite well from his paternal grandmother speaking it to him as a child. His father's family was from Lahore and had escaped in 1947 during the partition riots. The driver took Harry's overnight bag, but left Harry to carry his briefcase and the plastic packet containing the sweets and fabric. He drove him through the congested roads to his hotel. The Pearl Continental was a large modern hotel, with international guests filling the lobby dressed in business suits. The driver told him that he would be back to pick him up at lunchtime.

After a quick shower, Harry changed his shirt and ordered tea. He checked his e-mails while watching CNN, grimacing at the images of the wounded in an apparent suicide bombing in Iraq. He phoned Elouise and told her that he had arrived safely and would be in a conference for the rest of the day. His phone would be switched off, but he'd call her that evening again. She wanted to know when he was coming back, to which he replied, "Not a hundred percent sure, but most probably the day after." Her voice sounded strained to Harry as she said good-bye.

Harry dozed off in front of the television as images of his childhood in Delhi flooded his mind. He woke up in a sweat, startled by the ringing of the hotel phone on the bedside table. "Your driver is here to collect you, Mr. Singh," the hotel receptionist informed him. He thanked her and said he'd be right down.

The driver took him to a restaurant in the Old City called Cuckoo's Café. This famous restaurant was opposite the Badshahi Mosque in the red light district and housed in an old five-story haveli. Harry recognized the well-known owner of the establishment sitting at a table with a bearded man wearing a turban—much like the ones worn by the Taliban, Harry thought. They were in a heated debate with the owner, pointing to his paintings that decorated most of the wall space. Harry gazed up at them and realized why the debate was so vehement; the paintings were obvious portraits of prostitutes. Harry had heard of the artist, who was well-known in the international art circle for his rather unorthodox subjects. His mother was a sex worker. The more conservative elements in Lahore disapproved of this business, but it was still frequented by both tourists and well-to-do Pakistanis.

A waiter seated him on the top floor. The restaurant was already full. He ordered a Coke and placed his mobile phone next to him on the table. After five minutes, a gray-haired, balding man, wearing black trousers and a half-sleeve white shirt with a striped red and navy tie, sat down heavily on the chair opposite him.

He smiled as he greeted Harry formally by shaking his hand.

"Dr. Malik, you're looking well," Harry said, noticing how the slightly built man was sweating profusely. He used a napkin folded neatly on the table to wipe his face.

"Thank you. It is very hot. What a relief it would be if the monsoons could come early this year." The doctor ordered a mango lassi and continued, "She is better, and I've told her of your visit. This cheered her up immensely."

"I'm glad to hear that. Will we see her today?"

"Of course, but let's have some lunch. Forgive me for bringing you to this heinous place, but the food is good, so we have to turn a blind eye to these wicked paintings." He gestured at them with an annoyed expression, keeping his eyes downcast.

Harry had no appetite but ordered a chicken kebab with naan. They made small talk, and when the food arrived they ate in silence. The plates were cleared, and then the doctor asked Harry, "Did you bring the cloth?"

"Oh, yes, of course. It's right here." Harry picked up the plastic bag and gave it to the doctor. "Did your wife like the piece I got her last time?"

"Yes, yes. Thank you, it was exactly what she wanted. The merchant has been supplying her family for many years, and he knows her taste well." The doctor looked around impatiently. "So I think we should go. We will tell the driver to wait here for you. I'm afraid we'll have to go on foot now."

Harry paid the bill, and as they left he saw the owner giving a large brown envelope to the man he had been arguing with. *Even morals have a price,* Harry thought as they left the restaurant.

The heat was intense as Harry hurried after the doctor. The streets were swarming with people and bicycle rickshaws. Heavily made-up women were hanging over balconies, some singing in sweet, childlike voices. Towering men with fearsome expressions glared at Harry while he kept his eyes trained on the doctor's back as he led the way. Perspiration was soaking his shirt.

After about a mile, they left the red light district and were in a more residential part of the Old City. It was filthy, with leaking sewage mingling with the daily waste of the overpopulated residential quarter. Some beggars lined the side of the street listlessly, but jumped up when they saw Harry and the doctor, lamenting and wailing. Harry ignored them, and when an old woman dressed in rags grabbed him by his trousers, the doctor lashed out with his right hand and whacked her on the head, sending her staggering and falling in the oozy muck face-first.

Harry was shocked by this reaction and said, "It's OK, you don't have to hit her. She's just an old woman."

The doctor looked at him with narrowed eyes; then he smiled amiably and said, "She is a well-known pickpocket in the area and not as old as she pretends."

He continued walking and stopped in front of a faded blue door, knocking. The door was opened by a scrawny youth, who salaamed respectfully and showed them inside. A large desk was in the corner of the room with some bare wooden benches lining the remaining walls. A middle-aged woman dressed in a washed-out pink salwar kameez sat in front of a desktop computer at the table. Files bound in gray cardboard folders littered her desk. A toddler sitting on his mother's lap was sucking on the end of her dupatta, a small frown creasing his silky baby complexion.

Harry smiled whimsically as he remembered his mother scolding him for wetting the edge of her pallu. His ayah had been more patient, laughing at her tattered pallu while hugging him to her small frame, smelling of woodsmoke and incense.

"Come with me. She has been sedated but wants to see you," the doctor said, walking toward a metal gate with a long, narrow passage behind it. The scrawny youth unlocked the gate with a large, rusty key hanging on a chain around his neck. The weight of it had chafed off some of the skin on his neck, leaving it inflamed with raw infected tissue emanating the sweetish-foul odor of sepsis.

Harry held his hand in front of his nose and avoided touching the boy as he squeezed past him. The boy looked ashamed, as if he was aware of Harry's discomfort. The pain in his eyes made Harry feel like a villain, and he admonished himself quietly for it.

Horrific screaming came from some of the rooms behind the closed doors. Some sections were eerily quiet, but the stench of carbolic soap and sour-smelling mildewed floors and walls played havoc with Harry's digestion. He swallowed his saliva, which tasted bitter, and looked around frantically for a bathroom.

The doctor knocked on a door at the end of the passage and was ushered in by a small woman dressed in full burqa. An iron bed stood against the wall under a tiny, broken window with shards of glass lying menacingly in its old wooden frame. On the faded floral single sheet, a woman lay staring into space while muttering incoherently to herself in Punjabi. Her long, dark hair was streaked with gray and hung around her face, matted and dull. On the opposite wall an ancient-looking wooden air-conditioner droned on, not really cooling the oppressive heat in the room. The only other furniture in the room was a plastic chair, which the burqa-clad woman had vacated. A glass of unfinished tea sat on the dirty floor next to a torn copy of a Bollywood film magazine.

Harry approached the woman on the bed tentatively, placing the plastic bag containing the sweets next to her. She continued staring at the ceiling, and it was only after Harry nudged her lightly on the arm that she turned her head and looked at him. Her eyes didn't seem to register his presence, but then she smiled. Tears were streaming down her face as she held his face in both hands.

"My son, my son," she said in Punjabi, her voice hoarse with emotion.

CHAPTER 19

Harry took his mother's hand and noticed how much thinner she had become. Since the discovery of his parents' deceit, he had been sending money regularly to this asylum. With an annoyed frown, he wondered whether the funds were being used properly. He sat down on the bed and watched her as she cried, mumbling softly. Feeling desperately sorry for her, he wished he could take her out of there, but they wouldn't allow it, not yet.

The revelation of this discovery almost three years ago still managed to traumatize him, and staying calm was an enormous effort. He thought about his life until this moment, about what he thought to be the truth and how that truth had erupted into a thousand lies. After the tragic death of his parents, Harry had decided to return to Delhi. It wasn't difficult convincing Elouise, as the luxury of having cooks and servants appealed to her greatly; it was one they couldn't afford in America. The girls were less excited, but appeased when they managed to get admission to the

American school.

The Indian government had snapped him up and gave him a post as researcher at their nuclear program in Mumbai, agreeing that he could take up residency in Delhi.

In May of that same year, he had been invited to deliver a lecture at a conference in Lahore. He was impressed with the high standard and efficiency of the conference. On the second-to-last day, he had the morning free and decided to explore the Old City. The hotel had organized a driver and guide for him. Yusuf Ali Khan, the guide, was elderly and dressed like a Muslim cleric. He took him to the Badshahi Mosque, where they had sweet, milky tea at a canteen opposite the mosque. That was when the old man started asking personal questions. Harry had become angry, telling him that it was none of his business. The man had replied, "But you see, it is. I am interested in your family, because I am your family."

"What are you saying?" Harry said, looking at the old man, trying to judge the situation, wondering if this was a scam of sorts.

"I am your uncle. Your mother's brother."

"My mother was an only child. She had no brothers."

"Your real mother did," Yusuf said simply, a small, triumphant smile tugging at the corners of his lips.

Harry sat very still, staring at the minaret of the mosque. Yusuf was watching him expectantly. Harry turned to face the old man and said, "Why don't you tell me—that was your intention all along, wasn't it?"

Yusuf Ali Khan smiled and bowed his head slightly, seemingly unperturbed by the scorn in Harry's voice. "Do you mind if I speak in Punjabi?"

"Go ahead."

Taking the last sip of his tea, he wiped the layer of wrinkled milk, which had formed on the cooling tea, from his straggly gray beard. He scrunched up the paper napkin and threw it on the pavement. Then, as if addressing a large audience, he turned to Harry and said, "My story starts in Lahore on the eve of India's and Pakistan's independence.

"My parents worked for a wealthy Sikh family. My father was their driver, and my mother was ayah to their three children. My mother also bore three children, two boys and a girl. My brother died of fever when he was only two years old.

"The family was very good to us. Mr. Jashpreet Singh insisted that we join his children when they received their lessons from the English governess they had employed. My father was against this, as he was already planning a future for me in Islamic religious studies in the new independent Pakistan. I was sent away to Peshawar to attend such a school. My sister remained with my parents.

"When it became clear that independence was going to be violent, Jashpreet Singh started packing up his family and home and left for Delhi. Because of this timely decision to move his family, they escaped the unbelievable bloodshed—neighbor against neighbor, friend against friend, religious differences a reason to fight until death. My father was hacked to death with a meat cleaver by the Hindu butcher in the market. My mother couldn't find his head. She asked some fellow Muslims to help her with the burial, but the blood shedding was like a strong narcotic; they had all gone mad, killing and raping, mothers hiding their daughters inside the wheat sacks in their pantries.

"Jashpreet Singh had come back to collect a forgotten document, much to his wife's distress, but he was a fearless man. He found my mother sitting under the fig tree with her headless husband. He helped her bury him under that tree in the garden. That was when my mother begged him to take my sister back with him to work for the family and raise his grandchildren. Without a husband she could not offer her daughter anything, not even safety from the bloodthirsty hordes. He hesitated, but the fierceness of my mother's resolve convinced him, and he took the eight-year-old girl back to Delhi.

"Because of Jashpreet Singh's clear thinking and planning, he had managed to transfer most of their funds to India and had acquired residential and business properties. The family settled in well. My sister, Soraya, was well taken care of. She joined the children during lessons but was confined to the servants' quarters with one of the old maid servants begrudgingly taking care of her. Soraya was particularly close to Ranjit, Jashpreet's eldest son. When he turned thirteen, he was sent away to boarding school. Soraya took up her duties in the household; it was the end of her schooling.

"Ranjit was sent to college in England. On his return, his parents had arranged his marriage to the only daughter of one of the Sikh ministers in the Indian government. Priya and Ranjit were married and continued living with his parents while he worked in his father's business. After they had been married four years, Jashpreet was delighted to announce that his daughter-in-law was finally expecting. That same year Jashpreet had organized a marriage between Soraya and the family's young gardener.

"It was a hot and humid night in August when you were born. The old family doctor delivered a son to Priya while the ayah from the neighbor's house delivered a son to Soraya, a healthy baby boy, born a few months early.

"In the early hours of the morning a wail, so loud and with such pain, awoke the pink-cheeked newborn of Soraya's as he lay suckling on her breast, opening his eyes for the first time. Soraya looked into those large, liquid brown eyes and knew that she would do anything for her son's well-being.

"Little did she know that this test was a mere few minutes away from realization. A knock had her young husband jump up and open the door, alarmed. It was Jashpreet and Ranjit. Ranjit's eyes were red and swollen from crying. When he saw the baby boy, he cried again and asked Soraya if he could hold him. She pulled her dupatta over her naked torso and handed the baby to him. Jashpreet sat down on the charpoy and spoke to Soraya in a gentle tone. He asked her if she wanted her son to have a future as a landowner and businessman. 'Of course,' she replied softly.

"Jashpreet told her that Priya and Ranjit had lost their baby boy; his lungs had not developed properly, and after struggling bravely to fill his lungs with air, he had eventually turned blue and died quietly, expelling the last wisp of life in a whisper against his mother's breast. Tears welled in Soraya's eyes as she looked at Ranjit, her heart aching for his loss.

"Then, as if in a dream, she listened and accepted Jashpreet's proposal. She'd give them her baby in exchange for his future. Her husband refused, but when Jashpreet mentioned an amount he had not even imagined, he assented. The following morning after having received his payment, he left, never to be seen again. Soraya would be his wet-nurse and take care of him, but he would carry the name of the prestigious household, Sardar Harmeet Singh.

"This arrangement worked well for a few years. Harry, as everyone began to call him, was a happy and easygoing child. He was the apple of his grandfather's eye, and when Jashpreet died of a heart attack, Harry was inconsolable. Priya adored her son and was extremely jealous of the obvious bond Harry shared with his wet-nurse. When Harry turned three, Priya started begging Ranjit to send Soraya away. Her excuse was that Soraya had threatened to tell the truth about Harry.

"At first he didn't agree, but eventually, to keep his wife from going insane, he sent Soraya south to a convent. Desperately unhappy, she managed to escape and found her way back to Delhi. The chowkidar was told not to let her in, and she howled for days, sleeping on the pavement outside the gate. After a few days, she was dirty and wild with grief and fatigue. The local imam was paid handsomely, and he took her to an institution for the mentally disturbed. Years later, he went to Pakistan and took her with him. By now she had somewhat lost her senses, and she accepted her life as a prisoner in a mental asylum.

"It was pure chance that I was reunited with her. A group of ladies from my mosque in Karachi was trying to create workshops within these few and secret asylums. They believed it would help these unfortunate souls. I accompanied them to Lahore, and browsing through the names of the patients, I recognized Soraya's name on the list. I was shocked, but happy to be reunited with my sister. It took her a while to remember me, but when the drugs they had been giving her had worn off, she became quite lucid and told me her tragic story. I decided it was my duty to track you down, and as Allah would have it, he delivered you to me."

Harry had been in shock, but had accompanied him to the asylum, where he met Soraya. She was so fragile, but when she had held him, her grip was fierce. The intensity of her embrace had frightened him. He had stayed with her for an hour, but she kept repeating the same words in Punjabi: "My son, my son, don't leave me."

When she fell asleep, Harry had asked Yusuf what he could do and if he could move her. To this Yusuf had replied, "It will be very complicated to prove that she is your mother. You might also lose your Indian citizenship and your inheritance. If any of your cousins get to know this, they may try to claim what your father left you. I think if you could find the time to visit her and help me with some business in India, I could possibly arrange something eventually."

"But I could just say she's my wet nurse. No one will think anything of it."

"Have you not noticed the state your mother's in? She's so happy to have found you. Do you think for one moment it's possible to convince her otherwise? She will give your scheme away. Please, trust me. I will find a way. You must be patient." The doctor looked immensely annoyed, and Harry decided to drop it.

A sharp knock on the door shook Harry out of his thoughts, and he watched as a young boy entered, carrying a tray with a steel bowl of watery lentils and a couple of chapattis. He placed the tray on the side of the bed and started spooning the lentils sloppily into Soraya's mouth. Harry got annoyed and told the youth that he would feed his mother. With a shrug, the boy left and closed the door with a bang. Soraya looked up at Harry, her eyes shining as she opened her mouth obediently. Harry fed her carefully, using his cotton handkerchief to wipe her chin.

***

Dr. Yunis Malik closed the door to his office, using his right shoulder to push it into place so that he could lock it. The heavy door was threatening to fall off its hinges. He opened the paper package, pulling impatiently at the red string. Instead of opening it, he tightened it accidentally and had to look for a pair of scissors in his drawer to cut it.

The green silk was creased as he lifted it out. Spreading it on the floor, he pushed a chair to the side, oblivious to the dusty footprints he had walked onto the fabric. He stared fervently at the intricate embroidery. Then, as if recognizing something important, he fell to his knees on the fabric, his index finger outlining a section of the embroidery. He studied it for another ten minutes, muttering something under his breath as if memorizing it. Then, looking satisfied, he stood up and stuffed it into a metal bucket, which was used as a wastepaper bin. He poured some lamp oil over the fabric, and lighting a match, he threw it on top, the silk catching fire instantly. It burned in bright orange flames, which only lasted a few minutes. Dr. Malik opened the window and coughed slightly from the smoke in the room. He poured a glass of water over the remains of the fabric and poked it with a metal pole to make sure no part of it was recognizable.

With a sigh he sat down at his desk and dialed a number on the old-fashioned black phone on his desk. He spoke quietly into the handset, smiling as he replaced it and wondered vaguely if the physicist suspected that he was being used as a courier for the great caliphate.

CHAPTER 20

Having left on her fictional doctor's appointment, Elouise struggled to find parking in the road. A large house on the corner plot was being renovated, and bricks and building materials were piled high in the dirt road. She wished that she had Harry's jeep as she carefully edged the left wheels of the car onto the sloping mound of building sand. The driver's side of the car was uncomfortably close to the road. Worried about the core stability of the vehicle, she gingerly slid out of her seat, gently pushed the car door closed and locked it. With a sigh of relief—her feet now on solid ground—Elouise walked toward the house adjacent to the construction site. The metal gate was covered in thick dust, and she sneezed when the chowkidar opened it for her.

A young servant girl wearing her hair in a very long braid ran toward Elouise and smiled. "Madam Elouise, so long time not coming to see Bua ji. She be very happy."

"You're right, Deepa, it has been too long. Is she

resting?"

"No problem, wake up if sleeping. Very happy to see you." She led the way through the side entrance of the house, which was in dire need of a coat of paint. The passage was lined with old black-and-white photographs of every important occasion and family events. Elouise loved studying the photos taken by Harry's great aunt, recalling the stories Harry had told her about Pushpa's exploits.

She had been quite an adventurer in her day. Her brother, Jashpreet, gave her a Franka Rolfix camera, which he had bought on a business trip to the States, when she was seventeen years old. Pushpa had been enthralled and became a proficient photographer, much to her mother's despair. She had accompanied the men on their hunting trips and attended every polo match, her Rolfix at the ready.

It was during an international polo match between India and Argentina that she had fallen in love with the dapper and unbelievably handsome captain of the Argentinian team. He was besotted with the beautiful and spirited young girl and asked her father for her hand in marriage. It was a scandal the likes of which Lahore had not seen in a long time. They refused, humiliated to the core by this proposition. Sikh girls married into Sikh families and that was that. Jashpreet, who was very close to her, had tried to intervene, but to no avail.

She was sent away to England, to a finishing school of sorts. A seemingly demure, contrite young woman came back home. Her delighted mother started making enquiries about suitable boys, but Pushpa was not interested. In fact, she proved to be an embarrassment, behaving outrageously at every formal meeting between her family and the families of these boys. It was no surprise to anyone when there were no marriage proposals. She became a spinster and insisted on living alone, becoming the family's official chronicler.

Pushpa was sitting on her bed in front of a box filled with old photographs. She was sorting through them when Elouise walked in. Her eyes lit up with joy as Elouise touched her feet and said, "Sastrikal, Bua ji."

"What a nice surprise," she said in her cultured voice. "Come. Sit here next to me. I was just going through some old photographs for Reena. She wants to write a book on the family."

"Oh, that's a great idea. I'm sure it will be a best-seller. Of course, she wouldn't manage without you. I'm sure you know in which cupboards the family's skeletons are kept."

Pushpa chuckled softly. "What would you like to drink?" she asked, smiling impishly and looking at her wristwatch. "It's past twelve, so how about a gin and tonic?"

"No. I don't think it's a good idea, and besides, I'm not sure your doctor will approve," Elouise said with a wink. At eighty-five Pushpa's blood pressure was dangerously high. The old lady sighed, and with delicate, tapering fingertips she meticulously twisted the few straying strands of white hair into the little bun at the nape of her neck.

"Really, what's the point of being old and wise yet not allowed some fun?" She smiled ruefully, called Deepa, and said, "Well then, I guess tea it is."

After a polite exchange over tea and Britania biscuits, Elouise asked, "Bua ji, who was or is Soraya Khan?"

"Goodness, my child, I don't seem to recall that name. Why?"

Elouise frowned, hesitated for a moment, and then made up her mind to tell Harry's great aunt about her findings in Harry's study. With a guarded expression on her face, Pushpa listened intently to everything Elouise told her, especially about the letters and Koran hidden in his desk.

"And, no clue as to the origin of those letters?"

Elouise shook her head. "No. There weren't any envelopes. There was also no address in the letters."

"This is strange. I never expected her to contact him, but I guess with him losing both his parents, she couldn't resist," Pushpa said, looking pale and sad.

"What do you mean?"

Getting up from the bed, stiff and slightly bent, Pushpa went over to a small teak desk in exquisite rosewood inlay. She opened the top drawer, reached in behind it, and pushed a small button on the inside of the desk. A small side drawer clicked open very slightly. It was perfectly concealed in the intricate floral inlay. She pulled on the little drawer. With shaky hands she removed a small neat pile of letters tied with a green ribbon. Shutting the drawer, she went over to the armchair and sat down. Slightly breathless, she rested for a few moments, her eyes on the letters in her lap.

"Elouise, I'm going to tell you a story I have kept secret for thirty-eight years. I promised my brother, Jashpreet, but circumstances have changed and so I will break this promise. What you choose to do with what I tell you is your business." Pushpa shook her head slowly. "I feel quite relieved to be able to share this very heavy burden with you. You are young and strong, as I once was."

Elouise moved closer to her, perching on the edge of the bed. She jumped slightly when Pushpa called out quite loudly to Deepa to bring her a gin and tonic. "I think you should have one, too, my dear," she said, smiling at Elouise, who felt she couldn't—did not want to—decline this time around.

***

Carla was undecided about phoning Andrew and thought it best to wait for Elouise's return. When Harry returned home from the office, she heard him in the courtyard but decided to stay in her room. An hour later, Kishan served lunch in her bedroom. When he returned to take her tray, he was visibly disappointed at seeing how little she had eaten. "Food not good, Madam?" he asked.

"Oh no, of course not. It was wonderful as usual, but I'm not hungry today. Must be the heat," she apologized, a little embarrassed.

Carla heard Harry leaving again, and as she walked through to the kitchen to look for Kishan, Elouise arrived home. Flushed and highly agitated, Elouise greeted Carla, who barely had time to say anything as Elouise went on:

"We're leaving for Kashmir tomorrow morning. There's a flight at 9:20 on Jet Airways. I've booked our tickets."

In perplexed silence, Carla followed her to her room, but Elouise was in a hurry to leave again to pick up the girls from school. "Why Kashmir?" Carla asked as Elouise emerged from the bathroom.

"I'm sorry, I can't explain now. The girls have already called twice. I have to pick them up, and then I have to quickly pop in on one of my friends to ask if she'd mind looking after the girls for a day or two."

Carla followed her out to the car and said, "Is it official, our trip to Kashmir, or—"

"No, thank God you asked. You must tell Andrew and George if they call that I'm taking you to a spa in Bangalore. If they want to know which one, just tell them you haven't a clue. OK?"

"Of course," Carla nodded, a frown creasing her brow as she went to her bedroom, where she decided to call Andrew.

He answered on the first ring. "I'm so glad you called. I was about to call you."

"Oh." *Well, why didn't you?* she thought, slightly irritated.

"Would you like to have dinner with me tonight?" he asked casually.

227

"I'm afraid I can't. Elouise is taking me to a spa in Bangalore tomorrow. We have to be at the airport early, by seven tomorrow morning."

"I see. For how long will you go?" He sounded quite miffed, Carla thought.

"I'm not sure, two days at the most."

"I know this may sound a bit patronizing, Carla, but we really need to get out of here. Fortunately, I have been given a week's leave, but I have to get back to Kabul. We could go back to London together—spend a few days together. Reconnect, you know."

Carla didn't reply immediately—*What does he mean, "reconnect"?*

Andrew went on, hesitant now. "I really want to work things out. Please give me a chance."

"Let's talk when I'm back, OK?"

He sighed. "OK, I'll wait. Enjoy Bangalore."

She was quite uneasy when she said good-bye, wondering whether she shouldn't just go back to London with Andrew. But she instantly put her shoulders back in self-reproof, ashamed at her lack of courage. She pulled her red overnight bag from the top of the wardrobe in the dressing room and started packing.

Carla was awake at six thirty when the punctual Kishan brought her a steaming cup of tea. As it was already quite hot in her room, she sat on the cool veranda to drink it.

Elouise had come home quite late the previous evening. After dropping the girls, she had gone out for supper with some of the moms on the fundraising committee. On her return she was exhausted and asked Carla to be patient; she would explain what it was all about. Carla had waited up for her, quite desperate to find out what was going on.

But on seeing Elouise's resolve, she realized that she had to bide her time and be patient.

Dressed in khaki cotton pants and a white linen shirt, Carla was ready at precisely seven o'clock. She got into the car as the driver put her small suitcase into the trunk. Elouise was five minutes late, wearing jeans and a short cream kurti. She caught her hair in an untidy bun as she got into the car next to Carla. "Good, we should be on time," she said with a relieved smile. "Did you eat something?"

"No, it's too early for me. I'll wait till we get to our mysterious destination in Kashmir," Carla said with a hint of sarcasm.

Elouise laughed. "I knew you were going to bitch about this information block-out. I promise you I'll tell you everything as soon as we find a certain person in Kashmir."

"Do we know exactly where this person is, or do we still have to search for him?"

"I have the exact address, don't worry—and it's a woman, by the way."

Carla widened her eyes—a woman? Somehow, this was far more intriguing. "Oh. Young or old?"

Slapping her playfully on her thigh, Elouise said, "Wait and see."

There wasn't much traffic, and within half an hour they were at the airport. After checking in at the Jet Airways counter, they went to the lounge, where they drank cappuccinos and ate a couple of finger sandwiches. Carla was recounting her conversation with Andrew when Harry called Elouise. She looked tense, becoming more flushed in the effort to converse normally, and as she said goodbye, her hazel eyes filled with fear and sadness.

This is all my fault, Carla thought, wishing she hadn't come to Delhi. "Is everything OK?" she asked Elouise.

"Yes, Harry just called to tell me that he had reached his destination safely, and he'd be at the conference all day."

"Elouise, I'm so sorry for dragging you into this mess."

"It's not your fault. I have to get to the bottom of this. I don't think Harry is involved in anything sinister, but there's definitely something strange going on." She smiled at Carla and continued, "Have you heard from George?"

"No, I haven't. But he's just respecting my wishes, so I shouldn't feel so down, right?"

"You really fell hard, didn't you?" Elouise said, smiling.

"Don't embarrass me. I think that's our flight they're calling."

"You're right. Let's hurry; we still have to clear security."

Carla stared down in fascination at the scenery below: the city seemed quite dwarfed by the expanse of the famous Dal Lake and surrounding verdant hills. In the distance the snowcapped peaks of the Himalayas rose majestically through the dense white clouds—like chess pieces, Carla thought, God stalling for checkmate.

The airplane touched down at 10:35 in Srinagar, ten minutes later than the scheduled time.

As they waited at the taxi stand, Carla noticed a number of military personnel as well as policemen. It was only when she scanned the crowd that she realized that she and Elouise were very obvious—the only Westerners. Carla knew from an assignment for CNN that tourism had dropped to practically nil after the spate of kidnappings by Islamic militants fighting for independence from India in Muslim-dominated Kashmir.

The cooler climate, at least fifteen degrees cooler than Delhi, was welcome.

"Kashmir used to be the preferred summer destination for most Indians, but since the terrorist attacks, the tourist industry is struggling to survive," Elouise explained to

Carla.

The Innova taxi drove them through the city along the lake, which had houseboats of all sizes moored to the banks. "I read somewhere that one can rent them," Carla said.

"Harry told me that his paternal family owned a houseboat they used only in the summer. It was really the British who introduced this houseboat tradition to the Indians. They were not allowed to own land so they built houseboats."

Cruising down the long driveway leading up to the Grand Palace hotel, the taxi driver pointed to the Zabarwan Hills on the one side and the apple orchards on the other. The hotel architecture was stylishly European. Noticing Carla's interest in the building, he said, "This was famous palace of Maharajah Hari Singh. His uncle Pratap Singh build it.'"

"I see. When was it converted into an hotel?" Carla asked.

"I think in 1950s, sorry, not know," the driver said, laughing self-consciously.

After checking into their rooms overlooking the manicured garden, the Dal Lake in the distance, they met back in the lobby.

"I'm afraid we can only see her this afternoon. She asked us to come at three," Elouise said, disappointed.

"That's OK. I'd love to explore a little. What do you say?" Carla asked.

The driver who had brought them from the airport was still in his car, and when he saw the two women, he rushed to them, offering his services. Elouise negotiated an all-day rate, to which he agreed with a beaming smile. He suggested taking them to the city center on Residency Road. It was a broad, busy road, shops and restaurants lining its sides. Elouise asked him to drop them off at one of the many handicraft shops. Carved walnut furniture and smaller items like trays and jewelry boxes interested Carla. She decided to buy a jewelry box with a concealed compartment.

"I wonder what you're planning on hiding in there," Elouise said while she picked up some papier-mâché boxes, hunting scenes beautifully painted on them. "I think my girls would love these. They can store treasures in them—what do you think?"

"They're lovely."

The charming shop assistant insisted on showing them their selection of hand-embroidered cashmere shawls. Seated comfortably on a long bench, the young man unfolded dozens of them. They were far more reasonably priced than the ones Carla had bought in Delhi. She was unable to resist a cream-colored pure pashmina, embroidered in a delicate beige and duck-egg blue floral pattern. Elouise admired a taupe-colored one embroidered in burnt orange. Carla insisted on buying Elouise the shawl and, after a brief battle of words, presented her friend with the gift.

Satisfied with their purchases, they didn't go into any more shops but strolled casually down the road. At one o'clock, their driver picked them up and suggested they lunch at Ahdoo's. According to him, it was the most famous eatery in all of Kashmir. The restaurant was part of a hotel and unassuming in its typical Kashmiri décor of silk carpets and walnut paneling. The waiter spoke perfect English and suggested they try the Wazwan buffet. They agreed readily, their appetite now stimulated by the aromas emanating from the kitchen.

Carla's mouth opened in surprise when the waiter carried a brass tray almost the same size as the table filled with at least a dozen different dishes. Another waiter placed a basket of flat breads, like naan, on the table.

"This looks great, tuck in," Elouise said, breaking off a piece of bread and dipping it into a dish that looked like chicken curry.

Carla tried the lamb on the bone and said, "This is so good." Each dish contained some form of meat or chicken, even the vegetable dishes. "Somehow I don't think a vegetarian would like it here," Carla laughed.

They ended their enormous lunch with Qahwah, Kashmiri saffron tea. Elouise leaned back on her chair and said, "I am so full; I need to sleep."

"No chance of that, it's two thirty. Is our mysterious lady not expecting us by three?"

Elouise looked at her wristwatch and said, "Gosh, you're right; we'd better leave."

They paid what seemed to Carla like a ridiculously low amount for all the food consumed and found their driver. As Carla was about to get into the car, she caught sight of a man staring intently at her. He looked away quickly, feigning absorption in a street sign. There was something oddly familiar about him, and as she sat down she realized that he had been on their flight from Delhi. He had not wanted to change seats with a pregnant woman who needed an aisle seat. The hostess had asked another man a few rows back, who graciously obliged. Frowning, she decided that it was just coincidence and better not to alarm Elouise.

Elouise gave the driver the address, and as they drove down Residency Lane, Carla noticed that while most women wore a head covering there were few burqa-clad women about. Once they were out of the city, they drove along the lake until they reached a beautiful park called Nishaad Garden. Quaint, European, period-style houses on large grounds surrounded it. The air was crisp and smelled clean.

They turned into a cul-de-sac and stopped in front one of the houses. Spectacular rosebushes crowded the relatively small front garden. Fruit trees, similarly crowding the back garden, branched high above the pitched roof of the bungalow. Elouise instructed the driver to wait, as she had no idea how long they'd be. He seemed quite happy and jumped out of the car to open the door for her.

They entered the property through a small wooden gate and walked down a stone path to steps at the veranda of the house. Elouise was about to knock when a slightly built woman in her late sixties or early seventies opened the wooden door. Her hair was steel gray and knotted in a bun at the back of her head. She wore a dove-gray salwar kameez suit, with the sheer embroidered dupatta covering her head.

Elouise knelt down to touch her feet, but she pulled her up by the shoulders and said, "Welcome, child, please come in."

She turned, and they followed her into a living room furnished with a large silk carpet and a carved settee and chairs in walnut. The upholstery was faded, but the overall ambience was warm and inviting. Elouise introduced Carla to her without mentioning the woman's name. Carla looked at her friend with an annoyed expression, but Elouise just ignored it.

The woman called a young servant girl and ordered something in Urdu. She folded her hands in her lap and smiled sweetly. Something in her expression reminded Carla of someone. A polite exchange ensued, Elouise congratulating her on her excellent command of English.

"Thank you, I was very fortunate as a child. An English governess and a retired British army officer and his wife were my neighbors for many years."

The woman, noticing that Carla was studying a painting and squinting to read the artist's name, asked, "Do you like painting?"

"Yes, I do. I'm not good at judging art, but this is really beautiful. Who painted it?" Carla asked as she stood up and inspected it closer.

"Actually I did," the woman replied bashfully.

"Wow, I'm impressed," Carla said as she read the name in the corner: *Soraya 1979.*

CHAPTER 21

Andrew stared hard at the boiled egg and decapitated it rather aggressively with his butter knife, drawing the curiosity of the Scandinavian tourists at another table in Claridges coffee shop. Quite oblivious to their interest, he dunked his toast into the soft egg and chewed without much appetite. His conversation with Carla the previous evening had unsettled him. That he might lose her was a thought that filled him with cold dread. "I'm such a fool," he muttered, not noticing the subtle, knowing glances at the neighboring table.

"Good morning, did you sleep OK?" Leila asked as she sat down at the table. She was wearing running shorts and tennis shoes.

"Good morning, and no, I didn't. Did you go running?" Andrew asked her.

"I tried to, but it's way too hot. I might go to the health club and use the treadmill after breakfast." She ordered coffee and said, "Have you heard from Carla?"

"I spoke to her last night. Elouise has taken her to a spa in Bangalore for a few days."

"That's strange."

"Why?"

"With all this stuff going on, I can't imagine her doing that."

"I don't know; it's kind of typical of her, running away from problems."

"You know her best." Leila drank the coffee quickly and said, "Anyway, I'm meeting someone at the Oberoi hotel for lunch today. He's an old family friend who moved here a few years ago. You're more than welcome to join us."

"I was thinking of finishing that piece I was writing on Pakistan's duplicity on the war on terror for *Time* magazine."

"See how you go. I'm leaving at one; let me know, OK?" She pecked him on his cheek and walked away. Andrew, along with most of the men in the restaurant, admired her toned figure as she exited.

Andrew made good progress with his article and decided to join Leila after all. He met her in the lobby, and they took a taxi to the Oberoi hotel, which was only a ten-minute drive. During the drive, Leila received a phone call from her friend saying that something had come up, and he wouldn't be able to make lunch. A little peeved, Leila asked Andrew if he still wanted to have lunch there, to which he agreed readily.

After clearing hotel security, Leila showed Andrew the bookstore in the lobby. They were well-known for large coffee-table books. Andrew was smiling mischievously, paging through a copy of *The Revised Karma Sutra*, when Leila told him to put it down and handed him a book by William

Dalrymple called *The City of Djinns*. "This is a great book about Delhi; try it."

Andrew bought it, and they walked toward the restaurant at the end of the lobby. Comfortable seating stretched along the right hand side of the lobby, overlooking the sparkling pool. Halfway along the couches, a man sitting alone, paging through a hotel magazine, looked up.

Leila smiled awkwardly and said, "George, what a nice surprise."

"What are you doing here, holiday or business?" George asked genially.

"A bit of both, I guess. Let me introduce you." She turned toward Andrew, who leaned forward to shake George's hand.

"Andrew Riseborough," Andrew said, introducing himself, horrified at his trembling hand.

George smiled and shook Andrew's hand firmly. "George Alexander, nice to meet you. So you two know each other?" he asked with a studied expression.

"Actually, we're colleagues. Andrew is a reporter with the BBC." Leila appeared calm, but Andrew was having trouble trying to remain composed.

"Are you here for lunch?" George asked.

"Yes, at Threesixty," Leila replied.

"That's excellent—you don't mind if I join you, do you?" He directed the question to Andrew while putting his arm around Leila in a protective gesture.

Andrew was tense and irritated by George's intrusion. He asked Leila if that was OK with her, to which she replied, "Sure, if you don't mind."

Defeated, Andrew said, "Of course not. The more the merrier."

George and Leila led the way with George laughing affably at something she said. A few paces behind them, Andrew was struggling with mixed emotions. He'd never thought of himself as the jealous type, but his bowels were in a knot. When they got to the door of the restaurant, Andrew leaned forward to ask the elegant hostess for a table, but she had already turned her doe-like eyes on George to ask him if she could help. George requested a table overlooking the garden.

From this point on, Andrew's dislike for the suave American intensified. Bristling, he adopted a defensive mental stance. When George asked the waiter for the wine list, Andrew asked for one, too. Leila watched in trepidation as the sparring reached an untenable psychological stalemate. Andrew would not back down, insisting upon a French Margeaux. All the while aware of the consternation in Leila's eyes and that the situation was now clearly getting out of hand, George relented.

She shot him a look of gratitude and then launched a discussion on Delhi. Didn't they think that the weather was unseasonably hot? George listened, bemused but not offering any comment. Andrew drummed his fingers on the edge of the table. When the waiter brought their lunch to the table, they ate engrossed in a silent world of private speculation.

The chicken, prepared Japanese-style, was delicious. Andrew thought it tasted like cardboard. George, on the other hand, was enjoying his rogan josh, in his hands like the locals. Leila opted for sushi, even though George warned her about eating raw fish in the Indian summer. "I'll be fine. I have an excellent constitution," she said with stoic resolve.

Arching his eyebrow, George responded, "Then who am I to stop you?"

As they ordered coffees, George's phone rang. On studying the screen for a moment, he decided to answer it, mouthing an apology to them.

"Yes, Kumar." George listened intently and then, frowning deeply: "Are you sure? Did you wait for the next flight?"

He listened again and said, "Stay put and check out the spas; you might have missed them. I'll check on this side." Placing the phone on the table, George turned to Andrew. In a grave tone he asked, "Andrew, do you know where Carla is?"

His ears flushing red, Andrew started spluttering in indignation. Calmly, George held up his hand and said, "Please, now is not the time. What did she tell you?"

Swallowing hard, Adam's apple pronounced, Andrew said with deliberation, "Elouise was going to take her to Bangalore for a few days to some or other spa. That's all she said."

"Well, they didn't arrive in Bangalore. My chap was at the airport," George said.

"Are you having her followed?" Andrew asked him, his cheeks now flushed with anger.

"Yes. It's for her own protection, I promise you."

"How did you know she went to Bangalore? Did she tell you?" Leila asked George.

"No, my guy in Delhi asked her driver after he dropped them off at the airport. Elouise had told him that they were leaving for Bangalore on the 9:45 a.m. flight on Jet Airways. Bangalore is famous for its health spas, so I assumed that that was where they were going." George called for the bill, and before Andrew had a chance to take out his wallet, George had his AmEx ready, giving it to the waiter and telling him to add a twenty percent tip.

The CIA are such generous employers, Andrew thought with sarcasm.

George signed and, getting up, said, "Let's go to my place. We can try to find her together. Are you guys OK with that?"

"Of course," Leila replied, getting up. "Andrew?"

He looked up sullenly and said, "I'm coming."

George sat in the front of the jeep next to his driver. He

made a couple of calls, but Andrew didn't understand the language he spoke in. Leila told him it was Pashtun and Hindi. When they arrived at George's house, Sunil showed them to the study and asked if they would like tea. They declined. George then gestured to the leather armchairs in front of his desk. Taking his seat behind it he said, "Thanks for coming. I'm really sorry about all this." After a moment he stated the obvious: "I suppose I owe you an explanation."

Andrew pursed his lips and said, "We know about Carla's kidnapping, as well as your and the CIA's involvement."

If George was surprised, he didn't show it; he looked at Leila and asked, "I suppose he got this from you?"

Leila looked down at her clasped hands in her lap. She sat perfectly still. Then with an apologetic smile, she looked up and said, "I had no choice, really. I owed it to them."

"But this was top secret; only a few agents had clearance to this."

"I think Langley should keep an eye on your agent in Pakistan. He's drinking more than he should."

George said with a look of incredulity, "He told you?"

Looking bashful, Leila replied, "Not in so many words. He let something slip about Andrew's wife and then, as you know, the CIA is responsible for my specialized training in extracting information."

With a knowing smile, George said in a serious tone, "That's pretty disconcerting information you've given me. I'll have to ask you to put in a report."

"OK, but please cover my butt. I'm not exactly Miss Popular with the director since that little fiasco in Syria last year."

George smiled and said, "Don't worry, it will blow over."

Feeling left out Andrew turned, somewhat petulantly, to George and said, "Please explain. Exactly what's going on?" To this Leila nodded her head in agreement.

"Sure, but what do you guys know?" George asked.

"I saw her file," Leila said. "You recruited her to spy on Harry Singh. The details of her kidnapping and rescue were there, as well as your successful honey trap." She looked at Andrew quickly. He was pale and felt nauseous. Leila continued, "The exact reason for all this was not forthcoming, but I gathered it's something pretty important."

"Well, that's a relief. You didn't find out too much," George said.

"But you are going to fill in the blanks, aren't you, George," Leila stated rather than asked.

"I guess we're in this mess together; we might as well try to make the most of it. Andrew needs to be cleared." Addressing Andrew, he asked, "Please tell me you have not been involved in any subversive activities during your youth."

"Of course not, why?"

"If Langley is to give you clearance, we need it fast."

George's mobile phone rang. He picked it up and said something in Hindi, listened intently, and then in English said, "You're quite sure, Srinagar? OK, thanks for that." He then switched off the cell phone and said, "Kashmir. They were on a Jet Airways flight this morning for Srinagar. The flight left twenty minutes earlier than the flight for Bangalore."

"Why Kashmir?" Andrew asked, perturbed.

George looked for a number on his phone and said, "I don't know, but I'm certainly going to find out. In the meantime, please sit tight and let me know if you hear anything from Carla. As soon as I have clearance for you from Langley, I'll fill you in. My driver will drop you back at your hotel."

Leila started to protest, but George gave her a firm, meaningful look. "OK," she said, "but please keep me informed. I could be of much-needed help."

George smiled and called Sunil to show his visitors out.

CHAPTER 22

Carla tried to alert Elouise to the name on the painting, but she went on chatting about her daughters. *Of course! Elouise knows...* Carla realized, frowning. *But how?*

The younger woman servant came into the room carrying a tray with a porcelain teapot and matching cups and saucers, while an older woman carried a plate of cookies. The older woman asked Soraya something in Urdu. Smiling kindly at her, she said in English, "It's quite all right, Mona, I'll pour."

The tray and plate of biscuits were put down on the square walnut coffee table. Soraya leaned forward and stirred the tea in the pot. "Mona and her daughter have been with me since I first came to live here more than thirty-five years ago. Her husband's family wanted to kill her baby daughter, as they were a poor family who couldn't afford to keep a girl. Naturally, she wouldn't hear of it. She bravely managed to escape, saving her baby. I was fortunate to offer her safe concealment. She has, in return, been loyal in service and companionship."

"I believe infanticide is still happening in parts of India today," Carla ventured as she was handed her tea.

"A terrible statistic, I'm afraid," Elouise commented.

"Elouise, I didn't quite catch the name of our hostess earlier," Carla said as she finished drinking her tea.

"Oh, I'm sorry, I didn't introduce myself properly to you. I just presumed Elouise would have told you," their hostess apologized, "My name is Soraya Khan."

Carla looked knowingly at Elouise while Elouise explained hastily to Soraya, "I wanted to meet you first before explaining the whole situation to Carla, and to be honest, I was hoping to hear the story from you."

"Oh, I see. Of course I would love to tell you. I have not ever told this to anyone." Soraya scrutinized Elouise's face and then, as she closed her eyes, shifted into a more comfortable position in the armchair.

"My parents both worked for a wealthy and powerful family in Lahore. They had three children, two boys and a girl. We were also three children, but my brother died when he was just a toddler. Mr. Jashpreet was kind to us, and I was only four when he allowed my brother and I to sit in on their children's classes taken by a young English governess. Ranjit, the eldest, was very kind to me. In fact, my older brother didn't like this very much. I was devastated when Mr. Jashpreet decided to take his family to India. I cried for days and begged my mother and father to ask them to take us with them, but we should have known that they would never agree.'

Soraya cleared her throat and, lowering her tone, continued, "Oh, the unspeakable violence; it was horrible. The rioters killed my father, and my mother was desperate. And then, as if God willed it, Mr. Jashpreet came back. My mother pleaded with him to take me back with him. She knew that she could offer me no future in the newly independent Pakistan. My brother was studying in a Madrassa in Peshawar. Mr. Jashpreet was kind and relented. He took me with him, and I joined his household in Delhi.

"One of the old maidservants took care of me. But she didn't like me much. She begrudged the time I spent with the children. When Ranjit was sent to boarding school, the English governess left, and his brother and sister were both sent to school. A good Indian education was needed now that India had finally gained its independence from Britain after more than two hundred years. I started working in the house, but missed Ranjit terribly. Years later, after his studies abroad, he came back. He was so handsome and worldly. Within days, his parents announced his engagement to the daughter of a powerful family. I cried for days. You see, I was madly in love him and had been all my life.

"His wife, Priya, was nice, but I think she resented me—always finding fault with my work. Ranjit defended me, but of course, this made matters worse. It was during Diwali that the unthinkable happened. Ranjit had organized a party with fireworks. He had a peg or two too much. Priya refused to attend, as they'd had a row over something or other. He asked me to hold one of the devices while trying to light it. It exploded in my hand and burned it quite badly. Ranjit was deeply remorseful and offered to drive me himself to the hospital. He stayed at my side while the doctor bandaged my hand.

"When he took me home, the festivities had come to an end. He saw me to my tiny little room in the back of the servant quarters. It was very quiet. He laid me down on the charpoy and covered me with his woolen shawl. As he walked to the door, I called him back and thanked him. It must have been the longing in my voice or eyes that made him turn around and kiss me with such passion and yearning that I thought I would die of love. The few hours we spent together felt like heaven. He left quietly, and in the morning I found his note scribbled on my small notebook. He apologized for what he had done and asked my forgiveness. It wouldn't happen again, he wrote. I was desolate but knew there was nothing I could do about it. I returned to work and tried my best to avoid him.

"A few weeks later I discovered I was with child. I told Ranjit, who in turn told his father. They asked me to keep it quiet, and Jashpreet arranged my marriage to the young gardener. He was a sweet and lovely boy, unaware of the deception. Priya fell pregnant that same month, and I was miserable. However, the thought that I was carrying my love child with Ranjit made it bearable. My son was born in August. He was most beautiful. Ranjit and his father came to my room while I was nursing my newborn, suckling with such strength and greed. I was so happy to see Ranjit, and when he held our baby in his arms, I thought my heart would break with love and pride. Jashpreet then told me that Priya's little baby boy had died. The doctor only managed to save her life by performing a hysterectomy on her. She would never be able to bear children again. He and Ranjit then made me a proposition I couldn't refuse. My son would have the name and status of a powerful family. He'd marry well and have a future. This was something I could never have given him growing up in the small, cramped servants' quarters.

"I was employed as his wet nurse, and so I was able to watch him grow. He was such a happy child, loved to distraction by his family. My husband ran away with the money paid for his silence. We had to pretend it was my son who had died. Ranjit's sister helped with the arrangements.

"When Harry was four, I realized that Priya resented my being there. I tried to stay away from Harry, but he was always crying for me. Priya, who was suffering from depression, told me one day that she couldn't live like that, knowing her son loved me more. She was going to expose Harry as Ranjit's illegitimate son. Of course I couldn't let her. My dreams and aspirations for my son were my reasons for living. I told Ranjit and his father that I would go away. They tried to dissuade me, but we all knew that it was for the best.

"A month later we drove here to Srinagar, where they bought me this beautiful house. They set me up with a monthly income and servants. The neighbors were told that I was a widow who had lost her family during independence. I was happy here and stayed in contact with Pushpa, Ranjit's sister. She told me everything. I recorded every little detail of his life."

Soraya stood up and fetched a large leather box from the table next to the fireplace. She opened it and showed the wedding photos of Elouise and Harry. The box was filled with letters and photographs of Harry from a very young age to some as recent as those taken at Chanda's birthday party. Carla sat still, mesmerized by the story.

"So you have never tried to contact Harry after all these years?" Carla asked.

"No, of course not. I've been tempted but have always believed that if God wanted it, it would happen," Soraya answered simply.

"Then how can we explain those letters?" Elouise asked, frowning.

"What letters?" Soraya asked.

Elouise explained it to Soraya, who listened quietly, and when she mentioned the Koran, Soraya said, "That sounds like mine. My father gave it to me. I can still remember him writing my name in it. It went missing some years back. I was playing cards at the club. I had given my maid and her daughter the afternoon off to shop for a friend's wedding. When I returned, the front door was slightly ajar. I thought that the maids had returned, but they were not yet home. There was no obvious sign of an intruder, except that this box had been placed back to front on the table. You see, I am very particular about such things. In the evening, when I usually read my Koran verses, I discovered it was missing from my bedside table. I then looked through the house, but this was the only missing item. We all came to the conclusion that it was some young Hindu boys trying to cause trouble."

"What year was this?" Elouise asked.

"I'm not sure, could be three years ago."

"Two thousand seven—that's the year Harry started getting those letters," Carla said.

Soraya's eyes were dark with concern. "I don't understand. I've never told anyone my secret." She closed her eyes and pulled the end of her dupatta over her head as if to block out the world, lost in reminiscence. "My Pataka—I used to call him that. He was as bright and lively as fireworks. There were, I think I told you, fireworks the night he was conceived." She smiled melancholically. "Pushpa told me his grandfather continued calling him that after I had left."

The younger woman came in with a fresh pot of tea. When she saw the leather box, she suddenly averted her eyes. Carla, who was watching her, noticed this and whispered to Elouise, "Maybe this girl read the letters in the box."

Elouise whispered back, "But they are written in English."

When she left the room, Elouise asked Soraya, "Did your maid's daughter get some schooling?"

"Oh yes," Soraya said proudly, "from me. I taught her to speak and write English. Sometimes she reads the English newspaper to me."

Carla and Elouise exchanged a knowing look. Carla nodded and Elouise leaned forward; speaking softly she addressed Soraya. "Is it possible that she read your letters from Aunty Pushpa and maybe passed that information on to someone?"

The shocked Soraya blanched. "I suppose it's possible, but why?"

"Do you think you can ask her?" Elouise said gently.

"Yes. Yes, I can and I will." Soraya rang a little brass bell, which summoned the young woman. Her mother followed closely. Soraya spoke to them in a stern tone. They were shaking their heads, vehemently denying the obvious accusations. Mona kept quiet and said something to her daughter in a quiet but stern tone. The daughter started crying and fell at Soraya's feet, clutching them and kissing them fervently. Soraya sat very still. Her eyes were dark. Mona fell to her knees and touched Soraya's feet, crying loudly, on the brink of hysteria. Expressionless, but with an uncharacteristic coldness in her voice, Soraya said something. Mona stood up and dragged her daughter away.

Carla watched Elouise, and after a few uncomfortable minutes Elouise finally broke the silence. "Soraya, what happened?"

Soraya sighed and said, "I feel so betrayed. It was Mona's daughter who betrayed my trust. She read the letters and then disclosed the contents to a young, handsome man at the mosque she was trying to impress. He was intrigued and asked her to find out as much as possible. To please him she did and told him everything. A week later he had disappeared." She started crying. Elouise stood up and sat next to her, holding her awkwardly in her arms. "Please, my child, find out who this pretender is."

"I will, and when it's all over, I'll bring Harry to meet you. If that's all right with you?"

Soraya smiled and said, "You know it will be."

"What are you going to do about Mona and her daughter?" Carla asked, worried.

"I'll let them stew for a while, but I won't dismiss them. I need them more than they need me."

Elouise smiled and said, "It's getting late. I'm sure you want to get ready for your dinner."

"Won't you stay?" Soraya asked graciously.

Elouise looked at Carla, who shook her head and said, "Thanks, Mrs. Khan, but we need to get back to the hotel. We had a very early flight this morning, and I'm so tired, but I promise to stay in touch."

"I understand. All this must be quite overwhelming. You take your time, and if and when you think the time is right for you to tell my Pataka everything, I'll be ready." Soraya got up a little stiffly and showed them to the front door. Mona had disappeared. Carla wondered how much they could now be trusted, now that they had been exposed.

The sun cast a sliver of pale salmon across the lake in the distance. A crisp breeze rustled through the leaves of the large chinar tree in the garden. The scent of apples and pine needles permeated the late afternoon air.

"It's lovely up here. I think I would love to come back here someday soon and spend a month," Carla said as they walked to the car. Their driver had reclined the front seat to its maximum and was fast asleep. Bollywood music was blaring loudly from the car radio, and when Elouise nudged him he jumped up with wild-eyed fright. When he had composed himself they drove off.

Carla put her head back against the neck rest and said, "I'm exhausted. That was intense."

Elouise laughed softly and said, "I'm sorry I didn't tell you anything, but I wanted to be sure. This discovery certainly doesn't explain what Harry is up to, but one thing is for sure, someone is pulling the wool over his eyes. I'm determined to get to the bottom of this."

" I agree. Any ideas?"

Sighing with her shoulders hunched, Elouise said, "No, not really, but I think the key to all of this is in his computer files. We need to crack that password."

"I agree. Let's work on it tonight, and if all fails I have a friend in Cape Town who is a bit of a hacker—we could e-mail it to him," Carla said.

Elouise yawned and closed her eyes. "I need a power nap."

Carla smiled and looked out at the changing scenery with interest. The driver wanted to know what they were planning for dinner, but Carla told him they'd be dining in.

She turned her head slowly while watching some young boys playing cricket at the side of the road. The batsman hit a terrific shot. The ball arched high in the air and then came straight down in someone's garden, and a motorcyclist behind the car ducked instinctively at the ball's trajectory through the air. He was not wearing a helmet and must have been afraid of being hit. As he sat up, Carla recognized him. It was the same man she had first seen on the plane and then on Regency Street. She quickly turned to face the front and then sat very still. *This can't be a coincidence.* Deciding not to alarm Elouise, she casually leaned her head against the window so that she could watch the cyclist in the side rearview mirror. He was weaving from side to side. He seemed determined to stick close to their vehicle, risking a collision with a truck as he hurried through a red traffic light. *Could he be one of George's?* Carla wondered, but dismissed the notion, as she believed that a trained CIA surveillance team would avoid being visible—making their presence so obvious.

When they reached the hotel driveway, the motorcyclist passed them and sped off toward the lake. Carla frowned, and when Elouise woke up she told her all about it. Elouise did not seem worried and said, "If he was really following us, he would've followed us right here to the entrance, don't you think?"

Carla decided to let it go. Elouise asked the driver to

pick them up the following day. He smiled merrily as he accepted her generous tip and said he'd be there at exactly eleven a.m. They went up to their bedrooms and agreed to meet in half an hour in Carla's room.

When Carla reached her room, she unlocked her suitcase and removed the laptop, plugging in the charger before she took a shower. In the hotel bathrobe, she opened the door for Elouise thirty minutes later. Elouise had changed into fresh clothes, but she looked tired.

"Hi, sorry I'm not dressed yet. I won't be long. Come in," Carla said.

Elouise sat on the bed and switched on the television while Carla changed into a charcoal linen dress. "One of Sanjay's copies?" Elouise asked, smiling.

"Yes, I'm so glad I had them made. Are you ready for dinner?"

"I am. Let's go."

The waiter suggested they try a Wazwan dinner, but after explaining that they had been to Adhoo's for lunch, he suggested the fresh rainbow trout caught in the cold mountain streams of Kashmir. The fish was delicate and full of flavor. Elouise hadn't heard anything from Harry, and after dinner they went to Carla's room, where Elouise tried to call him. His phone was switched off. Carla placed her laptop on the bed and accessed Harry's hard drive. She clicked on the "Soraya" file and sat staring at the blank password space.

"Elouise, any new ideas?"

"Not really. Let's try 'mother'—no. How about 'biological mother'?"

"What about that name they called him, Packet or something?" Carla asked.

Elouise laughed. "Pataka, it means 'fireworks' in Hindi."

"Yes, try that."

Elouise typed it in and shrieked when it was accepted:

"We're in!"

Carla sat down next to her as they watched the files opening. It looked like data taken from the BABA institute in Mumbai. "How's your physics?" Elouise asked Carla.

"Probably as good as yours, which means that I don't have a clue."

They continued scrolling down the page and found a file with names and places written in some kind of code. "What the hell...?" Elouise said as she looked at a file containing a scanned copy of her notes on the fashion show fundraiser she was working on at the American Embassy School compound. There were also notes on the security procedures, as well as a sketched plan of all entrances and the general layout of the theater where the event was to be held.

Carla was shocked. Looking at Elouise's fixed expression, she knew that her friend had figured it out. "You were planning to have a special guest of honor, weren't you?"

Elouise nodded and said in a shocked tone, "Surely he's not involved in this. There must be a perfectly acceptable explanation—"

"But what? Elouise, why did he keep it so secret? I'm afraid I think he's involved, willingly or not. We have to stop him." Carla reached for her mobile phone.

"Who are you going to call?" Elouise asked in a quivering voice.

"George. Do have any other suggestions?"

"I think we shouldn't call; maybe your phone is bugged or something. Let's get back tomorrow as scheduled and confront him in person. We could then show him that we got into the files."

Carla bit her bottom lip. "Are you sure?"

Elouise stood up and took Carla's phone from her. "Trust me, it's best. I'll wake you for breakfast at about eight, OK?" She kissed Carla on the cheek and left.

Carla lay down on her bed, staring at the ceiling, regretting the fact that she had agreed not to call George. The whole thing was rather unnerving. It was almost certain that Harry was involved. Why did he have this information if not to pass it on to someone else? He had discovered his real mother's identity. What could be the connection, if any? Carla closed her eyes as she tried to empty her mind, eventually falling asleep.

※ ※ ※

She was relieved when Elouise called to wake her the next morning. Bleary eyed, she joined Elouise in the dining room. She only had a coffee; she had no appetite. Elouise was also toying with her eggs and said, "I'll check us out and meet you at the entrance. Our driver should be there by now."

Carla fetched her suitcase and waited in the lobby for Elouise, who asked the doorman to call the driver on his PA system. They moved toward the blue Innova taxi as it appeared in the driveway. The turbaned doorman opened the back door of the car for Elouise. Carla got in on the other side. When the driver turned around, they saw that it was not the driver from the day before.

The somewhat younger man extended his open palm in a gesture of appeasement and said, "Madam, my cousin Ahmed wake up this morning with bad, bad stomach. All night in toilet. He ask me to take nice American ladies to airport." He smiled, and Carla shrugged. Elouise frowned.

"OK, but I have already fixed a price with your cousin," Elouise said.

"No problem, Madam, you give me same, no problem."

As they drove through the apple orchard, Carla remembered a nightmare she had had the night before and told Elouise.

"How horrible, but at least you slept. I didn't sleep a wink," Elouise said, leaning back against the seat and closing her eyes.

After fifty minutes, Carla realized that they should have reached the airport. She looked out the window and saw a signboard, but it wasn't indicating the route to the airport. She caught sight of the driver watching her in the rearview mirror and said, "How much farther to the airport?"

He smiled and said, "Not far. See, there's my cousins waiting for lift. I stop for only one minute please."

On the side of the road stood two men dressed in jeans and black T-shirts. They were carrying faded olive backpacks. Carla froze, the hair standing on end down the back of her neck. She frantically shook Elouise, who woke up to Carla whispering in her ear. As Elouise started to protest, the driver stopped the car and unlocked the doors. The men jumped in on either side of the two terrified women. Dirty rags smelling strongly of some kind of chemical were held tightly over their noses. Carla tried to pull the man's hand away from her face, but within seconds she lost consciousness, overcome by the fumes.

CHAPTER 23

Harry kissed his mother on her forehead. She had fallen asleep after only a few mouthfuls of dhal. It bothered him. She'd obviously been overmedicated. *I hope this nightmare will be over soon,* he thought and asked the burqa-clad nurse to please keep the sweets for his mother. She stared greedily at the packet, and he wondered if his mother would be lucky to have any. Resigned to the thought, he left the room and walked down the dirty corridor to Dr. Malik's office. The doctor was sitting behind his desk, studying a folder. Looking up, he smiled at Harry and stood up.

"I hope you enjoyed your visit with your mother," he said.

"Actually, I wanted to speak to you about her. She seems to be very disoriented. Is she not overmedicated?" Harry asked the doctor.

The doctor's reply seemed to hold something of a threat. "We know what we're doing. You concern yourself with what you know best. It looks like she will recover and in time, I'm sure we will find a way to get her out of Pakistan."

Harry looked at him for a few seconds before replying, "Of course, Doctor. Will you accompany me back to my car? I don't think I'll find my way very easily."

Smiling, he said, "Let's go." The doctor was hurrying, and Harry had trouble keeping up. He left Harry at the car and headed toward the mosque.

Harry stopped at the hotel, picked up his overnight bag, and checked out. He arrived a few hours early for his flight but made himself comfortable in the business lounge with a couple of international newspapers.

Yunis Malik was in a tearing hurry. *If only the Indian hadn't asked me to accompany him back to his car,* he thought, irritated. The courier was already at the station, ready to take the train to Islamabad. If Yunis missed him, he would have to wait for the following week to deliver this message. The caliph wouldn't like it. Even though he didn't quite understand the message encrypted in the embroidery on the fabric the Indian had brought, he instinctively knew that it was of utmost importance.

Yunis flagged down a taxi and gave the driver an extra one hundred rupees to go faster. The driver increased his speed, but the traffic was too congested. They inched forward at a snail's pace. Yunis was beginning to hyperventilate. Sweat was pouring down his face. He could feel his blood pressure rising.

The traffic eased off slightly. He breathed in deeply and muttered quietly to himself, "Must make it, must make it." The taxi came to a sudden stop, Yunis sliding forward on the plastic seat covers.

"What now?" he shouted at the driver, who had closed

his ears with both hands and looked up to the heaven, his eyes rolling backwards.

The taxi had crashed into an emaciated, dirty brown cow. Yunis opened the door and looked at the cow bellowing in pain. A gash on the animal's leg had exposed a pulsating major artery that was pumping blood into the street. A bicycle slipped in the sticky mess; the rider fell. The scene was like something out of a horror movie. The man covered in the animal's blood was gesticulating at the taxi driver.

Yunis, who was out of the car by now, stopped to stare for a few seconds. The crowd was pointing fingers at the driver; others were laughing. Yunis started running. His breathing was ragged, but he kept running. Almost crying from relief, he saw the colonial building that housed the train station. He dragged himself onto the platform, but he was too late. The 4:45 p.m. express for Islamabad had just pulled out of the station. Bathed in perspiration, he sat down on the filthy platform floor. Tears of frustration streamed down his face.

After ten minutes or more, he stood up slowly and walked toward the phone booths. He dialed a number in Abbottabad, a town about 150 kilometers from Islamabad. "Only in an extreme case should you call this number," his handler had said. *This is one of those,* he affirmed inwardly.

Somewhere many thousands of miles away, a computer picked up the signal. It was diverted to the dark listening rooms of Langley. An operator looked up from his computer screen, grinned, and jotted down some coordinates. He walked hastily toward the director's office.

Arriving back in Delhi early the following morning, Harry took a taxi to his bungalow. The chowkidar saluted him and then ran to wake up Kishan. Within five minutes Kishan appeared and asked Harry if he'd like tea.

"No thanks. I'm going to have a quick shower. Tell my driver to be ready at seven."

At precisely seven, Harry left with his driver. He gave him the address for the container depot in Tughlaqabad. The roads were empty, and they reached it within half an hour. A guard checked the car and asked for their bill of lading. Harry asked if Mr. Ramesh Gupta was on duty. Assuring him that he was, the guard directed them to a makeshift office in a container unit. Harry told the driver to stay in the jeep. A small, mustached man wearing a drab brown uniform looked up from the Hindi newspaper he was reading and asked grumpily, "Yes, what's your business?"

Harry didn't introduce himself; he simply handed the document to him. Squinting at it, the guard frowned, and then his attitude changed. "Ah, yes, of course, please follow me, sir. You have someone to help you carry this consignment?" he asked respectfully.

"Yes, I have someone, but it is not very heavy. I should manage fine."

Removing a large key from among a tagged bunch, the guard unlocked the large steel padlock. He heaved open the heavy steel doors and said, "Please go ahead. You know what you are removing today?"

"Yes, thank you."

While Gupta returned to his office, Harry removed a small device from his pocket and switched it on, scanning the entrance of the container. He peered at the reading, and satisfied that there was no evidence of a radiation leak, he returned the scanner to his pocket. Using the light from his mobile phone, Harry started looking for the suitcase hidden in the sacks of South African maize meal. Some of the sacks had split open, the flour spilling in a deep pile on the floor of the container. He finally heard the clank of metal after poking several bags of flour. Using his small Swiss army knife, he cut open the sack and found the steel suitcase; it looked like it might contain sensitive camera or video equipment. He lifted it easily—it didn't weigh more than twenty kilograms—and draped several empty sacks around it. He locked the container and put the suitcase in the jeep, returning the key to Gupta. Thanking him, he handed him a wad of one-hundred-rupee notes.

Harry dialed a number on his mobile phone as he sat in the back of the Jeep. A deep male voice at the other end said, "Tomorrow morning at nine you need to drive toward the east gate of Delhi. You'll pass a small hotel called Delhi Gate Inn. Your driver must drop you there and leave. Introduce yourself to the receptionist as Dr. Tuglak and wait. A man by the name of Uttam will collect you and bring you to me. You are to hold onto the case, and don't allow anyone to take it from you. Understood?"

"Yes. Of course," Harry said, frowning. He wasn't comfortable with the idea of going without his driver.

The following morning his driver dropped him off at the Delhi Gate Inn. He asked the driver to go home; he'd call him later.

The reception at the Delhi Gate Inn was cramped and smelled of ammonia and old oil. The woman at the desk eyed him with suspicion. Candy wrappings lay scattered among the untidy batches of invoices on the desk. The woman's dyed-black hair was oily and pulled back into a bun so tightly that her eyes slanted upwards. Harry introduced himself as Dr. Tuglak, and she told him to take a seat on a worn-out red leatherette couch. He kept his hand protectively on the suitcase next to him. The woman gave it a curious look but didn't offer to store it. She made a phone call and spoke softly into the handset, pausing to study Harry for a few seconds. Nodding, she replaced the handset and smiled at him for the first time with crooked, red, betel-nut-stained teeth.

Five minutes later a well-built young man with short-cropped hair, wearing jeans and a black T-shirt, walked through the door. "Dr. Tuglak?" he asked Harry.

"Yes, and you are?"

Smiling, he said, "You can call me Uttam. Please come with me."

A yellow panel van was parked at the uneven curb. Uttam opened the doors and helped Harry lift the suitcase inside. The interior was bare, except for one seat. Metal chains, boxes of scrap metal, and rusty nails were piled up on the one side. A middle-aged man wearing a pathani suit and skullcap smiled at Harry and offered him the seat. Harry protested politely, but the man was very insistent, pushing him rudely down onto the seat before squatting on his haunches on the floor of the van.

Uttam reversed carefully into the ongoing traffic but managed to pull away safely. *Thank goodness,* Harry thought, worried about his consignment. The driver turned east toward Ghaziabad. The industrial town in Uttar Pradesh was only twenty kilometers from Delhi. Their progression was slow through the congested morning traffic. They passed several factories manufacturing railway wagons and advanced electronic products for the Indian armed forces.

At a busy intersection the van turned left and headed toward the old part of the city where the populace lived in closely built apartments. Clotheslines strung between the buildings dripped soapy water onto the car's windshield, drawing a couple of expletives from Uttam. He stopped in front of a wooden door and blew the horn. The door opened immediately. A young man dressed in jeans got in beside him, and they sped off. After a few more twists and turns through the narrow streets, they found themselves on a dirt track, abandoned factories and warehouses along the way.

The van stopped in front of a large metal gate. A chowkidar opened it and waved them through. Uttam parked the van in front of an abandoned warehouse. The terrain outside was uneven and littered with industrial waste. Uttam opened the door for Harry, and he climbed out, carefully passing the suitcase to Uttam, who introduced the newcomer to Harry as Ali. They walked toward a relatively new-looking steel door fitted with a sophisticated combination lock. Uttam punched in a code, and the door opened.

They entered the large space, which was well lit with naked fluorescent bulbs hanging directly from the steel ceiling beams. Large steel tables lined one side of the floor, and on the other side two women wearing hijabs were seated in front of industrial sewing machines. A dummy stood to the side, modeling a vest in coarse handloom cotton. Thin nylon rope held a small throw pillow in place around the waist of the doll.

When they saw Harry, they looked up and stopped sewing. A tall youth got up from behind the table and embraced Uttam and Ali, who turned to Harry and introduced the youth as Dr. Nizaam. "Hi, how're you doing?" he asked in an American accent.

"You're American?" Harry asked, surprised.

"No, I'm Palestinian. In a skirmish on the West Bank, Israeli soldiers killed my parents. I was only six years old when I was sent to live with my uncle in Los Angeles. Later I went to UCLA where I qualified as a chemical engineer."

Harry smiled politely, his eyes scanning the table where Nizaam was working. Some technical drawings and neat packets of wire as well as small boxes resembling detonators filled the table. Nizaam noticed Harry staring and said, "Please, come. I'll show you what I'm working on."

Harry walked toward the table, still carrying the suitcase. Nizaam looked at it and said, "Great, you have it. Let me take it from you." He put in on the table next to his own briefcase and turned his attention back to Harry, pointing out the components of the bomb he was working on. "So, as you can see we are assembling a conventional bomb of shrapnel that can cause the most fatalities. But the added component, which you so kindly procured for us, will make it possible to cause some major psychological damage." He threw back his head and laughed, his laughter reaching an effeminate pitch.

The events of the past two days had taken their toll on Harry, but he somehow managed to control his feelings of disgust and agitation. He stared without expression at Nizaam as he walked to the suitcase. Nizaam's excitement was almost tangible in the cool, air-conditioned space.

"Let me," Harry volunteered when Nizaam tried to open the suitcase. "It has a combination lock," he explained, while punching in the short code. He lifted the lid, exposing the metal container, which lay cushioned in between gray foam. Red warning signs against nuclear radiation were painted on the metal container.

"What is it?" Nizaam asked, almost breathless.

"Caesium-137. The same radioisotope used by the Chechen rebels in Moscow in the nineties. Of course, it didn't detonate, but it certainly scared a lot of people," Harry said.

"How many kilos?" Nizaam asked.

"Seventeen. It should be more than enough for at least five bombs."

"Good. Well, I'm going to move it into a safe area to work on, and Uttam and Ali will take you to him." Nizaam closed the suitcase carefully and walked toward the back of the warehouse through a metal door. Uttam took Harry by the elbow and led him in the opposite direction through a wooden door and down a cement staircase.

He knocked on the timber door at the bottom of the stairs and then entered. A towering man dressed in white kurta pajamas sat at a desk staring at the smoke rings he was puffing in the air. He was holding a Cohiba Behike Cuban cigar elegantly in his right hand, while his left hand hovered limp at the wrist over a crystal glass next to a tall bottle of whiskey. He gave Harry an imperious glance and pointed his cigar hand to a chair opposite him. Harry sat down, reluctantly. This was definitely not the man he had expected to meet. Something in Harry's expression must have betrayed his thoughts, as the man smiled at him, condescendingly.

"A great army general once said, 'To beat your enemy, know him intimately, copy his ways, live his life, and then strike him when he least expects it,'" he said in a sonorous voice, watching Harry like a striking cobra.

"Yes, I believe that to be true," Harry said in a guarded tone.

Guffawing, the man stood up and walked around the desk. Putting his cigar in his mouth, he swung his hand back and slapped Harry hard on the back. "I'm Nadir. We've spoken on the phone."

Harry, wincing at the rough welcome, said, "Of course, I recognize your voice."

Nadir walked back to his cognac-colored leather chair and sat down heavily. Taking a crystal whiskey glass from a tray on his desk, he poured a tot and handed it to Harry.

Shaking his head, Harry said, "No thanks, I don't drink."

"Oh, what nonsense. This is a twenty-five-year-old Talisker. Not easy to get hold of in India." He pushed it closer to Harry and affecting an affable tone, said, "Cheers, and thank you. We are finally ready for the final phase in our operation." He lifted his glass to his mouth and iterated a hollow "Cheers!"

CHAPTER 24

The van tilted precariously to the side of the steep mountain pass. The jolting shook Carla out of her drug-induced sleep. She had a splitting headache, and her vision was blurred. As she blinked forcefully and rubbed her head vigorously, her vision cleared marginally. Her hands and feet were tied with nylon rope. She was lying on her side, and her hipbone was hurting as the van lurched and rocked on the narrow road. Through sheer willpower she managed to turn onto her back, and the pain in her hip began to ease gradually. She turned her head and saw that Elouise was also slumped on her side, still unconscious. Staring at Elouise, Carla began to remember, putting together the puzzle pieces bit by bit. A familiar feeling of dread gripped her, her nerves so tightly wound that her breathing was labored.

"Elouise, Elouise, wake up. Can you hear me?" she shouted over the van's noisy engine. But Elouise didn't stir. Worried about her, Carla managed to wriggle toward her.

She laid her ear against her chest and listened carefully. She couldn't hear Elouise breathing. As she tried to find a heartbeat, cold sweat poured down Carla's face. *Maybe Elouise had a reaction to the drug,* she thought in a panic. Tears welled in her eyes as she felt hysteria rise in her. Her breathing became more labored and irregular.

A sudden jolt knocked Elouise's lolling head sharply against a metal box, and her moan had Carla sighing with relief. It was then that she was able to think more rationally. The engine was deafeningly loud. *That's why I wasn't able to hear a heartbeat.* Moving closer to Elouise, she managed to nudge her repeatedly. Moaning again, Elouise opened her eyes only to close them again. Carla was desperate.

"Wake up. You must wake up, Elouise," she shouted loudly and then, to make sure they were indeed alone in the back of the van, she quickly scanned it. Reassured, she prodded Elouise again on her shoulder.

"My head, it hurts like hell." Elouise slurred the words, her heavy-lidded eyes squinting in the dim light. There were no windows in the van, but sunlight filtered through some of the cracks and holes in the metal sides and roof. Their watches had been taken, and there was also no sign of their luggage or purses.

"It looks like it's still daytime. How long do you think we were knocked out?" Carla asked her.

Looking at Carla with annoyance and surprising wit, given that she had just regained consciousness, Elouise said, "I wouldn't know. This is a first for me."

Carla managed a nervous giggle. "Of course, but if you had to make a calculated guess?"

Elouise frowned. She didn't answer Carla. Contorting her body, which caused a lot of groaning, she managed to find a more comfortable position and sat propped up against the side of the van. "Get yourself to that crack and smell the air," Elouise said, nodding toward the corner of the van where a steady line of light was streaming through.

Carla looked at the gap, frowned, and said, "At the cost of sounding like a dumb blond, what am I supposed to smell?"

"The air, you idiot. Is it morning or late afternoon air? Do you smell other cars or dust or tarmac? These are all clues as to where we are," Elouise said impatiently.

"OK, I get it." Having observed Elouise's heroic effort, Carla pushed herself up against the opposite side of the van. She reached the crack and, looking back at Elouise, said, "I could just try to peer through it, you know."

Smiling hesitantly for the first time, Elouise said, "OK, peer then, but you still won't know if it's morning or late afternoon."

Carla closed her left eye tightly and looked through the crack. The van was moving fast, and it took a while for her to focus. They were traveling on a tarmac road in an appalling condition. In the distance she could make out blue-gray, snowcapped mountain ranges. A transport truck decorated in the subcontinent's garish style came into her line of vision a couple of hundred meters away. The road they were on made an obvious sharp turn as it meandered down the mountain pass. "We are definitely going down a mountain pass. Needless to say, I don't recognize the mountains in the distance."

Then, sniffing theatrically, she said, "The air smells warm, but there is a crispness to it." Carla looked around at Elouise in mild surprise and said, "It's morning air. Afternoon air would be muggier and maybe balmier."

Elouise moved toward a crack and peered through it. 'I think you're right. That means we were knocked out all night and possibly driving through the night, judging by my bruised and battered body."

"Where do you think they're taking us?" Carla asked.

"It's difficult to say. Kashmir is mountainous all around.

I'm trying to remember its layout. It borders with Pakistan, China, and India. Let's hope we're not heading for Pakistan."

The van started slowing down and stopped. Carla peered through the crack and said, "I don't see anything. Looks like we've stopped on the road."

Then they heard someone talking, and the next minute the doors of the van opened. A young man dressed in jeans looked inside, and on seeing the women conscious he called to someone named Hassan. Another young man, dressed in a traditional kurta pajama, joined him and addressed them in English.

"You come." He motioned to them impatiently to get out of the van. When he noticed them struggling to stand up, the denim-clad man jumped in and untied their feet, helping them up. They walked stiffly, and both women groaned as they got off the van.

The sun shone brightly, and the sky was clear. The air was thin, which meant they were still relatively high on the mountain pass. The road was quiet. Hassan took Carla by the arm while the other man led Elouise away to a large bush on the side of the road. Carla was lead to the opposite side. She was afraid; their intentions weren't clear, and her head was filled with thoughts so hideous she tried her best to banish them and stay calm. *Violently raped, our throats slit by a large Afghan choora; thrown down the steep mountain pass; a trail of our blood darkening as it congeals in the summer sun.* Carla trembled as her imagination played havoc with her nerves.

Behind an unfamiliar bush, Hassan untied Carla's hands and told her, "Make business. I not look, but wait here." He tried to smile but was unsure, so he just turned his back on her.

Realizing how badly she needed to relieve herself, she squatted shakily behind the bush but managed quite well.

She pulled her pants back on hurriedly, and the moment she stood up, Hassan was at her side, leading her back to the van. Elouise was already inside, drinking from a bottle of mineral water. Hassan gave Carla one, which she took and drank from thirstily. He walked around to the driver's cabin and returned with a plastic bag, which he tossed to the young man who was tying up Elouise. He took out a packet of cookies and gave it to her, then gave the packet to Carla, and they ate ravenously.

Speaking English for the first time, the young man said, "Proper khanna next stop if not make any trouble. You understand?"

Elouise nodded eagerly and said, "Yes, of course, and, uh, please don't tie us up. We have no intention of escaping—we don't even know where we are."

He looked at her, frowning, and then he said something to Hassan, who also frowned. Hassan addressed the women: "No trying running away, you understand. I have weapon." He lifted his kurta and showed them the semiautomatic tucked into a leather belt.

Carla glanced worriedly at Elouise and said, "Promise, no trying to run away."

The young man untied Elouise, and after giving them both a warning look, he locked the doors. The van pulled away, skidding on the gravel, and then they were back on the narrow pass.

"Thank God they didn't tie us up again," Carla said, and then, sighing, asked, " Who are they and where are they taking us, any idea?"

Elouise shook her head. "No idea, but at least we're still in Kashmir and it looks like we're heading south. If we were going north there'd be more snow on the mountains and the temperature would've been cooler."

"So which country borders on Kashmir's south?"

"India and a small portion of Pakistan. My guess is that

they're taking us back to India."

"Let's hope so. We should've told someone the truth about our trip. Who's going to look for us now?" Carla said, despondency creeping into her voice. "Why did they kidnap us? Do you think this has something to do with Harry?"

Elouise pulled over some sailcloth stacked in a corner of the van and lay down. "I don't know, let's try and get some rest. My head's still hurting and fuzzy. No point trying to plan an escape until we know where we are and what their intentions are."

Carla managed a brave smile, marveling at Elouise's maturity and composure. She was scared, really scared. Closing her eyes tightly, she tried not to think too much of her predicament as she made an effort to fall asleep.

～～～

Nadir made Harry nervous. He sipped the whisky but hardly tasted the aged liquid. This man looking like a Mafia don had somehow completely thrown him; the mission now seemed tainted. The short hair on the back of his neck prickled, and he rubbed it with his free hand.

"Let's get to business," Nadir said as he poured himself another scotch. "According to Nizaam, the radiation won't cause many casualties, but it will contaminate the area, causing psychological damage, and there will also be huge economic implications. I believe they have to tear down the buildings and dig up the ground all around it. Is this also your thinking?"

"Yes, that's true, as we won't use more than a couple of kilos of the radioactive material in each bomb. How many are you planning to use?"

"Probably only two. America is scared shitless of a 'dirty bomb.' We want the conventional bomb, which we will pack with maximum shrapnel, to cause the deaths, especially the death of the guest of honor." He laughed raucously.

"The venue will be heavily guarded. What's the plan to get them through all the metal detectors and searches?" Harry asked.

"You don't worry about that; it's all sorted, all taken care of. Go help Nizaam with the bomb. I don't want us to blow up before the mission." Nadir began chuckling.

"I need to get back home by evening as my wife will be back, and we have to get out the country for a while." Harry said as he stood up.

A dangerous dark light shone in Nadir's eyes, but in a benevolent tone he said, "Of course, of course. Now let's get this damn thing assembled." He walked out with Harry following him.

Harry was now deeply disturbed. He cursed himself inwardly for getting involved in such a dangerous imbroglio. He wasn't a killer, and much as he sympathized with the more moderate elements, the anger that had once consumed him had been dissipating for some time. *What a disaster. I have made a terrible mistake.*

Carla didn't manage to sleep. Her brain was in overdrive as she considered every possible option. After a couple of hours, the van slowed down, and peering through the gap, she saw that they were on the outskirts of a city. She woke Elouise, who looked through the crack and confirmed her theory.

"Do you recognize it?" Carla asked.

"It's not Delhi, but let me see if I can spot some license plates." Elouise squinted, concentrating hard. "It looks like we're still in Kashmir. I think it's Jammu."

"That's near the Indian border, isn't it?"

"I think so."

The van stopped, but no one came to open the doors. After about ten minutes, it drove off through the city and stopped on the outskirts. The doors were opened, and they were let out to relieve themselves again. They were given chicken kebabs and roomali roti. The food was strangely appetizing, and Carla licked her fingers as she wrapped the chicken in the roomali roti and ate with relish.

It was hot in the van, and they were both perspiring. Luckily their captors had left a couple of extra water bottles in the back. As the van inched forward again, the driver taking care to avoid rocks and potholes in the precariously narrow roads, both women were listless, dread hanging like a tangible canopy over them.

"We should scream our heads off when we reach the border post," Carla said, and Elouise agreed. But the heat and their semi-dehydrated state lulled them into a deep sleep. When they woke up, it was still hot, but dark. The noise of transport trucks honking and brakes in need of services screeched and whined.

Looking through the opening, Elouise said, "I think we're in India. I can see dhabas with Indian names on them."

Carla moved closer and said, "Thank God. At least it feels closer to help."

"Well, I wouldn't be too sure, Carla. We're in serious shit."

"I know. Oh God, I'm scared. Who are these guys?"

"I reckon they're the ones who got Harry involved in whatever they're planning. They followed us from Delhi, so they've been onto us all along. I think they would've left us alone if we hadn't made these discoveries," Elouise said as she drained the last bit of water from the plastic bottle. "I'm so thirsty and hot. Right now I just hope we stop soon. I need to get out of this van."

The van slowed down and took a turn onto what felt

like a completely different road. It was quiet. Other traffic noises had died down. "Do you think we should scream for help?" Carla asked Elouise, who was peering through the gap.

"Pointless, we're in some abandoned industrial area. I can't see any lights or sign of people." The van stopped, and they could hear some muffled conversation. Then they heard a metal gate opening. The van drove through and stopped. Both women held their breath. Carla could hear her heart hammering in her ears. Her blouse was soaked through on her back, and her hair was literally dripping with perspiration. The van's doors opened, and the slightly cooler night air brought much-needed relief. Hassan was holding a rechargeable lamp in his right hand and with a nod of his head indicated that they should get out.

Carla made eye contact with Elouise. The question in her face was quite obvious to Elouise, but she shook her head and whispered softly, "We can't escape, not now."

Carla stood up stiffly and followed Elouise out of the van. A tall young man met them with a sardonic smirk. He said something to Hassan, who grabbed Elouise and held her still while the man tied her hands behind her back with a cable tie. Carla inspected her surroundings as discreetly as she could. She noted the three-meter-high wall with barbed wire on top of it and two guards armed with semiautomatic weapons standing at the metal gate. She turned her head slightly and swayed toward the corner of the gray cement building, which was cut off from the front with a fence. A guard, slightly behind her, with a weapon slung over his shoulder had a fierce looking Doberman on a lead. The dog growled and started barking. His handler made no attempt to quiet him down. Foaming at the mouth, he bared his teeth and snarled.

Carla snapped back her head as Hassan grabbed her hands and the young man tied her wrists together. The cable was too tight, cutting cruelly into her flesh, but she resisted the urge to complain. The men were in an obvious hurry, whispering to each other urgently as they looked at the women.

"Do you understand them?" Carla asked Elouise.

"Not very well; they are speaking Punjabi or Urdu. I think they're arguing about where they should put us."

Hassan went through a steel door and returned, accompanied by a woman wearing a hijab. Taking both Elouise and Carla by the arm, he steered them toward the side of the building. The guard with the Doberman unlocked the padlock and let them through. The dog growled at them, and as Carla passed the animal, she could feel his hot breath on the back of her legs.

The grounds were poorly lit, and Elouise stumbled on the uneven path, which led around the back of the building. The woman unlocked the door to the building with a key worn on a chain around her neck. The door opened to a small, dark room with stairs leading down. As they descended into the dank basement reeking of sour smelling sweat and urine, Carla's throat closed up and she started to cough, her airways demanding oxygen. Hassan whacked her on her back just behind her left lung. She cried out in pain and fright, but her airways unblocked and she breathed with greater ease. Alarmed, Elouise stared at her. Carla smiled feebly and said, "I'm OK."

Images of her detention in Old Delhi flooded her mind, but she was determined to shut them out, concentrating instead on her surroundings. The basement consisted of a large room, furnished with mattresses and a couple of plastic chairs. It was littered with empty soda bottles and paper plates. Stacked tiffin boxes in stainless steel sat in a cardboard box. A passage led off to smaller rooms.

Carla and Elouise were shoved onto a mattress covered with a mildew-stinking cotton sheet. Elouise asked them to please untie them, but they ignored her. Hassan filled a plastic bottle with water from a small basin and tap in the corner of the room and lifted it to Elouise's mouth. She hesitated for a second, but then drank quickly. They offered Carla water and she did the same. The woman in hijab showed them a small room containing a toilet and basin, but she did not untie them. The woman walked to the room; picking up the tiffins, she left with Hassan and locked the door.

It was pitch-dark. Small windows lined the one side of the three-meter-high walled basement. Lying down uncomfortably on the mattress, Carla stared at the windows and said, "Do you think we could fit through those?"

"I think so, but I'm pretty sure they're barred. Anyway, how do you think we'll get up there?" Elouise asked, her voice low.

"Well, one of us could stand on the other's shoulders and squeeze through. When through, she could pull the other one up with a rope made from this stinky sheet."

Elouise started laughing, much to Carla's surprise. Feeling indignant, she asked, "What's so funny?"

"I'm sorry, Carla, it's just, how are we going to do this with our hands tied up?"

"At least we have some idea, and now we know we have to get out of these cable ties."

With a sigh, Elouise said, "You're right. Any bright ideas?"

"Not yet, but believe me, I will think of something," Carla said bravely.

They lay quietly while Carla tried to scan the room for something sharp that could cut the ties. Exhausted from straining in the dark, she finally closed her eyes and tried to sleep.

Harry rubbed his eyes and looked at the time on the Patek Philippe watch that Elouise had given him as a wedding gift. It was past two in the morning, and he and Nizaam had just finished assembling the bombs. They would ask the women to sew them into the vests in the morning. Harry had been angry when Nadir insisted they finish the work before he was sent home. He'd phoned Elouise on her mobile, but it was switched off, and when he phoned home, Kishan told him that Elouise and Carla hadn't yet returned. This calmed him down, and he instructed Kishan to call him the minute Elouise returned. But that had been hours ago. He cursed himself for not paying attention to Elouise when she'd told him with whom she had left the kids.

"OK, Nizaam, I'm going home now. Nadir knows how to contact me if you need anything," he said, and walked toward the exit. They were alone in the warehouse, but Harry detected the faint aroma of the Cuban cigars Nadir smoked. Nizaam was hovering at his desk, looking toward Nadir's office expectantly. The door opened, and Nadir walked out with a cigar in his right hand.

"There you are. All OK?" he asked in his booming voice.

Nizaam's easy confidence dissolved, and quivering, he replied, "Yes, sir. Dr. Singh wants to go home now."

Nadir turned his powerful body around and, narrowing his eyes, appraised Harry. Harry stepped back involuntarily as he recognized the cold menace in those dark eyes.

"My dear doctor, what's the hurry?" His voice was sweet like a ripe mango, but with the guarantee of a hard stone pit inside.

Harry felt ice-cold fingers caressing his back, and he had to control the urge to make a run for it. Knowing that maintaining a controlled calm was his only hope of some kind of escape, he licked his dry lips and said evenly, "I promised my wife I'd be back before this evening. She'd be worried sick. She will start asking questions."

"I'm sure you'll be able to dodge those," Nadir said with a cunning smile.

"You don't know my wife; she's...unbelievably stubborn." Harry was now trying to keep his voice light.

Throwing back his head, Nadir laughed and said, "So they are, indeed, so they are. He gave Harry another unpleasant slap on the back and continued, "It's so late; spend the night—I want you here in the morning when we sew the bombs into the vests."

Harry started protesting, but the threat in Nadir's eyes stopped him short, and he said with as much disinterest as he could muster, "OK, where will I sleep?"

"Nizaam will take you to the sleeping quarters."

Smiling nervously, Nizaam said to Harry, "Come with me." He led Harry upstairs to a small room, almost filled by a charpoy and a small nightstand. An old air-conditioner droned noisily, but to Harry's relief, quite effectively in the corner. A bathroom with a shower and toilet was down the passage. Some of the rooms' doors on either side of the passage were open, and Harry detected the sleeping forms on charpoys and mattresses.

Nizaam waited outside the bathroom for Harry to complete his ablutions and then followed him back to his room. He said good night and locked the door behind him from the outside. Harry ran toward the door and banged on it, shouting, "Hey! Open this door now."

Nizaam replied quietly, "Please understand, it's better this way. It's for your own protection." He paused and continued, "I'll unlock it myself first thing in the morning, I promise."

Harry turned his back angrily to the door and reached into his pocket for his phone. It wasn't there. Seething with frustration, he sat down on the bed and thought of Elouise and his girls.

CHAPTER 25

The call came through at midnight. George had been asleep but came alert within a split second. Listening carefully for a few minutes, he said, "Thanks, I'm onto it. I'll report back in twelve hours." He replaced the handset; then picking it up again, he dialed a number.

"Yes?" a woman answered.

"Leila, sorry for the late hour, but we have to meet soon. My guys in Kashmir can't find Carla and Elouise."

"Did you manage to get clearance for us?"

"Yes, I did. Are you up to it?"

"Of course. I'll wake Andrew and see you in fifteen minutes."

"I'll send my car—don't take a taxi, OK?"

"OK." Leila hung up, and George got out of bed. He called Kamal and told him to fetch Leila and Andrew from their hotel. Pulling on a T-shirt and jeans, he walked to the kitchen and started making coffee. His face was somber as he tried to figure Carla's whereabouts. He took the coffee and cups to his study on a tray and sat down behind his desk.

He switched on his desktop and entered a secure CIA Web site. Accessing the satellite map page, he typed in some coordinates and waited impatiently for it to load. While studying the images, he heard Kamal arrive and enter the house. He knocked softly on George's study door and stood back respectfully for Leila and Andrew to enter.

Leila was wearing gray track pants and a white tank top. Her long dark hair was tied in a high ponytail. She smiled as she saw the coffee, said, "Great, just what I needed," and poured herself a cup.

Andrew was frowning and, without greeting George, fell into the armchair. Leila asked if he wanted a cup of coffee, but he declined her offer. George thanked Kamal and said he could return to bed—he'd call him again if needed. Kamal touched his hand to his heart and head, bade them all good night, and left silently.

"So you haven't found Carla," Andrew said, the accusation in his tone not lost on George.

"No, I'm afraid not. We picked them up in Srinagar—they were staying at the Palace hotel. They had hired a driver for the day. He told my guys that they had behaved like normal tourists, and then they visited an old lady at her house in an upmarket residential area of Srinagar. He dropped them off at the hotel and was to take them to the airport the following morning, but he received a message that they were to take the hotel transport provided for them. We checked the hotel, and they had checked out in the morning and taken a cab to the airport, but they didn't board their flight to Delhi."

"What did the hotel taxi driver say? Where did he drop them?" Andrew asked.

"That's the problem. They didn't take the hotel transport. The doorman remembered them and said they went with a car and driver he hadn't seen before, but they had obviously prearranged it."

Andrew leaned forward, put both his hands through his un-brushed hair, and said, "Oh my God, I hope they weren't kidnapped. A colleague of mine covered the Daniel Pearl kidnapping in Pakistan in 2002; those guys were ruthless."

Leila put her hand on Andrew's shoulder and said, "Let's not get carried away. They could've changed their minds and persuaded the driver to take them somewhere else."

"I'm afraid I don't think so, Leila," George said. "I contacted the friend with whom Elouise had left the kids, and she said she spoke to Elouise the night before and they made arrangements for her to pick up the girls in the evening. Needless to say, she didn't pitch." George looking at Andrew with an expression that was guarded but sympathetic.

"And Harry?" Leila asked.

"He was followed to a container depot in Tughlaqabad where he picked up a box or suitcase. He returned home and hasn't left since"

Andrew sighed loudly. With slight irritation in his voice, he said, "George, I believe you got clearance for us; please explain to me what the devil is going on."

George considered this request for a few seconds. Then he said, "You realize, of course, that what I'm about to tell you cannot be divulged."

Andrew nodded. "Of course. I just want to find Carla and get her out of here."

The passion in his voice bothered George, and he had to remind himself that the stakes were high, and he couldn't allow personal feelings to interfere. He poured himself a cup of coffee, which he drank, grimacing, as it had gone cold.

He looked at both of them and said, "After Korea, I returned to Afghanistan. The search for Bin Laden was still on, and our new president along with the new CIA director made it our top priority to find him. The president was committed to pull out of Afghanistan, and the only way he could do it—to save face and not piss off half the American electorate—was to achieve one of the main aims of the war on terror: Osama Bin Laden's head on a stake." He paused and took a sip of water.

"We stumbled onto some intel regarding Bin Laden's preferred mode of communication. He uses a network of trusted couriers to bring him messages in person. We intercepted a communication and discovered the nom de guerre of the courier. I was flown to Guantanamo Bay to help some senior Al Qaeda members jog their memories a bit—"

"Torture?" Andrew interrupted, surprised. "I thought the US banned it. I know the Bush administration issued a special directive allowing it only in extreme cases of national security, but the new administration categorically vetoed it."

Frowning, George said, "When a whole nation's security is threatened and a little water boarding gets you some crucial info, then quite frankly I don't give a damn."

"Yes, but—"

"Andrew, do you want to waste precious time debating this issue, or do you want to find your wife?" George's eyes were now flashing with anger.

"Of course. I'm sorry; please continue," Andrew said, sufficiently chastised, it seemed to George.

"Now where was I?"

"You were in Guantanamo, assisting certain prisoners with their memory," Leila said diplomatically.

George looked at her in mild amusement and continued, "Well, we didn't discover the courier's identity, but we did manage to put together some facts that led to the discovery of his identity pretty soon after. We traced him and his family and then asked the National Security Agency to place them and all associates under electronic surveillance. This was when Harry popped up on the radar. He was seen meeting with several suspects here in India, as well as in Pakistan. We were all confused, as he is a Sikh. As you know historically, Sikhs waged huge battles against the conquering Moghuls in Northern India to remain unconverted. However, after further investigation, we discovered that he was visiting a mental asylum in Lahore. It turned out that his mother was a patient there. As far as we knew, his Sikh parents were both killed in a road accident in Kashmir. Suddenly the picture looked a bit different, and we had to find out what was going on. He was working for the Indian nuclear program—"

"So when Elouise failed to give you what you needed, you turned your attention to Carla," Andrew said scathingly.

George ignored the comment and continued, "As I was saying, he had access to India's nuclear reactors, so we couldn't ignore this or simply think of it as a coincidence."

"And then you came up with the brilliant plan to have Carla kidnapped and drugged so that you could rescue her and gain her trust so that she could spy on him," Andrew said.

"It was not planned that way." George stood up and said, "I'm going to make another pot of coffee. Leila, do you mind helping me?"

Leila looked at him in surprise and said, "Of course not." She followed him to the kitchen.

George closed the kitchen door and said, "Leila, I don't think we can work with this guy. He's way too emotional, and he could compromise the entire mission. Something big is going down, and he's making me nervous."

Leila placed her hand on his arm as he put the coffee

percolator on the stove. "Don't be silly. He's OK, really. He's a brilliant war reporter, and I've seen him do some crazy brave stuff. I think there's a conflict of interest here. You guys are after the same woman."

"No, it's not tha—" Smiling sheepishly, George said, "'Maybe you're right. Carla is special. I can understand why someone would fight for her."

Leila frowned and said, "George, to be honest, I think you should be careful."

"What the hell's that supposed to mean?"

Giving him a knowing smile, she turned around and removed the coffee from the stove, pouring it into the silver pot. Irked, George closed his eyes for a second as he tried to regain his composure. Then, as if they had been discussing the weather, he smiled and said, "Good, looks like I made a perfect pot. I think Sunil stashes his cookies away somewhere here." He looked in the pantry and returned with an old-fashioned tin box. Leila carried the coffee and fresh cups while George followed her with the tin of cookies.

Andrew stood up politely and took the tray from Leila, placing it on George's desk. Leila poured the coffee, and they helped themselves to the raisin cookies. George, who was sitting on the armrest of Leila's chair, finished his coffee and returned to the other side of the desk. He switched on his computer and said, "I have some satellite images over Srinagar. My guys are watching the Delhi airport, as well as the border posts in Kashmir. There's not a whole lot we can do right now, except keep our phones on and hope one of them makes contact."

"Maybe Andrew and I can go to Kashmir and ask a few questions. The lady they visited the day before their disappearance might know something," Leila said.

"I guess there's no harm, but stay in contact with me at all times. I have a couple of guys there who could pick you up at the airport and assist you. I'll give them a call. Anyway, you guys better get back to the hotel and try to sleep for a few hours before catching the 9:30 flight tomorrow morning. Please take a taxi, as I will be busy with Kamal." George stood up and walked them to the door.

The scraping sound of the key turning in its lock woke Harry. Sleep hadn't brought him rest but a relentless assault of nightmares. He sat up as Nizaam came in with a glass of milky tea. "Good morning, I got you some chai," he said cheerfully.

"Thanks," Harry said gruffly, looking for his phone. Nizaam handed it to him. "I need to phone home. Where can I get a signal?"

"Try downstairs," Nizaam said casually. He had scrambled the signal the day before, but had decided to not tell the doctor and alarm him further.

Harry moved around, and when he got closer to the door that led out to the back, he picked up a weak signal. He dialed Elouise's number, but the signal was not strong enough. The door was locked, but the key was in it; he unlocked the door and stepped outside. Early morning sunrays peeked over the gray cement buildings, warm against his skin with the promise of another hot summer's day. He moved to the side of the building as the signal grew stronger. At last, with most bars showing, he dialed her number, but it was still switched off and went to voice mail.

While dialing Kishan, he noticed a row of windows. He strolled toward them and peered down into the basement. It was dark inside, and it took a few seconds for his eyes to adjust to the dimness.

Harry's blood turned to ice as he saw his wife lying on a dirty mattress on the floor. Her hands were tied behind her back. He banged on the window and shouted, "Elouise, Elouise, it's me, Harry."

Elouise sat up confused. She nudged Carla next to her to wake her up, then looked up, squinting against the bright morning light. Her mouth opened in shock, and she started saying something, but Harry couldn't hear her. The hot, stinking breath of the snarling dog behind him chilled him to the bone. Keeping as still as possible, he moved his head sideways and saw that the dog was on a leash. He turned around and saw the guard straining to control the fierce Doberman.

Ali appeared. With a savage expression matching the dog's, he grabbed Harry roughly by the shoulders and heaved him into a standing position, tying up his wrists with plastic cable ties. Ali turned him around and said, "Dr. Singh, after you," pushing him forward toward the door.

Harry was terrified for himself and his family. *What is Elouise doing here?* Ali steered him toward Nadir's office, then knocked and pushed him forward. Nadir looked like he had just woken up. His eyes were puffy and he was grumpy. "What now?" he bellowed.

Cowering slightly, Ali said, "We found him outside. He saw the prisoners."

Harry jumped in. "Why is my wife here? She knows nothing, I swear. I demand that you release her immediately."

Nadir looked at Harry with a raised eyebrow. Amusement played at the corners of his mouth, and then he laughed, a deep, ugly cackle. His eyes bored into Harry, and then he slapped him with the back of his huge hand. The force of the blow had Harry staggering backwards; he would've fallen, but Ali caught him and kept him upright. A trickle of blood ran into his eye, as the diamond ring on Nadir's index finger had cut the tender flesh above his eye.

Nadir rubbed his hand absentmindedly and then he said, in a voice filled with scorn and loathing, "We don't need you anymore, my dear doctor. We will manage without you, and for your time and trouble we will make sure that your suffering is quick."

"But what about my mother? You promised to get her out of that rat-infested stink hole in Lahore. We had a deal."

Sitting down heavily on the chair at his desk, Nadir looked longingly at the bottle of whisky. Sighing with regret, he opened a drawer and took out a Cuban cigar instead. He unwrapped it slowly, with what appeared to be infinite patience, and said, "That old, fetid whore? She's not your mother. She's just a disgusting prostitute, her mind so weakened by venereal diseases that she believed you to be her long-begotten son. Quite touching, actually." He dragged the smoke deep into his lungs.

The color drained from Harry's face. Ashen, he stormed forward with a ferocious, almost inhuman scream, but Ali stopped him, forcing him to his knees by kicking him savagely in the groin. Harry lay writhing in pain, tears of frustration and self-condemnation flowing freely. When the throbbing pain started subsiding, he struggled onto his knees and said, "Please let my wife go. You can do whatever you want with me, just let her go. Please, I beg you."

Nadir, who was drawing on his cigar with deep, intense pleasure, suddenly stood up and walked toward Harry, who was now on his knees, his shoulders hunched, head thrown back, and eyes squeezed tightly shut. Nadir kicked him in the gut. Harry folded, gasping for air. His head started spinning; his eyes now stretched wide and unfocused, black spots impairing his vision. In a hazy red fog of pain, he heard Nadir's orders. "Lock him up with our prisoners and then start clearing the floor."

Harry felt Ali dragging him by the feet. His head scraped and bounced in the pitted unevenness of the cement floor.

With her heart pounding and a rush of blood to her temples, Elouise forced the words: "Carla, did you see him?"

"Who?"

"Harry!"

"What? Where?"

"There—at the window. He was kneeling and knocking on the pane. He looked straight at me."

"Then where did he go?"

"I don't know, must be trying to rescue us. Oh my God, he must be careful."

"Let's get up," Carla said.

Back to back, Carla's feet against the wall and Elouise's heels wedged in a large cavity in the cement, they got back onto their feet. As they made their way to the basin, the door opened, and Elouise screamed. Harry was bound and being dragged on his back into the room. He had a deep cut over his right eye, which was now completely swollen shut.

Elouise ran toward him, asking, "Are you OK?" Turning his head painfully to the right, he looked at her for a brief moment, and then down at the floor. Ali threw a package of cookies on the bed and, taking out scissors, cut the cable ties. He barked the instruction—"Eat. Quickly!" Elouise had no appetite, but Carla shoveled a couple of cookies into her mouth. Ali shot a mocking questioning glance at Elouise, but she shook her head. He shrugged, tying her up again and then Carla. When he got to the door, he stopped for a moment, looked at them strangely, and then walked out, locking the door behind him.

Elouise kissed Harry on his cheek and said, "Come sit down." He followed her to the mattress, which Carla had kicked against the wall. Backs to the wall, they slid down to the floor. Harry was silent. Elouise waited for him to speak and then asked, "How did you find us?"

"How did you end up here?" Harry asked, the stare in

his left eye boring into her with as much intensity as his tone.

"It's quite a story."

"Please tell me."

Skipping the details of Carla's and George's involvement, Elouise told Harry how she had discovered the truth about his mother. Harry's expression now was one of incredulity and utter horror. He started crying. Soon he was sobbing, loud, mournful sounds that bounced off the walls of the vast basement. Elouise began to weep, and Carla, her eyes now averted, felt the weight of their grief. After the tears, Harry and Elouise lay close to one another.

Suddenly Harry sat up. "There's something I have to tell you, and you're not going to like it."

CHAPTER 26

Harry's narrative began with the events that had deeply affected him throughout his life. Elouise was already familiar with much of it, but was now hearing things that she either never knew or had only been told a few days before. Carla listened with great interest but felt her skin beginning to prickle with apprehension. Harry was depicting a much wider, more complex context of people and activities quite beyond the personal experiences of the everyday successful businessman, husband, and father. The heinous world of criminal activities and, in particular, that of regional and international terrorism was unfolding. Finally, his voice trailed off.

Elouise and Carla sat hunched in shock and disbelief, horrified by what was being planned there, where they were being held captive. Carla was overcome with a sense of dread by the fact that Harry knew about it and that he was deeply involved. She no longer felt compassion for him, not even pity. Elouise had long since turned away from him, inexpressible pain distorting her features. He pleaded with her, but she seemed not to hear him.

Then he was quiet. His head rested in defeat on his chest, tears streaming down his face. The silence was oppressive. After what felt like an eternity, Elouise said, "We have to do something. Harry, if you want to redeem yourself, we must stop this."

Harry looked up, a glimmer of hope in his eyes. "I know, Elouise, I know." With an assertiveness that startled both the women he said, "Carla, how tight are your cable ties?"

"Well, actually—" Her voice cracked; she coughed and continued, "They tied it so tightly the first time that I remembered to keep my wrists a little apart this morning when they tied me up again."

"Do you think you could wriggle a hand free?"

"I'll try."

Elouise was also struggling with her ties and said, "Imagine it's a bangle that's too tight. Mine aren't as tight as yesterday, either. I might have a chance."

"Keep trying. We only need one pair of free hands." And getting to his feet, Harry said, "I'm going to look around to see if I can find something sharp."

Carla had rubbed her wrists raw; gritting her teeth, she persevered.

Elouise stopped and said, "Listen, I think someone's coming."

Harry ran back to the mattress and sat down. Ali and the guard and the dog were at the door. He unlocked it and came in, saying, "Get up. Come." He pointed toward the stairs and walked ahead.

The morning was hot, but the sun not yet overhead. Carla judged the time to be between ten and eleven. They were shoved through a metal door, and the cool air-conditioned interior was a welcome relief. The enormous, brightly lit room was a hub of activity. Young men wearing jeans and black T-shirts were packing boxes, while women in hijab and older men in kurta pajamas carried wrapped packages carefully out through the front door.

An internal door opened, and a gigantic man with an unlit cigar held between his teeth stormed out. With a forbidding look, he strode toward Harry, Elouise, and Carla. He looked from Elouise to Carla for a few seconds. Then laughing, he said, "Ali, you bloody fool, why didn't you tell me we had such beautiful company. I could've entertained our guests." He leaned toward and drew his face level with Carla's. She shrank back in terror. He touched her cheek, gently running the back of his index finger down the contours of her face. With a sneer, he pinched the skin on her cheek between his fingers, drawing blood. Screaming, she fell back against Elouise and Harry.

This brought on another bout of raucous laughter. "What a pity, such lovely ladies." Turning to Ali he said, "Lock them upstairs until we're done." He then strode out the main door and called to someone outside.

Carla and Elouise looked questioningly at Harry, but he shook his head as Ali led them up the stairs and into a different, smaller room, a single filthy blanket crumpled on the cement floor. Elouise asked for water, but she was ignored. They were shoved inside with so much force that they stumbled and landed in a heap. The key was turned in the lock behind them.

The room was not more than two meters square and was oppressively humid. A small, brick vent was the only source of light and air. It looked and felt like a cell. Carla sat down heavily on the hard floor and said, "Shit, shit, shit. Now what?"

Elouise burst into tears, sobbing loudly. Harry was distraught, half mumbling to Elouise or himself, "What have I done? I was such a fool. Please, please forgive me."

Carla, slightly embarrassed by the display of such raw

emotion, walked to the door and, putting her ear to it, listened to the commotion downstairs. Harry came up next to her. "What do you think they're doing?" Carla asked him.

"I think they are clearing out. My guess is that they will move closer to the target area, disband the nonessential members for the time being, and get ready for their attack."

"What are they going to do with us?"

Sighing, he lowered his voice and said, "I don't know, but either way we must try to escape. We know too much. I don't think they'll kill us soon. They might still need me. There could be complications with the dirty bombs. After the mission, who knows?"

Elouise wailed loudly. "What about my babies? Oh, Harry, how could you? I hate you!" She started screaming hysterically.

Carla bent over her and said, "Please, Elouise, now's not the time. We have to get out of here."

Elouise, curled up in a fetal position, was whimpering like a mortally wounded animal. Harry tried to approach her, but she screamed, and he retreated. They sat motionless for a while. Then Harry got up and started shuffling along the walls. He told Carla that he was looking for something sharp.

After a while, Eloise turned her head to Carla and said, "If you manage to get out alive and I don't, promise you'll take care of my girls. Get them to my parents in the States."

"We'll get out of here. One way or another."

"Oh, if only I could be as optimistic as you."

"Shh!" His ear to the door, Harry said, "I think they've left. I heard two trucks or vans leaving." He turned resolutely. "We have to get out of here."

George walked into the control room for the fifth time in

an hour and said, "Hey, Jim, found anything yet?"

The bespectacled intelligence specialist sighed and said, "George, I told you I'll call you the minute I find something."

George ignored him and walked toward the screen of satellite images. He looked at the date and time on the right-hand corner and said, "There he is, leaving the container depot. What is he carrying?"

Peering at the screen, Jim said, "Looks like those metal camera suitcases."

"OK, next?"

As he scrolled forward to the next day, George stopped him. "He's getting out." They watched him entering a building. A well-built man followed, and then they both exited a few minutes later, getting into a mustard-yellow Tempo Matador. Jim zoomed in to read the license plate, but the angle made it impossible. The Tempo headed east, and then it stopped again in a congested residential area. The buildings were very close together, laundry hung on a line between them, impeding their tracking of the van. They picked up the signal again five minutes later and followed it to the train station. A man dressed in kurta pajamas got out of the driver's seat. He walked to the back of the van and opened the doors, and a youth dressed in a pathani suit jumped out with a suitcase.

"Zoom in on that suitcase," George ordered.

"Not the same one; this one looks like black nylon," Jim said, adjusting his glasses.

The youth touched the older man's feet and walked into the station. He turned around to wave, and the older man got back into the driver's seat and drove off. He drove back to the residential area and parked in a narrow lane. He got out alone and entered a building.

"No one else has gotten either in or out of that van for eighteen hours," Jim said, pursing his lips. He fast-forwarded the images to eighteen hours later: the same man got into the van alone and drove away. "No sign of our Dr. Singh," Jim said and leaned back in his chair to drink the rest of his coffee from a mug printed with the CIA insignia.

George rubbed his eyes and sat down next to him. "My guy intercepted the youth on the train to Amritsar. The suitcase contained clothes and religious books." He sighed; frowning, he said, "So our Dr. Singh is either hidden somewhere, or they changed cars. Have you trained the satellite on the yellow Tempo since?"

"No, we haven't. We've been watching the residential area, and some of our local field agents have been checking it out, but no sign of him or the yellow van."

"We're missing something," George muttered to himself. "Let's go back to the images from when they entered the residential area."

Jim sat forward and went back to the images of the yellow Tempo as it turned into the area.

"OK, I want to go through it frame by frame. Show me how to do it, and I'll take over from here," George told Jim.

Shrugging, Jim said, "Sure, no problem, but don't be disappointed if you don't find anything."

Realizing that by doing this he was questioning Jim's professional skill, George added, "I'm sure you did great, but you know what they say: 'two pairs of eyes.'"

Getting up, Jim said, "Yeah, whatever. I'm going for a refill. You want one?"

George nodded distractedly. He was now single-minded in the scrutiny of each frame. After an hour, he took a break and called Leila. They had arrived in Srinagar and were heading toward the bungalow registered in the name of Soraya Khan.

"Any progress on your side?" Leila asked.

"No, I'm afraid not. Anyway, keep me posted. And, Leila, keep Mustafa with you at all times. He's got your back.

I don't think I'll have the resources to find you guys if you go missing, too."

Leila laughed, assuring him that he had nothing to worry about.

George returned to the screen as an image of a laughing Carla appeared in his mind. His heart skipped a beat, and he reprimanded himself silently for this fleeting indulgence. He resumed the examination of the video.

After another ten minutes, George finally had a breakthrough. A white bed sheet, which was hanging on a line across the two buildings, blew off in a little crosswind. It fluttered down onto the yellow Tempo and was pulled off a few seconds later. It was then that George noticed a very similar van next to the one they had been tracking. The second van passed the other one and a few minutes later exited onto the road for the station. "I got it!" George shouted, and Jim ran back into the room.

"What?"

"We've been tracking the wrong Tempo. Look here." He went back to the frame and showed Jim the image framing the second van. "The van Singh was in stopped for a few minutes, and this one drove out with the satellite tracking it. The other one would have carried on to its destination without satellite detection."

"Geez, you're good. Now I need to get general satellite footage of the whole area and see if we can find the other van."

"Will there be coverage?"

"I hope so," Jim said as he contacted the Air Force Satellite Control Network situated at the Consolidated Space Operations Center at the Vandenburg Air Force Base in California. He spoke to a few operators, giving them the coordinates, and waited. George paced up and down, checking on his field operatives constantly. He looked at his watch and saw that it was past one. Feeling hungry, he asked Jim if he'd like a sandwich. Jim was in conversation with an attractive female officer at the base via satellite, and he gave George the thumbs up. George made for the exit, but Jim called him back. "We found something."

George rushed back to Jim's side as images of Ghaziabad came on the screen. "We got this from the Indian air force. They've been watching Ghaziabad since 1995 when Kashmiri rebels, then known as Al-Faran, kidnapped six Western tourists in Jammu and kept them there in an abandoned warehouse," Jim explained as he typed in the time line. When he zoomed in, the images became clear. Jim typed in the exact coordinates of where he and George had last positively identified their target. They saw the yellow Tempo heading to the station, and then less than three minutes later the other van drove out and followed a road to an industrial area. The buildings seemed abandoned.

The door opened, and a petite blond woman in her late thirties said, "George, the ambassador wants to see you now."

George looked at her briefly and said, "Charlene, not now. Be a honey and tell Richard I'll be there in ten minutes."

"Now! He has that look in his eye."

George ignored her and continued staring at the screen. Charlene sighed and said, "Fine, I'll leave without you, but for your information, Dicky dear got a big fright when the Indian Minister of Defense called him a few minutes ago."

George looked up, alarmed. "What?"

Smiling flirtatiously, she turned around and said, "Coming?"

Jim looked at George and said, "Oops, that was fast."

"I don't want the Indians involved right now. Shit. Jim, please continue with the surveillance, and when that van stops and Singh gets out with the suitcase, call me. Understand?"

"Sure. Chill, man, we'll get them, OK?"

George breathed deeply and said, "I hope you're right."

With renewed effort, Carla was tugging to pull her hands free, but not making much progress. Elouise had by now calmed down and lay listlessly on the floor, staring into space.

"I think I found something," Harry said and called Carla over. "Here, feel here. What do you think?'

Carla squinted in the gloom and saw that a portion of the wall was un-plastered. A brick was jutting out slightly, its protruding end quite rough to the touch. She turned around and tried to rub the cable tie against it. It was just sliding off, but then after a minute something stuck and she felt the tie hooking and scraping. "I think it's working," she said excitedly.

Harry knelt down, his face against the wall. "You're almost there; push harder."

Carla felt the release as the tie broke off, and she fell to her knees, crying for the first time. "Thank you, God, thank you."

Harry pushed hard against the brick, and within seconds he had snapped his ties. He helped Elouise up, guided her to the brick, and together they managed to free her hands. The three of them were now smiling with relief. Carla hugged both Elouise and Harry and said, "We're going to be OK, but we have to work together."

Nodding, Harry said, "Thanks, Carla. Let me try and do something about the lock." It was too dark to see anything as he felt around. "It feels like an ordinary Yale lock. All I need is something thin and sharp, like a hairpin." He looked at them hopefully, but they shook their heads. "Never mind, let's try and find something." He went down on all fours, feeling the floor.

"I've got something!" Carla shouted, making Elouise jerk with fright. She started fiddling inside her blouse. Concentrating hard, she pulled out a half-circle of white, plastic-coated metal.

Elouise stared at Carla, perplexed at first, and then, with sudden recognition, "Brilliant, the underwire from your bra!"

Grinning broadly, Harry said, "That's perfect. It should do the trick." He took it from her and started picking the lock. They stood expectantly at Harry's side,

and then they heard the click of the mechanism.

Harry pushed the door open and looked cautiously down the passage. "It's clear," he whispered. The three of them crept carefully down the passage, stopping at the top of the stairs. Harry walked down halfway and peered down. Turning back, he said, "Looks like no one's there; come."

Carla felt her heart beating in her throat. The only light now in the large room came from small windows close to the ceiling. Elouise ran toward the door. As she was about to pull on the handle, Harry shouted out in alarm, "No, don't!"

She froze in alarm. "Why?"

He hurried to her side and studied the door for a few seconds. "It's booby-trapped. Look, do you see these wires here?" He pointed to green and red wires spanning the top half of the door and around the door lock. He followed the wires and found the bomb hidden under an empty cardboard box advertising Sri Lankan bananas. "Damn, this is an enormous son of a bitch," Harry said, deflated.

Carla sat down quickly on a crate. She felt faint, her hopes shattered.

Elouise was the one now who seemed hopeful, and she asked Harry, "Can you disarm it?"

He looked at her gravely and said, "I don't know, but

believe me I will give it my all."

Elouise was staring at the door; abruptly she said, "What's that?" She pulled a piece of cotton fabric off something. It was a black plastic timer: forty-three minutes and twenty seconds, in red digits.

CHAPTER 27

Richard Summers looked up when George entered his office. His bottom lip was sticking out slightly like that of a petulant child. *Oh yes, he's pissed off,* George thought.

"Sit down, Alexander," the ambassador said curtly, "I want to know what the hell is going on. The Indian Minister of Defense is furious. He has found out that you're using their surveillance to monitor possible terrorist activities. They want in."

Frowning, George said, "No way, at least not yet. We can't blow it now. After almost a decade of searching, we finally have a lead. You need to speak to the CIA director and the president. I'm not the person to divulge anything at this stage."

"Then what do you propose we tell the Indian government?"

"An American citizen has gone missing, kidnapped, as we have received a ransom note. It's a crime ring responsible, with no link to any terrorist groups."

"Then they're going to want to involve their police force."

"OK, but we can stall them a bit. I think we're about to find something. Jim was going to call—"As George said that his phone rang—it was Jim. He glanced at the ambassador and answered it. Jim said he saw Harry getting out of the van and entering an abandoned warehouse or factory. George said he'd be there in a minute.

"Listen, Richard, please think of something to tell the Indians to hold them off. You're the diplomat. And please, I beg you, do not divulge the identity of the missing American. I don't want them to know we're onto Dr. Harry Singh. If you'll excuse me, I must get to the control room. Jim found one missing person, and I'm pretty sure it will lead to the others." Getting up, he said, "So we're good?"

Richard smiled feebly and said, "Go, I'll handle it. But you better keep us out of trouble."

George thanked him and rushed out.

Jim was glued to the screen when George entered the room. "Show me what you got," George said.

"Give me a minute; I'll rewind in a second. I'm on fast-forward. After they got off, Singh and suitcase included, no one has left the building. I thought I'd do a quick check to see how long they stayed in there."

George saw the two armed guards at the gate and the one with the dog at the perimeter of the premises. "When is this?"

"Still yesterday." Jim glanced at the time line. "Eight p.m."

At eleven p.m., a Tempo van arrived at the gate. Jim slowed it down, and they watched closely, squinting at the dark images. Two people got out of the front of the van. While one opened the doors, the other went into the building. A much taller person came out of the building, dressed in kurta pajamas and holding a lamp. He went over to the back of the van where one man was now helping two women out of the back. George's heart lurched. It was Carla and Elouise.

"That's them!" George shouted.

The taller man tied their hands. A woman wearing a hijab joined the two men, and together the three escorted Carla and Elouise around the building where they were pushed through a door. After a few minutes the woman in hijab and the tall man exited.

"Where is this place; do you have the coordinates?" George asked, his face a mask of serious concentration.

"Sure, let's see. It's north of Ghaziabad, which is east of Delhi about twenty kilometers. This is an industrial phase that was closed down by the local government, as the developers never required business rights. The land was supposed to be used for agricultural purposes."

"Jim, my man, you need to check every minute of that surveillance while I round up a team to go get them. If they get moved, you call me right away. Phone me on my satellite phone. You can send images through as well."

"No problem, you go, man. Go."

George was already out the door and on his phone. Speaking Pashtun, Urdu, and Hindi, he organized his team to rendezvous at his bungalow. He reached it within ten minutes and was met by a tall Afghan.

"Asef, salaam aleikum," George greeted him.

A large, well-built, bearded Sikh wearing a khaki-colored turban stood up and saluted George military style.

"Good to see you, Mohanbir."

As they spoke, a short but powerfully built man wearing a kurta pajama and a crocheted skullcap came in with Kamal. "Naeem Khan, glad you're back from Pakistan." They embraced briefly and then George said, switching over to Hindi, "Guys, Sunil will make you some tea. If you want to eat, please ask him to pack something. I'll change quickly, and then I'll explain the mission on the way."

He went to his bedroom and changed into a pathani suit and turban. Taking a tube of Neutrogena Instant Bronzing Cream from his bathroom cabinet, he quickly spread it over his face, neck, and arms. He walked back to his study and effortlessly pulled the bookshelf away from the paneled wall, pressing on one panel that slid behind another to reveal a neat, well-lit, deep concrete cavity holding a small arsenal. He handed the Israeli-made Desert Eagle semiautomatic pistols to Mohanbir, a former sharp shooter for the Indian Defense Force. Mohanbir distributed the handguns among them. The two UZI submachine guns were given to Kamal and Naeem. Mohanbir kept the highly accurate Galil sniper rifle, while George and Asef took the Negevs, light machine guns favored by the Israeli Army for their dependable maneuverability. Pulling open a drawer, George removed five US-made Armocorr, high-performance polyethylene bulletproof vests. From another drawer he took a hunting knife and a couple of grenades, which he attached to a belt under his long shirt. He tossed a couple to Kamal and Asef.

They walked to the car weighed down with weapons. Kamal got into the driver's seat, and George sat in the passenger seat next to him. He turned around to face his men and said, "This is a search-and-rescue mission. Let's keep the casualties to a minimum. Take utmost care with the two women we are hoping to rescue. I think we are dealing with a dangerous bunch. Don't underestimate them. At this stage of their operations, they will be tetchy and trigger-happy."

"Suicide bombers?" Mohanbir asked.

"Well, we're not a hundred percent sure, but if I was a

betting man, I'd stake my money on that."

For the rest of the journey they discussed their plan of action, studying the aerial layout of the complex Jim had sent George via satellite phone. The time was 14:10. It would take them at least another half hour to get to their destination.

***

Sweat was pouring down Harry's brow, and he asked Elouise for a rag to wipe it. He was concentrating hard, but he had not yet decided on how to disarm the bomb. Carla stood close, mesmerized by the digital numbers ticking down: twenty-nine minutes and ten, nine, eight seconds. "Harry, isn't there any other way out of here?"

He glanced at Carla briefly and said, "I only know of the two doors, and they are both booby-trapped. Search the living quarters upstairs. See if you can find a window without bars. Elouise, stay with me; I might need you." She nodded and tried to smile bravely.

Carla walked fast and inspected the small factory windows in the rooms. They were all protected with iron bars bolted deep into the outside walls. After examining all the rooms again for a second time, she knew she was wasting her time and went back downstairs. She was close to tears as she told Harry there was no way out.

Carla sat down on an empty crate next to Elouise, took Elouise's hand in hers, and the two of them sat in motionless resignation. Harry stared in disbelief and said, "Don't tell me you're going to just sit there. Do something; keep searching." He turned around and continued picking at the wires. He had managed to unscrew the box that housed the shrapnel and was trying to detach the plastic explosives tied with masking tape.

The brief respite and recognition of their vulnerability

was all Carla and Elouise needed to strengthen their resolve. They stood up and started scouring the factory floor methodically again.

"Go to the back of the room—there's a steel door there," Harry called. "We worked with the radioactive material in there. I think it's fortified with concrete to prevent a radiation leak in case of an accident. You may find something in there."

They ran in the direction Harry was pointing and opened the steel door. The room was bare except for some cut wires and strewn tools. An empty metal suitcase was lying open on a steel table.

Harry had followed, and inspecting the walls, he said, "I think it's reinforced concrete. I want the two of you to stay here while I go on trying to disarm the bomb. You have a better chance in here in case it detonates. Close the door and lie on the floor. Cover your heads with your arms." He turned around and ran back. Carla closed the door and noticed the guilt, pain, and regret in Elouise's expression.

"It's OK. I know we're going to be fine," Carla said, not believing a word of it but desperate to make her friend feel better.

At 14:16 Jim called George and told him that he had scanned the images up to present time, and at 12:30 the compound was cleared out. It was done quickly, and it looked like they were in a hurry. Two Tempo vans and an old black Mercedes Sedan had driven off with goods and passengers.

"What about Singh and the women?" George asked, concerned.

"It was difficult to tell for sure. There was a heavy pollution cloud hanging quite low. I saw two women leave, but they were dressed in hijab. I didn't identify Singh, but my guess is that they've either been killed or they were taken with them, as the guards also left. The dog is running around outside without its handler."

"Is the satellite tracking the vehicles?" George asked grimly.

"I'm afraid the Indian footage is not available anymore, unless they receive an updated report. The control center in California, however, is in the process of training our satellite on the targets. It should take about an hour."

"Damn, that's not good enough," George said, dismayed. "Keep me up to date. We'll check it out."

George was quiet when he broke the satellite connection and his men, knowing him well, respected their leader's silence. Kamal continued driving, while the men checked their ammunition as preplanned.

Finally George said, "We have an hour max to secure the building. Chances are it's empty, but I want you to collect every piece of shit you find. I want fingerprints and DNA samples, toothbrushes, hair. You name it. Understood?" They detected the slightest quiver in George's voice as he gave these instructions.

"Yes sir," they replied, almost in unison.

"In roughly one hour, we should have surveillance of the vehicles, and then we're going after them." George sat very still, but his mind was in turmoil. *If Carla is dead, I will never forgive myself.* Rebuking himself for involving her in the first place, he started feeling dizzy and nauseous, something that had never happened to him before, even on the most dangerous of missions. He could smell her, fresh, clean, but with an exotic sweetness to her scent. He banned the image of her ready smile. *What the hell is wrong with you, George? You're going to get yourself and your men into trouble if you don't start thinking clearly.*

At 14:40 the warehouse came into view. Asef and Naeem

compared the images with the ones Jim had sent and confirmed it was the place. It looked completely abandoned; even the metal gates were unlocked. Kamal stopped the jeep and got out to inspect the gate. It looked safe, so they entered. The men got out quickly and silently. They surrounded the building within a few seconds. Mohanbir positioned himself on the concrete wall a little farther away, but with a clear view of the building and its windows. Through his telescopic viewfinder he started scanning the building. George and Kamal walked up to the steel door, while Asef and Naeem scoured the rest of the building for any other entrances. George stopped dead in his tracks when he heard the sound of a growling dog, and then it was eerily still. He knew Naeem would have been responsible for silencing the animal.

George studied the electronic lock on the steel door and said to Kamal, "What do you think? Disable it or just shoot it?"

Kamal studied it carefully and said, "I don't know. What if it's booby trapped?"

"What's that sound?" George said as he held his ear against the door.

Kamal listened carefully and said, "I can hear it, too. Sounds like footsteps."

George whispered into his Multiband Inter Team Radio, "Movement detected inside building. Mohanbir, do you have a visual?"

"Negative."

"Asef, Naeem?"

"Negative."

George, standing with his back against the wall next to the door, started weighing his options.

Harry went cold on hearing the motor engine. He ran upstairs and peered through windows, watching in dread as five armed men jumped from a jeep with alacrity. *The death squad,* he thought as his stomach cramped. He ran to the rear as he watched them surround the house and then head back to the front. He ducked quickly when he spotted the sniper on a concrete wall about 80 meters away. With his heart hammering, he peered through the window again and watched the two men at the front door. The tall Afghan, was talking into his radio, and the other younger man, wearing jeans and a white shirt, looked up, scanning the walls. Harry opened his eyes wide in surprise when he recognized the man looking up, as Kamal, George's driver. He sat down and tried to think calmly. The suspicion that George worked for the CIA or NSA was always at the back of Harry's mind. *Could this be a rescue mission?* He hurried back to the bomb and saw that twelve minutes and six seconds remained until detonation. Making a split-second decision, he ran into Nadir's office, and finding a black marker, he scribbled a message on a sheet of printing paper and ran back upstairs.

Mohanbir was still monitoring the building. As he swept his telephoto lens back to the front windows, he saw the paper, with something written on it, held up against the window. Talking into his radio, he said, "Sir, I see something. Someone's holding a note up against the window."

"What does it say?" George asked urgently.

"Please help, doors booby-trapped with time bomb. Twelve minutes to detonation."

"Shit," George said and continued talking into the radio. "Naeem, get to this side; we'll have to help this guy disarm the bomb." Naeem was a bomb expert for the Pakistani Inter-Services Intelligence. George had recruited him in Peshawar after the November 2008 attack on two hotels in Mumbai. With suspicion falling on the ISI, he had become disillusioned and agreed to help seek out the traitors in the service. His intelligence gathering was crucial and proved to be of utmost importance.

Naeem was at his side within twenty seconds. "Can we communicate with the guy inside?"

George ran to a window about three meters off the ground. He went down on his haunches, and Naeem instinctively hopped onto George's shoulders. He stood up and, steadying himself against the wall, reached for the windowsill. Then he pulled himself up. "Do you have a visual?" George asked.

"Affirmative. An individual is pointing out the bomb to me. This window is not booby-trapped. I'm going to break the window." Using the back of his handgun, he smashed the window. "Identify yourself!" he shouted.

"Dr. Harry Singh."

"Are you alone?"

"No, my wife, Elouise, and her friend, Carla, are here, too. They are hiding in a reinforced concrete bunker. Can you help me disarm this bomb?"

"Yes. Stand by." Naeem had a good view of the bomb, using his Steiner binoculars. On his instructions, Harry carefully complied, lifting and separating wires. Nine minutes and thirty seconds remained.

Carla patted Elouise on the arm, trying to console her. "We're going to be all right." She closed her eyes and tried to think of her family. She pictured her parents on the wide veranda of their farmhouse, her father glaring at her mother as she chatted incessantly on the portable phone. *Always talking to your friends, what about me? Can't we spend a quiet evening together without your friends?* Carla smiled; oh how she missed them now. An image of Andrew drifted briefly into her mind, and then she felt rather than saw George. She remembered how he had kissed her in the swimming pool, the taste of chorine on his lips. *Could it be only a week ago?* The awful reality that this was in all likelihood the end of her life made her admit her true feelings for George. *I'm in love with him. The moment I met him he stole my heart. Is Leila telling the truth? Is it possible that he doesn't care, at all? Maybe I deserve this. I didn't give Andrew a chance to explain himself. I think I was secretly glad to have an excuse to fall in love with George.* Carla felt tears run down her face and onto her arm. She stared at the tears pooling into the crook of her arm; she felt like Alice in Wonderland, drowning in her own tears. *It can't be much longer now,* she thought, as an unnatural calmness engulfed her.

CHAPTER 28

Elouise startled Carla out of her reverie as she suddenly sat up and said, "Do you hear that?" She was frowning, an expression of hope and fear in her eyes.

The door opened; Harry ran in and half-lifted Elouise off the cement floor. He embraced her, whispering consolingly, "It's OK. It's over. You can go home to our babies." But Elouise stood transfixed. It was all too much, all too sudden to assimilate.

Carla looked up and saw Kamal with a tall Afghan walk into the room. The Afghan bent over and held his hand out to her. She looked at his face at first in bewilderment, and then her heart skipped a beat as she recognized the brown eyes.

"George?"

Smiling mischievously, he said, "At your service, ma'am."

She smiled, resisting the urge to fling herself into his arms. "You have no idea how glad I am to see you."

He helped her up, and they walked out onto the factory

floor. George's team was all over the place, inspecting and taking photographs. George and Carla got into the jeep. He made a phone call, asking for backup transport. Talking on his radio, he addressed Kamal: "Stay with the team. Hafiz is on his way to get you guys. Send Singh and his wife out, and stay vigilant."

Harry and Elouise hurried out and got into the back of the jeep. Elouise was still in a state of shock, shivering despite the heat. Harry tried to hold her hand, but she pulled it free.

"I'm taking you guys back to your bungalow," George told them. "We can pass by your friend who has your kids and pick them up on the way."

Elouise started saying something, but George cut her short. "Harry, I'm afraid I'm going to have to ask you to come into the embassy for questioning."

"Am I under arrest?' Harry asked.

"For now, in custody."

"George," Carla said in an urgent tone, "I don't think there's much time. According to Harry the terrorists are going to explode a dirty bomb in Delhi."

George's eyes hardened as he studied Harry. "Do you know where? When?"

Until now Harry had preoccupied himself with their immediate danger. He had for a number of hours forgotten about the terrorist plot. "I know they are targeting someone important. They never disclosed whom. I got an idea it's a head of state or a minister."

"Oh my God!" Elouise shouted. "It's the American First Lady. She's visiting India on a humanitarian mission. In fact, she will be joining Sonja Gandhi at our Fundraiser for CARE India."

"When, Elouise?"

"What's today?"

"It's Friday."

Elouise blanched. Drawing in her breath sharply, she said, "It's today at four p.m."

George looked at his watch and said, "It's three twenty. Where are they holding this event?"

"At the American Embassy School." Elouise started crying again.

George radioed Kamal and told them to head to the American School in Chanakyapuri. "When you get there, call me right away." Then George dialed a number on his satellite phone. He was driving very fast, weaving in and out of the heavy traffic. "Richard, it's George. We have a situation."

***

Anu pushed a ringlet of her unruly sable hair behind her ear. She walked from behind stage at the AES Theatre to check on the girls for the third time. Her two daughters were the same age as their American friends, Chanda and Zara. She hadn't wanted to bring the girls to the fashion show, but they had begged her, and with Elouise missing she thought it would be a good distraction.

Security was tight, but relatively discreet. Secret Service men dressed in dark suits had inspected the auditorium for hours. The school's own security manned the entrance and did body searches. There were two lines, one for men and the other for women. After walking through the metal detector and handing in purses, wallets, and belts for scanning, there were additional body searches for some. Women were searched discreetly behind the fabric screen.

"Are you still OK?" Anu asked the four girls as they sat chatting excitedly. They nodded sweetly, saying that they'd be as good as gold. Smiling, she walked to the entrance to ask when Mrs. Gandhi was expected.

A sweet, round-faced, heavily pregnant woman dressed

in a pale blue salwar kameez objected to going through the metal detector, arguing that it wasn't safe for the baby. The official called the supervisor, who told her she could avoid it, but she would have to undergo a thorough body search. She smiled broadly and said that was not a problem, thanking him politely. She waddled to the screen, and Anu smiled, touching her flat stomach, which wouldn't remain that way for much longer. She hadn't told her girls yet that she, too, was expecting a little brother or sister for them.

Hearing the sirens of a dozen police cars, she watched as India's political First Family arrived. Italian-born Sonja Gandhi, accompanied by her handsome son, Rahul, entered the auditorium surrounded by guards. Her mother-in-law, Indira, as well as her husband, Rajiv Gandhi, both had been assassinated during their terms of office as prime minister of India. A little shudder ran down Anu's spine, and she hurried forward to greet her. The headmaster beat her to it and insisted on showing Mrs. Gandhi to her seat in the front row.

The theme for the show was "A Green India," with the designers decorating the stage and ramp with hundreds of different shades of green silk, draped and entwined with meters of roped marigolds, tube roses, and jasmine. The effect was magnificent, and the exquisite fragrance of the flowers filled the auditorium. It was almost full, as the excited expats and well-to-do Indians took their seats. A flamboyantly dressed designer called Anu and asked her to find the sound engineer, who wasn't at his post. She hurried outside and saw him standing with the security men, smoking a beedi. Annoyed, she beckoned him. He quickly dropped the handmade cigarette and rushed to her. Anu, along with the security men and their supervisors, didn't notice the female security officer, having just examined a heavily pregnant women, disappear into the crowd.

The tall, bearded man rewound the tape for the third time. An image of himself staring benignly at the camera made him smile. A Kalashnikov rifle was slung across his shoulder as he talked into the camera, and a sand-colored sailcloth was strung behind him, giving the impression he was being filmed in a desert tent.

A young woman wearing a long robe and hijab walked in with a glass of sweet, milky tea and gave it to him. He nodded to his third wife, and she sat next to him on the wooden double bed and watched the video with sleepy eyes. Noticing her expression, he said in Arabic, "This is boring you?" Immediately on guard, she apologized profusely, sliding onto the floor and kissing his hands passionately. His eyes were now hooded and cold, no longer full of benevolence as projected on video. "Get out," he rasped as he pushed her away from him. Cowering, she backed away and ran down the three flights of stairs and out into the courtyard, protected by a five-meter wall.

The man stood up and stretched: four years he'd been living in this compound. He didn't get to go out, but everything they needed was right there. Why was his wife so disinterested, so weary of this life, so lacking in vision? She was, after all, the wife of the great caliphate, the man who would go down in history as the one who had defeated the corrupt and evil West.

He heard his adult son call him from downstairs. Walking slowly and massaging his arched back, he met his son on the landing. Handing him a manila envelope, his son said, "The courier is waiting for your response and tape. The operation should be over within the next hour."

Smiling broadly, the man patted his son on the back and said, "Tell the women to bring refreshments for our guest, and meet me upstairs in my bedroom. Switch the satellite channel to CNN; I'm awaiting their breaking news." At last, another lesson for America. It had been difficult, so many traitors of Islam cooperating with those pigs. He spat against the wall. It was his son who had given him the idea to use Nadir Khan, the notorious gangster and crime lord in India. He had no decent Islamic hair on his body, but no matter. As long as the rogue was paid handsomely, he was prepared to do whatever it took to get the job done. It was so easy: for all his notoriety, the CIA had no interest in the rat—he was India's problem.

His toes curling with pleasure, the man turned and walked back into the room.

George slowed down when he spotted the black Toyota Fortuner in the oncoming traffic. He stopped on the side of the road and watched the Toyota make a U-turn, stopping behind them. Two US Military policemen walked to the jeep and opened the back door.

"Dr. Singh, would you mind stepping out of the vehicle, please?" the burly soldier said politely. Harry's eyes looked at George appealingly, but George's face was rigid, like stone. Harry kissed Elouise on her cheek and climbed out slowly.

"What will happen to him?" Elouise asked tearfully.

"He'll be interrogated, and as long as he cooperates he won't get hurt. I'm afraid that the final outcome will depend largely on whether that bomb is detonated or not." George's face was grim.

Harry looked back over his shoulder at Elouise, mouthing the words, "I'm so sorry." Then he climbed into the back seat, his face contorted with grief.

Elouise smiled feebly at Carla and clutched her hand tightly. Within ten minutes they reached the house, which was very close to the American Embassy School. Carla wanted to stay with her friend, but George insisted that she should accompany him, as she was the only one who would now be able to recognize the terrorists. As he reversed out of the driveway, Elouise ran out of the house, screaming for them to stop.

"She took my girls to the school." Elouise wrenched at the door and got back into the jeep. George was reluctant to take her along. But, looking at his watch, he realized that there wasn't any time for delay, and they raced to the school.

Staring out of the window of the speeding Toyota, Harry's mind was in turmoil. His stomach heaved with every sudden turn or stop in the congested afternoon traffic. Fear gripped him like an icy hand squeezing his heart ruthlessly. He had trouble breathing and tried to rub his chest clumsily with his chin, his arms useless to him, cuffed behind his back.

How could he have been so stupid? Surely he should have realized that he was being duped. He was an educated man. As he sighed with despair, his mind was calculating the ratio of radioactivity in the auditorium. Anu's residence was fairly close to the school; hopefully Elouise would reach their bungalow in time. They should be safe there.

He looked up at the high walls and security of the American compound and felt a stabbing cramp in his gut.

I have to get out of here; I must know if Elouise and my daughters are safe. But in his heart he knew he had very little chance of seeing his family ever again. He'd never meet his biological mother and Elouise would hate him forever.

No one noticed the tears streaming down the terrorist's face as they led him into a secure cell deep in the secret basement of the immense property belonging to the United States of America.

Within minutes the school was in sight, but they were held up behind the entourage of vehicles following the black bulletproof jeep the American First Lady was traveling in. George was on the phone. "Of course I don't have concrete evidence. Singh has told me all he knows. Richard, he didn't know where, but think about it; it makes perfect sense; the American First Lady and the last heir of India's famous Gandhi legacy—it's definitely going to happen here. Richard, we need to evacuate the school." He listened for a minute, his face becoming flushed with anger. He slammed down the phone and said to Carla, "Bloody asshole, he needs time."

George phoned Kamal next. "How far?" He listened for a few moments, and then he said, "I can't wait. I'm going in; just get here, dammit."

He stopped the jeep and said to the women, "I'm going on foot. When you see Kamal and the team, send them in."

"I'm coming," Carla said and climbed out. George was already running toward the gate. Sprinting up behind him, she saw the alarm on the faces of the Secret Service men as George approached them. Pulling out their handguns, they commanded him to stop. But he ignored them and kept running. Carla closed her eyes and mumbled, "Oh God, no, they're going to shoot him."

George had by this time managed to pull out his badge and held it up, as they were now right in front of him, guns still drawn. He spoke to them, his voice loaded with urgency and authority. From a distance Carla watched them put their weapons back into the holsters.

George turned and called to her. He quickly briefed security, getting clearance for her, and then instructed her, "Carla, go inside and see if you recognize any of the terrorists."

She nodded and, accompanied by a Secret Service agent, entered the auditorium. It was filled to capacity with at least five hundred people. She walked steadily down the left side, studying the faces as carefully as possible. Making eye contact with the agent, she shook her head, and they walked toward the other side. The headmaster was making his welcoming speech. The stage was well lit, but the auditorium was a little dark. Out of the corner of her eye, she saw George enter. Elouise was behind him and it looked like he was trying to push her outside. One of his men with his hand placed over her mouth and half lifting her off the floor carried her out. Carla started looking frantically for Zara and Chanda. She had to get them out of the auditorium. Sweat was dripping through her eyebrows stinging her eyes. She wiped her face with the back of her hand and continued scanning the rows. And then she saw her.

Her heart was beating painfully against her chest. *Could it be? She looked so serene. Oh my God, she's pregnant. But she can't be this pregnant!* It was Nazeema, the young girl who had been held captive with Carla in Old Delhi.

George saw Carla staring at the girl. At her side in an instant he whispered, "Who is she?"

"She was from Hyderabad, sold by her parents and imprisoned in Ghulam Bazaar."

"Are you sure?"

Carla swallowed and said, "Yes, it's her. I'll never forget her face."

George spoke softly into his radio, and two more Secret Service men joined him. The three men edged closer to their suspect, their hands on weapons concealed in their clothing. Nazeema saw George, and her eyes stretched wide in fear. She looked around at someone behind her.

Carla's heart was in her throat as she recognized the corpulent eunuch from Ghulam Bazaar.

The eunuch stood up. He held a detonator above his head and shouted, " Don't shoot! Don't shoot!" The red laser dot from a sniper's rifle was on his forehead. George scrambled over the seats and knocked the detonator out of the man's hands.

One of the Secret Service men screamed frantically, "It's a Dead Man's Switch. Catch it! It detonates on impact." George reached for it, but a woman, screaming hysterically, jumped up suddenly and got in his way.

Everything was unfolding in slow motion before Carla. With eyes transfixed in a hypnotic stare, she launched into a desperate dive through the air. With her arms outstretched to the point where she felt they were being ripped from her sides, she caught the Dead Man's Switch in her grasping hands, millimeters off the carpeted floor.

A man carefully lifted Carla, and then George was at her side. The eunuch was overpowered and handcuffed. Just then, Kamal appeared at the entrance and led the team into the auditorium. The screaming woman, now aware of the new arrivals, threw herself down on the floor. Her screams turned to pitiable moans as she clutched her head in belated attempt at self-protection. George looked down rather quizzically at her and then turned back to Carla. Gently, he pried open her fingers and carefully relieved her of the deadly switch. He leaned down, looked at her gravely, and whispered, "I'm impressed."

Carla smiled, a flush of pride as much as the rush of adrenalin on her cheeks, but George was already calling Naeem to look at the detonator. Nazeema was standing between Asef and another Secret Service agent, wailing as they carefully examined the suicide vest she was wearing under her blue Kameez. Carla tried to calm her down, but the pupils of her eyes were abnormally dilated, and Carla realized that she was heavily drugged.

Bodyguards were escorting Sonja Gandhi and her son out of the hall. The American protection unit was encircling protectively around the visibly shaken American First Lady and hurrying out through another exit. The desperate headmaster was attempting a controlled evacuation, but if it weren't for Mohanbir's stern, deep voice, and authoritative presence, chaos would have ensued.

As the auditorium emptied, George told Carla to remain alert, to watch out for other members of the terrorist group. She carefully scrutinized the people as they filed out through the exits. As the last person left the hall, she sighed and sat down heavily on a chair.

"Where's Nazeema?" she asked George.

"Naeem has taken her outside to wait for the Indian military's bomb disposal unit. He seems to think it's not going to be too tricky to disarm."

"Please be gentle with her. She was not here out of her own free will, I'm sure of that."

"Don't worry, I'll make sure they treat her well."

"What about the terrorist group?"

"We are keeping them under surveillance. They'll be more useful to us this way. We believe they might lead us to a very important target."

Carla nodded. Her mind had emptied of all thoughts, and she just wanted to get home. Concerned, George said, "Come, I'll get Kamal to drop you back at Elouise's. She is going to need you. I have to get back to the embassy to appease the Indians. Richard's run out of ideas. I'll call you later. Keep an eye on Elouise; she's going to be fragile."

Carla looked at George and noticed how animated he was. *Duty to his country. His first and only love,* she thought, feeling strangely bereft.

CHAPTER 29

Arriving back at the Singhs' bungalow, Kamal had to get clearance from the Indian military guards posted at the gate. After confirming their identities with head office, they waved them through. Carla thanked Kamal, and smiling, he bade her farewell and left.

A plainclothes policeman opened the door for Carla. Somewhat surprised, she asked for Elouise. He told her that she was in her bedroom, and he would have stopped Carla from going through, but luckily Elouise had heard Carla's voice and called her over. They embraced and returned to Elouise's bedroom.

"Where're the girls?" Carla asked, kicking off her sandals and lying down on the bed next to Elouise.

"They're sleeping. Our house doctor came over and gave them each a shot. They're traumatized and asking for their dad."

Elouise started to weep, and Carla, sitting up, held her in her arms. She didn't have the words to comfort her friend.

"What's going to happen to Harry? I'm so afraid," Elouise asked tearfully.

"I'm sure it's going to be fine. The bomb didn't detonate, so I reckon they'll ask him about his involvement, and once they understand his motives, they'll be more sympathetic. There's no reason that he won't cooperate."

"I hope you're right. As much as I abhor his actions, I still love him. He's the father of my children."

Carla smiled and told Elouise she should stop worrying and get some sleep. Elouise agreed and lay down, closing her eyes.

Carla returned to her own room and had a shower. She was desperately tired, but the events of the past twenty-four hours kept playing in her mind, preventing her from falling asleep. Eventually she drifted off and slept fitfully.

She woke with a start. Disoriented, she looked around the room. Kishan was smiling broadly, standing next to her bed.

"Morning, Kishan, what's the time?"

"Good morning, Madam. It is ten thirty. Andrew sir waiting in living room to see Madam from nine o'clock this morning. But I tell him Madam verri tired and needing sleep."

Smiling, Carla said, "You're right. I needed to sleep. Where are Elouise and the kids?"

"In their room eating breakfast and watching Hindi film."

"Please tell Andrew I'll be with him in a minute."

Kishan hurried out, and Carla took a shower, dressed in a linen dress, and towel-dried her hair. Not bothering to apply makeup, she walked to the lounge. It was very hot.

Andrew, who was reading an old copy of Time magazine, stood up when he saw her. Embracing her a little awkwardly, he said, "Thank God you're safe."

She smiled and sat down on the wingback chair opposite him. "Who told you?"

"George. We came back late last night from Srinagar and met him at the embassy."

"What were you doing there?" Carla asked, surprised.

"Looking for you." He smiled coyly.

"Oh, Andrew, that's sweet. Did Leila go with you?"

"Um, yes, but please don't think—"

"I'm not. Don't worry. I'm so tired. I don't think I will ever again complain about mundane life. I've had enough adventure and intrigue to last me a lifetime."

"Have you given any thought about when you're returning to London?"

Sighing, she took a sip of the tea Kishan had left for her on the side table and said, "I'm going to ask for extended leave. I need a real holiday."

"Where will you go?"

"Not sure, it depends."

"On…George?" Bitterness had crept into Andrew's voice.

Carla blushed and replied a little brusquely, "Of course not. Whatever gave you that idea?"

After an uncomfortable minute or two of silence he said, "Carla, I'm truly sorry about Leila. Please give me another a chance."

Hesitating slightly, Carla said, "It's OK. I'm OK with it. I understand." She looked past Andrew at the garden, and then, not meeting his eyes, she said, "I'm not sure what I want to do. I'll need some time."

Andrew kept quiet and studied Carla for a minute; standing up slowly, he walked to her and kissed her cheek. "I'm going back tonight. I've booked you a seat on British Airways for London. It departs at midnight. If you can't make it, I will understand. But you must know, my heart will be broken." He stood up and walked to the door. Turning around he said, "Please be there."

Carla watched him leave, her emotions in tumult. The comfort of her home and life in London with Andrew was so tempting, but what about George? She had to see him. *This is so unfair of Andrew. Why can't he give me a week or two? What's that in the big scheme of things?* Sighing, she stood up and went to Elouise's bedroom. Elouise was sitting on her bed staring at the ceiling. Seeing her friend like this tore at her heart, and she wished there were something she could do to ease the pain.

"Everything OK?" Elouise asked her.

"Andrew came to see me and has given me a kind of ultimatum. He's booked me a seat on the London flight tonight, and I get the distinct feeling if I'm not on it, then he will take it as the end of our marriage."

"But that's awful. After all you've gone through! I think he's been terribly unfair. Unless…do you want to go back with him?" Elouise's tone was sympathetic.

Carla sat down on the bed next to her and said, "I need to speak to George. There are too many loose ends. To be perfectly honest, I need some time to get over him."

Elouise squeezed her hand and said, "Carla, go. Go see him. Clear the air; you'll never forgive yourself if you don't."

Smiling, Carla kissed Elouise on her cheeks and said, "You're right. I'll call him, and if he's home, I'll ask Om Prakash to drop me off."

As Carla was about to exit the bedroom, Elouise called after her, "Carla! Tell him how you feel."

Carla stopped and popped her head back in. "What do you mean?"

A mischievous smile played on Elouise's lips. "Tell him that you love him."

"How did you know?" Carla laughed.

Elouise studied her for a second. Then she said, "You're kidding, right? It's as obvious as day."

Carla blew her a kiss and returned to her room to get her purse and quickly applied a touch of mascara and lipstick. She brushed her hair and tied it up into a ponytail. She knew it was quite absurd to be happy right now, but she was, even despite a tinge of guilt for being happy while both Elouise and Andrew were in such limbo. As she was asking Om Prakash to bring the car around, she called George and told him that she was on her way to see him and asked if it was all right.

"No problem. We can have lunch together if you like."

"Sure, I'd like that," she replied.

"Carla, you might notice, and please tell Elouise, that we have discreetly placed some extra protection around the house. We've identified the leader of this group, and he's a pretty mean bastard. This all baffles us, as the rogue has never shown any sympathy with fundamentalist groups. He runs a crime racket involving bookmakers, drugs, prostitution, you name it. Anyway, we'll chat when you're here."

"I'll see you soon."

Om Prakash opened the door to the Ambassador and greeted her politely. Within five minutes he had her outside George's house.

"You can go back home, Om Prakash. I'll call if I need you."

"No problem, Madam," he said, wiggling his head.

***

George was standing on the veranda. He kissed her on both cheeks, and she felt a rush of emotion. Not seeming to notice, George led the way to his study. He asked her to sit down and took his seat on the other side of the desk. Carla felt a little dejected; she had hoped for a more intimate welcome. Rebuking herself silently, she thought, *What's your problem? You told him you needed time. Maybe it's all true. I'm living in a fantasy. He really doesn't care.* These thoughts made her feel ill, but she couldn't dispel the hopeful feeling in her belly.

Sunil was smiling from ear to ear when he saw her and brought her a cup of tea. George was studying her with a peculiar expression on his face. Then, smiling as if nothing had occurred in the past forty-eight hours, he said, "You look great. Are you well rested?"

His compliment caused her heart to skip a beat, but she answered him with composure she didn't feel. "Yes, I did, thanks. You must be bushed. Shouldn't you be in bed?"

He smiled and said, "Later. I was busy and still am with all these official reports. I had to include you in my report, but you're free to go. You are officially not a CIA asset anymore. Happy?"

Carla nodded and found that she was somehow disappointed. But she dismissed the notion almost as quickly as it had surfaced.

"Any news about Harry?"

"He's in custody; the CIA's debriefing him. I saw him last night, and he's holding out all right. How's Elouise?"

"Worried. Tearful. Please don't let her suffer. Keep her posted; I know you can trust her. What about Nazeema? Do you know where they've taken her?"

"For now, into protective custody. Then she'll be sent to a secure home where they'll try to rehabilitate her. It looks like she's been on heroin maintenance for the past three weeks or more."

"And then?"

"This is where your testimony will come in handy. You'll have to testify in a special classified hearing that she was coerced against her will into becoming a suicide bomber.

It's pretty serious, as her vest would've caused major damage. She was carrying seven kilos of Caesium-137, a major radioactive isotope in that 'pregnant' belly. To date, we've never had a dirty bomb explode, so how much radiation and damage seven kilos of Caesium-137 causes is debatable. The shrapnel was also pretty hectic. I'm convinced they would have succeeded in assassinating one or both of their targets."

"I still can't believe all of this."

"You're the hero. I'm sure the president of the United States will thank you personally."

Laughing, Carla said, "Oh please, it was pure luck, a reflex. You must know I grew up with three cricketer brothers who tossed that ball around me nonstop."

George laughed, and then in a serious tone he asked, "Are you going to hang around for a little while longer?"

Carla hesitated momentarily. "I don't know. Andrew came to see me this morning and asked me to go back to London with him. He wants us to leave tonight, but I'm not sure."

George's face was serious when he said, "Please don't believe everything Andrew tells you about me, Carla. He has somehow got it into his head that I had you kidnapped and rescued just to gain your trust. It's not true. Admittedly, I was interested in meeting you and possibly gleaning information about Harry while you were a guest of theirs, but I never meant to put your life in danger. I swear."

"And our relationship, was it part of the plan?" Carla felt her heart beating hard, but her voice was steady.

"In a way, but I didn't expect to develop such strong feelings for you, Carla." His voice was warm and sincere, and Carla felt her heart miss a couple of beats.

She was searching for the right words to explain how she felt. The little flicker of hope was burning brighter, and as she was about to reply, someone knocked on the door.

She turned around and saw a beautiful, dark-haired woman dressed casually in khaki shorts and a white blouse. Her dark hair lay in luxurious layers over her shoulders. "Oh hi, I didn't realize you had company," she said in a thick Italian accent.

George stood up and smiled. "Valentina, please come in. I would like you to meet Carla. Remember, I told you about her."

Valentina walked up to Carla and shook her hand, saying, "How wonderful to meet you, and thank you for helping us."

Of course, Valentina Nesi, the Italian woman who worked for the Trafficking Protocol, Carla remembered. She smiled and said, "Nice to meet you, Valentina. I do admire what you're trying to do."

"Thank you," Valentina acknowledged graciously. Looking at George she said, "I see that you are busy. I'm going to the Imperial Hotel for a massage. Can I ask Kamal to drop me off?"

Walking around his desk toward her, George said, "Of course, I'll just call him." He left the study and walked toward the kitchen.

Valentina smiled again and kissed Carla on both cheeks. "Ciao, Carla, and I hope to meet you soon again."

"Yes, me too," Carla said. As she breathed in through her nose, she recognized the perfume Valentina was wearing. It was the same limited-edition Chanel perfume she wore. "I have the same perfume," Carla said.

"It's gorgeous; I love it. It makes me feel like a principessa Indiana." Valentina left the study and waved. Carla sat down and waited for George.

He returned and said, "OK, so where were we?"

"Is Valentina staying here with you?" Carla asked, trying her best not to sound too peeved.

"Yes, for a few days. She has some work with an organization here."

Something was bothering Carla like a memory or dream playing on the fringes of her mind. That evening, after she recovered from her ordeal, she had smelled that perfume on George. *Oh my God, it must have been Valentina. George is sleeping with her. And me.* Carla felt sick; the bitter taste of bile stuck in the back of her throat. *What was I thinking? He doesn't care for me. I was just another "asset" to bed.*

"Carla! What's going on? It looks like you've seen a ghost."

Frowning, she tried to gather her thoughts and control her emotions. "I've changed my mind. I'm leaving tonight. You have my e-mail and phone number, so when I'm needed to testify or whatever, just let me know, OK?"

George, looking bewildered, said, "Oh, I see. Um, of course. I'll contact you. Are you sure you're fit to fly?"

She stood up and, forcing herself to smile, walked around the desk to him and kissed him quickly on both cheeks. He stood up, but before he could say anything, she was on her phone, calling Om Prakash, asking him to pick her up. She hung up and walked to the front with George trailing behind her. He looked like he was in shock and at a total loss for words. Om Prakash was there within minutes.

George opened the door for her, and as Carla got in, she said, "Well then, cheers, George. It was fun."

A despondent look on his face made her look away so that he couldn't see the tears in her eyes.

"Where to, Madam?" Om Prakash asked politely.

"Take me to Elouise Madam's travel agent. I have to confirm a flight."

Watching Carla leave, George experienced an aching loss, an unbearable void like a physical pain. He caught himself breathing fast and shallow, fully aware that for the first time in his life he was having a panic attack. He didn't want to lose her. He couldn't lose her. George Alexander, ordinarily calm and contained, did not have a single idea on how to persuade Carla to stay.

Jolted from his thoughts by a call from Valentina's girlfriend, he answered it and walked back to his study. "Buon giorno, Eva. Yes, I'm well, thank you."

Eva, Valentina's lover for the past ten years, said she hadn't been able to reach her for two days and asked if she was back in Delhi.

"Yes, she arrived early this morning. Her flight was delayed from Kabul. She's not here right now; she's gone for a massage at the Imperial Hotel's spa." He promised to ask Valentina to call her back later.

Exhausted, he sat down on the leather armchair in his study and closed his eyes, trying his best not to think of Carla.

Carla and Elouise had dinner in her bedroom. They chatted about their plans and tried to remain optimistic about Harry's fate. When it was time for Carla to go, Elouise hugged her for a long time.

"Will you be OK?" Carla asked.

"I'll be fine. I might even start writing again. There are awful things going on, and some exposure wouldn't be a bad thing. Thanks for telling me about Kishan's daughter. I will invest the money you've left her and get someone to sort her out. I just realized—you didn't even get to do what you came for. You must come back to explore your own family's history," she said with a grin.

"Yes, of course. So, I'll see you soon," Carla said and smiled.

After promising Elouise to stay in contact every day, Carla finally asked Kishan to take her luggage to the car. She rewarded the staff with a generous tip each and had to wipe away a tear when she said good-bye to Kishan. She felt like hugging him but knew that would embarrass him, so she simply smiled and walked to the car. The staff had all lined up along the driveway, and she smiled, touched by this wonderful send-off. Waving and blowing kisses to Elouise and the girls, she was on her way to the airport.

At check-in she tried to upgrade her economy ticket to business, but she didn't have enough miles on her frequent-flying program, so she left it. "I'll have plenty of time to rest when I get there," she told the check-in clerk.

He smiled and said, "It will be nice and cool in Cape Town. You won't miss the Delhi heat."

"That's for sure," Carla replied.

"Have a good flight, Miss Gill."

As she was going through the security check, she heard them announce the last call for the British Airways flight to London. With a relieved smile, she realized that she did not regret her decision. Andrew would understand, and whether he cared to admit to it or not, their marriage in effect had been over a long time ago.

She bought some Indian sweets and a coffee table book on India for her parents. For her nanny she bought a dark green pashmina, and miniature versions of the "Delhi taxi" for her nephews.

The boarding announcement for her flight was early, but she decided to board anyway. Judging by the line, it looked like a jam-packed flight. Finally on board, she sighed, disheartened that she had a middle seat between two large, potbellied men, guffawing loudly and already smelling of booze. Managing a brave smile, she packed her purse in the overhead compartment and sat down.

"Darn, I should've taken out my Ayurvedic pills," she

muttered to herself.

The man next to her said, "Excuse me?"

"Oh, sorry, I was talking to myself."

He gave her a curious stare and smiled. Carla put her head back against the headrest and closed her eyes. She must've fallen asleep, because when she opened her eyes she saw the plane slowly moving down the runway. An attractive flight attendant leaned toward her and said, "Miss Gill?"

"Yes," Carla answered, surprised.

"You've been upgraded to business class. Please follow me."

"Thank you, that's wonderful," Carla said quite loudly to her fellow passengers, who were glaring enviously at her. Collecting her carry-on luggage, she followed the flight attendant into the spacious business class section. She had the window seat with an empty seat next to her. Purring like a cat, she fell into the ample seat and smiled. As she closed her eyes, an image of George floated into her mind. A dull ache of longing and regret engulfed her. With her thoughts turning to Elouise, she wondered guiltily if she shouldn't have stayed a little longer.

"Excuse me, is anyone sitting here?"

Her eyes flew open, and she was gazing at George's smiling face. "I don't understand. Where's Valentina?"

"What do you mean by that?"

"Oh George, it's just… I mean, I figured it out. It's obvious you have something going with her."

"Are you serious?" George started to laugh, much to Carla's annoyance. "Valentina has never been my lover, if that's what you're implying. She has an Italian girlfriend, Eva, and even if they broke it off, I don't think I'm her type."

Carla stared at him and at first his words didn't make any sense, but then realizing her own stupidity and how she had jumped to conclusions, she blushed. The knowledge that this grand gesture of George's meant something; that he shared her feelings, overwhelmed her. With tears of joy rolling down her cheeks she unbuckled her seat belt and flung herself into his arms; cupping his face in both her hands, she kissed him. He was laughing, and as the flight attendant approached, asking them to take their seats, he said, "Let's sit down; we're about to take off for a much-needed holiday in Cape Town."

ONE YEAR LATER
SUNDAY 1 MAY 2011

*T*he gray-bearded man slept soundly, along with the rest of the household, which had grown complacent in the past five years since occupying the newly built compound in the quiet city of Abbottabad. Only the barking of street dogs disturbed the slumber of the retired military officers, doctors, and lawyers in the area.

This one-acre property, enclosed with high walls, topped with barbed wire, lay less than two kilometers from the military academy—Pakistan's answer to West Point. But even there, young cadets were dreaming of glory and power on battlefields.

In a field nearby, the whirring sound of two large black helicopters almost invisible in the darkened sky had two illicit lovers look up in surprise. Naked under their Kashmiri woolen shawls, they dismissed the helicopters as part of a Pakistani military training operation and turned instead to the warmth and pleasure of one another.

The sound of gunfire woke the bearded man instantly. He lay completely still, trying to fathom the distance and direction of the sound. It was very close. It was in his compound. His wife was awake; she sat up, her eyes wide with fear and questions.

Jumping out of the bed, he felt under it for his rifle, but with a sick feeling in the pit of his stomach, he realized he had left it on the landing of the second floor the day before. He heard his adult son shout for him to hide, but he had no time to do that or ponder on the attack. There was a rush of heavy boots on the stairs.

Instinctively, he pulled his young wife in front of him as a shield. If the attackers were American, they wouldn't dare shoot an unarmed woman. Then, with disbelief and awe, he stared straight into the faces of two American SEALS wearing night-vision goggles and pointing their Heckler and Koch rifles at his head.

They hesitated for a split second, and then the man on the left pulled his trigger. The woman, shot in her thigh, fell down, the crushed femur not able to support her weight. As if in a recurring nightmare, the bearded man watched as the second SEAL fired, and the bullet aimed at his head hit him in his left eye. The sound was deafening. Sudden strobes of blinding light zigzagged across his vision. Then, suddenly, the lights were switched off, and it was dark.

It was uncharacteristically silent in the Situation Room of the White House. The men and women sat with their eyes glued to the monitor as they watched the live drama unfold via satellite. There were no cheers or smiles when they saw their target go down. The president simply shook George's hand and said, "Thanks, George. Your help was invaluable, and I don't think we would have accomplished this task without you. The United States of America is grateful."

With a hesitant and somewhat embarrassed smile, George said, "Glad I could be of service. I'll be on my way then." He said goodbye to the pensive audience, and walking out, he took out his iPhone from his blazer pocket and dialed home. A woman answered and he said, "Carla, I'm on my way now—wait up. I have some-

thing to tell you."

AUTHOR'S NOTE

When I first started writing this novel, international terrorism had taken center stage in the public discourse and was increasingly represented in popular culture and movies. Yet human trafficking tends to flit in and out of the public consciousness and is often seen in the media as just another inevitable evil along with drugs smuggling or arms dealing.

Researching human trafficking shocked me. The prevalence and scale of the trade in vulnerable human beings is horrific and continues to grow. Governments appear to be ineffective in implementing protocols that might stem this growth. Exposure and awareness are needed in the fight against human trafficking. While I was writing this narrative, CNN broadcast, 'Project Freedom: Ending Modern-Day Slavery', which helped to highlight this crime. I hope more of such reportage will find its way into the media and galvanize governments and society to fight this heinous crime.

There are many individuals who were instrumental to this book being written.

My sincere thanks and gratitude go to my editor Claire Strombeck for believing in this novel from the beginning. Thanks also to Sukaina Walji for the invaluable feedback and editing. My sister Carin Murphy and best friends Lia Rattle and Preeti Kapoor were ever present with their enthusiasm and critical feedback, helping to shape the story. I will forever be grateful for your love and support.

My account of Kashmir would not have been possible without the help of Satinder Sethi, who painted it so vividly in my mind. Your time and stories are much appreciated. Thanks also to my dear friend Melody Deas for designing the beautiful cover.

To all my readers, you know who you are; thank you for reading the drafts and for your kind support. You gave me the confidence to see it through to the end.

Lastly, I'm so grateful to my husband Sabi and our four exquisite daughters, Somara, Sarina, Anjali and Carina. Without them, my life would be like boiled, unsalted rice.

Kirkus Reviews

THE DELHI DECEPTION
Sabharwal, Elana

In Sabharwal's debut romantic thriller, a 30-something South African journalist travels to Delhi, falls for a mysterious charmer and inadvertently becomes a pawn in a secret mission to uncover a sinister underworld of human trafficking and international crime.

Seeking to surprise her estranged, war-reporter husband, Carla arrives at Andrew's hotel room in Peshawar only to find him in a compromised position with a female co-worker. Reeling, she takes refuge in the Delhi home of her best friend, Elouise, an expatriate who's settled in India with her wealthy husband, Harry, and their two children.
As a distraction from her heartache, Carla, known for her exotic beauty, easily immerses herself in Elouise's daily life of leisure, elite parties and full-time servants.

While out on a tourist jaunt, Carla's fate, as well as the novel, takes a dark turn when she's kidnapped, drugged and nearly sold into sexual slavery. Just in time, George, an acquaintance with a shadowy reputation and no shortage of sex appeal, comes to the rescue. He reveals his true mission to her as part of an operation to catch those at the helm of this seedy venture.

For her part, Carla agrees to spy on Harry, whom George believes to be involved somehow. Soon after Carla gives in to her desire for George, her husband appears and begs for forgiveness. She's left in utter confusion, which is only magnified when Andrew and his aforementioned co-worker put George's motives and true identity into question.

The narrator's breezy tone and the characters' indulgence in frivolity contrast appealingly, if oddly, with the novel's darker depictions, as of the place where young women are subdued with forced drug use and then preened like living dolls and sold to the highest bidder. The detailed accounts of criminal activity, apparently researched by the author, seem to belong to a story not wholly unearthed here, though admittedly, it would be difficult to fully serve these nonfictional elements without overpowering the interpersonal dynamics, which ultimately drive the narrative.

A swift pace will keep readers hooked as the timely, intriguing plot unravels.

Kirkus Indie, Kirkus Media LLC, 6411 Burleson Rd., Austin, TX 78744
indie@kirkusreviews.com

New Book by Elana Sabharwal to be released in 2014

Of Rice, Love And War
By Elana Sabharwal

Set during the turbulence of the Vietnam-American war, a young French woman, Amelie, born in Indochina, is recruited to spy on the Americans for the Ho Chi Minh government in the North.

The brutal reality of war soon disillusions her and when she falls for an American Naval pilot, they discover a conspiracy that could swing public opinion and force the policy makers in Washington to end the war.